D1639591

A FEW FLOWERS FOR SHINER

Also by

RICHARD LLEWELLYN

★

HOW GREEN WAS MY VALLEY

NONE BUT THE LONELY HEART

RICHARD LLEWELLYN

★

A Few Flowers for Shiner

London
MICHAEL JOSEPH

First published by
MICHAEL JOSEPH LTD.
26 Bloomsbury Street
London W.C.1
1950

MADE AND PRINTED IN GREAT BRITAIN BY PURNELL AND SONS, LTD.
PAULTON (SOMERSET) AND LONDON

DEDICATED

to

ALL WORKMEN

A FEW FLOWERS FOR SHINER

1

Snowy Weeks was drying himself in the washhouse under the tower, listening to noon chiming on two bells, a big one that called across the rooftops of Torre Fiore in a hearty bellow and no nonsense about it, and a little one that followed a long time afterwards, creeping out among the glory still afloat with a little clonk from the side of its mouth. Between the two, Snowy filled in the count with stamps of his foot, sorry as ever that the other ten bells had been taken for scrap, though it made him happy to think of the old workmen putting that big one up there hundreds of years before knowing it would always be there, and making certain by building all round it, so that getting it out would mean razing the monastery. But the ten smaller bells in between must have come out easily as milk teeth, yet they made their absence known by pauses that annoyed like the jog of a nobbly elbow, until the big one sounded again and shook the walls, and the two crates, holding the plank, and the washbowl sitting on top with his toothbrush and paste, and tipped them all over the floor in a splash of grey water.

"There we are," Sergeant Whitmarsh said. "Saved you the bother of putting it down the sink. 'Course, if you will stand there all poetical, I mean, there it is. Bell struck?"

"Got one like it round our way," Snowy said, fishing in the drain. "And I reckon it's a marvel the way a bit of soap'll turn on you. Get it in your hand, and you're due a lovely wash. Let it go, and it'll either come up full of grits, else it'll find some dirty hole like this to slide about in."

"Almost human," said Sergeant Whitmarsh. "How long'll you be?"

"Don't want no encouragement," Snowy said. "I know when I'm welcome. Two ticks getting me shirt on, and I'm off."

They heard the birds come back in a breath of wingbeat and settle up there among echoing bronze.

"I'll have the cartridges here any day now," Sergeant Whitmarsh said. "Then there'll be steak, kidney and starling pie for dinner. So you'd best hurry back. I had a line from Shiner's missus."

Snowy knew there was something coming, and watched the wine cart lumbering along the dark street with only the patched red umbrella sticking up in the sun, wondering, and yet guessing in part of his mind what brought Sergeant Whitmarsh to look away in the yard.

"She didn't know you'd be out of hospital so quick, I suppose." Sergeant Whitmarsh spoke in the grudging muffle of a man with an unpleasant job. "She asked me if I'd do what you're going to. That's why we got Rosie ready, see?"

"I reckon the lads done a marvellous job on her." Snowy was comforted by the firmness of his voice. "I couldn't believe my eyes. She's as good as new."

Sergeant Whitmarsh nodded across at the refectory, busy with tool benches and spotted with working lights blinking with the movement of passing mechanics.

"That was the lads," he said. "Worked all their spare time on her. She was in a rare state."

"I was lucky," Snowy said. "Didn't ought to be here."

"She'll get you there, anyway." Sergeant Whitmarsh walked a pace or two, looking across at the orange groves, and down the street at white walls and crinkled rooftops, watching dust falling in fine gold from the wine cart's wheels.

"Here's your work ticket, and pass, and things," he said, wagging an envelope behind his back.

Snowy took it, running his thumbnail along the edge until it threatened to tear. What he wanted to say was building a honeycomb of corners inside that seemed to hurt mostly in his throat, and he realized in a frown of shock that he was still weak from hospital and not as strong as he thought. Looking at Rosie out in the sunlight puddling dark drips below her petrol intake, he heard the engines raving on the test-benches, and bacon was frying in the cookhouse, but it was no use trying to talk.

"So you've got all your papers," Sergeant Whitmarsh said,

knowing perhaps what was going on and trying to help. " And you'll have to keep an eye on 'em. Because if you ain't got papers, you ain't alive. You ought to know that."

" I've got enough papers to start a salvage dump on me own." Snowy was grateful for a chance to talk rough. " I hope the coppers can read, that's all."

" Won't have no trouble with them." Sergeant Whitmarsh spread the words with all the tired confidence of a veteran. " There's just one other little thing before you go, though."

For a single moment the sunshine was brighter and colours were clearer and silver freckled in the leaves of the orangery, and in that period Snowy knew, for all time, that what he feared had become a fact, and Sergeant Whitmarsh was only trying to break ground to get there. Yet while he appreciated the kindness, he was angry because of delicacy bobbing little curtsies in the sergeant's voice, for it emphasized the enormity of what was about to happen, besides showing that its probable effect on him was known, and he resented to the point of desperation any hint that he might be susceptible in any manner, whatever the circumstance.

" I knew there was a catch in it somewhere," he said. " Trot it out."

Sergeant Whitmarsh pulled his moustache until his upper lip was out of shape, closing an eye at the toecap of his boot on Rosie's off-fore tyre.

" This ain't me talking," he said primly. " The management says you've got to have a mate. So he'll be coming with you on this trip. See? "

" But why now? " Snowy asked, while anger was shrivelling, for he had known so well that some time or other this moment would come, and the knowledge had got heavier with the days, so that hearing it was at least relief.

Sergeant Whitmarsh made a clicking noise and stamped in the petrol patch, making an apologetic rite of pulling up his trousers and stuffing in his shirt.

" You'll be on your own for a few days," he said. " Get to know yourselves, like. Then when you get back you'll be able to go straight out on the road, see? No growing pains, no nothing. Just the job."

Snowy went round to the back of Rosie and let down her tailboard.

" All very well for you," he said, climbing up. " But it don't suit me too much."

" Ah, well." The sergeant's voice twined pain and comedy. " Nothing don't suit none of us in this lark, do it? There's nothing here suits me, chum. I've got to get back home to East Plumstead and the old lady first. That's where it'll suit me. I mean, we all got to make the best of it, ain't we? "

Snowy looked up at the change in tone, subtlest reminder that a favour had been granted as yet without a word of thanks, and saw an instant pattern of the work done and the hand of Sergeant Whitmarsh plain in all of it.

" Listen, Sarge," he said, folding his blankets carefully around a canvas package. " I don't know what to say to you or the lads. It's a bit too much, see? I reckon you're the best lot of blokes in the Eighth. I don't want to cause no trouble and sort of spoil everything. But you knew why I was going, so why does this new bloke have to be shoved on me? It don't hardly seem right. Do it? "

" Depends how you look at it," the sergeant said, and his grey eye followed a design on Rosie's painted canopy. " You're wanted back on duty, so you've got to have a mate. You're due for leave. So's this new bloke. The adjutant asked him. So when he said yes, there it was. Suits the management a treat. Whether it suits us or not don't matter, do it? "

" Where is this new bloke, then? " Snowy asked, not quite sure where to show his anger. " How long's he going to be? "

" He's here," the sergeant said. " And he ain't relishing the ride from the looks of him."

" Neither would you if you'd just heard all that," said another voice, in syllables flat as clogs come down on stone. " I'll not go where I'm not wanted. There's plenty of other places I can go on leave, d'ye know."

" Now look here," Sergeant Whitmarsh said, squaring himself up. " Don't you start. One in the family's enough. This is Craftsman Dodds, late of Number Five Depot. Where they make 'em, or bust 'em up."

Snowy thought he looked about thirty, but surprising grey hair bushed out of his fore-and-aft cap. He was brownly thin, lined about the mouth and eyes, and a new scar split his left cheek. Steel-rimmed glasses were bound bumpily with cotton half-way down and askew a broken nose, and his eyes were as pale as the metal, frowning a smile as though willing to have a joke or slip his blouse off and pitch in. He looked tired and a bit strange to it, like all new blokes, but well on his guard, treading it lightly, taking everything with a pinch of salt and ready to tell everybody what he thought without worrying what happened afterwards.

And nothing like Old Shiner.

" Craftsman Edmund Herbert William Weeks," Sergeant Whitmarsh said, looking at Snowy. " Tell you why we call him Snowy some fine day. What they call you? "

" As long as they don't call me late for me dinner, I don't mind, meself," Craftsman Dodds said. " Make it Bill. I'm a William, too, if that's not infringing his patent."

" Couple of you," said the sergeant. " Now you can have a marvellous time of it, a couple of Sweet Williams up in your little greenhouse in the front there, proper champion. All you want's a lump of maidenhair fern, and there you are."

Bill looked down at his pile of kit and winked up at Snowy on the far side of the sergeant to let him know that whatever he felt was being shared.

" Let's get out of it," Snowy said. " Make things worse, chewing the fat."

Sergeant Whitmarsh screwed up his mouth, jerking his head at the rear of the wagon, ruffling his moustache ends with the tips of his fingers, and Bill saw relief nearly in open laughter and content almost at the strut in the way he offered a cigarette.

" What about his pass, then? " Snowy called from inside the canopy. " Wait another couple of hours for that, I suppose? "

" It's in along of yours," Sergeant Whitmarsh said, halting the match on the striker. " See? You ain't looked, have you? I might just as well have give you last month's Part One Orders. And his rations are in and all. So's his canteen issue. Anything else you'd like to start grousing about? "

" Just asking, that's all," said Snowy, taking Bill's kit from him and hanging it up beside his own. " You had it all worked out, didn't you? Start now, can we? "

" You've got the freedom of Italy," Sergeant Whitmarsh said. " There's the gate. Turn right and keep going."

" Right back to Africa, if I had my way," said Snowy, jumping down. " I wouldn't give you fourpence for this hole."

" I hope you ain't been away too long to remember she's got a tailboard," Sergeant Whitmarsh said. " Give us a hand, Bill."

Snowy got into the cabin and sat for a while examining the luxury of eased muscles, trying to think how he felt. It was like the happiness of getting home, of being warmed by the familiar smallness of everything, and listening to silence like the stun of an unfelt blow; and yet it was different, for someone was missing, and his ears seemed to be stretching out for the sound of a voice that, try though he might, he could not wholly remember in tone or body.

He frowned, saddened into anger at himself, and impatiently trod on the starter.

Rosie spoke up at the slightest touch with the same old sound, just as he had always remembered; that, and the feel of the driving wheel with all the notches Shiner had cut in it, with a dab of red paint in the big notch marking the first Boche tank they towed out of Alamein—and he still saw the 88s bursting giantly in ragged rows of instant blue cauliflowers all round them —and that little crack in the screen up by the wiper where a piece struck through and burnt Shiner's knee, all came back in waves that hit him blithely in the face and made him want to laugh out loud.

The cabin door opened on the other side and Bill climbed in, dropping his fore-and-aft cap, and the grey hair fell over his eyes in a tangled, dusty offence of strangerhood and age.

Snowy pressed viciously on Rosie's button until she screamed, and then with an inward nod of sympathy took his boot away and let her breathe easy, listening to a friendly old tune softening as a lullaby, watching in his mind the play of her pistons, alert for any whisper of trouble; but Rosie was just as she had always been, sweet as a nut.

" Set? " he asked Bill, though he was looking at the gateway.

"Spanking," said Bill. "You've a very nice job here, you know."

"Mm," nodded Snowy. "Rosie's all right."

He let out the clutch, and as they started, Sergeant Whitmarsh walked ahead, turning to look up, and the bristles of his moustache and the tuft of hair curling out of his beret were gilt in sunshine, and he was laughing.

"Have a good time," he shouted. "I've put a parcel on board there. What we was talking about. From all the lads. Be seeing you, chummie. Bring us back a bottle, mind."

Snowy held up a thumb and closed one eye, putting his weight on the wheel, leaning far out of the window in pretence of warning traffic that he knew did not exist, watching a couple of women on the river bank draping sheets over cactus, and glad that Bill was looking elsewhere.

He knew what was in the parcel.

2

Bill lit two cigarettes and passed one over.

"Ta," Snowy said, without smile or look, and the cigarette went into a corner of his mouth and stayed there.

Bill undid the front of his blouse, leaning back, fidgeting himself into comfort.

"If it keeps up like this," he said, nodding at the sun, "we ought to be all right, didn't we?"

"Mm," said Snowy. "But you can't tell in this rotten hole what it's going to do. Never make up its mind. Give me the old desert every time. When it rained, it rained. When it was sun, it was sun. You knew what you was on."

"'s quite right," said Bill. "Give me good old Africa every time. Whatever I've said about it before."

"You there, was you?" asked Snowy, a little too distantly. "What doing?"

"Tank recovery," Bill said, and took off his glasses to polish them on his shirt. "When it was over, I had a go in workshops. Then I had another go at recovery in Sicily."

" That where you just come from? " Snowy's voice was light with the pretty airs of one engaged in major campaigns from inception. " Have a nice quiet time down there, did you? "

" I come out of hospital," said Bill, aware of his position. " I were at the Con Depot three months."

" Convalescent three months? " Snowy looked at him for the first time. " What you do? Break your neck? "

" No," said Bill. " Got one in the shoulder, a lump in me leg, and this one in me dial."

" Ah," said Snowy, and the difference in tone made Bill smile inside and far away. " Hard luck, that. Three, eh ? Greedy for glory. Where'd you collect 'em? "

" Outside Catania," Bill said. " The Sicily job, what everybody's forgot about."

Rosie moved over bumps and potholes in the wide macadam with the barest shrug of her springs; and thinking of the new paint coating her body, the scarlet hubs and rim nuts, and the masterpiece of buff and purple camouflage on her canopy, Snowy felt the pride of an owner leading a champion on her way to a show.

He slowed her through the littered street of the village, though not too much, afraid of urchins clambering aboard and throwing the kit out and then dropping off.

" Can't hang about because of the kids," he said. " There's millions of 'em. They're proper little terrors."

" They could do with a good toe behind 'em," said Bill. " Most of 'em can, in this country. Mucky lot."

The street was narrow, gloomy between high buildings, and chocked by market carts and barrows full of vegetables done up in nets. Mounds of cauliflowers blossomed whitely on stalls, and oranges spilled down to the kerb from piles inside the shops, with lemons, and tomatoes in string bags, and clusters of peppercorns hanging around the doorways, all the way up the walls, and framing every window among the flutter of washing. A little girl finished pegging, and hooked a thin leg around the iron railing of a balcony, staring up at the sky, unmoving.

" I wonder what these kids think about? " Snowy said. " They just stand there and look. I can't remember my two doing it. Me, either."

"I can tell you what it is with this lot," said Bill. "They're daft. Runs in the family. No hope for 'em."

"That's the R.A.F. canteen down there," Snowy said, nodding to the right. "Proper well off, they are. If there's anything going, they get it. I reckon they've got better blokes up top, meself."

"You've only got to look at our lot," said Bill. "They'd make you drip."

It was a long pull up to the highway through a road of houses in flower gardens almost hidden by trees with no sign of battle, but all the way along the walls a Hammer and Sickle had been stencilled in a threat of black.

"They'll go bolshy, you know," Snowy said, as though doubting himself. "It won't half be a do, and all. Bad-tempered lot, they are. Very hot blooded, what I've heard of 'em."

"Whatever happens to them'll never worry me," Bill said. "I hate them, and I hate Jerries. I always will."

"Same here," said Snowy. "So did old Shiner. You should have heard him."

"Who was Shiner?" asked Bill, sideways, under his spectacles.

"My old mate," Snowy said. "Ought to be sitting where you are. But he ain't."

Bill turned deliberately, looking out of the other window.

"That why ye didn't want me?" he asked.

Snowy nodded, watching the turning ahead.

Rosie ground up the bumps and potholes, and turned herself on to broad tarmac, and once away from shrugs and jolts she tremored her needle among the early thirties in a murmur of powered contentment.

"You can't forget blokes like Shiner," Snowy said, with anger shredding his voice. "How can you? But they'd like you to, though."

He watched the orange groves rumpling by, and a couple of children helping women bending stiff-legged in a plot of broccoli. A skimp of a woman, faceless under a burden of sticks, was walking on bony bare brown feet towards them. He could feel it had to be said because he knew it must.

"I didn't want you on this trip," he said. "I wanted to be by myself."

"Why the hell didn't you say so, first off?" Bill said. "I'd have understood. I'm not one of them back there. Of course you can't forget him, any more than I'll forget old Cob."

A little disturbed by rage colder than his own, Snowy stared ahead at the patchy smoothness of the tarmac, seeing the squad of Indian pioneers rolling pitch barrels down to the crater by the bridge, aware that the volcano wore a little white cloud like a busby over its head.

"I wanted to get out of it," he said, because he had to say something. "It's no good of arguing with 'em. Just get yourself worked up for nothing. That's the army. They've got you, one way or another."

"All ways," said Bill. "Coming or going."

Rosie picked her way over a short Bailey bridge, rattling the planks as she went, dodged in and out of a channel of pitch barrels, and settled down to the long stretch ahead. A dozen women carrying headloads of cabbage done up in linen were tripping along the near side of the road and their rumps bounced up-down, up-down as though they all belonged to the same woman.

"What happened to your mate, then?" Snowy asked, as ordinarily as he could. He was aware of Shiner laughing at him from the broken walls of another village sprouting from grass and bush on the skyline, and oleanders erect on yardsticks seemed to be talking to him all along the roadside, holding up armfuls of gay pink rags soft in the sun.

Over on the right, lemon trees ruffed a grey farmhouse, a simple block of stones piled squarely together, with an outer stairway to the upper room. But nobody, not an animal or living thing, moved near it, or among the trees, or in the fields, or along the road, or around, or about.

"They work hard, you know," Snowy said. "You got to give 'em that, any rate. I've never seen any of 'em at it, mind. But just the same, it gets done. And after all, you can't tick about that, can you?"

"They don't damn well deserve it," Bill said, fine as a hair. "They should all be chucked out of it, the lot of them. Like we were."

" Chucked out of it? " Snowy said. " Who chucked us out of where? "

" I don't know about you," Bill said. " But we got chucked out, all right. They've got a damn great aerodrome where we used to live. You ought to read my old mother's letters about 'em. Her sweet-peas. And her blackcurrants."

" Hard luck," Snowy said. " Bad as being bombed out, that is. We had it, couple of years back. I've still got the wife's letter. I don't know how it come past the censors. She's with her relations now. Her and the girls. But what we're going to do when I get home I don't know."

Rosie was bumping her way over a cratered stretch in a curse of changing gears. Dust flew white in sunshine, filling the cabin with a little world of stars that in settling lost light, fringing eyelashes in saffron, clinging to hair on knees and forearms, filling the nose with a quick powder that made talk a miller's burthen.

" All right in a minute," Snowy said through a handkerchief. " They got it bad round here. Ain't had time to clear it up."

" They ought to get a few Wops working," Bill said. " Grumbling about no jobs and no grub. Ought to have mended this months ago."

" Wops," said Snowy. " They ain't us."

" You ask me, it's the damn women do all the work in this rotten country," said Bill. " Lot of idle, chunnering, thieving good-for-nowts, that's all the damn men are. I've seen better in the scum of a wash-Monday."

" Some of 'em's all right," Snowy said. " We had a bloke with us, sergeant he was, picked him up at Sidi Rezegh. He never went a prisoner. He was the best mechanic I ever see. Proper upset when we had to send him home. Just stood there. Never said a word. Neither could we. Good bloke, old Rusty."

" Ah." Bill was looking through the window. " Had foreign blood in him likely. I can't abide any of 'em."

" I've got his address," Snowy said, perhaps in rebuttal. " We'll look him up."

Rosie grumbled her way over the cobbles of the village, moaned at farm carts turning out of the square, and, finding macadam again, drew in a rich breath and clanked them all goodbye with the loop of her crane cable.

" Listen, Snowy," Bill said. " Where are we supposed to be going? "

Snowy felt the notch slipping through his fingers.

" It's about a couple of hundred miles all told," he said. " I don't know the name of the place, but I know where it is."

" That's all that matters," Bill said. " Nice place, is it? Worth going to? "

Snowy felt he had to stop and turn back. A stranger sharing the trip was bad enough, but having the right to ask questions or make any comment was wormwood. An itch was in him to brake hard and twist the wheel at the nearest wall. But all the while he thought and felt, he knew futility, and a core, deep down, of cold rage began to spread in helplessness.

" It's a lovely place," he said, listening to himself. " Very quiet. It ain't quite in the mountains, but it's near. And the sea's marvellous. We ought to have a couple of nice days there. I know a few of the people."

" As long as you're happy, I am," Bill said, knowing something was wrong, but not quite sure how to approach it. " Ye didn't mind me asking, did ye? "

" 'Course not," Snowy said, feeling he was being unfair. " Only it's, like, special, see? "

Bill obviously did not. He was looking over the top of his glasses.

" Listen," Snowy said. " I've asked you once. What happened to your mate ?"

" Got his cards," said Bill. " He was sat just where you are now, and we got this tank out of a minefield. Then he fell on top of me. He was a fine bloke. Dead game, he were. Had seven wounds in him."

Snowy eased up and changed down. Rosie turned her square jowl into the shade of an orange grove and stopped there, humming for a moment. Then she screamed, and sobbed, and was still.

" I know how you feel, chum," Snowy said, loudly, in the quiet. " That's where we're off to. Where Shiner's dug in. We're going to put him to rights, seeds and plants and things. Tidy it up a bit."

He looked through the speckles of dust on the windscreen, watching little haloes of sunlight bright about the oranges on top of the trees.

Somewhere far over among the leaves a girl was singing, a few notes now, and the creak of something cooling under Rosie's bonnet, and then, a merest pinch of sound, a few more notes, sad as lilies.

" This party's too cheerful," Snowy said. " I reckon it's high time for a brew."

3

They sat in the shade of the orange trees, backs against the boles, scraping the earth to make a flat place for their mugs, watching meek scarves of flame twisting about the brew can. Snowy broke a match-stalk and dropped it in the water.

" I reckon it's marvellous how that little bit of wood keeps the smoky taste out of the tea," Bill said. " I wonder who thought of it? There's some rum talent knocking about, you know."

" Whoever he was," Snowy said, " he wasn't a First Army wallah. They wasn't in the brew business long enough to get their tins blacked over."

" As it happens," said Bill, through a sour mouth, " I'm a First Army man meself. You're one of them blokes thinks the Eighth took over from Nebuchadnezzar, I suppose? "

" The old hands have been at it so long they don't remember," said Snowy tiredly. " Who was he? Eyetie? Ol' Wavell stopped their gallop."

" Admitted, the Eighth done all the chasing," said Bill. " But we had to do most of the fighting."

Snowy looked down at his mug, reaching out a forefinger to touch chippings in the enamel as a lover of porcelain might trace a motif, tipping his head on one side with the preoccupied air of a father listening to ill-natured bawling from a distant cot.

" Oh, ah? " he said. " Where was all this chasing going on, might I ask? "

" Right round Africa, be all accounts," Bill said. " Except where we was. That's where the scrapping was. Did you know? "

Snowy scratched his head.

" You ask me, I reckon you First Army lot got too much of that there mepacrine down you," he said. " It knotted all your guts up, and perished all your brains, them as had some to start with. Now you're all getting jaundice, or else walking about spare. I feel sorry for the lot of you."

" I thought it was the Eighth started that damn mepacrine stuff," Bill said. " Kept their nasty passions down."

" The only passions we ever had was Jerries or Wops," said Snowy. " And the bloke who invented V cigarettes. One of them, and a cup of that compo tea first thing of a morning, you'd got a home-made flame thrower."

" You're right," said Bill. " One puff, and you cried yourself to sleep."

They were looking at the fire, each knowing from the weight of air that the other was thinking of something to say that would settle the issue there and then; but though neither wanted this heavy feeling, each would have seen the other burning before retracting a word, and so the feeling persisted, and in the green quietude it seemed to gain until it might have been hatred and not a mere duel of loyalties tempered hard in memory of dead men.

" Nobody's going to say nothing about the Eighth," Snowy said. " Not while I've got me breath, anyhow."

" Same here," Bill said. " I'm not having a word said about the First, neither. I saw too many damn good lads get smashed up. And no thanks for it. Couple of years, they'll all be forgotten."

" Christ," Snowy said. " They've forgotten already. They ain't going to bother about us, chum. They got their pockets to line first."

Bill saw bubbles gathering along the side of the tin and moved to pick up the tea and sugar.

" Half a mo'," said Snowy. " What you going to do? "

" Make the char," Bill said, a little surprised.

Snowy sat back. His attitude suggested that a fig for consequence was more than enough.

"Let's see you," he said. "I never had me tea with the First. They was always a bit too far away."

"Ah," Bill said. "In front of you, if ye'll look at the map."

"We had to come and give you a hand in the finish," Snowy said.

"That's quite right," said Bill. "Round the back. We had to let you in to give you a bit of encouragement. If it hadn't been for that bloke Monty ye'd never have been heard of. Did you know?"

Snowy looked up, searching for a gap in the crochet of leaves, and, finding none, closed weary lids.

"If poor old Monty ever hears that," he said, "the tank'll roll straight off his beret."

The girl was singing again.

Bill watched the tea settling on the water, moving, alive in the heat until it crept up the sides of the tin and threatened to overflow. Knowing that Snowy was watching, he let the leaf settle down until most of it was under the bubbles and then put the tin back on the fire.

"Done it all wrong again," Snowy said. "You never boil tea! It's murder."

"I thought you was still heartbroke about Monty," said Bill, and as the leaf came up he took the tin off and kicked earth over the fire, stamping the pile flat. "Wait till you get it in your mug before you start howling. How much sugar have we got? Sweet toothed, are you?"

"Yes," said Snowy. "There's plenty there. My old lady ought to be here."

"Married, are you?" Bill said.

"Eight years," said Snowy. "Four home, four away. She says she forgets what I look like. I've told her it'll be just the same when we've spit the candle out."

"Ah," said Bill. "Same here. It's been a long time, seems like. It'll be a bit strange when we get back, you know."

"Let's get back and find out," Snowy said. "I'll let you know after the first couple of days."

The singing girl reminded him of Liz in that old pink throw-on humming while she got breakfast ready in the dark mornings, with the fat rolls of her curlers sticking out all round her head, and that little tail of hair that her fingers always seemed to miss hanging down and curling up in a big O at the back of her neck. He felt its silken grind when he rolled it tighter to lift it where he could kiss the smooth skin, bending her head back till the curlers stuck in his cheek trying to cover her mouth saying Bertie, nooooo, in a voice like a baby that drove him half mad, feeling the words throb out of her under his palm, but it was no use on workday mornings. She always looked at the clock and pushed herself away and he could hear her saying ten minutes is ten minutes so think of it before the alarm goes off if you want me all that bad because I get the blame if you lose your job. I shall still be here tonight. Oh, look, Bert, your tea's getting cold. Bertie, nooooooo. Oh, Bert.

It was all in the quiet song.

" It's not that bad," Bill said, and held out the mug. " Try it."

" 'Tain't the char, mate," said Snowy. " I could go proper barmy at times, I could. Just thinking."

" Best not think," Bill said. " I've give up. In fact, I don't even like writing any more, and I used to write pages and pages. I can't seem to get hold of anything to say. It's like writing to somebody I used to know."

" Then you wonder why they start going out with other blokes," Snowy said. " You'd be sorry then, wouldn't you? "

Bill was looking down the road to distance beyond distance, aware of the ragged peak of leaves above, and the blue polish of tarmac ahead, but it all had been part of life for so long that anything he remembered seemed only a dream to be borne like the nag of an earache that became a nuisance only now and again by day but nearly always at night.

" Night-time I get it," he said. " It's a terror. Damn it, why've we started on this? How's the char? "

Snowy scooped his tongue tip around his top teeth, swishing the tea about the mug, looking down in patronage at once malicious but always impersonal.

" You're coming on," he said. " Everything takes time, though. You'll see what I mean when I make it. Make you thirsty, this would, in the desert. But it'll do to keep the dust down."

" Fancy that now," said Bill, sharing an admiring confidence with an orange just above his head. " I suppose ye'll be carrying a grain or two of that Alamein stuff round with ye? Taste it up a bit, likely? "

" Got more in me system now than you ever marched over," Snowy said.

" A nice dose o' salts'll cure all that for ye," said Bill comfortably. " My mother always said a tight belly makes a blockhead. Perhaps that's what's wrong with ye all."

" We done the job, chum," Snowy said without feeling. " And if we hadn't, the rest of you couldn't have got started. You're jealous. That's all that's wrong with you. Nasty complaint, too."

Bill was listening to the girl, hearing the doctor talking about Pet in just the same words. She might recover, of course, but a nasty complaint can go one way, or the other, so best not worry and let it take its course. The little brass slides on top of the bag clicked together, rattling the rows of tubes inside, then hat and bag had gone, leaving him watching a pill-box on the hallstand. Worrying will do nothing for either of you, in a voice with a fireside and good food in it, and then grey light from the open door caught him across the face and darkened again in a slam that made the silence worse, listening up the stairs at Pet, knowing she was listening back at him.

" I didn't mean it nasty," Snowy said, thinking he had gone too far.

" Had me mind on home," said Bill. " Funny, ye can't seem to stop, can you? "

" I'll stop when I get there," Snowy said. " And if they want me again, they can have me. If they can find me. But I'll make bloody sure they can't. You take that from me."

" We're not like men at all," Bill said. " We're like a damned lot of doped animals, wandering about. Worst of it is, I can't see a finish to it."

4

A little way off an American lorry pulled out of a side road and slowed to set down a soldier, and with barely a pause started on again, passing by in pleated draperies of dust.

"Ye'd swear somebody were after them for the rent," said Bill. "They must have something on their consciences."

"If we had the stuff, we'd be the same," Snowy said. "They don't have to worry where the next one's coming from. They believe in using things up. It's all there, waiting for them. It's us that's barmy."

"This bloke don't look none too bright, anyhow," said Bill, in a voice that was part of the leaf rustle. "Ye'd not send him far with a shopping bag and half a crown, would ye?"

The soldier was even shorter than Bill, narrow in the shoulder, and bandy, walking on the inside of his heels with an oddly deliberate placing and lifting of his feet, as if he feared somebody might take the ground away. He was looking at them with his head slightly on one side, perhaps asking himself a question, but a couple of yards away he stopped and smiled, and straightened his face. His eyes were fringed black with travel dust and veined with strain.

"Hi," he said, and smiled again.

"Hi-yi," Snowy nodded. "Lost your army, have you?"

"Right," the American said, without a smile. "I never felt so good."

"Try some?" Bill held out his mug, and, seeing the American hesitating, grinned. "I just put the poison in. Didn't you see me?"

"That's mighty kind of you." The American turned the mug handle to drink on the opposite side to Bill. "You boys going south?"

Bill nodded.

"Room for me?" the American asked, perhaps diffidently.

" 'Course," said Bill. " How far do you want to go?"

" Oh, well now." The American looked up at the oranges, showing the swollen veins in his eyes. " Down aways, I guess. I've been told there's nothing going on except a lot of peace."

" That's right," Bill said. " The war's up this end now. They thought it was time. They got tired of it down there."

" Me, too." The American passed the mug back to Bill. " That's good tea."

" See? " Bill said. " Outside opinion, that is. Unprejudiced."

" Something wrong? " the American asked.

" No, boy." Snowy waved at the grass. " Have a lump of conquered territory. We're taking a couple of minutes off for a break."

The American squatted against an orange tree. In among the olive-drab sprawl, seeping through the creases and rumples of waterproof cloth and gaberdine, Snowy thought he could see a smile, or the makings of a grin; and a notion that the American wanted to laugh, although his face was free of any sign except tiredness, made him stare, coldly, though without rancour.

" Something striking you comic? " he asked.

The American looked at him directly, for an instant with a matching coldness, and then he smiled, with little bubbles on the edges of his teeth, and looked up at the green spread.

" I was thinking what happens to you," he said gently. " The darndest things. When I was a kid, about the first thing I ever heard was the Boston tea-party, and the Redcoats burning the Capitol. I used to hate 'em. So the first thing you know I'm having a tea-party with their relations. In Italy, where my old man was raised, for God's sakes."

Snowy looked down at the bright top of the milk tin and knew without looking up that Bill was watching it, and that each had replaced the disc in mind as the other's face, for in deference to the rules of hospitality they were not openly staring at each other, but each had closed an eye, they knew, in a fat, cold wink.

" Where's that get you? " Snowy asked.

" About in the second grade," said the American, still looking at the leaves. " Along with Goody Two Shoes. Make you sore? "

" Nothing makes me sore, chum," Snowy said. " Except thinking of blokes at home who ought to be out here, and blokes out here who ought to be back home."

" O.K. with me." The American settled down, careless of the moss stain. " I'd sure like to be home."

" How long you been out? " Snowy asked, and looked up at him.

" Eight-nine months," said the American.

Snowy stood, dusting himself.

" Roll on," he said. " I've been out here nigh on five years."

He saw the bloodshot eyes widen, and the turning of a head.

" Ah, Jesus," the American said. " Wherever you go, it's grief. I've gotten so I don't care any more. I'd just go nuts."

" That'll be easy," said Bill. " Take it from me, there's better than us wearing strait-jackets."

" Can't do a thing about it," the American told the leaves. " Horsing around like a bunch of goons. If you can't use a gun, you're no god damn good."

" Make the best of it, that's all," Snowy said. " Blokes up the line are worse off. You infantry? "

The American got up, with both hands crushing his cap further down on his head.

" Yeah," he said. " I was. Right now I'm a tourist, and I'm headed south, if that's all right with you boys? "

Bill led a slow procession back to Rosie, with the American following and Snowy in rear, bending to evade the hiss of laden branches, wearing a garland of clinking mugs on his little finger.

" Know where you want to go? " Snowy asked.

" South," said the American. " That's all. But fast."

Snowy passed the mugs and the brewcan to Bill, and watched him hanging them on nails along the canopy supports.

" Got a pass? " he asked, trying and failing to keep denial out of his voice.

Out of the corner of his eye he saw the American smilingly shake his head.

" No pass," he said. " No orders. No nothing. Just me." His hands made an awkward move towards his pockets. " Still want me along? "

Bill gave the kits a final tidy pat, and then jumped down, pulling up his stockings like a schoolboy, and went round to the cabin without a look or a word.

" Deserted? " Snowy asked.

" A.W.O.L." The American took out a package of cigarettes. " Absent without leave, that's me, brother. Just couldn't take it any more."

Snowy nodded.

" I know how you feel, chum," he said. " Get in and make yourself comfortable. If we get stopped, don't forget, you got on when we pulled up for traffic. We never even seen you. See? "

" You won't get in any jam on account of me," the American said.

" Ain't afraid of that, chum," said Snowy. " We're Eighth Army. Nobody gets us in no jam. Up you get."

Snowy gave him a heave that carried him over the tailboard.

" We'll only stop for our own redcaps," he said. " They won't be no bother. So get down to it and don't worry about nothing. We'll look after you." He took the package of cigarettes, feeling an opulence of cellophane under his thumb. "Sure you can spare these? "

The American nodded.

" Off we go," said Snowy, and went round to the cabin. Bill was sitting with his hands between his knees, looking out of the window. The lines in his forehead spelt trouble.

" Hold tight," Snowy yelled, and shut the door. " Here's some Yankee cigarettes. They look so posh I'm afraid to smoke 'em."

" We're just helping him to be a damn fool," Bill said.

" You don't know what happened." Snowy let Rosie take the turn and watched the wheel come back to normal. " He knew what he was doing."

" And none too proud of it, neither," Bill said. " If he gets caught, we'll be inside along of him. Aiding and abetting."

" Who's going to catch us? " Snowy asked. " He's only got to say he nipped on at a traffic stop. 'Sides, he's probably done as much as any of them blokes back home."

" That's no answer," Bill said. " There's blokes back home's done their share, too. And women and kids. They can't duck a bomb, you know."

In a murmur of contralto overtones Rosie rocked herself along tarmac patched in mauve and blue always shadowed by the fringing orangeries below a curve of mountain lost in rumples of cloud. A tower stark on the skyline pointed from a little group of red ochre buildings with neither tree, nor garden, nor any sign of nearby green.

" Wonder who lives all the way up there? " Snowy was bending to look under the windscreen. " They must have my kind of relations, I should say."

" Probably a church, or some such," said Bill. " Superstitious lot, they are. Country's crawling wi' parsons."

" They've got a good job, you ask me," nodded Snowy. " The people's like mice. Look at this shower."

A procession of men and women among a scamper of children were coming out of a grove, and when Rosie slowed to give them way they stopped in a crowd, each brown face glossy with a well-sweated skin at rest, and eyes that even in the children looked as if they would never be surprised. Nobody wore shoes, and the knuckly stems of their toes were spaced like claws to grip the tarmac, looking up, waiting, with something of the feeling of sheep in a moment before they turn and bolt.

Women were dressed in black skirts, ragged at the hem from trailing the ground, with blouses of fady pink or blue, and their heads were bound in cloths tied under bulging plaits at the nape. Their babies wore little but a cut-down flour sack, and boys and girls looked like dwarf men and women in cast-offs, and the older men were in mixtures of threadbare army issue without buttons, so limp and patched as to want a special sort of shrug to keep them from slipping off.

Snowy leaned on the wheel, tiredly turning to Bill.

" How could this lot have the neck to go and declare war on us ? " he demanded. " Eh? We must have been in a fine mess. Bloody sauce, I call it."

" I'm not listening," said Bill. " I've seen all I want to."

" So've I," said Snowy. " But, blimey. I mean to say."

Children were clustering around the tailboard. He put his head out in time to see a girl reach up for a sweet wrapped in foil glittering like broken crystal, and the pale hair shone in her armpit. Instantly he saw Liz drawing the curtains in the morning, and sat back in the cabin, leaning his head against the cool leather, listening to the wild marvel of another song.

"What's up?" Bill asked, startled into sympathy. "Feel bad?"

"No, chum," Snowy said. "Just going scatty, that's all. Seeing things."

Bill opened the door and got down.

Snowy heard the talk without caring. He could see the garden, and feel the slats of the seat he had made for her bearing through and cutting him when she sat on his knee after the evening job with the watering can. Feel it all, see it all, so plainly, and helplessly.

Bill came back and sat down, bouncing the seat springs, and in anger the vision bumped out of his mind.

He let Rosie go, finding almost a satisfaction in the sound of her voice, as though she knew what he was thinking, and he patted the wheel as he might have stroked a mane.

"That Yank can't half parley the lingo," Bill said. "They was all over him. Specially the kids."

"Always will, for sweets," said Snowy. "My two used to go mad. My littlest one, she says to me one Sunday, we're out for a walk while the old lady's getting the dinner, see? She says, Dad, she says, passing a sweetshop at the time, we was, she's about three, sharp as they make 'em, she says, Dad, what do sweets taste like? 'Course, after that I got a choking-off from the old lady because they couldn't eat no dinner."

"Wish I had a couple," Bill said.

"What's up?" Snowy looked at him. "Wasn't you trying?"

"She can't." Bill was looking into the bowl of his pipe. "She's been laid up nigh two years. Best lass in the world."

"Hard luck," said Snowy.

Bill liked the feeling, but not the tone, for Pet's mother always spoke in the same way, as if she were being sorry from a height; and again he heard the iron-hinge whine of indrawn breath when she stopped talking about Pet, the last one of eleven, and always the weak one, but she brought that pay packet home every Friday night of her life since she were a twelve-year-old, and never knew the inside of a bed in daytime till just after she got herself married.

The whole family looked at him as if he were up to some game or other, but there was nothing he could say; and even when the doctor told them it was a blood disease in their own family they still looked at him as though they were telling him it was all his fault for not being more of a man. Ah, Will, the little voice was whispering again, why not get shot of me, useless lump I am. If I could only cook you a nice dinner, Will. I lie here and I think of a nice roast in the oven and roast potatoes. Oh, Will, why ever did you marry me?

Ah, Pet.

5

Private First Class Maximilian Montemuro sat on a bed-roll watching the road curving and recurving through cigarette smoke, accepting the jolt of Rosie's gait with schooled disregard, yet distantly thankful that it was tarmac and not an unpaved road that grizzled tunes beneath the tyres.

He watched the neons painting the roadway's sheen, hearing the jive outfit in the South-Sea Room giving with a warming comfort of sound that let him feel a part of a world that wanted him, where he felt safe and sure of a niche, able to tap his feet to its rhythm and feel the music roaming his head, maybe whistling counterpoint under his breath, sitting on a bar stool just watching the lights working miracles on the bottles until she came and put that hand on his shoulder from in back there. He felt her pat his cheek and bend over and whisper, Hi, and make the place swim around the way it never did for bourbon. Except maybe when she leaned on him so he could feel the points of her breasts, and then her perfume got crowded up high in his head, turning over and over, like a loosening spring inside there, whipping at sight and sound and hearing. He could hear himself saying, Hi, and kneeing out a stool for her, showing nothing, not even a smile.

But she knew.

She knew from the hand on his shoulder. He never could stop that shiver. He never wanted to. That was the feeling, and that was why he shivered, and he was shivering now, but not the same way.

She had to be there.

He got up, clinging to the bars overhead for support, and arm over arm went down to the tailboard and sat on the edge, breathing the colder air, watching the miles of green on either side of the road, conscious of nothing, thinking of nothing, feeling nothing except the want of her, and nothing else mattered, nothing else had meaning.

A few feet away, over a shudder of footboards and beyond the cabin wall, Bill was wondering where he was being taken. For years, it seemed to him, all kinds of people had been shoving him off to all sorts of places without asking an if you please or by your leave. It was a case of do this, do that, get in there, hop up here, or report to this or that place, all of it without asking him, or worrying about what he felt or thought or if he wanted to, or anything. They knew he was only a bloke in uniform, and They had him, They knew, only because if ever he got obstinate They could put him behind the bars; and They knew he was afraid of nothing except the disgrace of prison, so They played on it and did what They liked and They kept on doing it.

" I'm sick of it," he said, suddenly enough to surprise even himself. " Proper, thorough, sick of it."

" Quite right," said Snowy, helpfully, but equally surprised. " What of? "

" Getting chased about," Bill said. " Like a school kid. Go here. Go there. Get that done. Do this. Else take a court martial."

" Thinking of the Yank? " asked Snowy.

" No." Bill rattled his pipe against the brake, and Snowy saw tobacco flakes and ash fall on the polished embossure of Rosie's plates. He took off his beret and dusted the offence towards the door on his side, opened it an inch, and gave the little pile to the wind.

" Sorry," Bill said.

" It's all right." Snowy's tone implied a different answer next time. " Who was you thinking about then? "

" Us," said Bill. " Specially me. I'm a master man at me own job, I am. I've earned me own living since I were thirteen. Worked since I was eight. But here I am getting chucked about as if I were a tramp or a bloke as never done a hand's turn. Just because I'm supposed to be a soldier."

" Well, there you are," Snowy said. " What can you do about it? "

" I'm just sick and tired of being shoved about by a lot of people I don't know, that's all," said Bill. " If we was civvies, I'd black a few eyes for 'em. There's hardly one of 'em could earn a decent living. They don't know enough. But look what they do to us."

" I've thought about it, too, mate," Snowy said. " But it don't do you no good. Just get on with it. They've got you, any way you turn. Roll on, that's all I say. Once I'm out, they're welcome to try and get me back. Never again, boy."

" Same here," said Bill. " They can make the most of me now. They've had me once, but never no more. By God, no."

Snowy watched detour signs approaching and turned off on a bulldozed road through the heaped rubble of a wrecked bridge. Rosie made heavy going over the pounded earth and soon the cabin was filled again with a stinging dust. Snowy braked.

" Better ask that Yank to come in here," he said. " He'll choke, else."

" Good idea," said Bill, and climbed out.

Snowy looked up at the broken piers of the bridge, and, putting flesh on unseen bones, tried to see rubble back in its arches again, but it seemed a fairy tale. This heap of stones could never have been a tall bridge to be ridden over confidently day after day by ordinary people giving it no thought. Five spans across a river bed put there by unknown workmen, nothing more than rock, craftsmanship, imagination and time; and yet he seemed to hear it praying to be up on its legs again, shoulders spread and arms wide to take the homely burdens of the road that ended, chopped off short, a hundred feet up the cliff, in regular layers, pretty as a cake, of stone and concrete and asphalt, with a broken pot in a froth of weeds still crowning the end of the baluster.

Bill opened the door and the American got in with an air of belonging elsewhere.

" Say," he said, " I'm a nuisance around here. Why didn't you just go ahead? "

" Didn't want no dead Yanks on me hands, that's all," said Snowy. " Plenty of room."

" My name's Montemuro," the American said. " Call me Max."

" Snowy Weeks," said Snowy. " That's Bill Dodds."

" Hi," said Max. " I certainly appreciate this. Boy, did they make a mess of that bridge."

" Bloody shame," Snowy said. " You think of all the work there is in that lot. One big bang, and it's a brickyard."

" Those Krauts," said Max. " They surely have the knowhow."

Rosie mumbled over the soft roadway, barely keeping her front fork between the guide posts. Drooping lengths of tape blew in twists from iron stakes, and white signs screamed a red MINES among the weeds. Further on, where the cutting led up to the roadway, a pile of mines like solid iron wheels were stacked on the grass verge.

" Those things give me the pip," said Bill. " They get me down."

" Same here," Snowy said. " I've had all them."

" Ever hear 'em go off? " asked Max. " Like to scare the pants off you."

" Had one under this off-fore wheel here," said Snowy. " Blew me and my mate clean out of the cabin. Took the front axle and the engine out just like a cut of cold ham. There we was."

" Get hurt ?" asked Max.

" Deaf as a post for a couple of weeks," Snowy said. He patted the wheel. " She saved us. But that's only part of Rosie's doings, that is. Best drop of bus on the road. Ain't you, gel? "

For answer, Rosie nosed at the ramp in a growl of power and went up to the roadway in depths of content, rumbling in the very fat of virtue.

" See? " said Snowy. " Anywhere, anytime, anyhow. No trouble. That's Rosie."

" How'd she get her name? " asked Max.

" My oldest girl," said Snowy. " And my old Ma. O.K.? "

" O.K.," said Max. " My wife's name is Rosalinda. She just had a girl. Had a bad time."

" Hard luck," said Snowy.

He saw poor old Liz lying whitely still, hair stuck on her forehead with sweat, and blue shadows about her eyes, but the midwife quickly pinned his question with a forefinger. For just that moment he thought she might be dead and the barest notion of living on without her dried his mouth. He felt his face going cold; but then, seeming to feel him there, she opened her eyes and a smile came in those reddish eyeballs so unlike the eyes he thought he knew. Hullo, she said, but quietly. Hullo, my darling old matey, he wanted to say, if the spit had been there to loosen it. You and your bleeding bed, she says, you nearly done for me.

" Just the same with my dear old duck," he said. " I could have cut my throat. She had four days of it the first time. But it was all right the second time."

Bill felt that jealousy again, just as he had when the men at work spoke among themselves of those important moments when the nurse opens the door and the wife is seen fresh out of her pain, and by her side the child they waited for. He knew it could never happen for him, and somehow he could see Pet's face and the restless hands.

" She all right? " he asked.

Max nodded.

" I hope," he said. " That's why I'm taking time out. You can't shoot somebody and then produce a daughter, all in one day. A guy can't take it. Maybe some can. Not me."

" Supposing we all couldn't? " Bill asked. " What then? "

" We all don't think the same way," said Max. " Me, I think the way I think. You think something else. That's how it ought to be, and that's the way it is. So I'm headed south. You can drop me off any time you want."

" Listen," Bill said. " That's not what I meant. The rest of your lads are holding on while you're down here. If they all dodged out, what would happen to your wife and the kid? "

" I told you," Max said patiently. " Some guys can take it. I can, up as far as here. Then I have to walk. I don't know what would happen. I just know I'm sick of killing. Sick to my stomach. Yesterday I shot a guy, and, Jesus, he rolled over screeching, screeching, screeching, holding his belly. Next thing you know,

I have a message I'm a father. I can see her, and she's holding her belly, and she's screeching too. So I figure I'll take a walk. No straight lines any more."

Snowy saw the wide river again, and the pebbles poking out of the water. Rain was on the wind, bringing over the talk of a lot of Jerries doing their laundry under the chestnut on the far bank. He watched the hussar load his Bren, sliding the sights up, digging his toes in the grass, and then his fist tightened in a burst that made little fountains play in the water this side of the washers, and all the pink faces looked up together. Two dropped in the splashes, and all the others ran, except one crawling head down, dragging a leg. Someone was shouting and yet not shouting, high, and frightened, like a rabbit not quite dead in a trap, and somebody said it served the bastard right.

"We'll stop for some grub later on," he said. "I know a family down there. She can't half cook."

Max looked over Rosie's bonnet, thinking of her paintwork and bright metal, wondering how men could waste time painting and polishing and talking about food when right that moment some other mother's son was breaking his nails tearing at rock with given blood bursting through a hole in his belly.

"God damn it," he said. "I don't want to eat. I can see that boy."

"That's all right," said Snowy. "But you might change your mind. We've seen a few dead blokes, too, you know. Been one where you're sitting."

Bill remembered how cold it was that morning, lying there with his arms outside the bedclothes, watching the sisters push the dressing trolley from bed to bed along the ward. The Christmas paper chains tossed like the scurry of dry leaves across pavements, and the chatter of glass on the trolley reminded him of the milkman coming down the back lane at home.

He was thinking of Old Cob, and the dried flowers and summer grasses between the pages of his Bible, muniments of time spent at the roadside, or on tracks through the ploughland, or against the vines, or waist high in purple iris, raising his voice across the rough breath of hurrying traffic while water brewed for tea. *And I will make thee unto this people a fenced, brasen wall.* He heard the words and felt again the coldness sitting there listening, yet a different coldness from this that froze his arms and clamped each finger-tip in a slammed door. *And they shall fight against thee, but they shall not prevail against thee: for I am with thee to save thee, and to deliver thee, saith the Lord.*

And always, over against that well-remembered voice there lay another, immanent, yet strangely apart, deliberately pitched in some cool wilderness of the spirit that said Craftsman Cobbett died this morning. We were all very sorry. He went off quite peacefully.

The clinking trolley, the clatter of pans in the washup, the grey walls, and the smell of disinfectant on brisk hands pulling blankets over his shoulders, all morticed craftily into that other voice.

He could just see Old Cob, and his seven wounds, lighting his pipe, and stumping off peacefully to Paradise in search of a House of Many Mansions, foretold in a book of thin pages marked by flowers and grasses, and blessed by the juice of his fists.

6

Rosie took the landscape into herself as into a basket, throwing it away on either side, gentling the bends, and making nothing of hills and dips, meeting all the winds with a little sonant of remote contempt. She lumbered through the town's cobbled veins, whined displeasure when she took the corners, hummed her plainsong across the piazza, and bellowed at the crossroad when Snowy brought her short at a tail of priests behind a black procession of veiled women and children. Bill opened the window, letting in a wrangle of church bells among a chant of voices. Beyond Rosie's own chorale, they heard the frayed metal of an old priest's voice edging through a soft soprano shell.

" His best friends wouldn't tell him," said Max.

" Couldn't make themselves heard," said Bill. " He's spoiling the issue."

" Leave him alone," Snowy said. " Poor old bloke's only earning his money. Any case, if they all put as much in the job as he's doing, you wouldn't hear him at all."

" Damn Catholics," Bill said. " Ye'll have nowt from them except noise and trouble. Big churches and big slums. Fat shepherds, thin sheep. Look at 'em. Isn't one of 'em hasn't got a guts like a gasworks."

" I'm a Catholic," said Max.

" I meant the priests," Bill said. " I never meant to hurt your feelings."

" I don't have any," said Max. " People have been saying that about 'em for years. There's still an awful lot of Catholics."

" My opinion," said Bill. " Too many."

" This country didn't get in any mess till they started kicking the church around," said Max. " Now look at 'em."

" That's politics, that is," Bill said. " Trust the Catholics."

" Oy," Snowy leaned over the wheel. " Singing, dancing, gambling—except if it's a dead cert—any kind of blondes, and talking about religion ain't allowed in this saloon. Else I'll have to start slinging a few of you out in the road."

" What religion are you? " Max asked him.

" Me? " Snowy laughed, sitting lower. " None, chum. You ask me, it's all me eye. If it wasn't for some of 'em making a living out of it there wouldn't be none. I reckon we'd all be better off. That's that. I'd like to get my old dear a bit of that there purple, though."

Two ranks of priests in laced surplices and long purple gowns followed the crowd of women stretching across the road, with a group of choristers in front and a flanking of fatherly old men dressed in raggedy shifts. Many of the women wore shoes made from a wedge of cork tied at the ankle with cloth strips, and it was all they could do to get from one cobble to another without ricking an ankle, so most of them walked with their heads down, holding on to their veils, balancing as if they were walking on a rope.

But the chant never stopped.

Inch by inch, though without a turn of the head or any sign that Rosie had been seen or heard, the procession edged over, and once the channel was clear Rosie sang with them, and incense filled the cabin.

"Notice the young blokes don't take no part in it?" said Snowy. "They leave it all to the women and kids, seems like."

"Wops," said Bill. "That's them all over. Too damn bone-idle, that's why."

"My father was a wop," said Max.

"If it's only out of spite," Bill said. "I'll be bound to say something right in a minute."

"It's O.K.," said Max. "We don't mind it. Don't do a thing to the people. They still go to work. Still have kids. Build houses. Grow the stuff. You never saw country better handled, did you?"

"It's all right," said Bill. "But how many times d'you ever see a bloke working?"

"You'd probably see a whole lot more if they'd let 'em loose from the prison camps," Max said. "Two or three million, maybe. Two or three million men, rotting their lives away behind the wire. Jesus. No wonder these poor bastards pray. They have to."

Snowy found himself sympathizing with the savage undertone in the voice, and wishing that Bill could be persuaded not to open his mouth again, for in the granite of his eye and the knife powder in his voice there was constant challenge to everybody either to align their opinion with his, make divergence good by proof, or else keep silence, and Snowy felt that Max was not the sort to align or prove, much less keep silent.

Even the light in the cabin seemed tremulous with cross-shafts of feeling.

Bill was urging himself to think of something to say, nothing that might start another argument, but the longer he thought the worse grew the silence, until he was ready to give up thinking and fight, if only to alter the pressure of air.

Max was thinking of his father, pale from nightwork in the bakery, watering the window-box back home. He could see the hands puffy from long kneads in the dough-trough and the feet splayed from years of standing on puddled stone floors, and he heard the cough that sounded as though blades were fretting deep in his chest, and white stubble in the crack of his cheek when he smiled. Through time and distance he reached out an arm and put it strongly about the old man's shoulders, feeling a heat to defend the gentleness of his smile.

"My pa beat his brains out to bring up eight of us," he said. "All he ever wanted to do was grow things in the garden. He never did. He worked twelve, fourteen hours a day. My two brothers are lawyers. My kid sister's a doctor. So he's a wop."

"Talking about these blokes over here," Bill said. "Not in America. They're different. They change when they get over there, somehow, I suppose. And as I've said, I didn't mean to hurt your feelings. Anybody said anything about my old dad, I'd kill him. Plain enough?"

Rosie's headlamps nudged aside the children leading the procession, and among the upturned faces Snowy could see the two girls on the morning he left the house that last time and poor old Liz standing in the doorway, eyes silvered over, trying heavens hard not to cry.

Deliberately he geared his mind away, feeling the blood thicken in his head, perhaps conforming to Rosie's faster pulse, and then realized she was going more than fifty miles an hour in a street paved for cartwheels.

"Sometimes you've got to get out of it, quick," he said, excusing himself. "All them poor little kids. You can't bear it, somehow. There's nothing you can do. That's what narks me. It's always some other bloke's got to do something, and he's higher up, and he don't care, seems like."

"As long as they're comfortable, they'll not bother," said Bill. "If the work gets done, and their grub's on the table, why should they? They might go and spoil it for themselves."

Max found himself amused against his wish by the conflict and yet the apparent agreement between these two. The air of solid goodwill even in the heat of argument was a new experience that pleased and yet puzzled, and he found himself looking on like someone outside a glass tank watching a pair of Siamese fighting fish.

"You mean you'd want to help these kids?" he asked. "What about the women?"

"What about 'em?" asked Snowy. "Poor cows don't know which end's which. No grub, no soap, half the time there's no water, and no gas or coal. I don't know how they manage. But I can tell you this much. Liz wouldn't stand for it. She'd be out in the road, quick, copperstick in one hand, carver in the other. And I pity any poor bloke got in her way."

"Different blood," said Bill. "This lot's used to getting knocked about. Comes natural, so they put up with it. I'll bet the Americans wouldn't, what I've seen of 'em."

"Don't worry, brother," Max said. "They'll never have to."

Snowy sat up straighter behind the wheel, staring directly ahead, and deliberately pushed back his beret, rubbing it to and fro until his scalp stopped itching.

Bill sat rigid, watching the hair above his knees ruffling in a breeze from the open window. He had no desire to cause fresh trouble, but here was a real slice out of what he had always considered to be Yankee bellyfat, and there was much he wanted to say. The tone and the words made him feel right beside himself. He could see Pet sitting up in bed, pulling the curtains aside to make funny little noises at the ginger cat from next door tearing about in the garden, perhaps spoiling the precious crop, and he heard his mother grumbling about the way the world had gone to satandom since she was a girl, what with having to use milk powder instead of cream and frying up a lot of old muck instead of being able to give a lad a decent bit of steak to his dinner.

Snowy had that cold feeling again, the one that always came when he thought of Liz and the kids left without him. The thought of getting killed and never seeing them again always brought that icing of flesh and warm blood. He felt her arms in surprising woman's strength about him and the way she shook in wordless goodbye; and he could see her face, her cheek was soft for his kiss, and the joyous bulges of her hipbones were firm in his grip.

"You're lucky, chum," he said. "We've got to worry."

"Listen," Max said. "Don't get me wrong. I meant what I said. Our women don't have to worry. The country produces. We have the stuff. Do I have to say I'm sorry?"

Snowy shook his head.

"Best not talk about it," he said. "It's a rotten business. I got a wife and a couple of kids. If I get knocked off, what happens to 'em ? Not much saved up and nothing coming in. She don't want a pension. She wants me. As for saying you're sorry, it was the way you put it."

" Boasting," Bill said, and took off his spectacles almost defensively. " That's what it was. That's always been the damn trouble with you blokes. Always slinging your weight about. What you've got and what you haven't, and what you're going to do."

" So what? " Max looked at him with a wide eye.

" So give over," said Bill. " We don't want to know."

" Half a mo'." Snowy slowed down. " Listen; you Lancashire blokes, you're all the same. What don't suit you must be wrong. I reckon you've got a sauce, talking like that. Don't help nobody. Just get yourselves popular, that's all, 'sides making it bloody uncomfortable for everybody. Now you give over."

" Swell atmosphere," said Max. " I better get back in there."

" Stay here," said Snowy. " Nothing like a drop of fresh air sometimes. Blows the cobwebs off."

" I'm supposed to be sitting here like Joe Dripping, am I?" asked Bill. " Properly told off, so sit in your corner and suck your thumb ? Eh? "

" I don't want no arguments, that's all," Snowy said. " No nasty tempers. No need for it. Never was."

" But I wasn't arguing," said Bill. " I was telling him."

" There's your Lancashire for you," Snowy said. " They never argue. They tell you. And what they tell you is gospel. It's only when they get down my part of the country they ever get any sense knocked in 'em."

" Sense? " Bill put on his spectacles as though creeping out of a nightmare on all fours. " What, in London? If some of us didn't take ye a bit now and again, ye'd all be hopping about with your fingers crooked, daft as brushes. I notice none of you London blokes ever come up to Lancashire. Ye'd never last."

" See? " said Snowy. " And it's the Yanks do all the bragging. God stone my grannie's hat."

" Whose side are you on? " Max asked.

" Me own," Snowy said. " There's a lot of trouble caused by yap. Round our way they'll shut it for you. Be surprised what a push in the snitch'll do for a yap. Now come, the pair of you."

Somewhere within himself Bill could feel injustice burning craggy ash. There were things he wanted to say that seemed ungenerous, and others that were merely bad temper, and one by one they passed, thought, phrased, analysed, and in their passing left a thin froth of feeling, a sense of impotence that in weariness brought him to laughter.

"I can see the funny side of it somehow," he said. "I always have. It's no use. We're all daft as bloody poultry."

Max argued with himself for sitting there in silence just for the sake of peace and the ride. These two with their strange talk were creatures of another world, a breed well hated for the greater part of his life, villains of most of the history he knew, arsonists, rapers, cunning plotters and crafty schemers, unprincipled when it came to borrowing the riches of his country to keep a shaky empire from falling apart, with never a word of thanks and nary a cent in return.

"Look," he said. "If he can say what he wants, so can I. Some of that chow in back came from the States. We've been giving you all kinds of stuff, just like we did the first time. But, by God, we had to come over and finish the job, too, didn't we?"

"Now, listen," said Snowy, stroking the wheel. "This old bus, old Rosie, she's come all through the piece. She got a basinful when we landed here, and my mate got killed, and so did about a dozen blokes in the back there. They was all Yanks. It's no good of talking like that in here. There's too many of your own blokes listening. And my old mate. As for finishing the job, I reckon we'll all be there together. But not the way we're going."

"Beats me how we've got as far, if you all think alike," said Bill. "Anybody'd think you was damn' foreigners, the way you go on."

"But you guys talk as if nobody else was around," Max said. "Do you think we're still some kind of a colony?"

"Listen," Snowy said. "Ever hear kids squabbling over a couple of apples? Ow, look, Mum, she's got a bigger one'n I have. No, I ain't. Yes, you have. I just dish out a clip in the ear to my two. Pity there ain't somebody to dish out a few to some of us."

"I wish we spoke some other language, for God's sakes," Max said. "French, or Eskimo. Anything. Then we could quit being polite and just say what we want to. I'm sick of this kind of stuff."

"No more than we are, chum," said Bill. "We've put up with it long enough."

"Listen," said Snowy. "I'm in charge of this wagon, see? Now, I'm on leave, the first I've had for four years. I'm going to meet some decent people, have some decent grub, think about my family, and my mate. Old Shiner. If he was sitting up here, he wouldn't be arguing the toss. He'd be singing away there, enjoying life. How about it?"

"Suits me," said Max, and offered a cigarette.

"Ta," said Snowy.

"Much obliged," said Bill, and held out a lighter.

"Thanks," said Max.

"Now then." Snowy took off his beret to rub the dust off the windscreen. "Who d'you reckon this is?"

7

A woman in brown was walking almost on the crown of the road where the hedge was red in a sprawl of rambler rose.

She was walking slowly, not lazily, and erect, swinging one gloved hand, carrying a small suitcase in the other. The seams of her silk stockings cut her calves like a knife through a pear, but there was a hole in the heel of one, and the shoes were thick with dust. A handbag was slung on one shoulder, and a hooded bird perched on the other, held by a little chain.

"Strictly an up-town gal," Max said. "Low whistles really get the bird. Brother, that's class."

"It's a hawk," said Bill. "She'll never be gone rabbiting dressed up like that with a portmanteau, surely?"

"You'll be all right in here," Snowy said. "I'll look after you."

Rosie whispered up behind her to draw level, and then took a breath, preface, as it were, to spoken invitation.

Snowy leaned out of the cab window immediately above a brown felt hat turned up at the back, down in front, and saw the lace of her blouse; but she was looking up, and her eyes were brown, and freshness was in her skin not so much from its colour as from a quality that seemed to light the air around her, as though everything had drained through and dried away, leaving her to shine quietly in a place all her own.

"Er," said Snowy, and turned to Max. "Here, come on. You can talk Eyetie. Ask her if she wants a lift."

"Sure I want a lift," she called. "How far are you going?"

"Jesus," said Max. "Right off the main drag. Hullo there."

"Hullo," she said. "Don't all look at me like that, please. I'm on my way to see my husband. He's a guest of the Allies." She dandled the suitcase. "This is mostly food for him. And this is Li'l Abner," she said, putting her cheek against nervous plumage. "My protection. You'll never know how I needed it."

"I'd be a son of a gun if you didn't," said Max. "That why you're walking?"

"That's why," she said. "The ride finished just after lunch. The gentleman should have lost an eye. Lost his temper instead. So I still don't have any oil in my lamp. But I certainly have a mail order set of bunions. Don't your friends talk?"

"Not when we can listen to you," Snowy said. "If you'd like a lift, the door's the other side."

"That's British enough," she said. "But please don't let's have any of that Perfidious Albion stuff."

"Never heard of him," said Snowy.

"We're both married," said Bill. "Ye'll be safe enough."

"Oh no," she said. "That sounds kind of horribly dull."

"They've been out here since Eve wanted the core back," Max said. "You better watch your step, lady."

"Mind how you fall down these two," said Bill, holding the door open. "I'll take t' bag round to t' back."

She got in and sat next to Snowy.

"I thought soldiers weren't allowed to transport civilians," she said.

"We ain't," said Snowy. "Where do you want to go?"

"About two hundred miles south." She lifted her feet. "Mind if I take these off? I'm taking such a beating." She slid the shoes under the seat and shut her eyes, sighing. "That's heaven. I wasn't made for walking."

"Ain't there nobody round your way'll give you a lift?" Snowy asked. "No officers?"

"Plenty," she said. "But I don't need that kind of help. Certainly not after today. My name's Castelfalcone. Adela Castelfalcone, just in case you get stopped. Falcone." She lifted the shoulder perching the bird. "This. It's a falcon. I haven't any identity card, but I'm Italian by choice, if you want to know. I'm sick of catechism. Sick of the whole mess."

Her voice tipped up.

Snowy looked hard out of the side window. He could hear the kettle promising supper after they all got back from the park the night before he came away, and the kids were upstairs singing ride-a-cock-horse, hoping he might go up there and sing it with them on the bed. Needles was cleaning her face in her box by the fire and suddenly the kettle lid was rolling about the floor, and Liz was black against the gaslight, running over to him falling on her knees between his legs putting her arms around him, and he heard her saying, Take care of yourself, Bertie, in a small rough voice, swear you will. I couldn't bear it. Oh, darling, I hope other women ain't as soppy as I am. Blast the war. Blast the bloody war.

"Yes," he said. "Gets you down sometimes, don't it? This your first trip down here?"

"No," she said, herself, and cool again. "My husband's in a prison camp. I found out where he was, and I've been going down there ever since. On my flat feet."

"What, two hundred miles?" said Snowy. "Walking? What for?"

"Some kind of wifely devotion, I guess," she said. "It gets worse when you're older."

"Ah," Snowy said. "I wonder where them two've got to?"

He jumped down, wondering at the quietness, and went to the rear. Max and Bill grinned over fans of cards.

"Just happened to have 'em along," said Max.

"He's showing me stud poker," Bill said. "It's a lovely game."

"Why didn't you say you wasn't coming back?" Snowy demanded. "I've been waiting up there like Joe."

"Sorry," said Bill. "Max says she's a Princess."

Snowy glanced at the suitcase and the labelholder in Max's hand.

"It says here," Max said. "The Princess Adela Castelfalcone de Colavolpe. In black and white. Boys, it looks like we're having a big day."

"That's caused it," said Snowy, and stood considering. "You can't call her Miss, or Ma, can you? What can you say? Miss Princess?"

"I wouldn't bother, meself," said Bill. "Take it or leave it. That's me."

"Call her Babe," said Max. "If she's a Princess, she'll like it. If she ain't, she won't. Bill, I'm going to raise you just one cigarette."

"Suits me," said Bill. "Ye'll soon be smoking tinned herrings."

"Hold very tight," said Snowy, and went back to the cabin, noting the dust on Rosie's new paintwork, half sorrowing that there had to be any, half wondering why dust and other nuisances had to exist at all.

Rosie started with all the old eagerness, up, past the flowers, and into a mist the colour of lavender, and holes blown by the wind were filled with the bright green of pasture down on the plain. Mountains went up in clear air and then were lost in foam that never seemed to move, and just beneath the cloudline mile on mile of pines in dark clutter straggled down to a dreariness of bare stumps and skinned logs.

But nearer the road the mountainside was tidy as a park, patterned in olive trees terracing in steps dug out of rock, banked with stone, and filled with basketsful of earth carried up from the valley on the shoulders of other generations building themselves, all unknown, into green memorial.

Further on, Snowy turned the key and Rosie began to whistle under her breath downhill into the plain, along a road running between red earth in ruts that seemed to stretch to the horizon on both sides, turning like spokes on two great wheels all shining wet under drab light.

The Princess shivered, remembering the time before, and blistered feet and arms that felt numb from carrying the suitcase, thinking of herself, and trying to see herself on this road, one foot after another, a single figure ridiculously out of place, and not another soul in all the miles, in such dread of her lonesomeness that she might have wept to see any human being.

8

Snowy was trying to put aside awareness of the perfume and fighting to keep his mind free of silken feet wriggling enamelled toes just beneath his eyeline. In brief periods of changing gear he flinched from glossy calves and ankles like wrists, and kept his eyes on the road, remembering the night Liz let him take her stockings off, the laughter and the half-hearted struggle, the bloom of flesh in candle-light and wonder at its softness.

But the Princess Adela was wishing she had waited for the chance of the road, or anything except a trip accepted in desperation and now repented in angry impatience as moments piled, and the kilometre stones flicked by, for part of herself she had long thought dead was evidently, to her cold amazement, pleasurably alive.

This man sitting so near gave off an odour that belonged properly to the cloister, of health, clean clothes and cold water, the passive reek of a monk; and in thinking about his family, feeling quick sympathy for the wife and wondering what kind of woman could be waiting for him, and what change might be made in him, she was provoked to curiosity, turning to try and make him talk. But then, and abruptly, she was halted at prospect of a male caught in a cold moment of amenity to discipline, watching the road in grey-eyed vigilance, a natural creature performing an unnatural task, and yet accepter with dignity of all responsibility flung at him.

By making a business of looking in her handbag to find a mirror, and then pretending to use a lipstick, bending here and there to catch the sunlight, she was able to see the shaven tan of his skin, the paler lines beneath his eyes, the mouth pulled in from effort of mind, and a nose that had lost fine edge along the bridge. His hair was a dusty fairness that once was straw, the royal Saxon shade darkened by breeding in back streets grimed in an era of coal. The hands on the wheel were knotty in the finger, broad in the palm, at a glance the hands of a machinist, and the forearms were thatched with fine curls, and their shadow fell across his thighs, that moved, changing gear in a leap of muscle and then rested, tense, and she saw that the untanned flesh was white, sprung with hair that in the play of sun held warm lights, aspects of fire recalling the muscular gallop of centaurs and the glare of an eye in a lash of flame.

She was remembering a room hung with terracotta prints in little gold frames polished as far as an arm would reach, and above, dulled with dust and blotched by flies. She stood looking at them again, putting herself in place of the schoolgirl frightened by a green stare from cypress shadow, sorrowing for Lais in silent shriek of flight with her chiton held in the claws of grinning Pan. She thought of other times when fancy turned those images about and fear became expectancy, uncaring except for assault that in essence might prove delight, and ease from a new, uncertain pain, half felt and half surmised.

The falcon sought fresh hold, unhooking talons from the leather padding, shaking the little gold bell. She put up a hand, lightly stroking its warmth, smiling inwardly to think that had she been Princess a generation or two ago she might have had this commoner impaled and his entrails thrown in the mews for daring to disturb her peace of mind. But then the thought occurred that about the same time her ancestor might have been riding across the Iowan plain, and he, too, commoner and womanless in sought exile, might have carried this same brave scent of lonely men.

She moved impatiently, warming in a quick impulse of anger. She felt ashamed that she could be affected, the more since the cause, this quiet creature in crumpled twill, seemed unaware of her, and that, she found, caused deeper anger and a further self-contempt. In despair, she felt for words, if only to break thought.

"Wonderful day," she said, and frowned at herself.

"Generally is," said Snowy; "when it ain't raining."

"It's good for the land," she said, grasping at everydayness. "My garden's been crying for it."

"I always feel sorry for a garden," Snowy said. "You never know when it's had enough. My old mate always said a cabbage is just the same as you are. Just when you're enjoying yourself they close the bar. Give 'em the half-pint extra. It don't do you no harm, do it? If you was a cabbage, you'd raise your glass."

"Who was your mate?" she asked. "He sounds interesting."

"My mate?" Snowy hated the offhand enquiry in this new kind of female voice. A head lay heavily, and blood glued his fingers. "He wasn't interesting. Best bloke ever lived, that's all."

"Really?" she said. The strict tone, admirable in finer accents, was insupportable from a mere soldier, and even against her will she felt herself retiring along a crimson runner toward double doors and a bowing flunky.

"Yes, really," said Snowy, imitating her tone, but watching the road. "He got killed. I don't know why. It didn't change nothing. Everything goes on just the same. That's the part I don't understand. The best blokes in the world get killed. And it don't change nothing."

"I don't see how you can say that," she said, and he heard the edge. "Things'll never be the same any more. We shan't know civilization again in our time, that's obvious. Everything's changed."

Snowy wondered that a woman with such eyes and enamelled toes, wearing clothes that he knew Liz would have given her eyes to wear, could talk like it. He felt she had no right to complain.

"Perhaps it's changed for you," he said. "But it ain't changed for us. And it won't. Except for the worse."

"How can you be so sure?" She was touched by the ruin in his voice. "It's all going to be so democratic from now on, isn't it? I don't know exactly what they mean by that, but all the allies I've met tell me so. How's it going to be worse for you?"

" Listen, Mrs.," Snowy said, and hedged. " Sorry. Princess."

" Never mind all that," she said. " I was born in New York City. Let's start from there."

" Ah," said Snowy. " Well, listen. You can't go killing off blokes like Old Shiner by the thousands and then expect things to be better afterwards. Because who're they leaving behind? All the toe-rags. A lot of laceholes. That's who. And that's why."

" You're a little sweeping," she said, cold, watching a ravaged face through barbed wire. " Some of them have quite a conception of duty."

" Look here, Princess, or Miss, or whatever you like to call yourself." Snowy slowed on a cambered bend and leaned across the wheel to face her. " It's the likes of you that's half the trouble, giving yourself a lot of airs, there. More edge than a busted pot. If people like you'd done your job we wouldn't 've got in a war at all. Eh? A princess is a princess. Fairy-book stuff. My two kids 'll tell you all about princesses. Doing good and waving their wands. But I'll bet they don't talk like you do. And they ain't got that sort of voice, neither."

" Look," she said. " Don't let's fight about this. There must be a laugh in it somewhere if it's only Mama's flat feet. I can cry without any help from you."

" We was talking about Shiner," Snowy said. " He's dead. And it's half your fault, and a lot of people like you. Putting on the airs. Getting big ideas about yourselves. When it comes down to it, you want a lift just like anybody else. Trouble is, you don't happen to know it at the time."

" But listen," she said. " We did all we could."

" Oh, ah? " Snowy said. " Well, the rest of us didn't hear about it. Shame, ain't it? "

She was angry, impatient to leave him, anxious to meet herself again in the sanity of loneliness and exhaust herself once more in argument with conscience. She knew she might have done a thousand things, but at those times there seemed a thousand reasons why not, and so conscience argued, and so she answered until her mind was dulled with the clatter, and capacity for feeling was reduced to matters of physical pain, or bodily discomfort, and all other ideas and notions, right and wrong, good or bad, were shrugged aside as nuisances impeding the savage business of living.

Angrily she acknowledged his claim, and the jibe about the quality of voice and the manner of its use was added irritation, for she knew how completely her mother-in-law would refute any possibility of guilt, and in any event deny any right of criticism to a commoner. She heard again the voice of a languid, slightly-puzzled fowl, and she saw the ram nose, and the muddy eye, the savings-box mouth and a carefully piled torture of hair, and always the dirty finger-nails under the varnish.

The thought of that gracious creature exposed to this commoner's tongue was too much, and irritation flew in quick laughter.

"Sorry," she said. "Very sorry. I was thinking what the real princess would say to you. I'm a phoney. I only married a prince, you see."

"You done all right," said Snowy. "She make a better job of it? Wave a good wand, does she?"

"I'll say," she said. "The draught'd give you pneumonia."

"Ah," said Snowy. "We've got one like that in our family. She'll give the kids a couple of toys worth a tanner apiece and think she's bought the house. Come for tea, and stay for a month. When I've had enough, I give Liz the wink, and I come home drunk. Oho, then she's off."

"Don't tell me you get drunk?" She tried to imagine his face. "Surely?"

"I ain't had the chance lately," he said. "I can't like the vino. Out here, getting stewed don't mean so much. You only start yourself thinking that much more."

"You're lonesome," she said, and felt the brine in her eyes. "I can hear it and see it. I can even smell it. I'm sorry. I'm so sorry. Not just for you. I don't know what's got into all of us."

She was trying to see in her bag for a handkerchief. Snowy changed down to go through the village and then put out a hand, barely touching her knuckles with the tops of his fingers.

"Sorry if I said anything, Miss," he said. "We'll stop in a couple of minutes. Best grub in Italy, and a lovely family. Cheer up, gel."

9

He turned at the patio of the little hotel and Rosie lounged into the shade.

The sudden tears had surprised him. Moments before, the swank in the voice and the cold words seemed long streets away from wet eyes and a crack in the throat. He remembered Primula when she fell and grazed her knee, trying to stop the cry. He saw the drag at the mouth, the effort to blink away tears, and he opened his arms and gathered her, tiny, warm, smelling of her mother, and again he was filled with wonder that this little thing was his, looking to him for comfort.

"I'll go and find Ma Nincio," he said, looking away from her. His impulse was to nurse her as a little girl. "She'll look after you for tonight."

She looked up through her handkerchief, for the tone of his voice was suspect. She saw in his attitude, the slack shoulder and turn of head, a sympathy that was almost a caress, and, seeing, she melted inwardly in a manner that amounted to a hurt, and turned away.

"All right," she said. "I didn't know we were staying anywhere."

"Best to stop," he said. "I don't like these roads at night, not when our engineers ain't working on 'em. I like to see where I'm driving. You'll be all right. I'll look after you."

"I know it," she said.

A quick pride ran in him, almost the same quality as that when two little hands slipped into his on Sundays, years ago, walking down the road to get an appetite for dinner, the feeling of a real family man, running into people all making a fuss of the girls, and the two of them looking as if it was all part of the game, and him trying to look as if he only borrowed them for the afternoon.

The young Nincio girl saw him first and turned in a white flourish of petticoats, running into the back door screaming for Mama. A few men sitting in the evening sun at tables in the garden stood up waving their hands in greeting, and he waved to them, hurrying into the darkness of the house heavy with the fumes of barrelled wine. A bomb had blown in part of the front and rubble was still neatly laid in the passage, but he noted that the wall was patched in solid concrete.

Mother Nincio heard him coming and met him in the kitchen door.

The width of her had always been a joke, but now she looked so solid in welcome and promise of good food that Snowy felt ashamed to have joined in the laugh. She spoke no English, and she knew he spoke no Italian, but their form of address had long ago been settled in smiles, perhaps in a laugh, a shouted word or two, points of the finger and pats on the arm with no satisfaction on either side but an infinite contentment.

Their greeting was primarily long, moments long, loud laughter and a little jig among pats and slaps, until Ma pulled herself away to run across to a steaming pot on the stove. The other Nincio girls had come in, but they were maidens not given to hugging men and so were happy with a laughing handshake, all of them showing teeth so regular, of such whiteness, that Snowy was always reminded of the best china cups hanging in a row in the parlour cupboard that Liz only brought out for visitors.

The Princess came in, taking the falcon off her shoulder and letting it stand on her wrist. He noticed the raw scratches on her glove where the talons had struck. There were moments of silence while the Nincio family got over surprise, and then they all seemed to shriek together, running to huddle against one another in the darkest corner of the kitchen.

"Snowy," the Princess said, arranging the chain loops. "Don't let them know I speak Italian. I'll tell you why later."

"Right you are," he said and turned to Mother Nincio, trying to signify with hands and eyes that this was no monster but only a poor little bird. One by one, while the Princess soothed and whispered, and plumage lay still, the girls came out of the shadow and stood in a group watching Ma Nincio staring out of the window pleating the hem of her apron, obviously drawing up a plan for a special meal, muttering recipes, impatiently denying them as unworthy or unobtainable, and finally hitting on a selection to send the team of girls chattering about their business. She took the Princess by the arm and led her out, smilingly, with a nod for Snowy; and as they left, Max came in, followed by Bill carrying the suitcase. Snowy swung it out of his grasp and unbuckled the label.

" Tell you why later," he said. " Max, don't forget. She can't talk Italian. See?"

" That make me the official mouthpiece?" Max said. " O.K. I don't suffer."

" I'll have a stroll round," Bill said.

" Listen," Snowy said. " The Section stayed here ten weeks. She was a proper old dear to us, old Ma was. Her eldest girl married the corporal fitter."

" That's his hard luck," Bill said. " See you later."

Max stood, hands on hips, half nodding his head watching Bill go down the passage.

" Snow," he said. " That's a funny guy. He talks like he was living a hundred years back. I bet he never wore shoes till they got him in the Army."

" He's from Lancashire," Snowy said. " It's a terrible place, right up there in the wilds. I mean, you got to make allowances. We have to send expeditions up now and again to find out what's going on. Savages, that's what they are."

Bill heard them talking, but he let them get on with it. He went out for what he liked to call a quiet airing, up the main street and through the more inviting alleys of the little town, but it was all so much like many more he had known with nothing to take the eye, for the houses were just the same, all distempered a sort of quiet orange, and all the doors were closed and the windows were tight shut against mosquitoes.

It was getting dark without street lights, and the sky was blue down the cracks of the side streets, making everything look a bit chilly and wretched. He felt envious of the men he saw with a woman hanging on their arms, and he was angry that an Italian could have the comfort of a woman and he, a thousand miles from Pet, thrown out against his will, no comfort at all.

He turned about, seeing little except his loneliness and his anger that seemed to pattern all things in a far-off greyness, and went back to find Rosie.

In her bulk, in the sheer size and weight, there was some kind of satisfaction. She spoke to him of the clatter of machine shops at home and lines of tea-cans swinging on a firebar, and a crust of bread and a thick slice of mutton in a red handkerchief.

It was warm under the canopy, heavy with a smell of tools and oil, just like the backshed at home, and he could almost see Pet smiling down at him from her bedroom window. Just thinking of it gave him the feeling of looking through the family albums, full of relations out on picnics or gone to Blackpool for the day, all dressed up to the nines, three months' savings to blow and not a worry in creation except what they was having to their teas. He remembered the last Bank Holiday, when the family left him behind, and he struggled her chair downstairs to sit her by the nasturtiums, and the goldy red of them all shone in her face, making her eyes that much bluer, and she come up that pretty he could hardly believe it was Pet.

Holding the package of her letters tied with a ribbon from her hair seemed to bring her closer to him, until he could almost sense the heat of her by putting out his hand in the darkness.

Mandolins were playing somewhere, coming down gently as a veil over the other sounds of the night, but he heard the back door opening and light showed the paint design on the canopy. He was suddenly frightened of going in and seeing a lot of happy people. He felt he ought to be solemn about everything, without knowing why, except that misery made it so.

"Oy," Snowy said. "You there, Bill boy? Grub's up. Come on."

"Not feeling too bright," he said. "I don't think I'll bother, thanks."

Snowy put his head through the dust curtains.

"You all right, chum?" There was a frown in his voice. "Why don't you put a light on?"

"Don't want one," Bill said, and started feeling angry with himself. "Honest. I'm all right."

"I'll bring a plateful out, then," Snowy said. "That's easy."

" I'll have a go at the rations in here," said Bill. " I'd rather. Just leave me be."

He heard Snowy jump down.

" I'll come out and have a look at you later on." There was impatience, disappointment, and obvious regret hallmarked in the voice.

" Good night," he said, making it as warm as he could.

A distant door shut, and the mandolins seemed farther away. He felt a little hurt that Snowy had left him so easily, for he thought a harder argument might have overcome his mood, but against that he assured himself he had nothing to thank anybody for, and he was better off as he was.

A can of beef and a crust from the ration box took the edge off his appetite, but while he chewed he thought of what might be sitting on the table inside, and gradually he found himself getting angry with Snowy for not coming out again and lifting him bodily into the place.

And so he set himself for bed, tearing at the knots of his bed-roll, but in their innocence they tightly defied him, and he threw the stubborn bundle into a corner, leaning his forehead against cool tubulars, feeling as though a cage of cats were inside there somewhere giving him a good clawing.

In a rigor of self-pity he took each knot delicately between his fingers, finding them all idly responsive, so that presently he revenged himself by jerking the slackened rope away, and the flytail gave him a crack in the face for his pains.

Standing in the dark, feeling the weal for a moment, he had a devil's notion to set fire to everything in sight, but the very power of his rage brought on the giggles much against his will, and he billowed the blankets down anyhow in the darkness, slipped off his boots, and lay back, putting his spectacles in his cap, and, still grunting with laughter, went to sleep.

10

Snowy thought that one of two things might have upset Ma Nincio, either Bill's refusal to eat at table, or else when she knew they were staying the night, and it was hard to tell which, but her face appeared to fold in secret creases right under his eyes. It was plainer when the girls stopped laughing.

" I can't make it out," he said to Max. " She's never been like this since I've known her."

" O.K.," Max said. " Perhaps the war's gone too far north. They don't have to be polite any more."

Ma Nincio was standing at the stove under the open chimney, one foot on a low hob, watching the old kitchen-maid using a ladle in a dish of sizzling fat. From the look of her back Snowy knew his instinct was right.

" Listen, Ma," he said, as though she were Liz and he was in disgrace. " What's up? Eh? What have I done? "

She shrugged and went on watching the bubbles, reaching up for the salt canister, sprinkling, and setting the canister back in place. Snowy watched her movements, steady, studied, and knew it was hopeless.

" Max boy," he said. " If I could find the Princess, I've got a good mind to shove off, now. I don't want no trouble here. I don't know what we've done, but something's gone wrong. Anybody'd think we'd put a couple of the girls in the family way, wouldn't they? "

" Well," Max said. " That's still an idea."

" Don't bother yourself," Snowy said. " They're all as tight as galvanized pipes. 'Sides, ain't you got a girl of your own? "

" Yeah," Max said. " Boy, what I'd give to see her right now."

He threw his glass across the room and it burst in the darkness of the far wall, returning in a spitting grey and white concertina as the cat went for the door.

Mother Nincio made a soothing sound with round lips, and turned her head in a smile of annoyance, but her hands were still down the sides of her apron, and the old kitchen-maid went on ladling.

" What you do that for? " Snowy asked.

" General principles," Max said. " If I don't feel better pretty soon, I'm just going to tear up the joint."

He walked back to the sitting-room, bumping the lintel as he entered. Snowy tried to catch Mother Nincio's eye, but she was watching the ladle though he felt that in her mind's eye she was watching him.

Suddenly he was angry.

" All right," he said. " Keep your bloody grub. Treating us as if we just came out of the workhouse."

As he moved, her cap fluttered in a swing of the head that he knew beyond doubt came from regret, but before he could turn to her she was back at the pan with the salt.

He paused, scratching his chin, uncertain what to do, but the door was old, with a temper of its own, and given impetus by the cat had made sly progress toward a final inarguable slam.

The Princess woke from a nap on the sofa, cold and a little heavy in the head, regretting the early start that morning and the behaviour of her escort. Yet she found excuses for him, and while her fingers were busy with plaits she was laughing at the stare in his eyes when she pulled the bird away and he saw the blood dripping on his blouse. She felt a certain content and a note of pride that the movement of his pudgy hand had earned him that leap of rage when she wrenched off the hood and thrust the shrieking beak in his face.

The youngest Nincio girl came in with her underwear and shirtwaist neat from the iron and draped them on a chairback, but there was no smile this time, and though she paused long enough to pummel the cushions, she went out without word or sign and softly closed the door.

In surprise, the Princess made a face in the looking-glass. It occurred to her that something must have happened downstairs, possibly to do with the men, and a feeling came that she should not have stayed under the same roof. Spineless, she thought, for here Signora Nincio might think of her as some sort of camp follower and that, perhaps, might be the trouble. Yet the welcome and their kindness, this room, a hot bath, raw meat for the falcon, the smiles, and the happy conversation between mother and daughters was not in keeping with this bleak girl and her lack of response.

She hurried with her dressing and went downstairs through the empty restaurant to the sitting-room.

Max was asleep on the sofa, head back on the blanket, snoring. A half-filled glass of wine stood on the chair at his side. Snowy was writing under the candles at the table, looking up as she came in, hurriedly cramming the sheets into his pocket.

"Don't disturb yourself, please," she said.

"I ain't, Miss," said Snowy. "I been waiting for you. I'd like to get out of this place, if I could."

"What's wrong?" she asked, and nodded at Max. "Drunk?"

"No," Snowy said. "He only had a couple of glasses of that vino santo stuff. He needed it."

"Like I need a troop of camels," she said. "I'd be glad to get out of here, too."

She was cold at the thought of being a member of this party. She found herself disliking Snowy, hating Max, detesting the thought of the contempt Signora Nincio must feel for them, coarse, drunken, unfit for any society but that of the barracks.

Watching candlelight on the bloom of her cheek, he caught the faint fresh sting of her perfume, and knew the lace of her blouse was covering without hiding a suggestion of shadow between her breasts.

She looked up at him, recalled by an intent note of silence and saw his eyes; but though he turned quickly to pick up his cigarette, she knew and instantly felt fury that he should presume, and almost in the same thought realized him to be dangerous. She was frightened, inwardly, and the more determined to leave.

"I've been very grateful," she said, using her official voice. "But I really think I'll go along on my own from here on. It's not far, and there's pretty sure to be lots of transportation. If you won't mind?"

"All right, Miss," Snowy said, knowing the voice. "If I'd known this'd happen, I'd have took you right through. I thought you was a bit tired, that's all."

"What happened to make you change your mind?" she asked.

" Don't know," he said. " Beats me. One minute they're all smiles. The next they won't talk or even have a laugh."

" Somebody play around with the girls? " Her question sounded as though she was pointing a dagger. " That won't make you popular."

" We didn't," Snowy said. " And still we ain't. 'Sides, even if we did, it's got nothing to do with you. Has it? "

She looked him blankly in the eye.

" I just wouldn't want them to think I was one of this party," she said. " That's all."

" You ain't," Snowy said. " You're on your own. And you're welcome."

" Thanks," she said. " I don't want to sound ungrateful. But do I owe you anything? I mean, do you make a charge? "

He looked at her until she had to turn away.

" I'm sorry," she said. " I didn't want to go off and have you think I was expecting something for nothing. I'd rather you told me."

" You're about as kind-hearted as that sparrow of yours," Snowy said. " And he'd pick the tripes out of anything, wouldn't he? "

" Don't say that," she said. " Just leave me alone."

" You're blowed up like a barber's cat," he said. " That's all that's wrong with you. Full o' wind and whasname. But you are; you're lovely. That's all you play on."

She knew he was angry, though his voice showed nothing but a gentle jeer, and she realized in a sudden heating blush that he was playing husband whispering to a wife perhaps in bed as though, however remotely, he had made love to her a moment ago.

He wondered why he had never noticed before that she was so like Liz.

About the same size, and the same shape at the waist, but Liz was a bit thicker in the ankles. She wore her hair in the same way, in a big bun at the back, and some of her ways were exactly the same, of pulling down the front of her blouse between forefinger and thumb while she was talking, pinching the lobe of her ear, and catching her bottom lip under her front teeth, softly, so that delicate flesh went lightly pale and then hurried back to red.

He found himself looking at her and wanting to grasp her by

the shoulders and stand closely against her, drinking the joy of her tenderness, and it was all so easy to hide and disguise, until his voice broke and he had to catch at a sound slipping down his gullet.

Then he knew the secret was loose and open to her contempt. A gross feeling of nakedness was on him, and lighting a cigarette seemed some sort of cover, but he was glad to find his hand steady when he struck a match. He was happy in the thought that nothing in his appearance suggested what was happening in his mind.

Until he looked at her.

Colour had gone from her face, and somehow it was thinner. Her mouth moved, though the lips were still, but her eyes stared in wide fixity and the pupils were hugely dark in whites that held a tinge of blood and yet appeared dry.

His leg was swollen under his weight on the edge of the table, and candle flame hachured little spirals of gold in its thatch. She caught a glimpse, nothing more than a momentary picture of a limb in a gilt matting, and yet, despite the appeal of her normal self, she stood in a night and beneath her palm a cool rumple of grapes and a taste of salt in her mouth.

He was startled, not because she looked as she did, so much as to think she might be prone, and he watched her, fearing to move, for the thrust of surprise was not stronger than his fear of her and of what she might say and, worse still, of what she might do.

Her eyes shut and she turned her back.

Instantly he felt again that tenderness for her, sympathizing, seeing Liz, knowing perhaps something of the struggle, but he sat still awaiting a sign, and despairing, and aching, physically in pain to the point of sickness, and wishing Max in another world.

Quietly the door was pushed open and Mother Nincio came in, going to the fireplace with a tray of dishes, looking at Max as she passed and raising her eyebrows with all the force of a wise shake of the head.

He tested his voice.

" You still can't talk Italian, I suppose? " he asked. " You wouldn't like to ask her what we've done wrong? Just to satisfy yourself? "

She shook her head.

Snowy tried to catch Mother Nincio's eye, but she was busy in her work, and for perhaps the first time he wished that he could speak the language.

"Well," he said. "What between you and the old girl, we're having a rare old time tonight."

"Would you be kind," she said, looking not at, but near him, "and ask her if I could have some food in my room? Any time you want to go in the morning, just ask her to give me a call, will you? Good night."

"Good night," he said, and cursed himself, for without volition his voice had risen on the end of the word, making it into a question, an appeal, and a regret.

She heard the unexpected note as she closed the door, and smiled in the darkness, hurrying through the restaurant between the silhouettes of chairs piled on tables, like skeletons of happier times, and bumped into a group of men entering noiselessly in soft shoes.

Someone grabbed her, but she held a scream.

"Who's this?" a voice asked in Italian.

"Leave her alone," an old voice said, and she could smell the pipe tobacco of old Nincio. "An American with the English. She's sleeping here. She knows nothing. Nothing. Leave her."

The grip slackened.

"Very well," the voice said. "Away. Go away."

Old Nincio took her through the dark to the stairfoot. Mandolins began a sudden tinny thudding and a few men hummed a chorus. As on a signal the old man turned quickly, dragging at her wrist.

Through the window she saw Snowy walking across to the wagon carrying a tray. He climbed up and seemed to be speaking, and then jumped down, dusting his hands and walked in the lit path back to the doorway, and the closing door made the tables shudder.

The old man seemed to breathe the heavier, and the mandolins went raggedly silent, but a voice hummed after all the others had finished, out of tune and feeling for notes as a blind foot will hazard a step. The hand released her arm in a gentle shove, and as she went up the stairway she could hear by his breathing that he watched her.

She got into her room and stood at the door, wondering whether she ought to go down and tell the men, but the thought of Snowy decided her, for she knew that any warning would mean protection, and possibly a guard outside the door; and again she smiled to herself, for she knew the guard would be Snowy and none other.

She shook her head, and went over to the window, pulling aside the curtain, looking down into the patio.

Faintly she could see Rosie under the shadow of the far wall, ugly and square, and yet looking at her brought comfort of a sort, an argosy cargoed with memories from another world, sturdy with usefulness, and solid in readiness to serve, and for some reason she thought of the breadth of Mother Nincio.

11

Snowy was surprised when the door swung and the quiet group came in, but happier to see old Nincio and his three sons among them; but there were no handshakes or pats on the shoulder, and the unmeant smiles of the sons strengthened the irritant feeling of unwelcome.

The meal Mother Nincio had cooked was nothing by comparison with others he remembered, but the soup of thin spaghetti, the escalopes and buttered spinach, the salad, and the marsala custard all went down in the old style with a flask of chianti and then a thimble of black coffee.

Throughout the change of plates Max said nothing. He was haunted by a screaming, by a young face with an open mouth and eyes that looked into the top of a skull, by fingers stiff in hooks of pain; and never mind what he looked at he could still see the face, and the face was always screaming. The middle of his brain seemed caught upon the thought of burying his face in Rosa's lap and telling her, as she told the priest in that little box of carved wood back at the church. He could see her fingers slipping the beads and her mouth moving and the tender skin of her eyelids ruffling and smoothing. The desire only to feel her hand, or just to sniff the draught as she passed became a heat that made his skin crawl, with tautness in the spine and a suction of the belly.

" Snow," he said. " I have to get good and god damn drunk. I'm all in."

" That's all right, mate," Snowy said. " I've got a good mind to join you. There's plenty here."

" Fine," said Max. " You said you'd seen dead guys. When was that? "

" Not so long ago," Snowy said. " Still worried about the bloke you got rid of? "

Max nodded, looking into the wine.

" I can see his face in here," he said. "Wherever I look I can see it. That's terrible, ain't it? I must have shot a whole lot more, but I never did get to see 'em close to. I sure wish I never saw him."

" You'll get over it, chummie." Snowy could see Shiner lighting up and the question of his eyes in the flame. " The worst of it, anyhow. All you got to say is, if it wasn't him, it might have been you."

" I said all that." Max poured out another glass. " He's still there. And Linda. I know she'd hate me. She hates hurting people. She loves the earth. She even takes sugar in her bag for the horses. Jesus. I'm all mixed up."

" It'll work out all right, chum," Snowy said. " But you're going to be a bit unlucky for news, ain't you? "

" News? " Max sat struck. " Linda. Why in hell did you have to think of that? Something might have happened. I wouldn't know. She might be screeching now, god damn it. Hey, you." He swung his chair round to the group of men near the fire-place. " Come on. Give us a picking on them things."

He spoke to them in Italian, and one after another they swung their mandolins over their knees, starting a quiet little melody that came strangely from hidden faces among rags, and strings quavering under fingers rough as claws.

Max drank down a purple flush as though it were beer and went to the flask for more.

" Boy," he said. " It's going to be good to get that dead feeling again. Like after a half bottle of rye, straight. And no chasers."

Snowy looked over at the group in a roundhouse pivot that

should have brought him to face them, but instead he overshot his mark and found himself staring at the door. The sound of the singing disturbed him. He was used to the fullness of their voices, and secretly he enjoyed their pride in reaching an octave and hanging on to the note till they were giddy and the room filled with rich sound, because then the hair on the back of his neck started tingling and life had a different look. But these men were too quiet, with a hint of mischief about them that crept into their voices, and despite the warmth of the wine he felt uneasy about odds of seven against two, but he decided that Max and he could handle them, for, though Max was short, he had big hands.

"Max," he said. "What you do in civvy street?"

"Civvy street?" Max closed an eye on a brilliance of double candles. "What I was doing before I was inducted? Druggist. Not soda jerk. I was once. Working through college. I got to be a druggist, make pills, medicines, cure sick people. Now I just kill 'em off. Hold your breath, press trigger. What you do?"

"Foreman fitter," Snowy said. "London Transport. The buses. The old red 'uns."

"Fitter." Max considered the word. "That's good. Just like a druggist. You fix the motors, I fix the guys 'at drive 'em. So we're partners. Open a business for man and machine. Just drive in. You empty the sumps, and I empty the colons. Clear their heads. That's all most of 'em ever want. A good purge. And, by God, can I fix a purge! Any flavour."

"This lot over here could do with one, from the looks of 'em," Snowy said. "I reckon they're out for a do."

Max slewed in his chair, cocking an ear to listen to the music, screwing up one eye, and shook his head.

"They're just bums come in for a warm," he said, and pulled out a ball of notes, wetting his thumb to peel off a couple, throwing the curly paper across the table. "Hey, Joe. Buy some chow for the kids. Hell, they don't have a light."

Papa Nincio was looking up at the lamp, nodding it might have been at a gargoyle on the wall of his mind. Nobody in the group made any movement.

"See?" Max said. "That ain't trouble. That's just hunger. Strictly from hunger. And you know what?" He picked up a knife. " I started in a butcher's shop. I was ten. Little fella. But I can still slice the best steak you ever saw. We used to hang 'em in the ice box, maybe ten days. Then they was blue. And you scrape all that blue stuff off and you put it on the charcoal grill. Man, you like to eat your mother's heart."

He took the knife with him across to the couch and put it on the chair.

" I just want to see somebody start something," he said. " I'll slice the arse off of him, that's all. Hey, Snow. 'm I drunk?"

" No more'n I am, mate," Snowy said. " One more for the road, eh? If you can still see it."

Max lay back.

" By God," he said. " I wished I was home. You wished you was home, Snow? "

" Do I? " Snowy said. " And I couldn't half belt the old lady tonight. It's a terror, this business, you know. You've only got to see a woman, and you're like a bloody weasel. I wasn't like this before. Can't remember it, anyhow. I don't know."

" You know something, Snow? " Max levered the other boot off with his bare toes. " War's just a lot of guys going around with a hard. And the girls doing wets in their pants. But a hell of a ways off. So you just got to keep on going around with a hard. That's no way to run any war."

" You get used to it," Snowy said. " I've often felt like a cock walking about with a bloke on the end of it."

The group seemed to have got up together. Old Nincio went over to Snowy and jerked a thumb upstairs towards the bedroom he usually slept in, but still without a smile or sign of welcome.

Snowy shook his head, pointing outside at about Rosie's position, and old Nincio nodded into the bowl of his pipe, and shrugged, and went out behind the others.

Snowy scratched his head.

" Old Dad and me used to be pals," he said. " We must have done something. But I can't think what it is."

Max started to snore.

Snowy went across and pulled the tasselled rug off the sofa back, draping it over him, and then felt his way out to the patio, and Rosie, and a length of wide leather seating.

He switched on the dashboard light to hang up his blouse and shorts, and put away his boots in the locker. His haversack went down for pillow, with a blanket over it, and a towel over that to take away the rough. Before he got in, he took the photographs from the rack and kissed the cellophane cover, hurriedly putting them back as though afraid someone out there in the dark might jeer at him.

" Good night, gels," he whispered, seeing the little house and the white gate and the trellis he built while he was on leave, walking through the darkness, looking in the girls' room, hearing Liz's sleeping breath from the room beyond. " We nearly done it tonight. Just the luck of the cards, that's all. Never mind. I can still face you. Not as it does you much good."

He lay down, pulling the blanket up, feeling the cool of the leather warming beneath him, and reached out to touch the steering wheel.

" Rosie, me old ducky," he said, " we'll get rid of this lot tomorrow. Relations and visitors, they're all the same. A bloody nuisance, all round. But that Princess. Ooh, dear. Never mind, Shiner boy, we'll be there. 'Night, Rosie gel. You're all right, ain't you, matey? Eh? "

His right hand slipped from the wheel, nerveless, yet now and again a finger jumped from impulse in the resting brain, causing a movement enlarged in shadow by the green glow on the dashboard.

Outside, not many yards away, more than a dozen pairs of eyes, themselves catching light, had watched him since he shut the door, and from behind the curtains of her window in the dark room the Princess had watched them all.

For minutes on end the group stood under the fig tree, looking, and then moved away.

She saw them open a cellar trap and haul bales and sacks into the patio. They opened the coach-house doors, but all she heard was the fig tree shaking itself out of the day's heat, and she saw a truck manhandled into the open, and loaded, and roped, and again the men grouped, humping shoulders to push it out in the roadway and down the hill, all within the fig tree's indolent fuss.

In the distance the engine started.

She saw the hand clench, grip the blanket, and pass beyond range of light, and while she chilled with fear that he might waken, she threw an apology across the darkness to him, with a mental nod at Signora Nincio, believing she knew the reason for a warm welcome but a cold stay.

His hand came back in the light, at that distance so much like a baby's to be kissed and put inside the warmth, that she was almost tempted to go down and see if he was properly covered, but instead she laughed at herself.

As she settled the pillows it came to her that this feeling for Snowy was possibly not for the man, but for the male she sometimes had dreamt about, and not for sake of manhood as for a man's body, not in spirit of love, but in desire of orgasm. She refused the idea, but it recurred and she turned on her side, crossly pulling the bedclothes with her, and, cupping her chin on a lip of quilt, fell asleep in a wish.

12

Dawn was still blue, with ice in the wind, when Snowy heard the primus being pumped. He got out and clattered in unlaced boots to the rear, rubbing his hands and beating his chest. Bill was half shaved. A tub of water rumbled heat beside him and the brew-can wisped on the stove.

"'Morning," Snowy said. "Feel all right?"

"Fine." Bill was looking in a chip of mirror about two inches by three. "Plenty of water here. Have some tea in a minute. Hear anything funny last night?"

Without his spectacles, Bill's eyes seemed twice as big, and bright as glass. Snowy looked at the lathered tan of his face blued by the light of the primus.

"A lot," he said, helping himself to washing water. "Which you talking about?"

"I thought I heard a lot of blokes tearing about here," Bill said. "Another convoy, or something."

" You was dreaming," Snowy said. " Why didn't you have a look? "

" I were too comfortable," said Bill. " They couldn't have done much, any road. I'd disarmed her and shorted her ignition. They couldn't have got her far."

" Blimey," said Snowy. " D'you know, that's the first time I've ever put her in anywhere without seeing to her. I must be going barmy. I shall have to start looking round meself."

Their voices awakened the Princess.

She lay for some minutes enjoying the rise and fall, the acute difference in quality of voice and diversity of accent, and after a while she thought herself listening, not to a couple of men, but to an old parchment suddenly speaking in lines of script, thick and thin, then an unexpected little twirl, and more thick and thin, and then a glorious flourish when they used words she had never heard.

She got up and went over to the window.

" Ah." Bill's voice was curtained by towelling. " Ye've to be that careful how you rid a lamb. Ye've to take it from t' ewe, and get out on it, a matter of miles, and ye've to have a cart, or something, else she'll follow ye. And wherever ye killed that lamb, if she can find a smell on it, hide or hair, she'll set herself down, she will, and she'll dorm there. That'll give y'away. She'll shop ye."

" Go on? " Snowy sounded airily amazed. " Is all this up round your way? "

There was a pause.

" Well," Bill said, with a sniff. " If ever ye've a mind to a bit of lamb, take my advice. Else ye'll find yourself doin' a fine, fat, fourteen fresh 'uns backside of t' grating."

" Ain't much difference between that and what we're doing," Snowy said. " Come to look at it, we're cooped."

" Good morning," she called. " When are we off? "

They looked up at her. In that light their faces were masks outlined by the rippling blue flame of the stove. Both men were lumpy with muscle, but to her surprise Bill, though a foot shorter, looked the lumpier of the two.

" Morning," Snowy said. " We're just getting a shave here. Be some tea ready in a minute. Want some hot water? "

She had a quick fear that he should have any excuse for coming near her, even though she was impatient with herself for thinking it.

"Don't bother, thanks," she said. "There's plenty here. I'll be right down."

The voice from overhead brought Mother Nincio from sound sleep into the stifle of her pink apron, taking a few moments to find out where she was, pulling it off her head, setting her combs, getting up from the kitchen chair and stretching her arms in thankfulness for the quiet. For other moments she listened, and then looked out of the window, watching Snowy throwing water over himself. She nodded, and smiled, and went to call the girls.

Max pulled out of nowhere, listening to the scrape and clang of firedogs next door. He lay for a while piecing things to form a whole, bemused at the misery it brought. Sitting up started new pains, and desire to sleep again and be out of it. He went over to the window, seeing Bill whitely roughed in light from a handlamp spannering deep in Rosie's bonnet, and the strain of his movements, the power in the turning arm, and the bright play of light on his spectacles brought again the disquiet, the true pain, the nibble of conscience deep down but unheeded, the thought that a world was running without his help, and yet suffering without complaint for want of the mite he could do.

Strangely, he felt the desire to do that mite even more than a nausea to be out of it and have done. He wanted the quiet pleasure of feeling sharp again in a starched coat among the bottles he knew by touch. He wanted to know his hands were helping raise a levee against sickness, and he liked knowing the responsibility of preparing hundreds of prescriptions every night and the duty of sealing the wrappers in a sweet finality of burning wax.

He caught at a memory of risen spirit on the night when Rosa looked through the mahogany pigeon hole. First he saw the hand, and the nails without paint, and thought of music, an arpeggio swift in paradise, but he was listening to her voice in a fall of petals about her without hearing what she said. She said it again, and took her hand away, and then he looked up at her, and some part of him was dead, and some other part was being born in its place, felt in turmoil and lack of speech, for she was glory only dreamt of, and so beautiful that to be this side of the counter was misery in itself.

He beat the butts of his fists together, trying to match the inner torment with an outer pain, but then he heard the bump of footsteps and the creak of a turning handle, and he took up his cap, walking towards the patio door, afraid to show his face and yet unwilling to concede the thought of flight.

" They're human, same as everybody else," Snowy was saying. " Just depends how you treat 'em. I suppose she didn't like you staying out here. The grub wasn't good enough. That's what she thought, and I don't blame her. Just like my old duck. Straight up in the air. No use talking to her. I knew the signs. But it made me look such a mug."

" Pity," Bill said. " Where's Max? "

" Ah," Snowy said. " Ain't too ripe this morning, I bet. Go and rake him out in a minute. Then we'll have a go at Rosie. Eh, gel? " He patted the tailboard. " Get her nosebag on, and mess her about a bit."

" It's all been done," said Bill, in the tone of a critic martyr. " I went over her first thing. She were a bit cluttered in her plugs."

" Ah," said Snowy, feeling Rosie's eyes large upon him. " I bet she wondered who it was."

" She stayed quiet enough," Bill said. " What'll y' have for breakfast?"

"What I've had for years and years," said Snowy. " A drop of good old Eighth Army brew. I can't eat of a morning."

Max held up his hands and groaned.

" Please," he said, in a voice ribbed with sleep. " Just coffee. That's all I want. Hot. No milk."

Snowy took charge of the primus.

" Sorry," he said. " There's no coffee. Just sprog."

" Don't know it," said Max. " But I'll take it. The way I feel, death is plenty of laughs."

" Sprog," said Snowy. " There's some calls it tea. Others say char. But when it's made by them that's served their time to it, and I mention no names, present company barred, it's sprog."

" I'll get things straight, up front," said Bill. " I'd rather be poisoned unbeknownst, thanks."

" Put some life in you," Snowy called after him. " Raise your standard of living, this will."

" Where was he last night? " asked Max. " I never did see him."

" After that second glass I don't reckon you saw anything very much," Snowy said. " He kipped down in here. He's a bit worried about home, I think."

" Me, too," Max said. " Boy, what I'd give for a mug of coffee. One mouthful, I'd probably get rid of the mice. They just trailing me around."

" Couple of quick sips of this," said Snowy, pouring the tea. " You'll have the rats. Desert rats. They'll sort your mice out."

He took a mug to Bill, and stood watching him polish the windscreen. The glitter inside the cabin and the overall cleanliness outside told of a practised hand and plenty of elbow grease. Snowy felt his heart going out to a workman.

" Here you are," he said, lifting the mug. " I shan't know myself behind that windscreen today. Like my old lady's parlour windows."

" First Army style, that is," Bill said. " We liked to know what we was doing of, d'you see? "

" That's the difference," said Snowy. " We knew what we was doing of. All we worried about was who we was doing. How's the sprog? "

" Do to bath the baby in," Bill said. " What's her majesty going to drink out of? "

" Ah," said Snowy. " Best behaviour, and no larks. My new mug. I just got it out of the straw."

" I don't hold with this Princess business," Bill said. " It's a lot of damn scrimshanking nonsense."

" Don't tell her," Snowy said. " She'd set the canary on you."

" Best thing the Americans ever did," said Bill, treating the glass as though it were part of the scrimshanking. " God rid of the lot. Plain Mister and Missus. And that's it for everybody."

" She's an American," Snowy said. " She only married it."

" Took the wrong advice, I've no doubt," said Bill. " There's plenty of damn fools about."

" I can see you'd be a good bloke to go in a strange pub with," Snowy said. " Get drove home on a copper's barrow, the pair of us. Watch it. She's here."

The Princess took plenty of time to button her gloves, looking all round the patio, slightly surprised to find the fig tree, last night a misshapen crawl of whispering shadow, this morning was a friendly old thing, sprung with fruit blue as lapis.

Snowy looked taller, perhaps thinned by cold, still in wrinkled twill pants and short stockings, with the air of a boy not yet fit for trousering, but his eyes were old enough, and with amusement she noticed his unwillingness to look at her.

" Good morning, Snowy," she said. " How did you sleep? "

" I got a wallop from a flannel hammer, Miss," he said. " Like some tea? "

" Love some," she said. " Good morning, Bill."

" 'Morning," he said, still polishing. " Likely we'll be having another fine day, then? Sun's coming up a fire ball again."

" What part of England are you from ?" she asked.

" The cream of it," he said. " The red rose county. Lancashire."

" I don't think I was ever there," she said.

" Ah, well," said Bill. " You've only touched foreign parts, then. Wasted your brass."

Max came from the washing tin rubbing his head.

" Good morning," she said. " How's the rest of the family? "

" Costive, penitent, and trachomic," said Max. " I ain't even getting respect from the mice. And that's new."

" I have a tablet in my bag," she said.

" I'll suffer," said Max. " I deserve it. Couple of glasses, and I'm a dead duck. That's bad."

" I agree," said the Princess. " I don't know what they thought, but I wasn't awfully impressed."

" Somebody ask you? " The towel dropped to his side. " Can't a guy get high once in a while without a lot of squawks? "

" I'm sorry." She turned her back, in half a mind to go inside the house. " I just don't want to see Americans disgracing Uncle Sam's Army and making people believe they're no good."

" So O.K.," said Max. " Drop dead."

" You're just ashamed," she said. " I'm glad."

" What did I do? " Max looked up at Bill. " I drink a couple of glasses, so I'm crucified? "

" Half a mo'," Bill said, and climbed down. " If you're coming with us, ye'd best get some bells ringing. We've not long. There's no time for a damn row."

" That's right," Snowy called. " Cup of tea, here, Miss. Just time to drink it."

" Coming," she said. " I haven't had tea in an age."

" God damn women," said Max, and leaned against the fender, making no attempt to wipe his face. " Was I bad last night, Bill? "

" Don't think so," Bill said, putting the tools away. " Any road, it's all over now. Don't worry. Get dressed."

" Me," said Max. " Disgracing Uncle Sam. Even the mice took off."

" Ride behind with me," Bill said. " Leave her be. Ye know what women are! "

As though letting the wind freeze his wet face were part of his punishment, Max buttoned his shirt and scratched his hair back with his finger-nails.

" I could write a tag for her," he said. " Let's go."

Snowy came round to the tool-chest and bent over Bill's shoulder.

" Listen," he whispered, helping to rack the tools. " I'll have her up front, see? We don't want no ups-and-downers this trip. She'll get off this afternoon, then we'll have some peace. Don't half take on, don't they? "

" She's right," Bill said. " He knows it, and all."

" You don't know nothing about it," Snowy said. " You wasn't there. Heard about the Smiths? "

" No," said Bill.

" Lived in the neighbourhood," Snowy said. " Ma, Pa, four boys, seven girls. Saturday night, when the pubs turned out, Ma'd set about Pa and put him on his trousers for a starter. Then the boys'd set about Ma. They've had to call the fire brigade to dig her out of the blowhole before now. Then the girls'd have to go at the boys, yelling and hollering, tearing about all over the house. Next morning, black eyes galore and half of 'em crippled for the week. Never quite come to a hanging. That was the Smiths."

" Well, what about 'em? " Bill felt himself on the end of a line.

" Well," said Snowy. " Everybody'd have a go at everybody else, come one, come all. But just let one of the neighbours stick his snout round that door, and the whole family'd drop tools, pitch in, make sewer bait out of him, and then get down to it again. Keep it all in the family was their motto, and no strangers by request. That was the Smiths, round our way."

" You mean," Bill said, " let these two get on with it? "

Snowy patted his shoulder.

" I've always said there's nothing wrong with you First Army blokes," he said. " When you've been with us long enough you won't be able to tell the difference."

" That's what's been worrying me," said Bill. " You and y' Smiths."

" All aboard," Snowy shouted.

Bill took the suitcase and swung it over the tailboard. Max turned away from it and sat on a case of rations.

" I'm not striking for her," he said. " I'm no lackey."

" Neither am I," said Bill. " But a woman's a woman, d'ye see? My mother always said if there comes a time that a lad won't offer a helping hand to a lady it's come time to knock the roast potato off of his dinner plate."

13

When Rosie started up she was easier, quieter, and in her voice a note that made Snowy frown, but then he remembered that Bill had been at work and realized that all day yesterday another mind had been noting her faults, accepting his boasting without a word, and this morning the jobs had been done before he awoke, leaving him to look at himself and feel silly, and, worse, disloyal to his old pal. She seemed to be chuckling away to herself, jeering at him. A fine way to treat me, he could hear her rumbling, fine goings on, I must say, and you call yourself a driver. Snowy Weeks, tck, dear, dear.

" You're quite right, gel," he said. " I'm very sorry. Shan't happen no more, I give you my davvy."

" I'm glad of that," said the Princess.

" Talking to Rosie." Snowy smiled at her. " It's all right, Miss. I always talk to her. Fair's fair. She talks to me. I let her down this morning, see? So now she's paying me out. She's calling me everything."

" Lots of curious things happening around here," she said. " Do you have any idea what happened last night? "

Snowy had put the matter out of his mind. On all previous visits there had been hot water for shaving, fresh fruit, hot rolls and big basins of coffee before starting out, with all the family and half the town in the yard to cheer them on their way.

But this morning not even old Nincio had shown his nose out of the door, even to hand over his lighter for a fill of petrol, knowing he could have a gallon.

" Tell you the truth, Miss, I'm a bit worried about it myself," he said. " Hope we ain't parted bad friends. I reckon they got narked because old Bill wouldn't go in. They're very touchy. I suppose the Eyeties are like that."

" Yes," she said. " Why wouldn't you let me talk to him? "

" Look, Miss," said Snowy patiently. " He's fed up and far from home like a lot of us. Talking don't do no good. Old Ma Nincio, she must have took it the wrong way. But I'm sorry just the same. Old Ma's been a good pal to us. Lovely cook, too."

" That all you think about? " she asked. " Cooking? "

" Makes a happy house, good cooking," said Snowy. " You don't get that unless you've got a good girl. There's half the battle. All you want then is a good job and something to bring home every Friday. Health and strength, a bit of garden, and a few kids. Then get down to it."

" Is that what you want? " She seemed sad.

" I've got it," Snowy said and took a wallet from the rack over the wiper. " I've got two girls, an' all. Pair of beauties. That's Liz, took on Rosie's seventh birthday. That's Primula."

" Lovely name," she said. " Whose idea? "

" Liz's," he said. " I wasn't too keen at first. But if you could see her, you'd say same as me. I took one look at her and I says that's the only monniker for you, my girl, I says."

She handed back the photographs.

"It's fantastic," she said, perhaps to herself. "You go on hating people for a long time, then you find they're just as human and so kind. My husband hates the British. So I hated them, too. It's all crazy."

"Like us," Snowy said. "When we was coming over here from Africa."

"Were you Eighth Army?" she asked.

"That's the only Army there is, Miss," he said. "And what we wasn't going to do. Burn the country out. Make your volcanoes look like a kitchen stove. Give all the girls ten kids apiece. As for loot, we was all going home millionaires. What happens? Before we was off the boat hardly, we're giving 'em petrol to get fires going, chocolate rations, soap, cigarettes. And the women and kids was lining up at the cookhouse. No, it's no good."

"Bunch of softies," she said.

"That's right, Miss," said Snowy. "Too many kids of our own, I suppose. You can't bear a kid crying if it's hungry. I don't care who you are. But it can't last much longer."

"Please God," she said. "Then you'll go home."

"Yes, Miss," he said. "That's where I'm off to when all these clever blokes have stopped all this sort of nonsense. And they won't get me out of it in a hurry, I can tell you. I'm browned off with this lark."

"Perhaps Signora Nincio feels the same way." The Princess was looking inside her bag. "Perhaps she's had all she can take, too. People dropping in without warning aren't any blessing. Food's scarce, you know. And she cooked for Lucullus."

Snowy leaned down and turned the key. Rosie puffed her cheeks and lay still.

"That settles it," he said, and opened the door. "I'm just going to give her a nice big kiss like I've always done."

"Go to it," she said. "Give her one for me."

Snowy went across the patio and turned at the doorway.

"Bill," he called. "Here you are. Job for you."

He heard Bill jump down and rattle across the cobbles. There was health in the sound, sparkled by the hobnails, and the corridor seemed lighter. He felt unsure of himself and jumbled inside, for there appeared three parts to the problem, starting with himself as an Eighth Army soldier deriving certain dignity from battles fought and won and requiring proper respect from a conquered people; himself as Snowy, known to the family for many months as one of the section billeted on them in greatest comfort; and himself, the family man. He was remembering the days when mail came, feeling Mama Nincio's hand on his arm sending him to that little room on the other side of the house where it was so quiet that even the wallpaper made a noise, and the door opening, and Mama Nincio coming in with a tray of coffee and a glass no bigger than a little finger full of cognac; that, and a smile, and a gentle shaking of the arm that held the letter, for with three sons in prison camps and no letters in two years she wanted him to know she knew what letters meant.

He opened the kitchen door.

The old kitchen-maid in black going brown, with a big white bow tied on the bump of her skirt, looked round and wiped her hands on the cloth hanging down from her apron. The youngest Nincio girl looked up from a bowl of beans; but though she seemed surprised, her hands went on cracking the pods with the sound of a kiss, and the beans poured on the metal in ripples of purest kitchen music.

Snowy had never tried to learn Italian or even to use the few words of general pidgin minted by an army's daily need. Somewhere in his mind lay a thought that learning another language might take him even further away from Liz and the kids, and so any foreign talk addressed to himself he treated as so many clouds of flies to be brushed aside or sprayed with an oath. Any conversation with a native, therefore, was compounded of winks, gestures with the index finger, and odd words having no meaning whatever shouted directly into the face of his partner, until the subject was forgotten or thankfully dropped; and since in this way he was able to get all he wanted on his own terms, as he often said, he saw no sense in burdening himself with a lot of natter that might only get him into trouble.

Faced with the maid, he merely stood and grinned, winked across at the younger Nincio girl to show there was no ill feeling, and shouted a greeting that murmured among the pots in the chimney recess, and brought Mother Nincio out of the storeroom.

" Ma," he said, going over to her. " I couldn't go off without saying the word, could I? Eh?" He pointed to Bill. " That's him. That's the bloke started all the nonsense."

" Well, I'll be damned," said Bill. " This all you wanted me for?"

" Go on," Snowy said. " Give her the word."

" Don't be so daft," Bill said.

He was listening to the beanfall. Pet always podded the beans sitting up in bed, holding the cullender in the cup of the bed-clothes, but her hands were white, thin, showing the bone to the wrists. These hands were brown, fat, and window light shone about the dimples at the finger roots. He was suddenly angry that this girl should have a full beauty, bearing promise for endowment of a family, and Pet, with beanpoles for legs sitting at home in darkness, with nothing more than promise of shop flowers at her funeral.

" I'm damn glad I never come in," he said. " T'hell with 'em."

" There you are, Ma," said Snowy. " He's saying he's sorry, see?" He pulled a face and crossed his eyes, holding himself about the midriff. " Bostoporus. Ooh. Speligric. Four a pound tomatoes. Eh? Just the job. No larks. Just the job."

" Justajop," said Ma, recognizing a term, she thought, of sympathy, finality, and general approval. " Poverino. Justajop."

" Don't let the section down, Bill," Snowy said. " All the boys got took care of here. Don't spoil it. Go on. Give her a smile. Do yourself a favour."

Bill noticed her bumpy hands, and saw again the little room in amber shadow from the lamp, and lace ruffs on the nightgown, and the box of purple velvet covered with sea shells. The resting hands were the same shape. He looked into Mother Nincio's face and saw the lines about the eyes and the patience there and knew that she, too, sometimes walked to and fro quietly in the corner, with those hands hidden in her armpits for warmth to relieve the ache.

He took her by the arms and kissed her forehead, sensing the cool of her surprise. There was no difference in feel, but his mother smelt of doctor's stuff and liniment and Ma had some sort of sweet smell, faint, like the smell of feathers.

" How's that, love? " he said, and knew from her eyes.

" Outside quick, 'afore she adopts the pair of us," said Snowy.

" I'd not mind it," said Bill. " She's as like my old lady as a couple of them beans." He prodded himself with his thumb. " I'll be in on me way back, Mother. I will. See? "

" Justajop," said Mother Nincio, still a little surprised at the change, but so used to the Inglese, that, as she often told her daughters, there was no astonishment left in life. Accept, give, depart, and that was all.

" So long, Ma," Snowy said, with a pat on her arm. " No ill feelings, eh? Just the job. Eh? "

He got out in the patio, waiting for Bill to catch up, and looked him in the eye.

" If you'd done all that last night," he said, " you'd have saved a lot of bother. Come over comic just now, did you? "

" Never you mind," said Bill. " You look after yours and I'll mind mine. And that's it."

Bill was a little ashamed of the exhibition, but prepared to defend himself on personal grounds. He felt sorry to have missed the dinner of the night before, not because of lost delights, but because those hands had cooked the feast, and he marvelled again that pain ballooned in knuckles gone pink and shiny could have any part in cooking dishes that met your nose at the front door, followed you through to the wash-house, and gave you no peace until you sat in front of that plateful with those knuckles pushing salt and pepper at you.

Sun was up behind the rooftops in the piazza, reddening the chimneys and running lemony paths down lanes between houses. Rosie sat in a blue stipple of cobbles, fat with content, in a glow of paint, glass and metal, and so handsome that Snowy felt pride, like a chill, run through him.

Her bulk seemed to hold all thought of home, the size of her, the cleanliness, the bonnet and headlights that always looked like the mask of a patient hound, the knowledge of what she could do and all the work she had done, of all the places she had known.

And Shiner.

" Looks a proper picture, don't she? " he said. " Old Shiner always kept her like that. Even in dead winter. I'm glad you made it up with the old girl."

" I'll tell you what," said Bill. " And I'll put it right first time I get near a workshop. Her front suspension's all wrong."

" Never been right since she argued with that mine," Snowy said. " And while we're at it, I may as well say you ain't a bad fitter."

" Thanks," said Bill. " You're not a bad driver."

" You're about as good as your tea," Snowy said. " Still a bit to learn."

" That's right," said Bill. " If you drove a wagon like you make tea, I'd wait for a bus."

" You got it down you, though," said Snowy.

" I had to," Bill said. " Me mother always said manners maketh a man suffer."

14

Snowy was glad to see Max sitting on the tailboard looking at the cold light of the sun, but he noticed the whitish strain in his face and the deep carving under his eyes. The tone he used to the Princess and the cut of her reply had been a surprise, for there seemed no effort on either part to be sympathetic; and though he could understand Max being angry at notion of disgrace, the harshness in both voices, however refined in one and rough in the other, was cut from the same piece, and he felt a strange disappointment, for he thought she might have been kinder and Max less savage, especially in front of strangers.

Max felt the hurt down in his marrow. He felt he wanted to fly right back up to the Line and pull his jacket open with both hands and beg some Kraut to pour the shells in there where it hurt so much. Rosa was in his mind, and the baby, a girl, someone beautiful, a new somebody from God knew where, born in pain, with drugs and soft words among crackling linen and shrubs from a Nisei garden.

He watched Snowy and Bill come out in the patio, and knew by the pitch of their heads that they were talking about him, and suddenly hot mud was bubbling inside, and he threw himself over the tailboard and ran to them.

" Listen," he said, with each gripped in a handful of flimsy twill. " By God, I don't want you guys talking about me, see? I don't want it. I had enough."

Snowy felt the trembling of nervous strength in the hand, the eyes were white all round the pupils, and the lips were bluish, tight over the teeth.

" We wasn't talking about you," Bill said, in sharp complaint. " Damn it all, have we got to ask you what we're to talk about? It's coming to something, I must say."

" Half a mo'," Snowy said. " Don't start creating. Now look, Max. In about half-hour we'll stop and have some breakfast, see? So jump up in the back and let's get out of it."

" As long as you both got it right," Max said, but the grip was loose. He was frowning at the back of his eyes. " You got something to say, say it to me. Don't get me mixed up with that broad up front. Princess, my ass. She ain't even people."

" That's her lookout," Snowy said. " Come on, 'fore Pa Nincio starts telling us our fortunes."

" Stay here as long as we like," Bill said. " He can't say nothing. Enemy territory, ain't it? "

" Look," said Snowy. " See that wagon? Soon as I get up the front, I'm off. If you want to stay here talking about your rights, that's your hard luck."

He went to the cabin feeling empty. Every word, every gesture, all the events of yesterday and this morning would never have happened had he been by himself, and it all seemed to be harming the memory of Shiner.

He waited until the two had climbed up, and then got in, and, despite his misery, he saw with a certain inner jump that her legs were doubled under her, and two silk knees bulged in the dark of her skirt. Above the aroma of petrol the shadow of her perfume moved about, never enough to be breathed deeply but always on the edge of an indrawn breath.

" Well? " She held her head on one side. " Did you give her one for me? "

" Yes, Miss," he said. " It's all right. All smiles this morning. She got narked because Bill didn't go in. That's what it was."

" You're probably right," she said; and saw the shadows under the fig tree.

Rosie took the corner and went up the hill with barely a murmur, making him wonder what sort of magic had been done while he slept. He tested her, smiling to himself, knowing that another mind behind him would be intent, smiling as he smiled, listening to the music of her, noting, comparing, deciding, and then he gave in and simply drove her by the book, taking pleasure in his handling, hearing a voice always at his elbow laughing with him in deprecation of his pride.

She watched him for a little while, puzzled by the delicacy of his movements, but then she realized that he was part of the machine, thinking with it, living in it, using its engine as he used his body and with as much sympathy, and in turn this monster was part of him, using his brain and his energy; the two were one and the machine was alive, speaking a language he understood, feeling, thinking, working, all in a quiet pulse, itself product of a mind, restrained, harmonious, of matching grace to these urbane certainties of hand and foot.

" What kind of language do you talk to this old lady? " she asked.

" Any kind, Miss," he said. " Depending on the time of day, and how I feel. Make your hair curl sometimes."

" I mean," she said, " do you use horse talk, or baby talk, or just something you dreamed up? "

" No, Miss," Snowy said. " Just plain talk, like we are now. She knows. I suppose you reckon that's a lot of toffee? You should have heard old Shiner. There was a line of patter for you. She'd answer him back, too."

" Oh, please," she said.

" I mean it." Snowy said it seriously. " When you get used to engines they'll talk to you. Tell you all their troubles. And you can tell 'em all yours so you're real pals, see? You do things for them and they do little things for you. Cuts up just nice."

" For instance, how? " she asked, and settled down to be fooled.

" Well," he said. " Take Rosie. She was at Alamein, Tobruk, Derna, Tripoli, and Sfax, and she even got as far as Algiers. She come right through the lot. She'll boil you up a lovely hot bath, turn on a fan to cool you down, fry your grub for you, rev you up a light to read with, lift anything out of anywhere, push anything, pull anything. Top of all that, she's a lady. Never give me a minute's trouble. No lip, and no back answers. Good as gold and twice as useful. That's Rosie, and she knows it."

She looked at the ridge of mountains, knowing that on the other side the gates would open and the same guard would ask the same questions, and show her into the room that smelt as though thousands of mice had been skinned under the floorboards and left there.

Then the wait of half an hour, and his arrival, pale, unshaven, in clothes gone shiny down the front from rubbing the table as he rocked, staring the greylong day at a procession of wishes, and she heard wildness, pressed in a mould of patience in a voice that she must listen to for three hours, and three hours tomorrow, and the next day, and then goodbye, and the journey home.

And meantime, this centaur with rubber hooves and a hide of steel would be riding the Appian Way through the valleys, and up the mountains, and along by the sea.

She found herself envying the mobile peace of his little glass cave.

From sympathy, Bill had turned aside any attempt at talk though he knew Max was bursting to pretend all was well, as blokes did when they lost a fight by knockout, trying to laugh it off to show they were not hurt or even surprised, but you could tell by that little sore place in their voices, like a nick in the crack of a finger that you ought to cover up, that made you feel sorry for them though you never showed it.

But women had sharp tongues and plenty of time to think, what with washboarding and ironing, quiet little jobs lasting a long time, that gave them plenty of space to look at things and make up their minds. He was sorry for Max because he knew how it felt to get a tonguing in front of everybody and not a word to say in return.

That was what led to murder, because from feeling that aching and bleeding inside you to picking up anything handy and letting fly was the job of a moment that all the police and judges in creation would never stop, and the funny thing, it seemed to him, was that women either knew it and gloried in boiling things up to that point, as though they enjoyed being frightened and taking the risk, or they just did it to please their sense of being the boss, like saying Yes and turning over ready for the job, or getting in on the wrong side of the sheet and saying No, and not budging. But both ways they were stroking a thin boiler that one day would burst, and the end would come either in a police court or cemetery, or perhaps half in each, with tears all round and everybody the wiser.

"Boy," Max said. "They certainly have a lemon crop. I didn't know they had this kind of country around here. The way my old man told it, they had a desert, pretty damn cold in the winter and nothing to eat except octopus, and lots of wine for some other guy to drink. Times must have changed."

"There's nowt much wrong with the country," Bill said. "It's the people. The way they carry on."

Max looked over miles of groves down in the valley on one side of the road, and all the way up the steep cliff on the other. The dark green bushes ran in trim tier on tier, shapely as though clipped out of metal, lit with yellowing fruit in profusion that seemed to heat his cheeks, all housed under awnings of straw matting. No inch of soil seemed to have missed the hoe, for where groves stopped kitchen gardens bloomed in every shade of green against black earth, and flowers sprang in reds and blues about the little huts with a stare from sunflowers among the frills of hollyhock.

He felt baffled by the approach of a mind that could look at so much work, every cut of it by hand, and then condemn the people as idle.

He remembered the quarryman up above the little port in Tunisia, an Arab in an old striped shirt and patchy trousers, and a felt hat pulled down so the bow came between his eyes. The muscles in his forearms were like rubber tubing, swelling up and going down with each crack of the long-headed hammer, curved like a pick, that beat, beat, beat, on a chisel deep down in the rock, and with each beat the fist turned the chisel, beat again, steel on steel in rock, turn, and beat again, with knees gripping a saddle of stone and shoulders hunched in momentary tensings of muscle, beat and beat, with the bow of his hat between his eyes, and beat, beat again. Then he pulled the chisel more than a foot out of the hole to feel down with a long stem of steel with a little spoon on the end, bringing up a scrape of powder. Then in with the chisel again, and beat, turn, beat, turn, beat, minute after minute without pause, a human clock ticking off its life in steel beats measured by the effort of lifting the hammer all day and every day through the years.

Whatever happened elsewhere in the world, any day from then until he died, his knees would be gripping a saddle of rock while he beat the seconds, and the minutes, and the hours in steel on stone, where it was so quiet that you heard the fall of a little scrape of powder, up there in the white sun.

"You ever get mixed up with the Arabs?" he asked.

Bill shook his head.

"They're a bunch," Max said. "Some of 'em's the dirtiest sons of bitches I ever saw. Just plain lousy. But I saw others, and, boy, they knew how to work. They were good."

"Never had a lot to do with 'em," Bill said. "The only time I ever saw 'em they was digging up the ration tins we'd buried. Bloody dirty lot. And thieve? They'd have your lugholes if they weren't tapped on. Worse than this crew over here."

"Well," Max said. "If you had nothing and you got hungry, you'd probably look around, too. You have a wife, don't you?"

"Yes," said Bill. "But I've a trade, and all. I work, in civvy street. I don't scrounge about waiting for other blokes' leavings."

"I'm no bum, either," Max said. "But I might have been. I had a good home, I guess. These people got no kind of life to make 'em know better. It's work, work, work. Look at all that work."

"You stick up for 'em," Bill said. "I'll not stop ye. I like a bloke'll stand by what he thinks. But it don't alter what I think."

"But listen," Max said. "Suppose you tell me what else they could do with what they've got? Can you see where they could grow any more, or dig any more? Could you improve what's there?"

"It's none of my business," said Bill. "So I don't know. But I do know I don't like 'em. I don't like the way they go about things. I don't like the language, and I don't like the country, or the skies over it. Now then."

"I wonder what they think about you?" Max said, almost to himself.

"I don't give a damn," said Bill. "Think what they like. One day I'll get home. Then they can all think what they bloody well like, and see if I care."

"Hell of a way to live, brother," Max said. "No wonder some guys got to do the killing."

"I mind me own business," Bill said. "Got nothing to do with me, none of this hasn't."

"You're just using up space and good air, and you're paying no rent, that's all," Max said. "That's why I have this Kraut screeching away inside here. I never wanted to pull that trigger. I was telling myself all the time, don't do it. He's too young, God damn it. He's a little runt, maybe eighteen. He's half of my age. Eighteen, I was playing ball in the back lot. And I have to kill him."

"Likely we'll have to kill a few more before we're done," Bill said. "When the rot's in the wood, ye've no more to do but chop t' tree for kindling."

"Ah, Jesus," Max said. "I'd give any kind of money for a cup of coffee."

15

Rosie was on a gradient leading up between the high banks of a road newly cut in rock. He put her in bottom gear, and as though doubting herself she went up to the square of blue sky framed on three sides, and on the crest turned in a bellying right hand on a hairpin going far down into a wide valley.

"My God!" the Princess said. "I wish life was always as good as this."

"This is one of the reasons I didn't go on last night," Snowy said. "You never know what's in front of you. Lovely job, ain't it? South African engineers. I watched 'em. Jerry filled the river with the old road."

Mauve shadowed the mountains and ruffs of mist hung from the sleeves of smaller valleys, grey in shadow, pink in light, and a pink cast lay over all the palm of earth, split by a wide river of muddy milk that curled once just below, and then went across the valley between miles of trees, green where the sun tipped, but black all the way to the yawn of the rivermouth and the stains of fresh water catching light in the sea. On top of a hill walled about on the far side, a village looked as though held up there on stalks of smoke; but further down, beyond help of the ridge, the vineyards came under the flutes of the wind and turned their coats pale or dark with every puff.

Almost at the foot of the last hairpin Snowy rounded within a fraction of the parapet and braked hard.

A man in a raincoat was running up to meet them, waving his arms in appeal that carried a comical degree of hopelessness as though, having made up his mind that what he was doing was silly, he had to persist if only to clear his conscience.

" This is your job," Snowy said, and brought Rosie close. " Ask him what's up."

She leaned across him, looking down at an old face slack with cold and ready for sleep. She spoke for a little, and the old man replied as though in gentle apology.

" They've burst a tyre down there," she said. " They've got a lot of women and children with them. They've been there since yesterday."

" Tell him to hop up," Snowy said. " See what we can do. Can't promise nothing, though."

She spoke again, and the old man climbed up on the step, smiling as a well-thrashed child given a piece of toffee.

Rosie ambled down the further stretch and turned the last corner, and Snowy saw how the tyre had burst. The lorry had skidded across the road and lay tipped against the cliff. A group of men stood looking over the parapet at the river. The road was strewn with shelters built from crates and bales where women sat among groups of children, nearly all of them asleep.

" Proper bright lot," Snowy said. " Tell 'em to get the rest of that stuff off the wagon, will you? "

Bill came round and looked on, with his hands in his pockets.

" Going to clear the road? " he asked. " Best thing is to shove the lot over the cliff."

" Get it right side up, first," Snowy said. " Then if we can't mend the tyre we'll give 'em a tow."

" Wasting your time," Bill said.

" See them kids? " Snowy put Rosie in reverse, watching the driving mirror. " Starved with cold, they are. Get busy on the crane, will you, chum? "

Max sat on the roadside watching Rosie waltzing into position. He was afflicted by a sense of hopelessness, for it was plain to him that the plight of these people was a mere multiplication of his own, weary, homeless, at mercy of grudged charity and the caprice of passing strangers.

The Princess went over to him.

" I'm sorry if I was rude a while ago," she said. " Morning temper, I guess. I shouldn't have said it. I need a seltz. I'm sorry. Truly."

" O.K.," he said. " I may as well get used to it. They'll throw the book at me one day. A seltz won't cure that one."

" You're not in any mess, are you? " she asked, and sat beside him on the parapet. " Anything I could do ? I know most of the top brass."

" Brass can't do a thing for me," Max said. " I'm A.W.O.L. Right out of the line. Sound good? "

" After this morning I'm saying nothing," she said. " Do these boys know? "

" Surely." Max stood up, stretching. " And that don't make me feel any better. They have me tagged as yellow. Fine thing."

He walked over to Bill and watched him adjust the crane chains under the axle, handling the heavy links as easily as rope.

The men in the party stood together, looking on. Each face was cast from the same mean mould, and Max bit his tongue to keep from shouting at them, for they stood so miserably, filled with apprehension of some tragedy about to happen, and all trace of spirit was gone, leaving behind ciphers stricken as olive trees, in the same attitude of frozen appeal, but without the saving promise of harvest to come.

" For God's sake, lady," he said. " What kind of people are these? What are they standing like that for? "

She looked down at her shoes, comparing the toes, appreciating fine work on the welting. The fury in his voice affected her. Something of somebody else was there, the strength of passion and the frustration, the pride, and again the sense of shame.

Bill fixed the chains, and stood by to signal the turns. In a deep breath, Rosie began tugging the steel body out of its hole in the rock, making the sort of noise that reminded people of their teeth; and when Bill shouted to stop her, a child cried loudly in the quiet, and the helpless sound flew up blatant as a banner.

" All right, my pretty," Snowy called from the cabin. " We'll have you out of it in half a tick."

Bill was looking at a wreck of gashed rubber under the rim.

" Ye'll not do a lot with this," he said. " They've no spare, neither."

" Right," said Snowy. " Load this lot on Rosie, and tow 'em down to the nearest town. That's easy."

" I don't know why we don't run a delivery service and have done," said Bill. " Going against common sense, this is. Ye'll get no thanks, mind."

Snowy turned away, wishing heavily for Shiner and his willingness to have a smack at anything, anywhere, anytime, anyhow. Hungrily, angrily, he wished for the warmth of the big smile with the broken front tooth and the happy eyes that always said more than the words. He was unused to paltry denial and hesitant help, or of turning away from urgency on scores of personal comfort or difficulty of any kind. Orders, routine, had never made any difference to Old Shiner, for if ever there was any reason to think a job was due to be done then it was done, and that was the word, and it was all just the job.

He sat in the cabin and lit a cigarette, and became irritably aware of a new sound outside. A glance in the driving mirror showed the rear crowded with men and women loaded down with crates and suitcases, handing them up to someone inside. But they were all laughing.

That was the sound, and even though it came from white faces lighting scared eyes, still it was laughter, and the gay disturbance pricked a harshness within and suddenly he was unworried again, and aware that all was well.

This, in a new lift of heart he knew, was what Shiner might and could have caused and what would have been from the first had he been there. He could see him standing in the road picking up one of the children, and laughing at the mothers, and he could hear him talking his dozen words of Italian to the men, scolding them, making them grin with him, and then would have come the work of lifting and packing and towing.

It was happening now as it would have been then, and he was glad, for at that moment he was almost certain he could open the door, slap Shiner on the back, and then set about getting the kids fixed up with hot soup.

But it was Bill up there stacking cases, not Shiner.

16

When the women had climbed in and the children had been lifted up, all the men got on and crushed in except the old man in the raincoat.

" Snowy," the Princess said. " This is Professor Casalonghi. He's sick. Could he ride up front, do you think? "

" Certainly, Miss," said Snowy. " Anything else you'd like? "

" Yes," she said. " I ought to tell you how much they want to thank you for all this. They've been here since yesterday morning and they never had a hope of getting out till tomorrow, if then. They're all university professors and their families. They thought you were going to throw this whole thing in the canyon. So they want to thank you."

" Tell 'em it was Shiner, Miss." Snowy turned to the truck on tow, hearing the laugh plainer than her voice. " All his fault. All aboard. You all right, Bill? "

" Right, here," Bill called, behind the wheel in the other cabin. " She won't stand much speed, mind. She's well down, y'know. And this brake's none too clever."

" Leave it to Rosie," Snowy said, and slapped her panels on the way up.

" Snowy," the Princess said, " you're a kind soul."

" That all, Miss? " Snowy said. " Not much, after a hard life, is it? How's the old Professor feeling? "

" Pretty low," she said. " The university's a ruin. Most of that stuff in back is books. They haven't even a house between them all. I just don't know what's going to happen in this country."

" We're all in the same boat, Miss." Snowy felt the strain on the tow chain, and put Rosie comfortably in her stride. " Personally, meself, I ain't worried about universities. They've never done no worrying about me. But I ain't got a house neither. Bombed out. By these blokes, and their kind pals up top, there."

" If you feel that way about it," she said. " I don't know why you'd want to help out."

" No use all of us getting awkward, Miss," Snowy said. " My old mate reckoned if you help somebody, somebody'll help you. He was a sailor 'fore he got caught in this lark. Third engineer, he was. He reckoned we're all the same. Black and white, brown or yellow, don't make no difference. If you can do the job, do it. If not, don't muck about."

" A very sensible philosophy," said the Professor. " One that appeals to me."

The Princess glanced at Snowy in surprise. Again he saw the clear skin, the flower of her mouth, and the smile in lively brown eyes, and feeling disturbed his mind. She looked round at the Professor, and sunshine put bright copper twists in the bun of hair.

" Professor," she said, " you've been holding out on me."

" Madam," said the Professor, " in these days it is better to be discreet and ignorant than to show one's learning and to be snubbed. We are not without experience in this matter."

" Come far, have you, guv'nor? " asked Snowy.

" A long way," said the Professor. " I am very grateful to you, and so are my colleagues. You are the first of our Allies to show us courtesy, much less kindness, because, you know, scholars in wartime are a nuisance. Unless of course they happen to be scholars of chemistry or physics. They achieve a brute value. Unhappily, we are not."

" Unhappily? " she asked. " Would you rather take a hand? "

" As chemist or physicist, yes," the Professor said. " It would give me great joy to fashion some noble weapon, something simple, as effective as the Socratean bowl, for example. And then to use it, and to have the honour to rid this cockroach existence in universal sleep. Those who come after might learn from our mischiefs. At least they would not be urbanised animals at the mercy of any jackboot. Not little cabbages to be thrown in a heap to rot."

Again she caught a hint of somebody else's voice, but the mildness of the tone made the meaning worse to bear. She tried hard to think of a subject away from bitterness, but noticing the white growth of beard she realized he was unwashed perhaps for days, and possibly ashamed of his appearance, and tears came in defiance of her will.

" You speak English well," she said, and marvelled at banality.

" I have many English and American friends," said the Professor, smiling at something on the side of the road. " I have taught in England and America. With a little study of the literature, naturally."

" My father was at Harvard," she said. " I'm wondering if there's anything else that's stupid I can say. How did all this happen? "

" First the Germans, then the Patriots, then the English," said the Professor, reading a catalogue and with as much emotion. " The Patriots, our own people, were the worst. The Germans let us live in the cellars while they fought upstairs. The aeroplanes drove them out. The first English tanks passed us. Then the Patriots came in and we were confronted by a number of young ruffians who accused us of consorting with the enemy. The English came in to use the buildings and they sent the Patriots away. Then they sent us away. Very simple."

Snowy was watching the road and listening as he might to a radio set. The quiet voice, so like those on the radio, caused him little surprise. It was a voice from a world he knew about, but did not know, and it carried an accent that he knew and did not trust, of people living in the same world but in another part, supposing themselves to know a lot, and doing nothing about it.

" You've had no more than a lot of us back home," he said.

" 'Sides, you ought to have thought about it before you started the war. That's the time to be sorry."

" My friend," the Professor said, looking steadily at the road, " we were as helpless as idiots in an asylum. As you were. One day, war is unthinkable. The next, we are at war. What is one to do? "

" God damn," she said, and her voice shook like a bare branch. " God damn it."

" I agree," said the Professor. " But there seems little hope that He will. After all, we make excellent damnation for ourselves."

" Well," said Snowy. " If people like your sort can't do nothing about it we've got a fat chance, ain't we? Me and my missus and the two kids? How do we go on? Who starts it? That's the blokes I'm after."

" No use looking at me," she said. " I didn't want any war. I don't know anybody who did. Oh, I don't know. What's the use? "

The Professor shifted on the smooth leather as though changing position might ease despair. The voice of the driver, sharp with contempt in a rough dialect of English, stuck a thorn in his mind. There seemed at first so many defences and yet there were none. Responsibility must rest with someone in position to authorize, though, he impatiently told himself, it was not for a scholar to interfere in politics, but to train young minds to build themselves in verities : yet there seemed futility in a process that ended, whatever the intention, in death or mutilation for some and chaos for the remnant.

" I can't make it out, somehow," Snowy said. " Nobody wanted one. But we had one. How's that? "

Ploughland on both sides of the road greened to skylines miles away, broken by cypresses shooting blue cones from the walls of a cemetery full of little houses topped with crosses. Cattle stood in reeds behind the farm at the edge of a stream with rows of birds perching on their spines, and a white cart scrolled with flowers held up its shafts as though appealing for the warm body of an ox; and as they turned, the lamp alight in the empty shrine on the roadside glimmered for a moment, red as a mouth.

17

A soldier was lying right across the road, using the restful level of the tarmac instead of sharing the ditch with flies, and when Rosie was well round the corner he turned to watch her perhaps expectantly, hands under head, smoking a cigarette, but he made no move until he heard her easing down, and then got up, slowly putting his beret on, buttoning his blouse, fastening his belt, lifting a pack on his shoulder, strolling around to the cabin, and looking up, coaxing the cigarette to the other side of his mouth in a roll of his jaw, and standing there as though time was only something like mustard, to be used on things, little or much to suit the taste.

Looking at him gave Snowy the same feeling as waiting outside the front door, with his key on the washstand upstairs, and everybody gone over to Walham Green for tea at Aunty Laura's. The eyes were deep grey, almost blue, with black pupils that seemed to spin inside themselves first round one way and then round the other until they merged in two spins, each in an opposite direction, and in looking there might be caught, as through a crack of light in heavy timber, the smallest notion of a certain sort of smile.

" Glad you're one of our lot," he said, in a voice that never stayed two syllables at a time in the same octave. " How far you going? "

" Who are you, and where d'you want to go? " asked Snowy, looking down at him, irritated as much by the tone as the leisureliness.

" I'm Nipper Dincott," he said, on the same level. " Know any more now, do you? Eh? I'm Harry Freeman. How's that? Or Charlie Peace. Do you any good? Take your pick. Who am I? "

" Sweeney Todd," said Snowy, without feeling, and with a blank face. " Where you off? "

" Crystal Palace," said Dincott. " Any good? "

" Jump up," Snowy jerked his thumb at the rear. " Drop

you at Lewisham High Street. Mind how you go. Got the family aboard this morning."

"Ought to started earlier," Dincott said. "Be dark 'fore you get there. What's your mob?"

"The Lolloping Twelfth." Snowy looked at the badgeless beret. "The old Duke of Muggin's Own. What's yours?"

"D.P.A." He was looking at the Princess, and sliding the cigarette between his lips. "Dincott's Private Army. I see you've got yourself a lovely lump of fiddle there."

"If you want the lift," Snowy said, feeling the enquiring pressure of her eyes, and an overall vexing, "you'd best trot your body."

"Nipper never trots," he said. "That's for blokes took short. This is my style, look."

Snowy watched him climb up as if a lifetime lay ahead, and Rosie freewheeled down the little hill.

"Hard case there," he said. "Have to watch him."

"I couldn't understand a word he said." The Princess looked at Casalonghi for agreement. "Where was he from?"

"Somewhere round Crystal Palace, I suppose, Miss," Snowy said. "That's in London."

"But you're from London, too," she said. "I understand you well enough."

"Ah," said Snowy. "But you've got to know London, Miss. Lot of people there. They all talk different, see? Mile End's a lot different to Kennington. Battersea's nothing like Camberwell. Mayfair's more your line. The posh lot."

"Posh." Casalonghi rolled the word about. "I don't know this word."

"Posh," said Snowy. "All about. You know. High class." He jerked his head at the Princess. "Like her."

She looked away, frowning a smile.

"An extraordinary language, English," Casalonghi said. "Glass and granite, and fine wine and thick soup. Nine-tenths of a magnificent vocabulary is barely known, and certainly never used. Such a word as 'posh' is preferred by the common run, I suppose, because it has a curious effect on the ear, and of course an important brevity. So the stranger takes its place and everyone is happy, except the poor scholar. Pity him."

"You don't do so badly," the Princess said. "You have very little in the way of accent."

"Bad accent, I think, is due either to a bad ear or to lack of respect for the medium," said Casalonghi.

"What about me?" asked Snowy. "I don't know so much about bad ears. I've had a few thick 'uns."

"Yours is a dialect, not an accent," Casalonghi said.

"Me?" Snowy almost braked Rosie to a standstill. "Dialect? Well, God starve the bookies' orphans. This ain't a dialect, Mister. I ain't having that."

"It is English of a kind spoken in a part of London," said Casalonghi. "A dialect. I'm sorry, my friend. Dialect."

"You're talking about Bill, you are," Snowy said. "There's a dialect for you. Pure Lancashire. You can hear the tripe and onions. You don't tell me I've got a dialect just because you talk Two Bob Return? Blinkin' neck."

Rosie was running through a gorge of red stone bright with bushes offering fresh green to goats that vaulted the rocks in flight, only so far, and then nosed at branches with a motion of the lips that was nearly a kiss.

Snowy eased over the crown and looked behind to watch Bill on the end of the tow rope, ignoring a small log in the roadway. The near front wheel passed over it, slightly tipping the cabin, and to save herself she put out a hand and the palm rested a full moment on a surge of muscle padded by bristling silk that even under her weight felt crisply alive. She took her hand away and reached up to put a soothing finger on the falcon's plumage.

"I'm so sorry," she said.

"'s all right, Miss," said Snowy, surprised at an alien touch. "It's only me. All home grown, prime quality. Lovely stuff."

She saw the slightest movement in the netted paths under Casalonghi's eyes, and, sensing her embarrassment, he felt shame for lack of facial discipline and forthwith nodded at laggards among the goats.

"The Song of Solomon, I think, says, 'How beautiful are thy feet with shoes, O daughter of Israel'," he said. "It might have been sung for the goat. Have you ever noticed the symmetry of a goat's hoof?"

"I hadn't made all that study of it particularly," she said.

"Strange." Casalonghi was staring up at a glow behind the crest. "Not long ago we insist on the sanctity of goats. A symbol of potency and insatiability. And because they give milk and flesh and even suckle the children, they are valuable members of the family, and they live in the house, and so they acquire a reputation for inoffensive usefulness. Then they have this little beard, like the patriarch, and men begin to call them wise because they look on the comedy and tragedy of family life, and, whatever they see, they are silent. And the goat becomes a little god. But that was in the days of poets. Now we have emerged from the dark ages, and goats are meat, milk, cheese and wool, little machines that smell and make money. We are so enlightened, and progressive, so utilitarian. And so abominable."

"Goats you may have," she said. "Give me mutton. Or pork. I'd just love ham and eggs right now."

"Shan't be long, Miss," said Snowy. "I've got some in there. I love bacon and tomatoes myself. The smell's nearly as good as the grub."

"Poor nose," Casalonghi said. "Such a buffoon. But in eating, and drinking, and certainly in love, always an aristocrat. And often forgotten. We shall all be glad to have baths."

"I'm so sorry," she said, turning on impulse. "How long have you been on the road?"

"Nearly three weeks," said Casalonghi. "The children are exhausted. Two of my oldest colleagues died a week ago. With almost the last lire in our pockets we bought that camion. The truck. If we had not, we should still be in the refugee camp. Refugees, you imagine? Displaced persons. My dear Princess, these are terms of such disgust. I have come to detest charity, and the women who dispense it. Your sex, if you permit me, in uniform are no longer women, but females. And such females have nothing to recommend them except their genitals."

"That's strictly a male idea," she said, in a surprisingly cold tone. "What plans have you for the children? Could I help?"

"We shall stop at the next town," he said, and his hands made small circular gestures of helplessness. "You must pardon me. One forgets oneself. When I think of those people, I am lost."

She heard tiredness, age, impatience with adversity and anger against circumstance thickening to hysteria. A little froth had formed in the corner of his mouth.

"When did you all eat last?" she asked.

"Yesterday," he said. "It is terrible that this should happen at the end of my life. Everything has gone. Work, and pride, and hope. Now I must see children starve. It is a crown upon my work."

"Cheer up, bloke," Snowy said. "The next place is just round the corner. Then we'll have some breakfast, and get that bus seen to."

"You are very kind," he said.

"I ain't," said Snowy. "I'm only sorry for them kids, that's all. I got no time for blokes like you. If you'd won the war, you'd have been over there giving us a dog's life. As it is, you lost. And you're snivelling. Well, you keep on, chum. Blokes like you let it happen. Now get on with it."

Casalonghi closed his eyes, thinking of the labour and bloody hands with pick and shovel down in the cellars, the mustiness, and the rough smoke of tallow in the tunnels, and whispers of encouragement to passing shapes burdened to the chin with books stolen away from the library upstairs, and the triumph of a bottle of wine drunk over laid stone and hidden treasure.

For nothing. An instant sweep of flame and a black bursting behind the eyes, and the books, the effort, and the dream were of the same dust.

That.

And this workman speaking with the aptitude and the accuracy of a talking doll. The life, the true life that had gone, all the years of work and learning and ambition and ideals, the dream of a new system of learning, the emergence of another type of mind, all, every thought and effort through the years thrown on the midden by this English fellow, product of an industrial phase bred in ignorance and trained to the machine, permitted rational speech by accidents of commerce and politics with an intelligence built on the catcalls of school historians and parochial journalism.

A line of willow trees foreshortened to one, and wheeled out on the other side in a ballet line of shock-headed oldsters, each peering down mumchance at its reflection in the river as though dissatisfied with the set of its wig. She seemed to feel the hurt of the Professor coming from his swaying body, and knew that some part of shame was her own. Again she was angry with this quiet mechanic for speaking in such a manner to a scholar, a man of peace life-long, and now homeless, penniless, looking for a place to rest and store his books. The destruction of all the pleasanter parts of life, the unhurried, ageless things seemed sketched for her by this unhappy man fleeing ruin in a worn-out machine.

Snowy was angry with himself for having picked the party up, of wasting a thought on the Princess or offering to help any of them.

Listening to them talking, nobody would have thought of Shiner, or guessed what Liz had said in her last letter, or that a couple of trips ago Rosie had carried more than thirty of the lads sewn up in their own blankets down to the cemetery.

It all went on just the same, and nothing changed no matter what happened.

18

Bill kept strain on the tow rope, unwilling to put weight on the brake, trying to keep as far from the parapet as Rosie would permit, for the road edge was crumbling under her rear wheels, bringing splendid dreams of a double plunge into the chasm and a riotous death under the waterfall.

From time to time he looked up at the crowded faces in Rosie's rear. At first he tried smiling and winking at the children, but they stayed flatfaced, looking at him with big eyes that had no whites. The adults hunched together, rolling with the turns, saying nothing, with never a smile among any of them, and an old woman in black, sitting up higher than the others, with her hat tilted just a little and grey hair falling down one side of her face, stayed awake, staring over the roof of Bill's cabin to a place that seemed a long way away.

Max watched Bill taking a bend on the gradient without using the brake and yet keeping the chain taut, and again admired his control and at the same time felt that sense of uselessness.

Everybody else seemed to be doing something useful. Even the Princess had acted as interpreter at a time when he felt he never wanted to hear another human voice, but when he joined the group and wanted to talk to them nobody answered, and he knew they distrusted him from the way they hunched their shoulders, gripping their coats across the chest with both hands as though fearful of losing another rib.

" Snow really has a bunch of misery aboard there," he said.

" Ah," said Bill. " Even the damn kids are all turned forty, from the looks of 'em."

" Probably want some chow," Max said. " I wonder how mine's doing."

" You've not put yourself in much of a place to find out, have you? " Bill watched the faint reflection on the windscreen and saw the movement from the corner of his eye. " Why don't you go on back and find out? Ye'll feel better."

" Why in hell can't you talk when somebody wants to know?" Max sat up ready to jump. " I know what I want to do."

" Ye don't think you're the only bloke that's gone for a breather, do you? " Bill was absorbed in taking a narrow hairpin leading to the road on the plain that ran straight as a white rail for many a mile. " Take it in time, that's all ye've to do."

" I did that," Max said. " I still am."

Bill smiled.

" But you're not all that happy," he said. " When I come out of hospital I couldn't face the thought of going back. So I bunked. Had a fortnight off. They never knew I'd gone."

" That's different," Max said, leaning back. " They'll know about me. I'm for the stockade. You didn't act like you'd been adrift ?"

" Why should I? " Bill turned to him. " Listen, chum. I know how you feel because I've had some. D'ye see? "

" What made you go back? " Max asked.

" It didn't seem worth all the nonsense," Bill said. " After you get away out on it ye start thinking of all the lads and such-like. So before you know where y'are, you're calling yourself everything and wishing y' could get back there quicker'n what y' come. D'y'see? "

" Right," said Max. " When are you guys going back? "

" Three days' time," said Bill. " Why? "

" I'll string along," Max said. " Set me down where you picked me up."

" Fair's fair," said Bill. " Glad to."

" Why did you tell me? " Max spoke as though he were some way off.

" Stop your nasty temper," Bill said. " Y' can't be let walk about like one of Pharaoh's plagues here, and us on holiday. 'Tain't right."

They were running into the outskirts of a small town hidden in the forearm of a hill. One narrow street was lively with people, most of them unseen and part of the deep shade, though in the sun groups of women wore a black velvet corsage with black skirts bunched up over red petticoats and the men wore the same old mixture of grey military tunic and worsted trousers, but everyone moved slowly, as though walking was as much as they could manage. The houses were all grey stone, perhaps built at the same time by the same man, and the shutters were back from all the windows, with untidy scrambles of bed linen hanging over the sills or flung anyhow over balustrades. Shops were all shuttered, but outside two of them lines of women wearing cloths over their heads were waiting as though they had been there forever with baskets as empty as their eyes. And everywhere barefoot children sat by the dozen in the gutters all in the same sort of rags, with the same mudstains from toe to crown.

" I've never seen so many kids in my life," Bill said. " They breed like rabbits."

" That's how they come off the line," Max said.

" I don't hold with it," said Bill. " They can't afford 'em."

" We probably can't afford hurricanes," said Max. " But we get 'em. They just are natural, that's all. It's what happens when you get next to a girl and you hump her. Boom, it's a kid. These folks just live natural. Period."

" Poor little devils," Bill said. " I'd be ashamed to face the neighbours. Look at 'em. They haven't seen soap and water since they got whelped, any of 'em."

" Doing all right," Max said. " Soap and water don't make all that difference. Your grandad didn't have the plumbing, either. And your grandma made her own soap. Twenty years, these'll have families, too. That's more hands around the farm. Less work for the old man."

"You stick up for 'em," Bill said. "I don't mind that."

"I'm for 'em," Max said. "That's why. I can't stick around and hear 'em torn up. I get mad. I can see my pa everywhere around here. Same face, same eyes. I know how he's worked. These old guys are just the same. Look at their hands."

Rosie put her nose round the corner of the piazza, and Snowy coaxed her between the town hall steps and the fountain to reach the open door of a blacksmith's forge, where two Ages lapped. A leather bellows grew a little rose of flame in rear of a concrete pit and the tool benches of a garage. A wrecked German staff car in green and white camouflaged with rust showing through lay on its side helplessly showing tyreless rims. A distant odour of burning hoof overrode petrol fumes, yet not strong enough to smudge the outline of her perfume.

Snowy wished her gone and went back to Bill.

"Cast off, chum," he said. "Max, ask 'em in here if they can do this job, will you? I'll help 'em with patches, but I ain't got a lot of time. I'm behind already."

"O.K.," Max said, and jumped down.

"Bill," said Snowy, helping with the cable, "I'm coming round to your way of thinking, mate. Hear 'em talk, you'd think nobody had anything wrong with 'em. They was nattering about goats, if you please. Goats. God settle me."

"I told you," said Bill. "I wouldn't give 'em eye room. Get rid of 'em. Except Max. He's all right."

"Winning all his fags off of him, are you?" Snowy climbed up on the winch. "Nothing like giving the guests a nice doing. Makes 'em want to come again."

A crowd of children had gathered thick about them, standing still, pooling their stares in a vacuum of curiosity resting on quiet, broken by the voice of a harridan, shrill as the rub of a blade on glass, across the hot width of the piazza. Snowy looked at the knuckly feet, thin shins and big kneebones, and the ribs showing through rags, and the colour of faces in heads that looked top-heavy, and the white movement of nits in stooks of hair. He looked up at the children being lifted over Rosie's tailboard, seeing fatter limbs and rounder faces and bodies that had weight.

He looked down again, and saw the hollows in cheeks and about the mouth, and shadows under the jaw, and the droop of hands over swollen bellies made him think of the paws of a drowned pup lying on its back in the tideway.

"Here, Bill," he said. "What's up with these kids?"

"The lot that had 'em, likely," said Bill, clamping the chain. "Why?"

Even in the midday heat Snowy was cold. Looking up at an empty sky, he was surprised to find himself shaking. He could see the two girls at the kitchen table and Liz standing over the stove.

Bill bent down to look at a little girl, putting his spectacles on the tip of his nose.

"Well, Mary," he said. "What's to do, love? Eh?"

He straightened, staring down at her. With no smile or move or any light, the child stared up at him from a face the colour of faded paper, as dry in the skin, and lined for senility. Her eyes, a beautiful amber in that light, bulged from pits that would have held a thumb, but without spark, and she blinked slow as a bird.

"They're starving," Snowy said. "Just look at the colour of 'em. They are; they're bloody starving, mate."

"Well, damn it," Bill said. "I do believe you're right. Ye can see her poor bones."

"So what're you going to do for them?" The Princess was standing behind him. She was looking at the children and her voice was quietly normal as though she had asked for a match.

Snowy looked at her in surprise.

She showed nothing. She was looking at the faces all round and her skirts talked silk about her as she turned, but when she looked at him, waiting for his answer, he saw white lines down the sides of her nose, and though her eyes were calm she looked through scarlet lace.

"If I knew," he said, "I wouldn't be standing here."

"So now you know how the rest of us feel," she said. "Just don't keep hitting at people. We couldn't see this happening any more than you could. It didn't seem possible. Still doesn't."

She turned, with cheek bent to shoulder, and quickly went through the crowd, touching heads as she passed.

Not a child moved, and not a face had changed.

" Let's get some work done," Snowy said. " Let's get out of it."

" Hey," Max called from the garage. " Here's the boss. Who's paying for the job, he wants to know? "

" The Professor and his pals, of course," Snowy said.

" Who's he think we are? "

" Spare him a couple of gallons of gas," Max said. " He'll do it for love."

Snowy flung the spanner in the box. The effort gave expression to anger that had no words.

" O.K.," he shouted. " O bloody K. Give him his bloody petrol. Let's get out of it."

Max went inside, and Snowy had a glimpse of the Princess talking to the group of passengers standing among their baggage. She was looking at him between their heads with something in her face that seemed an appeal and yet was touched with some quality that jolted in sudden exaltation, for so often he had seen the look in Liz's eyes when things had gone too far for talk.

19

The townspeople were stopping to stare, and soon there were more adults than children, and their eyes clung to every movement with a look, profound but inept, that was only a stare in faces pulled too tight to the head, lined and shadowed, and horrid smooth over cheekbones and the nose. Closer to, the corsages were thin, with silver bloom where something of velvet was left, and the scarlet petticoats were stained, and the bundled skirts were greenish brown in the sun. But if the clothes were ready to fall, so were the bodies, for in that quiet circle the fragility of the person could be felt and the entire crowd seemed to have no more substance than so many hanks of wool.

An old woman held out her hand to Snowy, edging her toes with the dust hillocking between them in crawling fashion towards him. Her face had the surface of waxy crupp, and she looked at him at about the level of his cheekbones as if she were smiling inside, not at him but towards herself, and secretly, not for others to see. Her lips moved, but there was no voice, and as he stood quiet he seemed to feel her cooling inwardly and the veined bones of her hand went slack to her breast as though hope had gone and embassy was useless.

Snowy went closer to her.

" What's up, Ma gel? " he said.

" Hey, Snow," Max called. " Listen to this."

Snowy patted the old woman's shoulder, feeling the warm bone that was little more, and made onesided way through the crowd, smelling a stench of clothing worn until it might have been another skin. He went into the blue shade of the garage, blinking to find his way, seeing tools in purple settings and an anvil pointing its snout in a carpet of green cinders.

Someone was running and then he was grasped by the arms and a chin pressed barbs in his cheek.

" Snowy? " A voice between laughter and a question shouted in his ear. " Snowy? You don't remember? Rusty? Rusty. You don't remember Rusty? "

Max stopped short, watching the big Italian mechanic shaking Snowy as though he were a sack, and then Snowy seemed to wake up and his face split wide.

" Rusty? " His arms opened. " God stiffen the crows. Here, Max, this is Rusty. With our lot nearly two years. Rusty, that's Max."

" Hiya," Max said and shook hands.

" Bill," Snowy said. " This is him. I told you about Rusty. Remember the prisoner? Picked him up at Sidi Rezegh? Why, blimey." He turned to Rusty. " What with you and Rosie, I'm nearly back at Mersa Matruh. What're you doing here? "

Rusty gestured at the building.

" She's mine," he said. " Hell of a mess when I'm come back. Now she's not so bad. Not so bad, eh? Just the job. Come. We have nice drink, eh? "

" How about the job outside there? " Max asked. " You didn't want to fool with it just now? "

" How I'm going to do job without some tools? " Rusty opened his arms in appeal to the roof, bringing his palms together in a quiet gesture of prayer. " No tools. No gomma.

Niente. Nothing I got. Everything they take away. So what I do?"

"I'll get you all that," Snowy said. "All outside there."

"So," said Rusty, in a great calm. "Is easy, no? I do the job."

"That's all we're waiting for," said the Princess, from the doorway. "Else I don't know if we can hold these people from a riot. Snowy." She turned to him with a note in her voice that seemed to scrape. He could feel minute things happening to his face, changes he fought to stop, but they were happening all over his body until he could feel his will being eaten in a desire to show what he felt. "Won't you please see these people get away before you go? They'll be torn to pieces."

"Come on, Rusty." Snowy nodded at Bill. "Three of us have a go."

"What're they going to get torn up for?" Bill asked. "They're just as bad off?"

"They're better fed," she said. "These folks think they've got a truck full of food there. They won't believe it's just books. And I'm afraid for the children."

"Ah," said Snowy. "We'll take care of them. I wish there was a ration dump round here. I'd go and pay 'em a visit."

He went outside to Rosie and started unpacking the jack, and Bill unlocked the tool-chest. Max watched them, leaning against the doorway, knowing that she was just behind him.

"Why did you say that about the kids?" he asked. "Afraid of what?"

"Afraid they might eat them." The words pressed upwards through spittle and an effort to control breath. "Can you believe they'd do it? Oh, God. I can't bear to live any more."

"Lady," Max said, "I'll believe anything. Did you take a look at 'em? Anybody that looks like that, God damn it, they got a right to do what they want. Eat the lamb. They're so close to going over one more sin don't make such a hell of a lot of difference."

"Don't say that," she said. "It's terrible. Terrible."

"That's right." Max nodded, and, without turning his head, passed a cigarette behind, and felt it taken from his fingers. "It's terrible. But three, four hundred miles up there, they're eating 'em. Only they come in the larger size. What's the difference? Kill 'em and eat 'em, or kill 'em and bury 'em."

" Oh, don't talk," she wept. " Don't. Don't. It's wrong. It's horrible."

" Surely," said Max. " You bet it's wrong. But, lady, you ain't hungry."

The townspeople stood in a semicircle that took in the front of the garage and both wagons. The women seemed to have been edged out of the front ranks by the men, and Max watched a couple of them, with black beards showing the true pallor of their faces, wearing torn military uniforms that hung about them, slowly footing a way through the children, slyly pushing them behind, and waiting, and stepping forward another foot. Keeping his eyes on them without watching them, Max saw the creep movement happening all the way around within the orbit of his vision, the dark chins, and the lids of eyes all shut as men picked their way among silent heads, the gradual movement of children half pace by half pace to the rear, and the steadily growing frame of scarlet and black skirts neatly forming on the far side.

The silence gave deep tone to the tyre levers finding the rim, and emphasized the whistle of Rusty's breath, but the big Italian was weak. Snowy wordlessly took the tools warm from his hands and squatted down with Bill to hammer. As the first lever went in place, they exchanged a look, and each in sudden pity found sympathy for a man weakened to a point where he could no longer work.

Rusty turned away. Shame was a small animal chewing at him, but he knew he had no strength, even enough to lift any one of the children.

He straightened, slowly, watching Max sighting an automatic at the chimneys.

" O.K., Rusty," he said, with one eye screwed, and shifting the other to watch him. " I'm practising. You better tell some of these boys what's going to happen if they start something. A forty-five makes an awful big hole."

Snowy looked up.

" What's wrong? " he asked, and stood looking about. The faces of the nearest men struck fright.

" Better get your guns out of there," Max said. " We're due for trouble."

Bill pulled himself up in rear and unslung his rifle, bringing it from shadow into the bright light, making great play with the bolt to load the magazine. But his thumb seemed to miss the safety catch, and the crook of his finger found the trigger. The bullet whacked the warm air over the heads of the crowd, smashing a window high up in a house across the piazza in a plaint of splintering glass. Every head seemed pulled down in a vast genuflection and women screamed here and there, but without the shrill intent of urgent fear. There seemed a note of dismay, almost of sorrow, in their alarm, as if they had been waiting to scream for another reason.

" My mistake," Bill said. " Just to show there's no ill feelings, like."

Rusty went out to them as though to speak, but the circle had broken, and women were running away among groups of children, though the movement was odd, for the hurry was over in a few paces, and then came a breathless dawdle, and though fright had left their faces paler, perhaps, the same expression was back in their eyes, a groping in the spirit to prolong life without vigour.

Casalonghi stood in front of the group looking on with a smile that Snowy found hard to understand. He saw no reason for any sort of smile at that moment, yet it was in him to admire the spirit.

" What's up, mate? " he asked. " Got a feather round your neck? "

Casalonghi shook his head. He thought of Snowy as he might of a constable, a man confined to a particular function and a convenient means of keeping order, but without any other identity. His question therefore was not important, but it served an opportunity to express a thought.

" This is the true Italy," he said, speaking across Snowy to the Princess. " Now I am satisfied. It is normal for us to suffer. From the ages, from the barbarians, the land has been burnt and spoliated and our people have starved. We became a nation so. We built from suffering, and now we suffer again. I see the pattern. I am content."

" Nuts," Max said. " What the hell. You know what a cannibal is, don't you? "

Casalonghi still smiled.

" Certainly, sir," he said. " All my life. People eating each other. Each other's work. Each other's idea. But from the rottenness there will come good. That is the principle. From corruption is life. To eat is to live."

" Put the iron away, chum." Snowy looked up in disgust at Bill. " Let's get it done and get out of it. What's up, Rusty boy? "

Rusty was leaning against the enamel advertisement for petroleum. Contrasted with the sharp colouring, his fraying khaki shirt and trousers looked tired of the sun and, it might have been, part of another century.

" We don't have something to eat," he said. " For months, nothing. Not even the rat any more. No lorry. No car. No petrol. No horse. Nothing. Nothing to grow. Everybody they die. Everybody."

" Listen, Rusty," Snowy said. " Shut the place up. You can't do any good here. Come down with us for a couple of days, eh? Sake of old times? "

" It don't matter I close." A weakness of anger whistled in his voice. He was in the shadow and his footfalls were husky in cinders. " We got nothing any more. Hundreds of horses. Bovi. Cattle. The cows. Thousands we had. Now, not one. Everything they eat. Gone. So what we do? "

" Get your coat on, Rusty boy," Snowy said. " Let's get away."

Bill finished tightening the rim nuts and stood up, wiping his forehead on the sleeve of his shirt.

" I never thought I'd have to sweat for wops," he said. " I don't hold with any of this. It's daft. We ought to leave 'em in their own muck. It's nowt to do with us, this ain't."

" I'm a wop," the Princess said. " I have another little wop at home, and she's going to say prayers for you. Every night for years and years you can think of a little wop on her knees praying for you. All you did was help people out of a mess. You didn't have to. You just did. Thank you, Bill."

20

Bill ducked under Rosie's belly to escape the quiet voice. He had spoken not in cold blood but to make himself believe that what he did was simply an obligement that he regretted, product of his weaker, more pliable self, the part of his nature that could be worked on by any sly faker with a hard-luck story, the soft part of himself that he detested, that started tears rising in the cinema when it was sad, or when he saw a bloke hurt at work, or a little lad fallen down and cut his leg, or even a couple of kittens. It was the part that everybody poked fun at, that sometimes made him do jobs for other people without pay. It was the part that made him stop that day when it was raining and help Pet over the tram lines and then spend half the night repairing the engine of her cripplechair so that she could get to work in the morning, the part that loved carrying her upstairs, loved sitting on the bed watching her eating and then tucking her up afterwards.

But he hated it because everybody called him a fool for working for nothing and not looking after the future, and worse, that he was anybody's play and walked about half his time moon-gazing, about as soppy as they make them. He wished he had cold eyes and the sort of voice to make everybody stand up when he came in a room, and a nature that did nothing for nothing and ended up a millionaire.

"Ye'd best thank Snowy," he said. "He started it."

She went round to the cabin and looked up, watching Snowy setting the mirror.

"You want me to ride in the other truck?" she asked. "I'll be getting down just over the ridge. I wouldn't want to bother you any more. You've done enough. More than enough."

"It's all right, lady," Snowy said. "Jump up. We'll soon be there."

He thought he heard an angry word from Rosie and took away his boot to listen, but then he saw the Princess put a hand on the mudguard and the other with fingers spread against her side, and her eyes were staring, black, at the door handle.

The scream came from a throat tight with breath held moment by moment until ready to throw up despair in a retch of sound.

" Who's having a lark? " he said. " Who was it, gel? "

" Snowy," Bill shouted. " They reckon they can't find one of these kids here."

" No, please God," she said. " It can't be."

" Now listen," said Snowy. " There's no need to go barmy. If it's lost, we'll soon find it, don't you worry. Who's looking for it? "

" Nobody." Bill walked down, watching the brown faces ranked in shadow on the other side of the square. " The old bloke says it's no good of us wasting our time."

The Princess pushed herself away from Rosie and walked away as if she had weights on her feet.

" D'ye know what? " Bill whispered. " Max reckons they've done it in for grub."

" Go out of it," Snowy said, and hurried to follow her.

The group stood about a woman sitting on a crate in the sunlight. She raised her head as Snowy walked towards her, and he saw a face puffed in brutal fat of grief, and eyes that searched a colder world.

" Now then," he said. " What's the game? "

" Her child has gone," Casalonghi said, minimizing horror on an upward stress of voice.

" And you're squatting on your backsides? " Snowy looked down the turning behind the garage. " Come on. Some of you down here. Some of you down there. Max, you take this lot. Bill, you take them. I'll go through here with the rest. Rusty, you stay here. Get cracking."

Bill gave him a rifle. Rusty and Casalonghi explained to the quiet group of men, and they split up, hands still in raincoat pockets, mute from helplessness, looking at each other with eyes fogged by a sense of inutility.

" A bright lot, losing their kids," Snowy said. " I'd just like to see anybody lay a finger on one of mine. Didn't nobody see which way it went? Who're we looking for? Boy or girl? "

" A girl," the Princess said. " She was playing with the others. Then they couldn't find her."

" What was her name? " Snowy asked.

" Emilia," Casalonghi said.

" Right," said Snowy. " Start hollering for her. If you find the bloke, bring him back with you. I'll show you how to deal with him."

The groups set off in a chorus of shouts. Snowy led half a dozen men around the garage to Rosie, smiling to see her resting in good smells of petrol and oil. A movement inside the canopy made him frown.

" Who's in there? " he asked.

" Who d'you reckon? " lightly questioned a tremolo voice. " Cassamaranda? Queen of Sheba? Who d'you fancy? "

" Listen," Snowy said. " They've been and lost a kid round there. Come on out and give us a hand."

Dincott looked over the tailboard, and scraped his throat, resting his elbows comfortably on the riveted edge.

" That what all the nonsense was about? " he asked. " I heard somebody loosin' off. What's this kid's monniker? "

" Emilia," Snowy said, listening to echoing shouts in the next street, aching to reach up and pull that half smile into range of his fist.

" She's in here." Dincott nodded behind him. " Why didn't somebody ask the question? "

Snowy felt the eyes of the Italians on him.

" Don't know, mate," he said. " Let's have her out of it, will you? "

A little girl was lifted down, and Dincott held up her doll, lowering it slowly by its hands until it rested in the crook of her arm. She pushed a plait away and smiled up at him.

" There," he said. " Mended her dolly, kept her safe and sound while the nasty men was banging away and frightening her, and now she's off to the old lady. Arrivederci, bellina."

" Did you know she was being looked for? " Snowy asked, feeling a bubble had blown and almost hearing the escape of air. " Making us look like mugs in front of this lot! "

" Now listen," Dincott said. " I always mind me own business, and I take things very steady. That's where the trouble starts. Everybody tearing about. What for? You don't get no thanks for it."

Snowy walked away, almost ashamed to go back to the garage. The gabble had broken out again, and he heard the sob of women in laughter. Max met him on the corner.

" Boy," he said. " That had me going. I could see 'em with their napkins all tucked in, clear through to the coffee and toothpicks."

" It's funny," Snowy said. " While I was up there in the Line I wanted to be down here. Now I've got down here, I can't hardly abear myself till I'm back with the lads again."

" When you have to start worrying if somebody's going to use kids for the main dish," Max said. " I'd just as soon get back where they're somebody you have Christmas for, and like that."

" Changing your mind about this lot? " Snowy asked, nodding at the crowd, still standing in the shadow of the piazza.

" No," Max said, " I didn't change my mind. I just did a little figuring. These folk are back too far. They just don't know. We got to show 'em, and that's going to hurt everybody."

" I'd like to hurt a few of 'em," Snowy said, patting his rifle. " Only way to knock a bit of sense in 'em."

In the shadow of the truck, men and women looked as though heaven was round the corner. The little girl was in her mother's lap, ringed about by the other women, all of them talking, laughing and crying at once, but keeping hold of their own children, looking anxiously about moment by moment to make sure they were there.

Bill and Rusty pulled the jack from under the axle and started putting the tools away.

" All ready here," Bill said. " That were a proper damn sell, weren't it? "

" It were," Snowy said. " Don't let's waste time. This is our holiday, in case you've forgot. We can still be tooling about here for the next couple of months, and nobody'll bother."

He inspected the repair job, noting, he was surprised to find, with pride the evidence of Bill's work.

A little cough made him turn. Casalonghi was looking at a pendant and chain shining in his palm. A diamond flashed quick strokes of coloured light.

" Sir," Casalonghi said, " we are all in your deepest debt.

The mother and father of the child wish you to accept this article as a gift for your wife. For the remainder of us, we wish to present you with this small sum to drink our health at your leisure, in the knowledge that you brought joy to people who were hopeless. And may the Great God in His mercy send you and your friends back safely to your families, as you brought this little one to hers."

Snowy looked away, into the dark garage, aware that Max was watching, knowing without turning that the Princess was just behind him.

"We don't want the money, guv'nor," he said. "And I ain't taking nothing from her mother and father, neither. Thanks just the same."

"They'll be awfully hurt, Snowy." The Princess said it in a whisper hard with conviction. "Please take it. You couldn't do anything better."

"I don't want to take their stuff," Snowy said. "They got enough to do with it."

"Please," she said. "If you refuse they'll think it's not enough, or something awful. Please, Snowy. Be nice."

He was suddenly angry with her for asking him to be nice about a job he was ashamed of. All the bluster before the search, the bullying of the men, and the shouting afterwards seemed ridiculous when one question would have got her, safe as a judge, out of Rosie.

"Look, Miss," he said. "I don't want it. Matter of fact, they ought to give it to them out there."

"But they feel grateful," she insisted. "They have to show it."

"All right," Snowy said. "Let 'em feel it to their own kind, then. Not because we done anything, but them people out there wasn't the lot they were supposed to be. So pipe down, and let's get aboard."

"Snowy," she said, "you're so damned British."

"Yes, Miss," he said. "And all this is so blinkin' Eyetie."

He left Casalonghi pouring the jewel from palm to palm, catching pinpoints of light in his eyes as he passed into the sunshine. The quiet crowd still stood in the shadow on the far side of the piazza, black and dull red marking the block of women, grey and khaki among the men, with row upon row of brown faces turned always towards him. There came a feeling that they must always have been there, and always would, dull red and black women, green and khaki men, and mudstained children in row upon row of brown faces, silent, watching, waiting.

" They're giving me the creeps," he said to Bill. " Start up, chum."

21

The driver of the other truck backed into the piazza, followed by the group carrying suitcases and children, shepherded by Casalonghi.

He felt tired in a peculiarly new way, not physically, he thought, or mentally, but perhaps socially. He felt he no longer had the energy to deal with people, for something had happened to them, even the commonest of them, that permitted a low-born mechanic to refuse gifts and ignore felicitous speech from those that in another day could have denied him the right to raise his eyes in doubt, much less his voice in refusal. Thinking heavily of time to come, the new lessons in patience to be learnt, and the stubborn quality of ignorance to be endured, he felt himself too far gone in years, too drilled in other disciplines, to make the effort, and in realizing it the sunlight seemed a shade darker, and a tremor started in his walk.

" Soon as we come to the next town," Snowy said, " that's where we lose 'em."

" Half-way there," the Princess said. " That's where you lose me."

Her voice was abrupt, edged with dislike that he found hard to bear. She was staring ahead, and in a quick glance he saw her eyes were dry, yet bright with anger, but he was surprised to see she had used make-up, even to blue over her lids.

A thin disappointment chilled his mind.

The clear washed-away look that had made her so easy to approach seemed not even a memory, but only a mistake, for the added colour showed another order of woman, full of the authority of beauty that struck at him and made him silent.

He remembered Liz roaming about the house doing odd jobs in her morning glory of curlers and a splash under the tap, and the difference when she was going out for the evening and his feeling of pride in her looks after she shut the front door and they strolled down the road together. Time, trouble and colour made all that difference, just as it did with Rosie, yet here the difference made not for pride, but for something like fear.

"Let me know where it is," he said. "You'll be there."

She turned quickly, and caught the appeal in his eyes, and a quick thrust of pity alchemized her feeling to a silt of motherly impatience.

"I don't know what to say to you," she scolded. "You're so sweet one minute and so brutal the next. Why couldn't you have taken those little things gracefully? You'd have pleased them so much. Now they feel indebted to you. Everybody feels awful."

"You can't take things from people if you ain't done nothing for it," he said. "'Sides, look at them poor devils outside there."

"They've got nothing to do with it." She spoke as though she knew. "It's a different problem. That's a question of work and eating and drinking. I've talked and talked about it, but all I got was a dear-little-woman-just-what-the-hell-do-you-know-about-it look. And you can't imagine how that helps. You haven't just hurt these people. You've insulted them. They wanted to show you how grateful they were. Why do you have to be so rough with everybody?"

He wanted to shout in denial, but a sense of the uselessness of argument overcame anger, and he lapsed thankfully into driving Rosie, sending his mind across to Shiner, wishing he had never wasted a moment of thought or time on anyone else, and in among it all cursing himself for thinking about the Princess instead of Liz.

He had a sudden picture of her at home, sending the kids to the pictures for a quiet couple of hours, and then sitting down to write her weekly letter. The thought of her sitting there, among her worries, poking out the tip of her tongue in time to the movement of the pen nib seemed to cripple something inside him. But instead of feeling sorry for Liz, he found himself hating the Princess so much that he could have thrown her out of the cabin then and there, with no feeling beyond relief.

He saw her shiver, and sit straight.

"Too much draught?" he asked. "Shall I close the window?"

"No, please," she said. "I was just thinking of that child."

"You don't reckon they'd have done her in, do you?" he asked.

"I'll just say I'm thankful," she said. "If your other soldier hadn't taken care of her, I just don't know. That's all."

"That's the bold Mr. Dincott," Snowy said. "No use, I can't like him. Don't know what it is, but I can't."

Max looked over scarlet miles of alders bristling from the marsh on both sides of the road, and thought of fishing trips back home, the feel of a cork handle, the smell of trout, and the aftertaste of pumpkin pie in a headful of woodsmoke. A flash of sun on open water caught his eye, and in turning he became aware of Dincott, not watching, or even looking, but with all the benign intent of a poodle, setting eyes upon him.

"I've had a lot to do with you blokes one way and the other," he said, as if he had been waiting to be noticed. "You going down to the Forestry Company?"

Max looked at him side-eyed.

"I don't follow the line of reasoning," he said. "I don't understand you, either. You English, too?"

"Why's everybody so nosey?" Dincott looked up at Bill. "Your mate, for one. You for another. Now this bloke. Am I English? I suppose the Smoke's in England?"

"That's what they call London," Bill explained. "No wonder. Dirty hole."

"Hark at the weavers," Dincott said.

"The weavers 'll do more than talk," said Bill. "They'll weave you a couple ye didn't bargain for."

"Need a few more shuttles," said Dincott, "and the blokes to work 'em."

"We'll see when we pull up," Bill said.

"You two cookin' up a case of homicide?" asked Max. "Don't you have enough trouble?"

" This won't be a fight," Bill said. " It'll be a refresher course in holding your damn' tongue. He's highly due. I've not fancied his style since he got on."

" The way blokes talk," Dincott dreamed, looking across the river, " you'd think they was shop stewards to the Holy Ghost. They want to know. They demand to know. Who are you? Where d'you come from? What's it got to do with them? We're here, ain't we? We're all here on a little ball of dirt, going round and round so slow, it don't even make us giddy. Where do I come from? Where else is there to come from? "

" So? " Max asked.

" Don't bother," Dincott said. " Don't matter to me where you come from on a little ball of dirt. But I know where both of us are off to. That's what matters, don't it? "

" The answer carries no money," said Max. " Where? "

" Down the dark hole," Dincott said. " Six, by six, by three. And it don't matter how you mess about between now and your time to go. That's where you'll end up. And when you're there, where are you? "

" It's a conducted tour," Max said. " You tell us."

" You're in the dark," Dincott said, still dreaming across the river, with a water reflection lighting the pale eyes to make them almost one with the whites. " Down in the dark. With all them little wriggly things getting at you. I've often thought it pays us all out in the finish. All the questions, and shouting and screaming, and carrying on, there. Don't make no difference. They're waiting for you, down the bottom of the hole."

" I don't get the message," Max said. " What are you trying to tell us? "

" Nothing," Dincott said. " Either I say something, else I don't. I never try. I've give up trying. It takes it out of you. And you'll always find when you're asked to try, it's for somebody else's benefit. I don't hold with it. I like my benefit. In fact, if you was to ask me what I like best in all this world I'd say it was my benefit."

Max was listening to the voice with ears cocked, as the eyes sometimes follow a popping ball in the shooting gallery, first listening for the high notes and then for the lower, and in between trying to fit both to make a whole. The sound had a rippling quality, coarse as the interfold of wrapping paper, and yet, spread over words without emphasis or vocal strain, the effect was almost hypnotic.

Bill watched Dincott closely from boot top to beret and back again, for something about the man set the hackles rising, making the back of his neck feel as though a blunt blade were shaving upwards to the crown. The civilian boots with rubber soles, the thin stockings and specially made gaiters, khaki twill shorts freshly starched with the ironing gloss still on them, and a battle-dress blouse that never saw a quartermaster's store, were details that added in the tally of mistrust.

But the face annoyed him. It looked like a blancmange shape slightly fallen over on one side. The skin was loose, fattish, and too much of it for the bones, so that the nose tip sagged below the nostrils, the eyebrows at the outer corners of the eye slipped down, and the lower lip was a curve of veiny flesh, sometimes glistening, sometimes dry, depending on the roll of the cigarette. Long black hair was smooth under the beret, shaped by the barber to a razored fit at the nape, squared down the jowls in sideboards below the ear, all of it flat with grease, and some of it stuck out in thin splinters. The comb came out of a breast pocket for a run through, and a hand patted it all in place.

That was enough.

"Where you off to?" he asked, stung by the comb and the pats, and ready to start a fight.

"Where I'm going," Dincott said, putting the comb away. "And that's somewhere you don't know, so what's the use of me telling you? If you must know, I'm going to get married for a couple of days. None of this forever business. I don't hold with it. Takes it out of you."

"You married?" Max asked.

"I got your sympathy?" Dincott lit another cigarette from the stub. The package was American. "Yes, I'm married. She never liked me. Bit too heavy for her, I suppose. 'Sides, I was in the cooler too long. She got somebody else. She's something like that bit up the front, there. Your pal ain't so slow, is he?"

Max saw that Bill had not once shifted his eyes, and, worse, his feet had stopped swinging.

" Well," he said. " Say, that's interesting. You been in prison? "

" Certainly," Dincott said. " Rest cure. Good's a holiday. I've done a two and a five. Do some more before I've finished, I suppose. Out here, in there, it's all the same. People are still nosey. Who are you? Where you off to? What for? There's only one little difference. In there, you can't have a woman. That's all."

" Right back on topic number one," Max said. " Bill, what do you say we play some poker? "

" We're pulling up," said Bill. " Afterwards, lovely."

Snowy eased down in the village, driving carefully over the heavy cobbles, watching the men leaning against the church wall in something of unbelief, for all of them wore conical black felt hats with short brims, black capes flapped about their knees, their calves were bandaged in rough strips of black cloth, and ragged felt was wrapped about their feet.

" Blimey," he said. " Who're these geysers? "

" Local boys," she said. " Drop me just around this corner. Then I leave you."

Snowy thought she might be sorry from the sound of her voice, and thinking of her as she had looked at him the night before, and as she had looked at him over the heads of the group that morning, he found himself hurt in both memories, but he was unsure whether the soreness he felt was really for her or for Liz, and then he was certain without knowing why.

He was going to miss her, miss the colour, the shape and the perfume, the voice, the line of her face, the sound of her skirts, the way she spoke and how she laughed. Back in his mind he cursed himself for disloyalty to Liz, but he braced himself against the charge because in some way he knew Liz was losing nothing of him. This feeling was new, from some other part of him that Liz had never touched.

" Anything else I can do for you? " he asked, keeping his eyes ahead.

" See those people get to their town safely." She perched the bird more comfortably, and sat still, in a sigh. " I don't think you know what you've done for them. And thank you for being so sweet to me. Don't worry. I'm not going to offer you anything. I'm going to let you be proud."

"We'll be coming back this way day after tomorrow," he said. "Shall we pass you on the road?"

Somewhere in her mind a panic started, of notions, and imaginings, none of them round enough to drag out in the light and pull to pieces, but all of them fighting away inside, mainly, it seemed, to get away from him and never see him again.

"I doubt it," she said, using the official voice. "I'll be pretty busy, I expect. But thanks, anyway. Around here will do."

Snowy pulled up at a church, with a building one side, and on the other a long stretch of iron railing and barbed wire. The church had pillars in front and some steps leading up to a doorway hung with red curtains and flowers. The building at the side was old, and iron bars guarding the windows were falling out of their sockets, some of the sills had dropped in pieces in the yard, and creeper was growing over the roof.

"Bill," he called. "Let's have the bag here, matey." He reached up to help her down, nodding at the barbed wire. "They put him a nice way out, didn't they?"

"They did," she said. "Doesn't it make you mad to think they could keep human beings in a place like that for a couple of years?"

"They done it to us," he said.

"That's right," she said. "They did. But they weren't supposed to be Christians. Anyway, it's been fun. 'Bye."

"'Bye, Miss," he said. "Good luck."

Bill dropped down, reaching up to Max for the bag, but before he could take it Dincott had jumped, springing up from bent knees, lunging at him with something in his fist. Bill seemed to know about it, and with his arms still outstretched above his head, turned unhurriedly to meet him with a left arm that caught him over the wrist to parry the blow, at the same time grabbing the blouse, turning his right shoulder behind a punch under the ear that clicked like a cleaver on bone, watching the lolling head for a moment, and then letting the body drop in a sloth of arms and legs.

"Ah," said Snowy. "Somebody been talking out of turn?"

The Princess remembered the lumps of muscle lit in primus flame that morning, and shivered. The falcon made to spread its wings and she put up a reassuring hand, watching Snowy climb over the tailboard.

" Sorry, Miss," Bill said. " He asked for it."

" Thank you both for all you did," she said, looking away. " I can't thank you enough. Goodbye."

She lifted the bag and walked away, but then she heard Snowy jump down and begin running behind her.

" Here you are, Miss," he said, out of breath. " Never grow a big girl without your breakfast." He put three tins and a loaf in her arms. " Bacon, tomatoes, and spuds."

Touched, far and away out of reach of voice, she turned, but not quickly enough. He caught the flash and knew of old that turn of head, and blood seemed to burn inside his chest and behind his eyes, and his hands caught her by the arms. He turned her towards him in a clatter of tins and a rumpling of feathers.

" I shan't forget you," he said, and kissed the cool of her cheek, breathing her breath, feeling her pulling away, not by moving, but from tensing, and released her, carrying some part of her perfume with him that he could smell, that was hurting, dismally, all the way back to Rosie.

Dincott was moving his head.

" Chuck him in," he said, going towards the cabin.

" Not me," said Bill. " He's had his lift."

" Can't leave him there." Snowy felt happier to be angry about something. " Blimey, these people'll butcher him."

" I'd help 'em," said Bill, and folded his arms. " All he'll get from me'll be t'other half."

" Come on, pal." Max helped Dincott to his feet. " Next time you throw 'em in there, you want to check on your fix. You were out two blocks."

Snowy settled himself in the shade of the cabin on the cool leather in the quiet, sniffing the old, clean smell of a well-kept engine, and edging it, the sweet of her. For perhaps the only time in his life he felt discouraged. Something at the back of his mind was angry, but he was unable to tell what, since the real he that he knew kept on laughing at himself for thinking about her, and yet all the time he was laughing and someone else was swearing at himself, still another part was longing for her, just as he longed for Liz, but worse, somehow, because he knew that one day Liz and he would be together, but the Princess had gone for good, taking away with her that vision of a life he could only imagine for moments at a time, as though dreaming.

He had no proper notion of that life. It was something she carried with her, some promise of another way of living that he sensed and wanted, and knew he could never have. He felt cheated, and angry because of this cheating, restless, and violent in rage that other men could love and enjoy that life with women like the Princess, but never in this world could he have more than part of a dream.

Even the cellophane package of photographs sticking out of the rack did nothing to heal. Liz and the children seemed to have no part in that life, no personality in the world he sought, and he was surprised to find that he could think of them without feeling of any sort, not as though they were dead, but as if they had never lived at all.

22

Snowy let in the clutch and pulled up the hill, careless how he went, bumping over the stony road until thought of the package stowed in rear made him change down, and on the bend he swore.

The other truck had stopped in the middle of the road and most of the men and women were grouped about a small van tipped on its side, and borne down by packages and bundles that must have weighed at least twice its peak load. Casalonghi's grey head was in the middle of a knot of people at the roadside, and as Snowy climbed down he came across holding out his hands, and smiling.

"I'm sorry," he said. "So sorry. But this poor family is on the way to the wedding of the daughter. You see she has all her household goods with her, and they broke down. It is impossible to ignore. It is one of the minor tragedies, but very beautiful, no?"

"Bloody lovely," said Snowy. "I suppose you've got to stop in the middle of the road, have you?"

"The girl placed herself in front of us," Casalonghi said. "So we stop."

She wore a green scarf over black braids hanging below her waist, a purple silk blouse and a yellow skirt that barely reached her knees, and her feet were bare, with the toes curled under. She clasped her fists on her bosom and turned her face towards him, closing her eyes tightly as if in appeal to God Himself, and he heard the prayer shaking in her voice, the plea of a little one, a lost one, and saw Primula kneeling by the bedside, curling her toes.

"All right," he said hopelessly. "Shove the stuff on Rosie. Tie that pram on behind, and let's get out of it."

Max came up with an old man dressed in black still creased from the wardrobe, wearing a black felt mould that sat straight on his head like a pot with a lip.

"Snow," Max said, "this old guy says there's a gang of thieves operating around this locality. He doesn't want to leave that stuff. He'd just as soon take it along."

"Look," Snowy said. "It's all took care of. Tell 'em to get the stuff aboard, that's all."

Bill was leaning against the radiator drinking it all in. Snowy watched him for a moment, wanting to say something bright, but he was damped by an open-eyed blend of mildest surprise and utter disbelief.

"Ye'll not be running a ruddy hacking service, by any chance, will ye?" he asked. "I'd apply for a licence, and be shut on it."

"Look at the poor kid." Snowy nodded at the girl lifting a package as big as herself on to her head. "Every day of fourteen, and she's getting spliced. Then the bus breaks down. Can't let it happen, chum."

"We've not had a bite to eat today," Bill said. "Did you know?"

"Let's get 'em there," Snowy said. "Then we'll eat 'em out of house and home."

He pulled Rosie up to attach a cable to the van, and waited until everyone was ready. Rusty climbed in with him, wiping grease off his hands.

" Snowy," he said. " You be careful, eh? You get robbers plenty down here. When I see it stopping, this one, I think it's trick. Careful, eh? "

" They'll take one look at that Eight on the fender, that's all," Snowy said. " Soon as we've dropped this lot off, we'll find a nice place for a brew. Still cook, can you? "

" Give to me the stuff," said Rusty. " I cook."

" Who's these robbers? " Snowy asked. " Where they come from? "

" Everywhere." Rusty shrugged at the countryside. " Here, there, British, American, Canadese, German, Polish, Italian, everybody. All the armies. Deserters. How many hundred. And don't make mistake, they shoot. They don't make like gentleman. They make terrible things with everybody. With girls, specially."

" We'll keep an eye out for 'em," Snowy said. " Told the others? "

" They got two rifles ready," Rusty said. " But four men, that's no good, not enough."

" Don't worry." Snowy passed a cigarette. " We shan't be down here that long."

They went along a highway, by a beach of black sand scattered with rusted keels of landing craft, with petrol tins in red heaps, and piles of burnt stones to tell where men had waded ashore to dry themselves and feed. Houses were holed, and roofs showed their ribs, and windows were patched with traffic signs torn down when armies had passed by, but around them all the patient green was breathing in squares of garden, in the long galleries of the vineyards, up among the lemon groves and in the pasture patch. Most of the men worked stripped to the waist or in shirts of pale blue that seemed to call out in the sun, and women were in black, with skirts of blue or red, but pot-bellied children ran naked, close cropped, with big eyes, unsmiling as they passed.

Rusty caught Snowy's look and shrugged.

" Nothing to do," he said. " Nothing to do. When is come

the harvest, then we get corn for the bread. But no meat. No pasta. Niente."

They knew they had reached the bridal village long before they got there, for houses along the road were closed, people had left the fields, and the tarmac was dotted with families, all barefoot, but wearing black best, turning to look around at them, and then shout and wave as they passed. The village was built on the rim of a cleft in high rock, and all the front doors opened on to a drop into water green as glass, except for narrow paths that visited them, roving round and round from the stones above the beach to a castle sitting on top, with two windows full of sky and a pylon trellis spiking from the middle of the keep.

The highway narrowed through the houses, and Rosie had just room to bounce across the cobbles until the crowd was thick under arcades of leaves and flowers, and voices echoed a long shout of greeting. The van was unhitched, and Max and Rusty, with Casalonghi, were hard put explaining to dozens of people at once what had happened, but when the story was known, all on board Rosie must go into the house of the groom and eat, and drink to themselves and everybody else.

"We've been and landed ourselves, now," Snowy said. "It'll be hours before we're out of this."

"You should have thought of all that before," said Bill. "I thought you were in such a blinding hurry to get down to your mate."

"So I am." Snowy felt quick, white rage. "Listen; if you can't help things, don't say nothing. If old Shiner had been here, this is what he'd have done, don't matter who said no. So pipe down, and get on with it."

Women came round with bottles of wine, and glasses were passed over heads in the shadow of the noisy street, and as they were filled and lifted, a dozen toasts were shouted, and the glasses were filled again, and again the syrupy stuff went down.

"Hey," Max called. "We going to stop here, or keep going?"

"I reckon we'd better," Snowy said. "Else I can see us getting a bit dreamy-eyed."

"One more of these," Bill said, "I'll be telling 'em about me rich relations. And a fat lot of good that'll do."

They made way to Rosie, and found her engrossed in the chatter of dozens of boys standing about Rusty. Snowy helped Bill to stow the tackle, and when they went round to the cabin a crowd of elders grouped about an old priest were waiting for them.

"Snow," Max said, "they want to know how they can thank you."

"Now listen," Snowy said. "I've had my thanks. I've got a little kid nearly as old as what's-her-name there, and perhaps somebody'll do the same for her one of these days. So thanking you one and all, take Half A Dollar, A Lady."

He climbed in, and let Rosie clear her throat to open a gap in the crowd. Max got in beside him.

"Mind if I ride with you, Snow?" he asked. "I have a favour to ask."

"Get in, boy, get in," said Snowy. "Hope you brought the cigarettes and matches with you. Always scrounging, ain't we? Eh? Always on your ear for something."

"Hey." Bill got on the running-board and put his head through the window. "That bloke Dincott's gone. Rusty's had a look round, but nobody's seen him. Hide nor hair."

"Good riddance to bad rubbish," Snowy said. "I'd forgotten all about him. Right. We're off."

People were tearing down flowers and leaves, and as Rosie started they ran alongside, throwing them up from the street, showering them down from the windows. The bride stood in a doorway in her white dress, with the black hair combed out about her, ringed about by matrons all in white lace and velvet.

"Does your heart good, don't it?" Snowy said, and blew a kiss, and she caught it on tiptoe, holding her palm to her mouth with closed eyes, and the bridal gown swung white and silver in her kissing back of thanks.

"Just the job," Snowy said. "Now then, what's the favour?"

"Well," Max said, "I was wondering if you boys would think of going back the coast road and dropping me up there in our zone. It'll be way off your route, but it'll save me a lot of good time."

The question in his voice settled it.

" You tell us where you want to go, Maxie boy," Snowy said. " You're as good as there, home and dry. Old Rosie, she'll take anybody anywhere, anytime, anyhow. Won't you, gel? "

" I'm kind of worried about Rosa," Max said. " That kid back there in that white dress. Hell, I wouldn't tell anybody else."

" Remind you of your old lady, did she? " Snowy slowed to let the other truck catch up. " Me, too. I shan't forget that Saturday afternoon. She looked a picture. I could have eat her. When we got back, she wouldn't let me in the bedroom. Hadn't got her dress on, if you please. I says, come on, I says—I'd had a couple of light ales downstairs—I'll shove the blinkin' house down. Then my old dad and hers has to have a shouting match about what they're going to call the first grandson. So we had a pair of girls instead, and very nice, too. Same again, any time you like."

" Jesus, I'd give anything to be back there and see 'em," Max said. " I'd be willing to come back and do ten years, just for ten minutes right now."

The road went up in the mountains, and the sky was rolling grey, and mist blew over them, and presently they were crawling. In a clearing on the mountain side, a high barbed-wire fence protected a dump of stores. Italian police saluted as they went by, and a British corporal waved his cap from a hut window.

" Lonely job," Max said.

" Wouldn't have it as a gift," said Snowy. " Never see anybody, never go anywhere or do anything. Nobody to talk to. Poor fella."

On top of the mountain, when Rosie's voice eased from a moan to a purr, they passed a village grey as the mist, near a modern building painted a deep terracotta, wrecked by shellfire and roofless. Half a dozen stone houses were grouped in a little square paved with stones grooved and polished as though by hand, and Max waved at an old man with bandaged legs wearing a brown cape, and a little boy in a shirt that he lifted up to his chin as they passed.

" Proving he's got one," Snowy said.

Inside the houses, fires were burning in the middle of the floor, and brushwood piled in the porches. There might have been people round the fires, but the smoke was too blue and thick to see.

" These folks certainly live mighty close to the ground," Max said.

" Pity they don't dig themselves a nice big hole and make a job of it," said Snowy. " Not even a chimney. My old lady screeches about having no bathroom. If she didn't have a chimney she'd have something to rattle the cups about."

Down in the valley they were out of the mist and into the sun as quickly as the train coming out of a tunnel beyond the cornfields. The black engine puffing toy smoke and pulling a long line of brown trucks seemed out of place among the furrows of ploughland and the endless green order of the vineyards.

Through the trees on the other side of the river they saw the rooftops of a town with barely a tile in place. Walls were down, signposts were twists of rusted iron, craters still gaped in the streets, and lines of women were waiting at pumps with buckets and jugs.

Snowy heard the siren calling on the truck behind, and parked in the shadow of a building that looked like a school. Not a window was whole, and all the woodwork had been torn away. Books and papers lay in heaps in the yard half burnt and long sodden with weather, and piles of cans glinting with rainwater cluttered the corners below the main stairway.

Casalonghi walked into the yard and stood looking up at the unit signs of a foregone army scrawled on the walls, at smoke-stains made by petrol fires, and at the rubbish heaps.

" So," he said, " here begins the work. From corruption, life. It is good."

Snowy looked about in unbelief.

" What're you going to do here, then? " he asked.

" Live," said Casalonghi. " That is why we have come here. To live."

" I wish there was something I could do to help out," Max said. " Un colpo di mano. I'd be happy to."

" You have all helped greatly." Casalonghi turned toward the stairway. " Nothing to say. Goodwill and sympathy are surely without price today. Everything else is ruin and misery." His hands came together in a clap that hurt their ears. " Ah, caro mio. Povera Italia. Dio buono, che miseria."

He turned to the group of men and women waiting in the gateway, but a glance at their faces seemed to stanch his words. With a sign, he led the men into the dark doorway, leaving the women sitting on suitcases with their hands in their laps, and their children standing close, waiting.

" This is our chance," Snowy said. " We can get out of it, now, no questions asked."

" Going to leave 'em a little gas for fires? " Max waved at the children. " Get some dirt out of 'em? "

" Trot out the petrol, Bill boy." Snowy went toward the cabin. " Quick. I can hear old wha'sname coming back."

Bill put the cans on the parapet, smiling at the general turning of heads, pointing and going through the motions of washing clothes.

" Bimbo," he shouted, though they were only a few feet away. " Bambino. Fires. Cooking."

" You've been so terribly kind." An elderly woman stood up. " We can never thank you enough."

" Oh." Bill stopped in the half turn. " Speak English, do you? "

" I am English," she said, and looked at Snowy. " Old wha's-name is my husband."

" Ah," Snowy said. " Accidents will happen. We're in a bit of a hurry, see, Missus? Hold tight."

" Keep tha' pecker up, love," Bill called. " There's nowt wrong as won't come right, give it a bit of time, like."

They went out through the smell of dead streets, jolting over sprawling wrecks of buildings, crunching glass and woodwork buried under dust that seemed lacking energy to rise, watching grass sprouting from window-frames and tops of doorways. A few women worked among the stones, filling baskets, and carrying bits of furniture, all of them grey with dust, and when they were still only the dark intensity of their eyes to tell them apart from ruin.

" God damn it," Max said. " What's going to happen to them? What can they do? "

23

Snowy had seen the black dots for a long time before he spoke about them, wondering at first if perhaps they were something to do with his eyes, and then, nearer, he thought of sheep, but they were too tall.

But they were moving.

The road went across a plateau of rocks and gorse, mile on mile through mist that sometimes blew off, letting them see more miles beyond, and another road joining from the east in a narrow V, but each time the cloud lifted the black dots were nearer, all sprinkled along the other road, all of them moving towards the crossroad, but without any sign to tell what they were.

"All right, I must be barmy," Snowy said at last. "But they can't be people."

"I pass," Max said. "Might be a whole lot of priests. Or nuns."

"Can't be," Snowy said. "Ain't no faces on 'em."

There was no pink touch of the human face, or pink spots for hands, and no scissor movement of legs in motion. There was only a ragged procession of dots, all of them black, all moving, as though a faceless township had put itself in mourning for pilgrimage along a white road in a grey and violet moor, with a north wind to harry them and a mist to wet them through.

Snowy set Rosie into the fifties down the winding road and every moment the dots got bigger. Some of them were spreading into the main road, and groups were forming in the ditches on both sides, but farther on more and more dots with smaller dots attached to them were going over the rise.

Rosie went down a narrow cleft with the mist for company, and in the deeper notes of her voice they seemed to hear the pulse of their impatience, and the wiper beat a wheezy tempo in sympathy, bringing them steadily up the incline into a clear patch, and they saw the dots had grown to bundles of black clothing that flew in mewls of wind, sitting, standing, some lying down with others kneeling about them, and more again walking on, away from them; but though Snowy sounded the horn, not one looked round, not one of them moved or gave sign of hearing, walking, sitting, kneeling, lying or standing, black in clothes, face, hands, and hair.

Black.

" God Jesus Christ," Snowy said. " They're women and kids."

Some carried children in arms, or held children in hand, or walked with one or two holding on to their skirts, all grimed in plain black without relief of colour, and froth had dried leaving dull marks about their mouths, and their eyes were brilliant red with strain, in distance, except for play of light, not to be seen at all.

Snowy stopped just beyond a pile of used oil barrels sheltering a group, and put Rosie in reverse.

" What's wrong? " Max asked.

" Just seen something," Snowy said. " They can do with a hand here."

At the edge of the road a mound of black lay partly in the lap of a crone, and when Rosie was quiet they heard the groans, and saw teeth in white bars, and knew her for a woman far gone in labour and too tired to shriek.

" Let's have the primus out, Bill," Snowy said. " Light a fire, Maxie. Rusty, get the big can filled over there."

He climbed up in rear and got the washing tin and a clean towel, and set about clearing a space for blankets. The primus was alight, and water was on when he got down and went over to the group.

" She have a baby," Rusty said.

" Tell her she'll be all right," Snowy said. " Ask them if she wants to move inside Rosie."

The women shook their heads, and Rusty listened to them. He took Snowy and Max under their arms, leading them over to Bill.

" She is ready," he said. " One minute, one hour, it's the same. They don't like you to look. You not doctor, so don't look."

" We don't have to," Max said. " We got plenty to see."

" How did they get out here? " Snowy asked.

" They come from long way," said Rusty. " The army come to their place and put all on train. Eight days on train."

" In open freight cars," Max said. " They didn't even rate with cattle."

They looked along the road, and round about.

In warm pauses, when the wind dropped, children could be heard crying and the voices of mothers praising them, all among the brush of feet and the clatter of cooking pots carried on bent backs. A woman passed with five children, the eldest to her shoulder, the youngest in her arms. She walked with bent head balancing a bundle on her neck, and dragged a bag along the road, turning now and again, whispering to the children, each of them carrying a bundle, the smallest, a boy, carrying his in both arms, but only just linking the tips of his fingers, lifting his knees against the wind and holding in his mouth a piece of twine pulling a toy cart, and a golliwog sitting back in it, arms and eyes wide with love for all the world.

A young woman with a plait of fair hair breaking out under the cloth around her head faltered near the signpost and reached out to save herself, dropping her bag, watching the pots roll over the road, tightening her arm about the child she carried in a shawl wrapped about her body.

Snowy was first to reach her, unwrapping the shawl, taking the child away, and Max sat her down.

" Bill," Snowy called. " Get the milk out, chum. Got a customer here."

He perched the baby on his palm, lifting him so that the head lay in his hand, a warm ball, sharp with coal dust he could feel in the scalp. Little movements of nerves jerked in the neck, and light shone on a paste of tears and grime flaking from cheeks and in the corners of a milk-mouth. Dark eyes, big in the small face, looked down at him perhaps knowingly but without a smile, a direct blaming look, and a look away into the wind, and then a yawn up at the scud of grey clouds, showing one small tooth.

" How they treating you, son? " Snowy whispered. " Eh? Coming down a bit heavy? Getting you down, are they? "

The bundle moved and kicked, and a black hand with grit still in the hollows touched his face and held on to his nose.

" That's more like it," Snowy crowed. " Now give me one for your ma. Got to take it out of somebody, ain't you? "

" Here y'are," Bill said, handing him a mug. " Dip your little finger in it, and let him suck."

" How many hands have I got? " Snowy demanded. " Come on, Max. Dip up."

Max dipped and the baby sucked hungrily, kicking and grunting for more, and mothers stopped to watch and the children gathered, and the mothers looked at Rosie's bulk as though the wealth of the world might be hidden in her fatness, jewels of warmth, and food, and shelter, and the baby opened his mouth wider and slavered over the finger-tip, cried when it was dipped, and struggled when he saw it coming, and still the mothers gathered, and the children stood and stared with dripping noses and eyes wet in the wind.

" Snow," Max said. " What the hell are we going to do? We just can't let 'em go on like this. God damn it. Couple of hours it'll be dark. They'll die of cold."

Snowy was afraid to look down at the children grouping about him. He felt their eyes, and knew exactly how the mothers would be looking, and he saw the involuntary stretching forth of hands in pleading, and their withdrawal, and the glances, perhaps of shame as they looked away.

" Tell you what," he said. " I'll go back to that dump up the road and see if I can get some soup and stuff. Won't take long."

He gave the baby to the mother, and Max gave her the mug.

" Look," Bill said, and pointed. " See them barrels? I'll cut 'em apart with the blower and make a few baths. Ye've two more tarpaulins in there. We've put t'other round the lass that's having the babe."

" On," Snowy said. " Max, coming with me? "

" Try keeping me out," said Max.

Bill and Rusty were rolling barrels when they left, helped by some of the women and a tribe of children.

" What kind of a human being could do that to women and kids? " Max might have been asking himself. " You know a lot of 'em died in a tunnel? Open cars, in a long tunnel. Coal-burner locomotive and lots of smoke, so they choked to death. What do you know? "

"I know one thing," Snowy said. "I'm glad my old lady never see it. Come on, Rosie. Step it out, gel. Get some of your fat off."

Rosie did an average fifty on the open road, and, by-passing the town, climbed the mountain again, singing, Snowy thought, like a bird, and almost passed the wired gateway.

They climbed down under the stares of the policemen and went through the wire gap into the hut marked OFFICE. The smell of sweet groceries clashing with the lye of soap lifted their hearts as though their errand were already done, and both leaned over the counter drumming their fingers and whistling, no shadows in their sun, and millions tinkling to their credit.

"What do you want?" The voice was sharp, loud, and sounded as if it might have come from a lectern.

Snowy stopped on a high note and looked at Max, and from looking at one another they looked along the blocks of shelves heaped with packages all making gay promise, but neither could see who had spoken.

"Probably something on remote control," Max said. "These days they have those things. Don't make for comfortable living."

"I said, what do you want?" The voice was louder, with a varnish of refined impatience.

"Blimey," said Snowy. "It's Alice. Where art thou, gel?"

A movement from the shelves almost in front brought them upright, staring. One of the pigeon-holes framed the face of a young man wearing the collar and tie of an officer.

"Ah," said Snowy. "Afternoon, sir. We've come to see if we could scrounge some tins of soup and some biscuits and stuff for some women and kids down the road. They're in a shocking mess there. One of 'em's having a baby."

The officer moved from the frame and came out, a tallish figure in a British shirt and American trousers.

"What's your unit?" he asked.

Snowy knew the tone, and heard his plan crumble.

"About three hundred miles up the road," he said, putting his pass on the counter. "All we want is anything going bad, like, or rusty."

"They're in the middle of rough country south of here," Max explained. "We thought you might want to help out."

"What d'you think this is?" The officer was frowning, looking from one to the other. "Some rubbish dump? Let me see your work ticket."

Snowy kicked Max under cover of the counter.

"Go out and look after the wagon, Maxie," he said. "I've lost spare wheels before."

Max nodded his thanks and went out, watched by the officer from the corner of his eye, holding the pass meanwhile as a surgeon might hold a slide.

"Where did you get that vehicle?" he asked, touching the points of his moustache with his middle finger. "You haven't got a work ticket, have you? You'll stay here till I've telephoned headquarters. We'll see about you."

Snowy looked at the moustache, and the grease spot on the tie, feeling a rage that had its roots in contempt for anyone in uniform, so far behind the fighting line.

He went out, hearing the telephone bell as he went through the gateway, and got up in the cabin, starting off without a word.

"No use," he said. "Argue with 'em, and you're done."

"Snow," Max said. "A little guy was giving me the high sign just now. Here."

The corporal they both recognized was standing at the roadside, and as they neared he made a turning motion and pointed behind to a hidden entry. Snowy went in to a loading yard full of crates stacked higher than Rosie as far back as the rock face.

"Have some trouble up there?" the corporal asked.

"Trouble?" Snowy said. "He's phoning for the red-caps."

"No, he ain't," the corporal said, leading the way into a small shed. "He only thinks he is. I done a job on his phone. Man's a nuisance. I'll have him out of it 'fore he's much older."

"We came up for some soup and what-not for a lot of women and kids down there," Snowy said.

"Pity you didn't bring a couple of the prettiest of 'em with you." The corporal was pouring tea into thick mugs. "Trot 'em in there, and let him play the big soldier in front of 'em. You'd have got your soup."

"If we could have found 'em under the coal," Max said. "It'll take a course of steam baths and alcohol rubs to get 'em looking half-way human."

" Come by railway, did they? " The corporal seemed to know. " They often do. Get in a state, don't they? Still, they all get shook down somewhere. All sorts itself out, somehow."

The disinterest in the corporal's voice was impressive, and, looking about, Snowy felt something like respect coming into mind. The walls were hidden by dozens of photographs and colour-plates of women. The bed was loot from a civilian house with the bedclothes and the carpet. There was a brass lamp with a green glass ball, and an apricot plush cloth on the table. A radio lay on a pile of magazines by a leather couch full of cushions, and a harmonium with a hymnal in its clips grinned cracked brown keys in the corner. In the smaller shed a line of saucepans and racks of plates with a pile of crocks upturned on the rinsing-board underlined the smell of a baking cake.

" You're doing yourself a bit of good here, ain't you, Corp? " he said. " Home from home."

" What, here? " The corporal's face sagged helplessly. " You wait till I've got myself settled in. Bit of good? Lord love us, you should have seen me in Algiers. That was the place, boy. Had me own staff of servants. I had five wives. Fact. Five of 'em. The oldest was only nineteen. Proper little bag. She pinched me watch."

" How do you go on with this officer, then? " Snowy asked. " Working you one, is he? "

" Me? Him? " The corporal gulped his tea as if the words he wanted were at the bottom of the mug. " He don't even know what's going on. Wartime job, he is. Prefab. Terrific bloke for efficiency. There's four times the forms, twice the books and ten times the messin' about since he got here. Only half the work gets done, mind, but you can't have it two ways, can you? "

" Who do you boys supply? " Max asked. " Or is that top secret? "

" God knows," the corporal said. " The stuff comes in, and it goes out. That's all I know. Where, who, or why, I don't know."

" So you won't miss a can or two of soup, then? " Snowy made it sound as idle as he could. " Few bars of soap, bit of chocolate for the kids. Any bully you can spare."

The corporal shook his head, turning down his mouth in wealthy disregard.

" Help yourself," he said. " It's all there."

" Right," said Snowy. " If you don't mind, Corp, we'd like to get going. They're all out in the cold there, and it's getting dark, see?"

" This way," the corporal said, and went into the kitchen. A girl was plucking a chicken by the door with a fluff of down bobbing about her busy hands, landing in her hair and whitening her eyebrows. Another girl in a creased red blouse peeled potatoes over a tin, and Snowy saw the corporal pinch her rump in passing, and she squeezed her legs together, widening her eyes with her tongue between her teeth, and croaked, watching him go, half smiling over her shoulder, but the potato never stopped turning and the peel coiled down in a long brown band.

Among the crates outside, the corporal called a group of men in ragged shirts and old twill trousers, giving orders and pointing round about. Max stopped in Rosie's shadow, looking up at the evening sky, and offered Snowy a cigarette.

" Snow," he said, " these're the guys who really have what it takes. They know what they want and they don't let anybody stop 'em. Even the brass. Am I right? All the ways down here."

The men came back loaded with cases, and one by one the corporal checked them over Rosie's tailboard, and ticking off the last item, handed Snowy a list.

" If you do happen to get stopped," he said, " show 'em that, an' tell 'em to come and ask for me. Corporal Pardoe. That's me. And if you're calling back this way, pop in. Open house, long as you like. All Freeman's. Have a good time."

" Ta, Corp," Snowy said. " Shan't forget you."

Rosie turned out on the highway.

" And there was me," Snowy said, " feeling sorry for that bloke. Rajah of the big tin can. I ought to have knowed better."

" I feel kind of sorry for that lieutenant," Max said. " He has a rattler in his barracks bag."

" I don't wish him no harm," said Snowy. " I just hope it corpses him, that's all."

24

They saw the fires burning from the top of the hill in long rows of orange blots in a black terrain under the deep blue circus of night.

" Bill's been busy." Max spoke for the first time since leaving the dump. " Makes a pretty show, don't it? Till you think what's going on down there."

Snowy nodded.

All the way along, an element had worried him, a chord that recurred, a notion that slipped away even as he thought of it, and then returned in a new way. There had seemed a matter of pride in letting Max believe that all Britons lived on a bare ration without trimmings, but Corporal Pardoe's riches had made a fool of him. He felt resentment that one man should have all the comforts while an army of others got none, though the deepest wound and the one that hurt most was the thought of his access to women. He found himself cursing under his breath, and at the same time trying to find excuses, telling himself how unfair it was to spite a man so free with gifts. But never mind how he thought or what excuses he made, he found himself ashamed to discuss the corporal with Max, and it troubled him.

He switched on the headlamps, flicking them in a signal, and saw Bill waving his arms among a group waiting at the signpost.

" Got it all in the back, chum," he shouted. " Get cracking."

Long lines of women were forming in the darkness, and the cases were carried off on their heads. Rusty took a couple of tyre levers towards the fires and broke open the lids, doling out the tins as fast as hands could grab. Snowy took the case of chocolate under arm and Max came behind with the milk.

" Steady as you go, there," Bill said. " We've dug holes for the kids to sleep in. Ye'll be breaking your legs, else."

" How's the girl having the baby? " Snowy asked.

" They're over there in them rocks." Bill nodded into the dark skyline. " We wrapped 'em up in your gas-cape. They both went. Couldn't do much else. Some poor lad'll be heart-broke, I suppose, but we done the best we could. There's another of 'em whelping out now. She's had some soup in her, so I hope she'll do a bit better."

Fires had been lit in round holes, just deep enough to give shelter from the wind and support a seated back. Further up, fires blew under steaming oil barrels, and a tarpaulin had been rigged across rocks to shelter women and children splashing in hot water. Bill cut chunks of soap, throwing them at women, some naked in the darkness and others with wet clothing wrapped round their waists, and chipped a couple of bars into the barrels full of clothes. Nobody spoke, nobody stood, everyone seemed intent on a mission of their own. The only sounds came from the moorland, in the whine of the wind, and the crack of burning brushwood, a rasping of hobs on rock, and the slapping and wringing of clothes under the tarpaulins. Even the children were silent.

But when the tins of soup were hot and the men began to open them with their jack-knives a sudden shrill went up, loud in the quietness, and holes erupted small silhouettes scrambling into the whiter light of the headlamps and they felt the soft insistence of children's hands upon them, about their knees, at their waistbelts, and tugging the slack of their shirts.

" Hey, Rusty," Max shouted. " Go traffic control here, will you? Else we're going to be in the gumbo. These kids are God damn hungry."

Rusty and some of the older women pushed into the darkness and presently lines were forming, pans of all sorts were being filled, and one by one the children found their way back to a fire, holding up their pots for the biscuits Max tossed from his cap. Bill took soup, biscuits and tins of beef inside the tarpaulins to the women washing clothes, and by signs made them stop washing to eat, and then, in a fold of canvas by the fire, he put a pair of crutches under his arm, and lifted up a girl as though she were a child, carrying her to Rosie and putting her up in the cabin.

" Sit thee there, love," he said. " I'll have a lovely supper for ye in two ticks."

" What's going on here? " Snowy asked.

" She were brought down in a go-cart." Bill was opening a tin of bacon, and his sweat dripped on the lid almost in time with the cut of the blade. " I've never seen such a poor little wretch. She's crutched, d'you see? Can't walk. So I give her a bath and got her clothes boiled up and dried out, but the poor thing's ravening. She were frightened of me, first go off, but we're pals now. Aren't we, love? "

He looked up at her with the light on his spectacles, and Snowy saw the white of her smile from the dark.

" O.K., Bill boy," he said. " You look after her. Maxie and Rusty and me'll take care of things. I reckon you two done a marvellous job here."

" That was Rusty," Bill said. " I've seen blokes use a torch in me time, but the way that bloke cut them barrels was a rare treat. He's a grand lad, is Rusty."

" Ah," Snowy said. " Told you, didn't I? "

" Tell the lads I'm cooking supper for 'em," Bill called. " Even Rusty can't whack me at bacon and spuds."

" Don't forget the tomatoes," Snowy said.

" They've all gone." Bill settled the primus on a rock. " I opened 'em up to make soup for the lass that's having her babe."

For some little time the men walked about, watching the women settling the children, or holding babies while their mothers changed drying clothes, throwing wood on the trench fires, and generally getting the camp tidy for the night.

Rosie backed up to be a dormitory for some of the youngest children and older women, and a tarpaulin was rigged off her roof to cover the rest; and when Snowy ran the cables out, she started humming under her breath to put power in white points of light.

" That's the job," Snowy said, looking at row on row of sleepers. " We'll give 'em some more soup at first light, and then kick off for the next town. If any."

" That means we'll get back up north in about three more days," Max said.

" About that," said Snowy. " Why? You worried? "

" Yeah." Max pointed over to the small tarpaulin. " I've been thinking. My Rosa just went through all that. And the other kid, the one they buried. Day after day, we don't have any worries worth a damn. We really have it soft."

The baby came while the bacon still curled in their mess tins, and a gentle sound stirred the camp as though every sleeper had turned to draw a breath of sympathy with new life struggling head down in the steam of a barrel, and the men pretended in wrinkled foreheads and calm eyes not to have heard, but the girl in the cabin brought them afoot in a clatter of pans, pointing her fork at the rocks.

Lit red in firelight, a woman with a white cloth about her hair was splashing silver upon a child she held by the ankles, and the scoop and stretch of her fingers and the rain of lit drops might have been part of a witch's liturgy, for even as they stood to watch the spine arched, and a loud cry brought the woman smiling. She put a golden hand under the golden head, and they saw the white of happy eyes as she turned into the ark of the tarpaulin.

" That's one they don't get," Snowy said. " One to us. Take 'em over a mug of tea, Rusty boy. Ask 'em to drink our health."

" I'm going to have me a bath," Max said.

" Same here," Snowy said. " Ought to be lovely and hot by now."

The water was hot, but the wind was searing, the ground was thick with cold mud and they stuck it right through to a change of clothes only because the thought of women and children clean and asleep shamed them into it.

" Snowy," Rusty called, coming out of the dark with the empty mug. " You don't know what name they call the new baby. Proprio un' bellina."

" No? " said Snowy. " What? "

Rusty threw his arms apart in a kiss of rapture, and then looked back wide-eyed at the sleepers, hunching his shoulders, tenting his hand over his mouth.

" Rosie," he anthemed, in a rich movement of the mouth almost without sound.

Snowy looked up at her face in a gleam of glass framed by the canopy like the brim of a bonnet, and waved his hand.

" There y'are, Rosie," he said. " That's nice, ain't it? You're a grandma."

25

The morning was still green when Rosie pulled up in the wide street of the town, and by the time Snowy climbed down the others had lifted the smaller children off, and the rest had tumbled down on their own, and the dark street was alive with chatter and the scrape of skipping feet all going off in one direction. Snowy listened to the children, feeling lonely, standing on the kerbside watching them all go.

Max hurried round a corner farther up.

" Look," he said, " I found the place where they operate the civil administration. I'll wait around for the officer running the outfit and see what we can do. There's quite a crowd of women and sick kids around there. That cripple kid Bill's got in the push-cart, she wants hospital. Where'll you wait? "

" Round the back there somewhere," Snowy said. " But we're behind, you know."

" I can't stand to feel that useless," Max said. " You boys worked all yesterday, and I was on the sidelines. I want to do some fixing myself."

" Rusty and me'll knock up some breakfast for you," Snowy said. " If there's anything left."

He edged Rosie into the open gateway of a yard full of chimneys and porcelain sinks. The primus came out, and they put on tins of soup; and while Snowy was making tea, Rusty chopped potatoes and cut a stale loaf for toast.

" Funny," Snowy said, sitting on a sink, with his mess tin propped on a chimney pot. " It makes all the difference to have your grub decent, don't it? I don't know what my missus'll do when I get home."

Rusty opened his arms, losing a forkful of potatoes.

" For one month you are both in bed," he said. " So after, what it matter? "

Bill came whistling into the yard, and Snowy took his mess tin out of the hot box.

" You look real done up, chum," he said, surprised at the pale face. " How's that little girl? "

" Just left her in hospital." He wheeled a chimney into position. " A fine hole, I must say. They weren't going to take her because she'd brought no grub or bedclothes."

" So what did you do? " Snowy asked.

" Had a bloody row with everybody," Bill said. " Now she's in. She were crying when I left."

Rusty put his fork down and stood, turning his back.

" I find Max," he said, and blundered over straw packing and piles of fireclay joins.

" You ain't finished," Snowy shouted. " Half a mo'."

They saw him shake his head as he went through the gate. For minutes on end they ate and drank as though chewing and swallowing were a drill in curb of untoward feeling. Then Bill gathered the mess tins and started to wash up.

" I'm right sick of all this," he said. " The way things are run. But except for making yourself a thorough nuisance, you don't get anywhere. People don't seem to understand if you talk to 'em civilized. Ye've to shout at 'em."

" That's right." Snowy stood up and tightened his belt. " I'm just going round to shout at Maxie. Else we'll be here all day. In somebody's backyard."

He found Max just round the corner in the steam-heated lobby among gilt seats, and copper bowls fat with tall spreads of palms. Light fell grey from round windows overhead, and Max was standing on a compass pattern in the marble flooring with his cap dangling from his forefinger, looking up the broad stairway at closed double doors. The small figure in greenish khaki turned at his footsteps, throwing his shadow over the smooth floor, and without nod or smile turned again to watch the stairway. Snowy was reminded of a terrier waiting for the flight of a ball.

" Ready? " he asked, and heard a half-dozen voices fly in echo. " Where's all these women and kids you was on about? "

" They threw 'em all out while I was up there," Max said. " I got thrown out by a buck sergeant. I want to wait for the major."

" And land in clink," Snowy said. " What did you ask for? "

" Jesus, Snow." Max slid his boot in a screech across the marbling. " I wanted to get these kids taken care of. I went up there and they wouldn't listen. They have a whole bunch of floozies chewing gum and making coffee, and they wouldn't listen. They just wouldn't listen."

" Let's get out of it," Snowy said, and turned for the door. " This ain't our sack of spuds, chum."

" Bastards," Max said. " Bunch of fresh clerks all tricked out in new tans. Every office all stunk up with cologne. Some little crumb-bum says to me, Listen, soldier, she says, we have all the trouble we can take right now. Then this jerk comes in, this sergeant, and he says I'm interfering. I feel kind of weak. Maybe I'm hungry."

" Waiting for you round the back," Snowy said. " Then we're off."

While Max was having his breakfast, Bill finished some repairs, and Snowy cleaned out the rear, carrying the canvas packages round to the cabin. Rusty came back with a joint of lamb and a couple of flasks of wine stuck in a basket of vegetables, and sat in a corner, stripping the greenstuff for a later meal, looking at nobody.

" See? " Max pointed to the basket. " That's what I mean. Everybody does something or gets something except me. All I do is eat, and sit around. Ain't that dandy? "

" Your turn'll come," Snowy said. " Last trip south, gents. All aboard."

He backed out of the yard, and edged his way out of the town always with a feeling of unbelief.

The sunlit streets of shuttered homes, the shrubs in blossom, the glitter of fine shops and the slow parade of dressy women with nursemaids and polished perambulators and not a uniform to be seen, made him aware of his foreignness, almost as though he intruded. A look at these women, a glance from their eyes, centred and withdrawn, looking at him and through him, and the feeling of his right to be there by conquest was dead.

" How's all this? " he asked Rusty, nodding at a butcher's shop hung with sides of beef. " You're starving up the road. Fat of the land down here. What's the catch? "

"Transport," Rusty said. "And money. You think we could pay so much? These rich people. Run away. Soldiers don't come here."

The road went up through a valley full of lemon trees in long straight lines that, for precision, might have been drawn by a rule, and there were more cattle, red in pasture, and white in the plough, and for the first time they saw a flock of fat sheep down at the riverside, and the shepherd with bandaged legs and black cloak, fishing from the little bridge, mimed for a cigarette as they passed.

Snowy changed down when he reached the first grey pool.

A smell of sulphur came in on the wind, faintly at first, but then, as the pools became bigger on both sides of the road, the stench was raw as a smoking match. Ditches were filling with cloudy water that steamed as it ran, and vapour rose from wide stretches of rushes beyond, and all the way down to the sea.

He turned off on a sidetrack towards a grove of trees and a height of rock, coming out in a clearing outside an old windowless house.

Watched by the others, he went along a path, down a stairway and into the door of a building dug out of rock. The warmth, and the smell, and the water dribbling from holes into deep stone troughs seemed friendly as handshakes. He ran back up the stairway and waved them in.

"Finest bath in the world here," he said, pulling his shirt off. "Stink like a polecat, but it's worth it. Shiner and me stayed here. I been waiting for this."

"Where's Shiner from here?" Bill asked.

Snowy pointed to a hill about a mile away.

"Up the top of that," he said. "I'll go on and get things fixed up, then we can go in the town tonight and start back tomorrow."

"Want any help up there?" Bill took a long time to put his spectacles on the ledge. "You'll have tools as well."

"Come if you like," Snowy said. "Any good at gardening?"

"I can do me share," said Bill.

They came out of their troughs with whitened skins gone silken smooth, and muscles that felt like rubber. The sun dried them, and they walked about in the torn gardens, pulling flowers by the roots and taking cuttings from the bushes, wrapping them in sacks for the journey.

Rusty slipped quietly away to the little kitchen at the back of the old house to build a charcoal fire, and Snowy found him in front of it, knuckles at chin, watching the rise and fall of the goosewing fan, dreaming.

" What's up, Rusty? " he asked. " Something gone wrong? "

" I think of Shiner and the boys." Rusty seemed unlike himself, quieter, and in some way smaller. " Then I think of us. A man come from a long way to make something good. So then you put some flowers on the mountain. I don't understand what sort of life we got."

" All come out in the wash," Snowy said. " We'll be up there about a couple of hours. Then we'll have some grub. Eh? "

Rusty nodded.

Snowy went down the corridor, watching the sun spin silver in the cobwebs, wondering what there was to do for Rusty, aware all the time that the answer was out of reach and that all he could do was think about it, and that was all anyone could do, and end up where they started, just thinking.

" Snow," Max said. " You mind if I trail along? That bath did something. I really feel chipper. I just as soon dunk myself in rotten eggs, but it pays off. How'd you find the place? "

" Well," Snowy said, " we landed down the coast there, and the Yeomanry cleared the road this far, so the Section camped down here, see? Then we got a call to pull a Bren carrier off the road up the top of the hill. So Shiner and me went. We got up the top, and something hit us, and now Shiner's up there, I'm down here, and Rosie's over there. That's how."

" Are we taking her? " Bill asked. " Or walk? "

" Walk," Snowy said. " I couldn't drive her away twice, chum."

They set off along the path across the marsh, Snowy carrying the canvas packages, Bill with the tools, and Max with a bundle of roots and cuttings, waving at the goosewing flapping between the bars of the kitchen window.

They went slowly, testing the ground, up to their waists in a creamy steam that made them look as though they cycled on a cloud. The hill went up in terraces of vineyards, with a goat-track winding grey loneliness through walls of leaves; and as they climbed, the green scent blew about them, and when the wind was still they heard the scatter of the sea, and bells in quiet argument from a village down the coast.

" I'll have a smoke for a couple of minutes," Bill said, in a patch where a hollow log ran clear water in a pool.

" Right," Max said. " I'll toss a few pebbles and pretend I'm home."

Snowy went on up, angry at the talking he could hear, and Bill laughing, but then, whether it was the act of straightening his back, or taking a deeper breath, or if it was the shock of the little rock tower that startled him by sudden approach, there was no way of telling, but as though in climbing the hill he might also have climbed out of himself and that thick feeling of loss, he felt a sharp sense of change, of wanting to laugh and talk and make others laugh as Shiner had always done.

He put the package and the cuttings in the shadow of the tower, and looked about, surprised to find in himself an unwillingness to go any farther, and irritably he spat the thought away.

Olive trees lined the hilltop and their trunks arched over, going down on the other side in long lines until only foliage showed, and the black fruit speckled against the gloss of the sea, glinting little lights in the sun. Doves flew up, and he followed the white flight over the rock, where a steel hat was slung on a plank, with a cigarette tin in the middle of the shallow mound, and a little stone lion, lifted off a gatepost, on guard at the foot.

He walked over a pile of shell cases and jumped the rocks with cartridge clips still bright in the clefts, and went to stand by the plank, touching the warm metal of the helmet, holed at one side, with a broken strap, remembering its clatter on a night when it spun in the road.

" Well, Shiner boy," he said, " we're here. Me and the old girl."

26

Everything looked so ordinary and everyday, just as he remembered it, almost to a pebble as he had left it that morning.

The olive trees and the ploughland, the rocks and the little tower with pink flowers growing in the roof and weeds waving from the cotes, were memories printed sharp as wallpaper.

But the quietness was something he had never heard, or else had forgotten; and without wanting to, he found himself turning to look over his shoulder, glancing quickly to the side, or turning about to look through the trees, without knowing why or what he expected. He rubbed his forearms, trying to take a grip on himself, but despite it all the feeling gained until he was standing stock still, rigid and yet trembling, listening.

He pulled at himself as though tearing out a splinter, moving to put the helmet on a rock, throwing the tin in it, and tugging at the plank.

The doves flew up when he stamped over to get the packages, and he whistled at them to make more noise only to destroy the quietness he still could hear, that never had been part of Shiner or his memory.

He looked back at the little lion, and tried to imagine Shiner lying there, but in the quiet even his picture seemed unwilling to come. He rested against the jamb, glad of something solid at his back, feeling himself sweating in prickles under the eyes, holding the packages, fighting a sudden wish to be out of the place and run down hill in jumps and leaps, shouting as he went.

He heard Bill coming in a heat of relief that surprised him, and for some reason made him want to laugh.

" That you, matey? " he called. " He's here. Same as ever."

Bill got into the plough, and stood taking breaths, looking about.

" Ah," he said. " You picked a lovely place for him. I wish I could have done the same for Old Cob. I can just see him up here."

They went to the mound and pulled off their shirts.

"Dig it over, put the cuttings in, and bank it with rocks, eh?" Bill asked.

"That's it," Snowy said. "But I don't know why you should get a wet shirt over it."

"I had a mate, too," said Bill. "If a bit of digging'd bring him back, by God, I'd have the guts out of creation."

Using the pick in rock, and shovelling out the chips, or levering his weight on the shoulders of the spade, hearing Bill whistling under his breath as he squared the sides of the mound, and watching the cleared space take shape, brought Snowy a sense of calm, and a wonder at the period of fright, unfelt at any time before, strange, and now, with Bill's shoulders in the corner of his eye, shameful.

"Bill," he said, "I don't know what it was, but I'm glad you came up. It didn't seem like old Shiner up here at all. I got windy."

"Well, what else did you expect?" Bill looked up over his spectacles, crumbling dirt off his finger-tips. "They don't stay once they've gone. They're off out of it. All ye've got there's what ye remember."

They built the walls in a deep square, putting the little stone lion to face downhill, with the cuttings planted on the inside, and the flower roots about the mound; and while Bill cleaned the spades, Snowy opened the packages and handed over a wooden cross, thinking of Sergeant Whitmarsh and the men in the shops.

He watched Bill thrust it down squarely into the fine mould at the head, and then took the cotton wool from a glass dome, full of waxen flowers and fruit, with a marble scroll curling through the flowers, and SHINER in fine long letters cut in it.

"Well, now," Bill said. "There, that's what I call something, that is."

Snowy put the base in the middle of the mound where the cigarette tin had been, and settled it firmly, flattening the earth with his palms, feeling a roughness that might have been the serge of a blouse.

They climbed out of the square and stood off, looking at what they had done, and Snowy felt the pride rise in him, and knew that Shiner was laughing somewhere, for the feeling of wanting to turn and look about was strong, and only Bill, buttoning his shirt, stopped him.

"Funny," he said. "I still feel windy, somehow."

"It's natural," Bill said. "Ye've had him on your mind too long. If you was planted up here, ye'd not think much to it, would ye? Too far away. A town lad likes a bit of life."

Snowy took a box camera out of the folds of his blouse, and got snaps from all the corners, and squarely at the foot.

"I ain't too bright at this lark," he said, moving here and there, trying to coax the picture into the little window. "These are for his missus. I want to try and get some good ones for her. But I generally get their legs in and leave the rest of 'em off."

"Sometimes it's just as well," Bill said. "But it's a lovely job. She'll be that pleased."

The sun's eye was round in a rosette of light upon the dome, glowing in the new copal of the cross, gentling the colours of the flowers, catching odd points of silica in the rock, sparkling among the chippings of the pathway; and when Snowy started whistling as he turned the film, the doves flew up and settled to grumble in the trees.

He opened the cigarette tin and made sure the identity disc and pay books were inside, and put it under the helmet at the foot of the mound.

"There you are, Shiner boy," he said. "That's it. That's the lot."

He had a feeling that something was still to be done, but, think as he might, nothing would come, and he was aware, now that he put his mind to it, that his dearest wish was to leave the place, quickly and thankfully, and never to come back again.

He looked up at the blurred white bundles perching on the boughs, listening again to the quiet, wishing he had a prayer, some few words to say, some God to beseech or throne to approach, but the words stayed away, and the prayer was only felt, with anger at his helplessness, and rage at power that turned its face aside, and a heat of grief bit into him, that in this quiet place Old Shiner had to stay with a world going on without him, or knowing, or caring about him.

" Oy," he addressed the brightness overhead, with doves flying white in the blue. " You want to watch out. There ain't all that many of 'em. Please. Look after old Shiner. Hear me? "

His shout sounded foolish and only set the doves in the air again. He looked at Bill for help, but his back was turned, watching the way they had come.

" I had to say a word," he said, shamefaced. " I suppose you don't know none? "

Bill shook his head.

" Didn't you say a few words for that girl and the baby last night? " He remembered the movement of clouds beyond a dark skyline. " Couldn't you say 'em again? "

" It's a hymn," Bill said. " I don't know a lot of it. Gentle Jesus, meek and mild, look upon a little child."

In a round movement of the arm he took up the picks and shovels and went across the plough, behind the tower, and was gone.

Snowy hung his blouse over one shoulder, and picked up the canvas wrappings. It felt wrong to leave without saying goodbye, and yet silly to say it out loud to a lot of trees and doves, some rocks and a cross, a case of flowers and a steel hat.

There seemed nothing else to do but salute, and walk away, feeling empty, thinking of nothing, with the plough giving underfoot and the camera bumping against his elbow, realizing in bitterness that this was not as he had seen it, or what he had planned.

But when he turned to look back and found he was too far downhill to see the tower, something like gladness came and he felt thankful that Shiner was not in the quiet up there, and never had been since the night he carried him up from the road.

It was just a bed that had been slept in for a night, left rumpled in the morning, and now was fresh again, and suddenly he felt easy and memory was happier.

Max and Bill were waiting for him on the edge of the sulphur marsh, standing among the vapour lit whitely as though caught in a mirror-shine of bright metal. He saw their surprise to hear him whistling.

" Get tired of waiting, Maxie? " he asked, falling in step through the short reeds. " You ought to have come up there."

" No, thanks." Max said it as if he meant it. " I found fish in that pool. They hadn't any size, but they were fish. What I'd give to go fishing again. You do any, Snow ? "

" Yes," Snowy said. " With grenades. Then you catch 'em when they float up."

" Brother," Max said, " I ought to throw you in one of these stinkholes. Pa and me used to go fishing every Sunday in the old jalopy. And that reminds me. I heard cars go by here a while ago."

" From one of the base dumps, I expect," Snowy said. " It's a long run down this way."

" You going to hang on here tonight? " Bill asked. " That bath's done me a world of good. I could do with another."

" I thought we'd go over and see some friends of mine," Snowy said. " Very nice people. They've got a farm down there about twenty miles. The grub's marvellous. Ever had cold ham, green figs and melons? With a glass of vino? "

" You can have ham and figs," Bill said. " Makes me right queasy thinking of it."

" Rice and brown gravy," Max said. " Or a fine spaghetti with meat sauce and tomatoes."

" I suppose a nice plateful of tripe's about your mark, Bill ?" Snowy said.

" A lovely little sucking pig wi' an apple in his chops," said Bill. " That's if you don't mind. Tripe's all right when ye've had a late spell at work and you come home soaked. Filling and warming, is tripe. I could give a nice steak a damn good hiding at the moment."

" Rusty's got a joint in there," Snowy said. " We'll have a good old feed and a snore in the sun. Then we'll have another lovely bath, and then we'll go and see my pals, eh? "

" Sounds swell," Max said. " Start back in the morning from there? Or here? "

" Why not tonight? " Snowy sympathized with the unconcern in Max's voice. " Nothing to stay here for. Tomorrow night you could be hearing about your little girl."

" But you've to let us know how she is, mind," Bill said. " I'll tell you what. When we pass through that place, whatever it's called, we could bob in and find out how that other kid is, in hospital."

"You interested in her?" Snowy asked.

"Well, why shouldn't I be?" Bill said. "Nobody else in this wide world is. Hullo! What's up there?"

Bluish smoke was coming from the bars of the kitchen window as they turned the corner, and a smell of burning fat cut through the sulphur.

"Rusty's overkicked," Snowy said. "Else we're late and he's showing his temper."

They ran in the back door, but the kitchen was empty, thick with smoke from food charring in pots and tins.

"Rusty, you lazy bastard!" Snowy shouted. "Where are you?"

Max pulled a tin full of smoking ash from the oven, and Bill threw red-hot saucepans on the floor. Snowy ran down the corridor looking in all the rooms, but they were empty.

He stood at the front door, and shouted again, looking down towards the baths, hearing his voice, moments afterward, booming among the troughs.

But the place appeared emptier. There seemed more rambler than ever trailing reddish-green leaves farther over the ground, and far more space, as though something was missing.

Then cold struck, and he looked about unbelievingly, but it was true.

Rosie had gone.

27

Snowy pointed above their heads at the hill top.

"This is where I should have left her," he said. "Then I could have kept me eye on her. Serves me right."

Heat came off the tarmac and flared under their chins, burning under their brows, drying sweat as it beaded, leaving patches of rime. It was so quiet up there that Max could hear the blood rumbling in his ears, and the brush of their limbs against baked clothing was louder than the wind brittling through meagre branches in the groves.

" You can't trust 'em," Bill said. " They're all the same."

" Why would she be safe all the way up here? " Max asked, looking over the sea.

" We got hit just about here," Snowy said. " And just up there's where we carried him. I'll never get over old Rusty."

" Don't deserve decent treatment," said Bill. " None of 'em."

Max was surprised at the restraint, almost the sorrow, in both. Even when Snowy told them Rosie had gone there was no anger in his voice. His eyes were brighter, and white about the sockets, but he was quiet. One straight stare from Bill, and that was all. There was no cursing, no shouting, nothing to suggest anger in either, and they walked out of the old house, on to the main road where her tracks were plain, and went on walking behind her in the style of men weighed by conscience and aware that what they were doing was entirely their own fault.

" Beats me what the guy's going to get out of it," he said. " He can't hide a thing that size."

" A bloke as good as Rusty'd have her down in a couple of days," Snowy said. " Batten her up, coat of paint, three days on the road again, good as new."

" He'll have a job on that front suspension, though," Bill said. " And he'll have to be careful how he goes."

" He knows her too well," Snowy said. " That's the part that's narking me. Knowing her and knowing me, and he can do this. But I'll find him."

Max looked over at him, startled by an odd tone. There was nothing to suggest violence about Snowy at any time, and there was less under that sun, in the bone-hard creases of his twill, and hands held loose behind his back. But the voice fitted the droop of his shoulders, and the hanging head.

Anger at his lack of precaution, and shame, and a feeling of affection for Rusty were all mixed in Snowy's mind with a sense of having been disloyal to Shiner, and of letting poor old Rosie suffer for it, until he barely knew what to feel, or if he would try. The thought of somebody else driving her was bad enough, but to think of losing her altogether made him sad, though underneath the sadness there was blood.

He began thinking of taking Rusty's throat in his hands, and presently he was tearing the flesh off the skull, and beating the body against a wall. A whiteness took him that reddened the road and made his throat dry, and with it, a thought that beyond what else might happen, Rosie must be found.

Bill heard the motor first, and stopped.

They heard it in breaks of the wind, a chuffing that sounded like a steam engine.

Snowy made a dive for the roadside and tore at the grass about a stone.

" Stop 'em," he said. " Chuck these at 'em, but stop 'em. We want the lift."

They waited with a rock in each hand and as the awning arch topped the brow of the road, they got on to the crown. The truck was old, with solid wheels, and the windscreen was stuck across with tape.

" I'll put this through the middle of the glass," Snowy said. " You two sling 'em through the sides."

They ran to take position as the machine threatened in approach, but then it slowed in a whimper and the driver leaned out shouting from a walnut face, stopping abreast of them, talking to Max.

Rusty was leaning back in the cabin, with a bandage round his head, and as Snowy climbed up he opened his eyes, and nodded off again.

" Somebody hijacked him," Max explained. " So he walked to the village and found this, and the old guy wants to know how you're going to get gas. He doesn't have any."

" Get as far as Corporal Pardoe," Snowy said. " Then it'll be easy. Try the school, first."

Climbing into a machine that moved and shutting a door made all the difference to their spirits, but the fact that Rusty was with them made them feel even better, but humble at thought of their judgment.

" He never saw who it was," Max said, after listening to the driver. " He heard her going and ran after 'em, but something hit him. The old guy thinks it's this big gang, the one we've been hearing about."

" That's all right, chum," Snowy said. " They don't know it, but they've had it. I don't go back without Rosie, and I don't go back with her till they've been properly took care of."

"I'm with you," said Bill. "Right down to t'knuckle."

Max laughed at the placidity in both voices. The abrupt change in attitude was funny, in hot sun, coasting down a hill in a thirty-year-old truck with the broad blue of sea on one side, red and grey groves on the other, and mountains in a crag of green ahead. They seemed too lonely, too far away from everything to be sure of anything, but they spoke as though they were on their way home in Rosie with the job all done.

"O.K.," he said. "I'll string along for the laughs."

They passed nobody on the way in to the town, and the only people they saw were too far up the hillside to call, but every now and again the marks of Rosie's tyres were plain, especially on the bends where the road had been mended.

They got into the streets in the late afternoon. All the shutters were up and all the windows were closed, and even the trees had a tight look about them. Max guided the driver to the white building, and they stopped in front of the big door between the hanging flags.

"Who's going to do the talking?" Max asked. "They know me."

"I'll have a go," Snowy said. "I've got a pass."

"You also have salt," Max said. "And you know when to throw it."

Snowy went in to the big hallway. Nothing moved among the palms, and the silence made him feel he ought to take off his boots, but he went up the stairs two at a time, and thumped on the doors with his fist.

There was a rattle, and one side opened about a foot. A little man, in a grey jacket that shone like silk, looked at him over spectacles with both lenses cracked.

"Yes?" he said. "What is it?"

"We've had our bus pinched," Snowy said. "Can I see somebody?"

"There's nobody here," the little man said, in a voice fine as the edge on cut paper, using a tone that put Snowy exactly in his place. "Everybody's gone home, my man. I'm the duty registrar."

"You'll do, Dad," Snowy said. "I want the military police."

" No telephone lines," the little man said. " They've been down since you people landed. The only cars in the place belong to the officers. And they've gone home."

" Any trucks here? " Snowy watched him pulling a cotton out of the cuff of the jacket. " Where's your transport section? "

" There isn't one," the little man said. " Won't be for months. I'm afraid I can't help you. Everybody goes off in the afternoon. Too hot. I'm only here in case of something urgent."

" This is urgent," Snowy said. " I want to get the police after 'em."

" This area's outside military jurisdiction," said the little man, taking off his spectacles, and smiling as though he enjoyed it. " And there aren't as many civil police as we'd like. Not nearly as many. Not much to be done there."

" Well, who's the boss? " Snowy asked. " Where can I get hold of him? "

" Won't be in," the little man said. " And I couldn't possibly disturb him if he were."

" Listen, Dad," Snowy pushed the door open. " Where's the phone? "

" I'm not Dad," the little man said in a sudden blurt of anger. " Don't you dare take liberties with me. Now you get outside before I deal with you."

" Before you what? " Snowy bent down to look him in the eye. " Listen, Charlie, 'fore I paint the wall with you, where's the phone? "

Head to one side, the little man backed away with his hands up at his shoulders and his glasses hanging from his ear.

" You're all the same," he whispered, as though to himself, or to someone standing behind. " All of you. Brutes. I won't be chivvied by a lot of common soldiers. The more I see of you the more I hate you. Oh, God, how I detest and despise you."

Snowy stared at him, troubled by the slash of the voice, and the crouch like that of a dog under the whip, showing a glint of aluminium teeth.

" Where's the phone? " he asked, feeling a sense of indignity.

" I won't tell you," the little man said, and put his hands behind his back, holding up his chin. " Hit me. Go along. Hit me. You may kill me, but I won't."

Snowy looked at the shredded collar many sizes too large and brownish with days of wearing.

" Now listen, Dad," he said. " We don't want to fall out. All I'm asking is where's the phone? "

" I won't tell you," the little man said, but the whisper was getting louder. " I won't tell any of you anything. There are many things I know. Many things you'd like to know, and you can keep on at me, but I won't tell. You're brutes, that's what you are. Brutes."

Snowy looked about in alarm, for the voice wandered all round the building.

He ran down to an open door along the corridor, and went into an office carpeted in blue pile. Oil paintings squared the walls in gold, easy chairs were pushed back anyhow from a table heaped with files, and a sour stench of cigar butts blunted the smell from bowls of flowers.

He stood there, staring.

The richness saddened him, for this was part of another world that he could only dream about, where another kind of people lived, that were his own and yet foreigners, only because he spoke another kind of the same language.

The scent of flowers brought a memory of the Princess. This was the world where she was comfortable, in this smell, that was part of her, among statues and velvet curtains.

Looking down at his boots almost hidden in soft blue hair, he longed for her, wanting to sit in one of the big chairs and just think of her.

A sound at the door made him turn.

The little man was looking at him, perhaps with regret.

He put the spectacles on, and took them off, twiddled with the cord, and impatiently put them in his breast pocket, blinking, clasping his hands as though uncertain of their shape.

" I beg of you not to mention this," he said, looking out of the window with eyes that were yellow all round the ball. " I go off like that now and again. I don't like it, of course, and I'd get into awful trouble here if you complained."

" It's all right, Dad," Snowy said. " I shan't hurt you. Sit down, and put your poor old feet up."

" Look at me," Dad said. " I'm seventy-eight years of age

and I'm a Master of Arts. You'd think they'd create a position for me, wouldn't you? With all my knowledge of the people and the country. But do they? Duty clerk, if you please. A watchman, that's all I really am. That's what they made me. After the sort of life I've led. Really. Oh, really."

He sat upright in a chair by the door and put his hands on his knees. Two aluminium teeth shone.

" When I think of it! " The sharp voice was softened and he watched the ceiling as if noble history were under review. " All my savings and my home. Dear God, what have I done? And these brutes. These devils. They won't even give me food. I hate them. I hate them all. I despise them."

Snowy walked out and down the corridor. He heard a scuffle of worn leather behind him, and felt the tickle of horror close at hand.

The little man stopped a yard away, with a ragged smirch of moisture spread over his cheeks.

" If you've got any cigarettes, I'll buy them off you," he said. " And any matches you can spare. We can't get them. And I know you've got plenty of bully beef. I'll buy that, too. I'll buy anything you've got. Anything. Blankets. Or uniforms. I'll give you a very good price."

" Sorry, Dad," Snowy said. " That's your share of what I've got." He put a cigarette on the table, and went out of the door and down the stairway.

" My name's Outhwaite." The little man leaned over the rail, whispering in the vault. " Doctor Outhwaite. English enough, isn't it? As English as you are. English. You brute."

Snowy turned quickly enough to catch a small face with light on the forehead chewing its mouth at him, but then it had gone and the big doors slammed.

" Blimey," he said outside. " There ain't half a case in there."

" What you been doing? " Max asked. " Laying a couple of them drabs? "

" There's a loony up there," Snowy said.

" Not just one, brother," Max said. " They have an assortment."

" What about petrol? " Bill asked. " We can't go on without it."

"A place of this size," Snowy raged. "Two bloody great flags, and nothing but a loony to run it. Everybody either gone home or barmy."

A civilian turned the corner, coming toward them. Max hailed him and the driver joined in.

"He's a clerk in here," Max said. "There's an ambulance up at the hospital. They might lend us a little gas."

"Two birds," Snowy said. "Get Rusty fixed up, too. I don't like the looks of him."

The cloth had dried on his head, and his face was almost the same colour, deeply lined, with the corners of the mouth turned down, swelling out with each breath. Snowy got in beside him, slipping an arm gently under his dead weight, but there was no move.

The civilian took them to a white building marked with big red crosses on a hillside, and between them they carried Rusty inside the hall crowded with women in black all sitting among their bundles anywhere on the floor, silent, with the same look on each face.

An attendant in a torn overall came out of the box, looking at them, hands on hips, shaking his head. Max talked to him and got angry.

"He says the place is full," he said. "And they don't take soldiers, anyway. He wants us to go to the military hospital about two hours from here."

"Look," Snowy said. "You tell him we've had enough of getting messed about. Get a doctor down here in quick time, else they'll want another hospital round here, and a few new people to run it."

"That's m'boy," said Max, and sent the porter hurrying, with a run of language to follow him through the battered chromium doors.

Even while they were talking a sound had worried them, and now, among the quiet women, they listened, looking at one another, wondering.

"That'll never be blokes, will it?" Bill asked, looking at the ceiling.

"Too loud," Snowy said. "Too many of 'em."

Max talked to a woman sitting at his feet. Without looking

up at him, staring across the treetops towards the green run of the river, she answered flatly in a few words.

" We better get Rusty out of here," he said. " They're operating without drugs. They don't have any."

The porter held one side of the door open, holding a folded stretcher, waving them in. They lifted Rusty on to dirty canvas, and Max took the foot. The corridor was wide, and dark, and thick with people sitting and standing against the walls, some in long white shirts and bandaged, others with arms in cradles, all making a mumbling effort that sounded like prayer, or lifting their heads to groan in long breaths. None of the rooms had doors, and people were lying on blankets spread over the tiling, and a fist beat out of linen, and a nun in brown knelt in the light trying with strong motions of her mouth to make herself heard among the drone of voices.

The porter stopped them outside the only room with doors. Women and children bound to stretchers with straps were lined head to foot along the walls in a queue. An old man struggled helplessly, shouting, and a girl was trying to calm him with a hand over his eyes.

Max looked at Snowy and then at Bill, trying not to hear the screams coming down the stairway, and the girl sobbing when the old man shrieked with an open mouth among the low tones of prayers, hoping to forget the smell of choked drains, and trying not to see blood shining on the floor about the bin of cut limbs, with a small hand clawing on the rim and a steel wedding ring dull on its finger.

A young man in a linen wrap blotched red came out with the porter.

" Look," he said, impatiently. " What's the score? He can't be worse than a couple of hundred in here. We've got nothing to work with. What happened to him? "

" Couldn't you just look at him, doctor? " Snowy said. " That won't do no harm."

" We just don't have anything." The doctor knelt down and half undid the stuck cloth. " We have a woman here with gangrene in both legs. They both have to come off and we don't even have a cup of coffee to help her. There's nothing wrong with this boy except maybe a little concussion. Thanks."

Max lit the cigarette for him.

" Doc," he said, nodding at the corridor, " does this have to happen? As bad as this? "

" What's your guess?" the doctor said. " We just got here, but the way things look, we're not going to last. They're just people, that's the big trouble. Not important enough. Goodbye, now."

He went in, catching the end of his wrap in the swinging door and they heard the angry word as he pulled it clear.

" Why couldn't I have gotten into a mess like this? " Max said. " I ought to be here, not way up there. Here's where I'd do some good."

Bill stopped among the quiet women in the hall.

" I wonder where I'd find out what happened to that little thing in the pram," he said.

" You wasn't doing her a favour to get her in here," Snowy said. " Ought to have minded your own business."

Max talked to the porter, and they looked down a list.

" She went out this morning," he said. " He remembers the push-cart."

" Ah," Bill said. " Well, I'd rather that than this. I'm wondering how far she'll get."

He squeezed a lip in the fruit tin full of petrol the civilian had brought, and poured it in the tank. They tried to make Rusty comfortable, but the cabin seat was easy with age, and he was lax in sleep.

" I'm the littlest," Max said. " I'll hold him. You going to drive, Snow? "

" No fear," Snowy said. " Every man his own mare. This old bloke knows her."

They went through the town and wondered again at the riches of the shops and the peace of clean streets, looking at strolling women, and lollers under striped umbrellas in the pavement cafés.

" Funny thing," Snowy said, feeling the call of coloured lights flashing on urns and glass in the taverns. " I don't know I've ever seen as good as this back home."

" You want to come up north," Bill said. " Look round Blackpool, or Morecambe."

" I'm talking about a little place like this," Snowy said. " Look what's in it."

" You can have it," Bill said. " Give me home, that's all. D'you think our place'd stand a hospital like that? Helpless lot."

" That doctor was a Yank," Snowy said. " He couldn't seem to do much."

" Depends on the people," said Bill, waving at the strollers. " Look at 'em. Meandering about in their best hats, if you please. They'll get some wheels turning like that, won't they? "

" Eyes down," said Snowy. " This is it. Here comes the weather."

Moorland roughed out ahead in sharp grey and brown slabs spread with violet, sloping down towards the evening, and bluer mountains in distance, making him think dearly of his kit aboard Rosie, trying to turn away from the cold snout of the wind.

He found pleasure in imagining himself crushing the throat out of the thief and anyone else aboard her, and a vision of strange hands on her driving wheel brought him upright, swinging his fists.

He caught Bill's eye, and pretended he was beating his chest from cold.

" Getting a bit parky," he said.

" There it is," Bill shouted, pointing.

They were passing the holes and barrels of last night, among black rings of ash and the glitter of tins in rocky clutter.

Bill stood on tiptoe looking among the scrub, trying to mark the grave, but the sunset light deceived him, and then the place had passed.

The woman with the golden hands seemed far away.

" There y'are," Bill said. " Y' marry a lovely girl and have a baby, and a couple of odd files put the pair of 'em down in a place like this. No wonder blokes go mad. Supposing it happened to your missus? "

" Look," Snowy said, " we ain't got any kit; poor old Rosie's getting herself knocked about and old Rusty's a hospital job. And you're trying to make me laugh? Give over."

28

The town started among dusty gardens and broken walls, and went on growing wreckage until they turned the corner of the school.

" Thank God we left that petrol for 'em," Bill said. " But it'll be just like 'em if they've used it all."

They pulled up at the gateway among crowds of children. The rubbish was gone from the yard, and when Snowy went in he found all the floors clean, and tables with forms about them neat in a bare room. Sounds of scrubbing and hammering came down the dark corridors, and a couple of women were carrying tins of water that bumped against their legs, and their long feet were white against the tiling.

Max asked for Casalonghi, and went away with one of them. Snowy went out to Bill, standing by the open hood watching him cleaning plugs.

" I don't know what keeps the thing going," Bill said, as though the matter were out of his hands. " Ye could grow spuds in these plugs."

" Don't moan," Snowy said. " Spuds or not, we'd still be miles away without it."

" Ah," said Bill. " And Rosie's done a good hundred and fifty in the time."

Snowy let the hood down hard.

" Whoever he is, he'll pay for it," he said. " He'll pay to me."

Casalonghi came out with Max, and behind a couple of men carried the tins.

" My dear friends," Casalonghi greeted them with both hands. " We are so pleased. We used only very little. What can we possibly do? "

" Just one of these is all we want, guv'nor," Snowy said. " You've saved our lives."

" You certainly gave this place a going over," Max said, looking at the building. " What'll you do when you're all straightened out? "

Casalonghi pointed to the children.

"Make peasticks," he said. "We put some sticks for these little peas. Last night they were attracted by the fire. So many have no parents, so they are wild, and I watched them while they slept. Yesterday I was full of despair. Today I have work to do, and so I am happy. I owe so much to you."

"That was Rosie," Snowy said.

"Where's that truck of yours?" Max asked.

"It was sold this morning," Casalonghi said. "For such a large sum. But it will buy food and paper. We are very happy."

"But how're you ever going to get out of this place?" Max asked. "You're way off in the blue."

"There's a town just down the road here'd suit you," Snowy said. "Ain't touched. You could have a good time there."

Casalonghi put his hand on Snowy's shoulder and pivoted him towards the railings knotty with small hands and laughing heads poking through the spaces.

"I shall have a good time here, my friend," he said. "Training little peas. In ten years I shall be proud. Dead, perhaps. But proud."

"D'you think you're going to know, if you're dead?" Snowy asked, watching a couple of the women attending Rusty.

"Certainly," Casalonghi said. "Why not?"

"You believe in the after life?" Max asked.

"What is this, after life?" Casalonghi opened his hands. "After birth, I know. It is thrown away, and our life begins. If after life is the body we throw away in the ground, certainly. And then the life of new experience, new music and new knowledge. You have a most beautiful hymn, I remember: 'New every morning is the love.' It is the same. Ecc'."

"You really think They know what we're doing down here?" Snowy asked. "I mean, not only the posh lot. But ordinary blokes?"

"Shiner," Max said.

"What is this china?" Casalonghi looked from Max to Snowy.

"Shiner," Snowy said. "My old mate. He got killed."

"Why should he not?" Casalonghi said. "Dear friend, what do we know? Not even what we are. A little seed brings out a green shoot. Ordinary, not even for comment. Very well. Analyse the seed, the shoot, the ground that covers it, and the water to feed it. We know all about it? Then what produced the green shoot? Where is this analysis? What was the power?"

"Normal process of growth," Max said.

"A splendid title," said Casalonghi. "It means, with the most embarrassing precision, nothing."

"That's you took care of," said Snowy.

Bill came round wiping grease from his forearms.

"Good job I looked at it, else we'd been on fire," he said. "It's fair stuck up wi' muck."

"It moves," Max said. "And boy, am I grateful."

"How's Rusty?" Snowy asked.

"Comfortable," Bill said. "Muttering a bit."

"Soon fix that." Snowy shook hands with Casalonghi, and climbed up. "You've give me a bit of heart, you have, guv'nor. Good luck."

"Come back if you can," Casalonghi said, following them among a drove of children. "You will see a change. Thank God."

They left him in evening shadow with his arms wide over a group of children, moving his hands upwards and wriggling his fingers on either side in a virile flash of movement almost making them see the leaves growing.

"He ain't a bad bloke," Snowy said. "But he's got a job on."

"Like all the rest of 'em," Bill said. "Up one minute, down the next. Old Cob always said catch 'em young and ye've got 'em. Let 'em go, and ye might just as well fold your hands."

Night came down when they reached the gradient into the mountains and mist was grey ahead, coloured in low-power headlamps to an orange flux, giving only a yard or two of vision, and so the wagon crawled, lashed by branches on one side, shivering in all its joints, scraping its wheels on the stone parapet, and Snowy looked in shame across at Bill, huddled in the corner, feeling as though hands were wringing in his brain.

"You cold, Bill mate?" he said, and made his way across, grinding his teeth in the wind.

"No, chum," said Bill. "I were just cursing myself to think of poor old Rosie. I ought to have disarmed her. I had a mind to, and tossed it away."

"My fault," Snowy said. "I'd had her long enough. Never struck me, somehow. I'll pay for all your kit, though."

"Nay," Bill said. "Wasn't worth half a dollar. But I'm right sorry about your photos."

"I lay my hands on him," said Snowy, "it'll be his finish."

A pitching bump sent them rolling into the other corner with sore knees and bruised hands, and for a couple of seconds they stared at the risen flooring, pinned down by its motion, and then the wagon righted itself in a snap of breaking metal, and landed on the tilt.

"Axle," Bill said, and jumped off.

Snowy sat there for a moment, collecting rage. He went on all fours to the cabin window and pushed aside the flap.

"Rusty all right, Maxie?" he called.

"Sure," Max said. "I didn't know icebergs got this far south. What hit us?"

"It's a damn great stone in the road," Bill said, over the side. "And ye'll do all your travelling on shanks' pony from now on. We've had it."

The driver put the tips of his fingers together, waving them under Bill's nose, and chattered.

"Be off with your bother," said Bill.

"He wants to know what's going to happen," Max said. "His boss'll chew his arse off."

"We'll see him all right," Snowy said, and quailed from an instant picture of Sergeant Whitmarsh. "We'll give him a brand new 'un."

"Give that lamp just one more rub," Max said. "I'll wait for the carpet to show up."

They looked about, each thinking of Rusty. The driver shouted, and a man came running through the fog. His voice was rough, and even through the cold mist they smelt the wood smoke on him.

"He has a house up here," Max said. "Let's go."

They carried Rusty a little way up the road and into a house of one big room with an uneven earth floor. A square of stones laid near the middle burned a heap of brushwood, and smoke went up white through a hole in the roof.

An old woman sat behind the fire on a rush chair propped with its back against the wall. People were sleeping in their clothes all round the room, but when they saw Rusty was bandaged, a few women got up to help lay him flat, and everyone moved up in a stir of sleep and startled snores, and the movement seemed to shift warm riding smells of sweat and burning bracken.

While they were feeling the fire, Max talked across the flame with their host, watching the women at work on Rusty.

" He says Rosie went through here this afternoon," he said. " He thinks there was something wrong. She was slow."

" Suspension," Bill said. " They'll have to nurse her."

Snowy felt her under him, and she seemed to be talking.

" Ah, Christ," he said. " I wonder if she knows? " He saw Max watching him. " I suppose you think I'm cracked an' all, do you? Don't worry, chum. Engines know all about it. You try messin' 'em about. You'll soon see."

" They stopped at a house along here," Max said. " Did a job on her. They have a couple of trucks."

" Wonder what they was doing," Snowy said. " Let's go down and have a nose round."

They were led out and across the smooth paving of the square; but though the wind pushed at them through the mist, the guide had to stay close to be seen, and the edges of stones tripped them until it seemed that wind, mist and stones were set in malice against them.

" Fine hole to live in," Bill shouted, and it sounded like a child's cry. " Not even a damn lamp-post."

A gateway was dark in front with a chequered path beyond, and then the house shadowed over them. Heat blew in their faces when a door was opened, and the guide lit a tallow dip from fire ash brightening in the draught.

The windows were boarded with tea-chest lids, and sacks had been stuffed in cracked walls. A crumple of pale-blue paper was scattered about on the floor, piling near a couple of empty boxes that might have served as seats by the fireplace.

" Hullo," Snowy said, straightening a sheet. " Somebody else having trouble writing home? "

" ' Will, my own darling heart,' " Max read. " ' A letter by your dear hand has come tonight, and I were that starved of you I felt like one of them blackbirds when they opened the pie and they all began to sing.' "

Bill lunged, kicking aside a box to grab the page.

" By God," he said. " They're never my letters, surely? They couldn't be that heartless! "

The fireplace was filled with ash and burnt ends of timber. Charred paper moved in the chimney draught, and a piece of red ribbon lay across a log with its scorched end towards the fire. He went down slowly and picked it up, looking at it in doubt.

" Well," he said, " I'd never have believed it. Poor Pet. Just fancy, a man could do a thing like that."

29

The dump was black, without a sentry to be seen, and shouting was useless in the wind. Max and Bill waited at the main gate, and Snowy went down to the turning again, but the wire was too high and coiled too thick.

He looked into the darkness, raging at the night and the wind and his soaking clothes. He saw the other two, shading a lighter, coming down to join him.

" Three of us ought to shift something," he said. " Get hold of some bricks and try hitting the roof. Poor bloke's asleep hours ago."

" Right," Max said. " With a bunch of them fat-arsed broads. The way he suffers'd break your heart."

For minutes on end they threw rocks up in the darkness, but the wind was too loud for sound of the strikes to reach them.

Light bloomed white in the mist behind them, and in amazement they saw a car skid out of the top gate, in a seethe of wind, coming direct towards them and stopping, bonnet to gate in a racket of brakes.

" Who are you? " Snowy recognized Corporal Pardoe's voice. " Stay where you are."

" It's me, Corp," he said. " Here the other day. Got a couple of pals with me."

" Stand still," the corporal said. " I'll fire if you make a move."

" Now listen, Corp," Snowy said. " You know us."

" Certainly I know you," the corporal said. " We're looking for you. You're walking straight in that gate and I'm locking you up till the military police get down here."

A couple of carabinieri got out of the back of the truck, unlocking the barrier and swinging it aside. They presented their automatics.

" March in," the corporal said.

" Corp," Snowy said, " I'll take my dying oath I don't know what this is about. My pals'll tell you."

" They'll be telling the Area Commander tomorrow," Corporal Pardoe said. " In you go. And don't come the acid, else you'll never come out. I'm warning you."

Spite in his voice froze them, and they went in, feeling the wetness of their clothing, following the carabinieri, with the corporal walking in front of the headlights.

" I suppose you was trying to get the rest of the stuff, was you? " he said. " After all I done for you. Just copped unlucky, didn't you? You won't get a chance to kill nobody else, you murdering lot of swine."

Snowy stopped and turned, feeling the revolver hard in his belly.

" Corp," he said, " you can shoot me now, dead as a door knocker, and I won't lift me finger. I swear I don't know what you're talking about. My pals, here, the same. Who are we supposed to have killed? "

" The officer," Corporal Pardoe said, but his voice was not so strong or so sure.

" I'm Fifth Army," Max said. " United States. I want you to know right now we have no knowledge of any crime. I demand you get through to the Commanding General."

" Better still," Snowy said, " call up our unit. You'll soon see."

" What are you doing outside here then? " the corporal said.

" Somebody pinched my bus," Snowy said. " Put one of my pals out doing it. We left him up the road, and walked here to try and get an ambulance."

" Come in here," the corporal said. " Mind your ps and qs."

He turned up the light under the green glass ball. A smell of many fat gravies made them feel hungry.

" These two blokes ain't going to be too particular." The corporal waved his revolver at the carabinieri standing in the doorway. " They won't stand no nonsense. One of their blokes got knocked off as well."

" Sounds like a very handy lot," Snowy said. " What we want's the ambulance first, then the coppers. How about the phone? "

The corporal sat down.

" They was smart," he said. " They busted it. I've had to send a bloke by the short cut."

" Any idea how long? " Bill asked, but so gently.

It was the first time he had spoken since they picked up all the letters. Snowy turned towards him, but the words stayed where they were, for firelight rimmed the edges of his spectacles and the lamp globe reflected deep green ovals in them and it seemed in looking at him that he shook, not in the larger way of cold, but finer, perhaps as a child in sleep.

The corporal sensed a threat, straightening in the chair.

" I've warned you," he said.

" It's all right," Bill said in the same voice. " I just want to know how long it'll be before I can hope to be after 'em, that's all."

" They done a repair up the road here," Snowy said. " Took our kits out and went through 'em. They burnt his wife's letters."

" Well, I never." The corporal stared at them all in turn. Their soaked clothing seemed to reassure him. " I don't know what it's coming to. Couldn't have happened at an awkwarder time, this couldn't. Just when I was getting things taped. Now I'll have to start all over again, I suppose. What's that? "

Somebody was shouting outside.

" Another car out there," Max said, listening to the carabinieri talking. " A soldier. It's an officer. He wants to come in."

The corporal went to the door, looking out. A torch beam lit his face white.

"Anybody home?" a voice hailed.

"Who is it?" the corporal shouted.

"Weary travellers," the voice said, coming nearer. "How's it looking for a nice mug of char?"

"Bloke with the right idea," Snowy said.

The corporal came in with a wink and a rearward jerk of his thumb, followed by a girl in battledress blouse and skirt, wearing a beret. An officer's coat hung from her shoulders.

"Oo," she said, standing in the doorway. "Can't we have a bit more light? I can't see a thing."

"Another tot, darling," the voice said. "You'll see everything, plus the make-weight."

An officer came in and looked round the room.

"This the place we've heard so much about?" he asked. "The half-way house?"

"No, sir, it ain't," the corporal said. "It's a maintenance stores, and I'm in charge."

"Oh dear," said the officer. "That's a blow."

"That's shook you," the girl said. "Now what's the answer? I thought you said it was all laid-on?"

"We'll push on, darling," said the officer. "It's not far. Push on, as ever."

"Not before I've had a cup of something." She fell into a chair with her skirt over her knees, pulling down the hem with the little fingers of both hands curling away as though they had other more delicate work to do, in a glance from eyes having something of the polish of a sugared bun, that took in all the men without appearing to see any of them. "Oo, I am, I'm starved. As for that rotten truck! I've swore I'll never have a ride in another. Staff car, me, from now on."

"You're rather more able to choose, darling," said the officer, smiling in a turn-down of eyes and mouth, aware that others were listening. "But I don't think we ought to bother the corporal this time in the morning. Or what does he say?"

"'Course," she said, looking up at Corporal Pardoe, "he knows how I feel. Don't you, dear?"

Corporal Pardoe winked at Snowy on his way in to the kitchen.

Snowy looked at the other two, and one by one they got inside the little lean-to and shut the door.

" This is all me eye," the corporal whispered. " They come through at night because there's no patrol along the road to stop 'em, see? They hang on here for morning, then they get in the town when things are opening up. Dead clever, ain't they? "

" Kind of off-beat honeymoon? " Max said. " It's being done."

" This is about the umpteenth lot I've had here," the corporal said. " They're always getting me out of it, all hours. I mean, a joke's a joke. All right. Here goes."

He put the kettle on the primus.

Instantly in the blue flame Snowy saw the Princess, and in the heat felt again the warmth of her breath in a cleanly gust of memory that startled him. He was feeling for her what he had felt for months after leaving Liz. A raw place in his brain that never healed seemed to be rubbed every time thought turned to her, until even the thought of thinking about her would get him on his feet, trying to find something to work at and fill his mind. Bitterly he turned away from it, going over to lean against the washboard.

" Look," Max said. " We have this boy at a house a few miles up here. How about sending a cop with your driver and getting him down? "

" That's right," Snowy said. " They might lift him to hospital."

" They're going the wrong way," the corporal said. " Besides, I ain't finished with you yet."

" He might die," Bill said.

" That'll be two of 'em," the corporal said. " And a copper, three. But he was Eyetie. Who'd ever have believed it, eh? I'll admit I never liked that bloke of mine, but that never ought to have happened to him. I heard the gun go off down here. Time I got there they was gone. So was half the stores."

" No idea who it was? " Snowy asked.

The corporal shook his head, standing on tiptoe looking up at the groceries stacked on the shelf.

" Here's the tea," Snowy said.

" I wish there was a way of mixing it with a nice dose of salts," the corporal said. " I'd give 'em half-way house."

The girl called out and the floor shook as she walked to the door and pulled it open.

" Having a mothers' meeting in here, are you? " she asked. " Where's the tea? Talk about women gossiping, I reckon you men take some beating."

" Shan't be long, Miss," the corporal said. " You'll enjoy it when you get it."

" I hear you've had some trouble here today? " The officer leaned against the door, nodding at one of the policemen. " What's going to happen about it? "

" I'm expecting our police any time," the corporal said.

" Police? " The girl looked about the room, putting her hand in her back hair. " Oo. Don't like that. Let's have this tea and get out of it quick. I can't afford trouble."

" You a nurse, Miss? " Snowy asked.

" Me? " She laughed as though she had to, and straightened her face, pulling the overcoat on her shoulders. " No fear. Bit more sense than that."

The stillness of the grouped men worried her. A feeling coming out of them, that she could sense, in brown faces and soiled twill all shaded in greenish light, piled in emotion that might have been fear.

" Listen," she said, in pretence of tears. " What have I got to do? Faint before I get this tea? I could've made and sold couple of gallons while you've been playing about out there."

Corporal Pardoe went into the kitchen with an air of royal mission.

" Hold on," he said. " Everything takes time, Miss. This is very special."

" Major," Max said, " would you loan us your truck to go and fetch a boy up the road a piece? He's sick."

" Now look," she said, with upraised hand, " you American? "

" Yes," Max said, looking at the major.

" Why can't you use your own transport then? " she asked. " You've got plenty."

" We had it stolen," Max said. " What's the word, Major? "

" We can't do no favours," she said, with her eyes shut, " else we're going to be here all night, I can see."

" This is no favour, lady," Max said. " It's urgent. The boy has concussion."

" I'll drive," Snowy said.

" Oh no you won't," she said. " You keep out of it. Nobody was talking to you. Why should we go chasing all over the place? I don't see it's fair."

" How long would it take? " The officer asked as though he were afraid of the answer.

" Under the hour, all told," Snowy said, looking at her.

" I like that," she said, looking at the officer. " If you dare let that truck go, I won't come a step further, there you are. I never wanted to come in the first place. I could have had a lovely time up the rest camp, and done with it."

" Darling," the officer said. " If the chap's a casualty and anything happens, we might be carpeted."

" Christ," she said, and threw down the coat. " Nothing ever goes right with you. Pays me out for coming. All right. Do as you like."

The officer looked at Snowy, and they went out together.

" She's rather tired," the officer said, pampering his voice. " Must make allowances, mustn't we? "

Snowy got in the truck, feeling as though a happy light were on inside him, and drove off knowing nothing except desire to put Rusty in hospital and then get after Rosie. He was sure, without knowing a reason, that she could do her best to go slow, and the thought of that quiet mass frowning all round herself, and waiting with one of her little quirks to start trouble, for the thief sat like a jewel on a cushion in his mind, and through the darkness he smiled, but under the smile was an ache to get his hands firm on her driving wheel again, and, beyond, a blood wish to feel the tips of his fingers meet in a throat.

30

His head was sore with sleep when he pulled into the village. Dawn was pink and grey with pale blue stars, and the stones shone washy gold, but the houses sat among it all, doors closed and windows shut with worn steps and tattery roofs, glooming as sulky children left from play.

Snowy went up the steps with the carabinieri, pushing open the door, hearing a woman talking beyond the empty room jumping in light from the fire, with cooking pots in a row on the slabs. A woman came out wiping her hands, tucking hair into the headcloth, bobbing a curtsy and smilingly pointing to a room behind, standing aside to wave them in.

Rusty lay in a double bed, cleanly bandaged, looking at them with round eyes.

" Snowy," he said. " Amico. E."

" Blimey, I thought you was boxed," Snowy said. " How are you, Rusty boy? "

" I'm so good," Rusty said. " No pains. Nothing."

" D'you remember what happened to you?" Snowy asked. " Who hit you? "

" Nothing," Rusty shook his head. " Not yesterday or day before. Nothing. I see the sun, and lights. Everything else, I don't know."

" Is this man Italian? " the officer frowned.

" Yes, sir," Snowy said. " Sergeant mechanic."

" You've had the bloody sauce to drag me all the way up here for this? " the officer said. " I thought he was one of our own men. I never heard of such a thing."

" Come on, Rusty," Snowy said. " Show a leg. You're due for hospital."

" He's not travelling with us," the officer said. " That's an order. Outside, at once."

" Look, sir," Snowy said, " this bloke worked with us nearly two years in the desert. He's as much a part of the Eighth as I am."

"Don't let's have any of that nonsense." The officer turned impatiently in the doorway. "Get a move on."

On the wall above Rusty's head the crucifix turned another colour, and a dome was flashing in sunlight.

"Sorry, sir," he said. "Either he comes or I don't."

"I've given you an order," said the officer.

"That's quite right, sir." Snowy took out his pass and held it up. "I'm on leave, myself, sir. Ain't due back for a couple of days, so I've got plenty of time. I'll hang on here."

"Go, Snowy," Rusty pleaded. "Go, go, go."

The officer turned to the door and stopped, turned with half a mind, and turned again, frowning, beating his palm with the leather crop.

"Very well, now that we're here," he said. "Get him in the back, and look sharp."

"Thank you, sir," Snowy said. "Up you get, chum."

Rusty called to the woman for his clothes. One of the carabinieri went down the steps to thump on a door, but an answering screech seemed to come through the rafters.

Rusty was weak, but able to stand. Snowy helped him into the truck, signing to the carabinieri to roll down the blankets.

"You know why that bloke couldn't go without us?" he whispered. "He can't drive."

He went inside the room taking notes out of his pocket. The officer was bending over a pot with his stick under the lid, looking in at the steam. The lid dropped, spitting, in the fire.

"Damn," he said, fishing for it. "They do themselves rather well, don't they?"

"They know what's good, sir," Snowy said. "They don't mess about with tinned stuff."

The woman came out in the passage at his knock, looking up at him and down at the money; but though he tried to force it on her, a closing door and laughter behind it was all he got for reply, and when he pushed the roll underneath it was toed back to him.

"Addio, Mama," he shouted, and followed the laughing policeman outside.

Sunrise had freshened the hill's green, but the valley was still blue, and dawn wind brought watery eyes. He drove slowly, feeling each bump as if with Rusty's head, skirting hollows in the road, braking on the gradients, knowing that slowness was irksome but obstinate to the point of going slower than he might.

"Oh, come along," the officer said at last. "We can go faster than this."

"Well, sir," Snowy said, "if you'd like to drive it, you're welcome, sir. But this is the best I can do."

"I wish I'd known," said the officer. "You'd have been damned lucky to get me on any wild-goose chase."

"Very kind of you, as it was, sir," Snowy said. "It's my fault he came with us in the first place."

"Of course, it's against every kind of order to carry civilians," the officer said. "But you chaps never seem to worry about them as far as I can see. You're all too full of this Eighth Army tosh. Damned good job when it's all done away with."

"That'll never be, sir," Snowy said comfortably. "They can't do without us."

"Don't answer me back." The major turned and faced him. "And thank your stars you're down here and not a little farther up the road."

"Yes, sir," said Snowy, and dearly wished he could say something else.

He slowed on the rise up to the dump, for a military police jeep stood outside.

"Want to stop here, sir?" he asked. "I'll go up and fetch the lady. Save you a lot of questions."

"She's probably had to answer a few by now," the officer said tiredly. "Damn it. Always some frightful hoo-ha. Don't understand it."

Snowy pulled in behind the jeep, seeing an ambulance parked inside the turning. Down at the hut a couple of redcaps were smoking; and thinking of Max, his spirits fell. They looked at his pass and nodded him inside. A sergeant redcap in leggings and a raincoat was talking to the girl.

"Hullo," he said. "What do you want?"

Snowy showed him the pass.

"That's O.K.," the sergeant said. "You'll have to put a bit of steam on to get there in time, won't you?"

"I think I can manage it, Sarge," he said.

" Where's our truck? " The girl got off the sofa, picked up her coat and bag, and stuffed the beret under an epaulette.

" Outside," Snowy said. " Sarge, there's a pal of ours got concussion. I want to get him in hospital."

" Ain't one round here," the sergeant said. " Base hospital moved up the line day before yesterday. Nearest one's about hundred miles up Route Two."

" I'm off," she said. " So long, dear. Nice to have met you. Don't forget to call in."

" Ta-ta," the sergeant said. " Sorry you're going."

Snowy stood in the frowse of the room in a sudden thought of Liz and a clean bed; but even as detail built, the Princess took her place. He marvelled at himself, trying to shift her, but she stayed, and as she stayed the thought grew warmer, stronger, despite tiredness, until Liz was a shadow barely seen.

" I'm surprised at me bloody self," he heard himself say.

" Ah." The sergeant's brows were up, grinning in the glass, putting his crash helmet on. " You get like that after a time. Lovely feeling, ain't it? "

" Where's my pals? " Snowy asked.

" Yankee, and the other bloke? " The sergeant nodded through the yard. " They took the ambulance driver up the top for some grub. They've reported about your job. Very hard luck."

" What're you going to do about it? " Snowy asked.

" Report it," the sergeant said. " Nothing else we can do. It's gone, chum. You can kiss it goodbye. Dozens of 'em pinched every day. Where're you going to start looking for 'em? "

Snowy walked up the yard towards the store in rains of helpless rage, ready to rip the hours out of the day. The tone of the sergeant's voice hurt in his mind, for it was used in a manner that implied foregone surety. Even the heat of the risen sun was cold when it struck him that yesterday was a long time ago.

He stood still, staring, trying to think how she looked, how she felt, but it seemed too far off to remember.

" Hey, Snow." Max hailed him from the doorway of a store shed, chewing. " Where's Rusty? "

Snowy punched the air.

" I'm going off me chump," he said. " I left him in the truck."

" We left the baby on the shore," Max sang, passing him.

" It's a thing we'd never done before. O.K. I'll get him. Chow's up."

" Ah, Snow," Bill said. " What's to do? How's Rusty? "

" He's all right," Snowy said. " Anything been said about us? "

Bill shook his head.

" No." His voice was borne on a gust of frying fat. " Nobody's said a word. They think they know who it was. They didn't say anything."

He came from the oil stove behind stacks of tins, with a plate of bacon and potatoes, and nodded at a man sitting at the table.

" Ambulance driver," he said. " Come to take the body away. He's giving us a lift. How about Rosie? "

" The sergeant didn't think much of our chances," Snowy said. " I'm worried about her."

" We'll be lucky to see her again," Bill said. " Might have had a chance if we could have chased her. They've had time to dig her in now."

" Took her to pieces, more like it," the driver said. " Worth a fortune out here. They've got nothing like her. Make a very nice living out of it, some of 'em. Wonder we don't all do it."

" I'll find her," Snowy said. " And when I find her, I find him."

Bill took off his spectacles to wipe them on a loose sleeve.

" I'll not say a word," he said.

31

Max woke up in the dark of the ambulance while it was slowing to stop. Above his head a body sewn in a sheet bobbed stiffly on a spring bunk, making little itchy noises as though niggling over a voice it had lost. Sunlight beaming triple silver through the ventilators, a faint smell of iodine, an evenness of bouncy motion and a lilt of stretcher squeaks gave wakefulness the feel of a dream. With closed eyes he tried to make himself believe that only yesterday that clay had done all it could to make trouble, with its finger-tips fiddling the points of a moustache, recalling the tone of voice and the intent of a stare that saw nothing but its vision of itself with the aimlessness of an eye trained by many a rehearsal in the mirror, all, now, sealed in shoddy and tied with string.

Snowy woke up when they stopped, looking about, still chasing the tail-end of a dream, but unsure of the content.

"Rusty wants to get off here," Bill said. "It's where the wedding was."

Snowy frowned up at him.

"Want to get off?" he said. "You're coming back to the unit with us."

"No." Rusty shook his head as though it ached. "I got to mend the truck for the old man. Plenty work. And I get a doctor."

"All right," Snowy said. "Get the doctor. But come and find Rosie with us. If they've got another truck with 'em, it'll be yours. Then you can come back set for business."

A crowd of children danced about in the shadowed street, and windows were opening all the way down. Max went in the doorway with bunches of flowers and wheat over the transom, and stood in the cool patio, listening to a clock chopping off time in long, hard pieces that might have been piling in the corner.

An old man came out in his singlet, and opened his arms with a shout.

"The girl's dad," Snowy said. "We're in."

Max talked to a group of older men in a slate-floored room while the doctor was looking at Rusty upstairs. Snowy, Bill and the driver sat outside the ring, listening, drinking chianti and tearing at long crusts filled with salami and lettuce, trying to eat politely and at the same time smile at the groom's mother and half a dozen other women all chattering together. The grandmother, with lace all down her front, and a little lace cap, came in with the bride's dress over her arm, showing them its beauty in a rill of words, breaking off to curse under her breath and slap at the younger women when they tried to chase her away, but without altering her expression or level of voice.

"Hey, Snow," Max said, "this is news. Rosie came through here a while ago, and they say she was making plenty of noise. This other truck was in front of her. And there were a lot of guys in 'em."

" She can't be far off." Snowy put down his sandwich and stood. " Who're these other blokes? What're they like? "

The old man pulled a face at Max's question, looking round the table at the others. They sat still, looking at the floor.

" They're sure scared of this bunch, whoever they are," Max said. " They just do what they want. Anybody wants to argue gets a visit from twenty or thirty of 'em. This old guy says he don't want to talk about it because he can't use any more trouble. He has enough for a committee right now."

Rusty came in all smiles, with a tight black skull bandage, still shaky, but almost his old self.

" Testa di legno," he announced. " Wood head. Very hard, don't crack."

" Come on," Snowy said. " We ain't got the time for a social."

The driver was a quiet man with a grey eye, and few words. Hours of lonely driving slown down to soften the toll of travel on wounded men had rooted a habit of gauging speed from the texture of the roadside unreeling on either hand.

" Go faster? " he said. " How fast d'you want to go? "

" What you got? " asked Snowy.

" Hold tight," he said. " Speedometer's busted, but we'll see."

Snowy sat among the group in front watching the road, always conscious of passing scenery and the slither of tarmac, borne on a bump and sway of springs, listening to the motor going up and up to a whistle that tickled at the roots of his hair. He looked at the hands loose on the driving wheel, and then at the pale approach of tarmac, down at the boot creased on the button, and up again to the tarmac, sideways to the driver's calm face, and back again to the grey stream rushing between broad pennants where houses looked part of trees.

" Over eighty," he said, dry-mouthed.

" Over ninety," the driver said. " Bet you. She'll do a hundred and four."

" God forbid," said Max.

They turned out on a rich green width of plain, with a village on the skyline, and nearer to, lines of hutments inside barbed wire with sentry towers outside the fence.

" This is where you dropped the Princess," Bill said.

" Perhaps the sentries'll remember Rosie," Snowy said. " Let's ask."

Max heard the sheeted weight slide in accord with the stop and hit the back wall with its boots.

Rusty hailed the carabinieri guards and three-cornered chatter ensued, with everyone taking part except Bill, watching, with his chin on his knees and his spectacles up on his forehead.

" I keep on telling everybody," he said, " if they can't tow her, she can't go far. It's that suspension. It were only good driving kept her going."

" Ta," Snowy said.

" Worse than bad driving," Bill said. " Taking advantage of good nature, that's what it was. Bad driving'd found the fault in time to get a repair job on it. You'd have gone on till she died on you."

" When are you going to die? " Snowy asked.

" Any time after I've run a rule over the bloke as burnt them letters," Bill said. " And very happy."

" O.K.," Max said. " She can't be far. She broke down the other side of the town. Let's go."

They went in to the village, slowing for crossing files of girls going to church in white blouses and blue skirts attended by nuns, smallest in front and tallest in rear, a moving wedge of neatness and bright looks that went up the steps and into the darkness of the postern as a morsel enters the mouth.

" They say anything about our pal the Princess? " Snowy tried to make it impersonal. " I thought I heard something about Principessa while you was talking? "

" Right," Max said. " She raised hell. They put him some place else, or something. Anyway, she never got to see him."

" Fancy her coming all the way down here for nothing," Snowy said.

" I couldn't fancy," said Max.

" Nothing wrong with her," Bill said. " She just told you your fortune, that's all."

"'od blimey," said Snowy. " He's off again. Don't take no notice, Maxie boy. They say anything else ?"

" Started back yesterday," Max said. " She has the sand all right."

" I bet she was walking," Snowy said.

He saw the brown back going through the village and all along the pale grey road, changing the bag from hand to hand with a swing of the hips, looking round every time she heard a motor.

" I wonder if she might get a lift from the blokes that pinched Rosie? " he said. " She'd think it was us. Eh? "

Max looked at him in amusement. The big fellow, with the beard breaking through in gilt strokes and tired eyes never further than half-way from a smile, was in a state that reminded him of a gun dog off the leash pawing around with a pekinese out of the basket.

He watched the black beach scattered with rusted metal in half-formed flowers, like asterisks, each of them announcing a footnote of times, and dates, and names of casualties, and he tried to imagine what happened to the men, and the clamour of their minds a moment after they were sown in the blast to be for all time part of silence. It seemed to him that she might be thinking of them as she walked by, and they, perhaps, in some pale echelon, might be watching her, smiling at her strangeness.

" I bet your wife's going to be mad about Rosie," he said. " Better take an option on the dog house."

Snowy was jerked back in irritation. It seemed improper to think about Liz, but now she was in his mind with a jarring reminder of his disloyalty. He knew her joy of him, and felt her need, catching in a trick of light her shut-eyed smile when she was pleased, and the passing of her open hand, palm outwards, as she pushed her hair away. There the two women were, each clearly heard and seen, both in a struggle to possess his mind, and he looking on, rampantly aware of both, yet memory of the Princess brought a heat that ached, but Liz was only remembered from a sense of shame.

" I'll tell her about it when I've got her back," he said.

Alders, in miles of stiff red brush, gleamed in sunshine on both sides of a road built through the marsh in detour for the wrecked bridge. The river ran pale green about the stones, blue as the clouds below and a yellowy milk in the ford, with car wrecks among fallen trees on the near side, and burnt tanks frowning among wild flowers on the other.

Bill pointed to the gravel as they took to the water.

" There she is," he said. " That's Rosie, for a million."

Snowy looked over the side, watching the deep imprints of the tyres until they were among the rocks with the same feeling as looking at her photograph. Directly across, the landing strip went up into a lane cleared through the brush, but even when they were half-way over they saw there were no tracks, neither were there any further up or down.

" I should have gone to summer camp," Max said. " Who has Injun blood in the family? "

" It's obvious," Bill said. " She's built higher than us, so she could go all the way down-river without getting anything wet. We couldn't in this."

" Go through this place," Rusty said quietly, pointing at the lane. " From little boy I'm here. Please, what I say."

" O.K., chum," the driver said. " I ain't too anxious to splash about. She ain't made for it."

" Please, I want to see," Rusty said, sitting up.

" We ain't got a rifle between us," Snowy said.

Max showed the butt of his automatic.

" O.K., Snow," he said. " We still have coffee money."

The lane was deep with powder, milled a year before by passage of an army, and dust rolled up however slow they went, but Rusty stood on the driver's step among it all, looking across the miles of rippling scarlet, and then he tapped the driver's shoulder.

" Please," he said. " The only place she go is here. Half mile."

" O.K., Rusty boy," Snowy said. " Who wants to come? "

Bill followed Rusty down in the marsh, with Max behind.

" You might be hours," the driver said. " Me laddo in there won't keep, you know. The flies are getting nosey, look."

" Here." Snowy wrote on the door panel. " Supposing you get through to Sergeant Whitmarsh there. He'll cover you. Tell him what's happened. We could do with a few of the lads and some spares for that suspension. If we find her."

" Oh," the driver said. " I'll leave you this tinned stuff and some petrol. Do you? "

" You're a pal," Snowy said, and jumped the ditch. " Be seeing you, chum."

They went in file behind Rusty, over their ankles in black mud topped with a bright green weed that looked like shamrock, up to their knees in running water, but always in shadow of the alders that from wagon height had appeared bushes, and now were trees straightly orange and scarlet, high above their heads.

Cold winds blew through the brakes, coming off water in shadow, and they felt the river icy in their boots long before coming out on a sandbank, with the fresh brown of tyre tracks curving up at them and going on around the bend.

" Rusty," Snowy said, " you're a marvel. I hate the sight of you."

Max pulled out the automatic.

" Just to make sure," he said.

" I thought you didn't like shooting," Bill said.

" I don't," Max said, and turned crimson. " Especially kids half of my own age. But there's a guy back there. What did he do? "

" Whoa," Snowy said, and stood between them, turning to Bill. " Ain't you a bloody dream, eh ? Get people hung, you would. Come on, Maxie, mate. Let's find her."

Rusty was waiting for them at the top of a sandbank among dwarf willows, thumbs in his belt, standing among the long green feathers, laughing as wide as the bandage would let him.

" Ecco, la poverina," he said, pointing.

They ran through the water to him and looked into the creek.

Rosie was tipped over on her side, slanted up at the far end of a dune with her crane almost in the water.

Snowy ran all the way. Fierce hilarity was in him, but with coldness underlying that checked laughter, or when it came edged it to a cackle, or when he smiled changed it to a grin rounding the corners of his mouth. He put his hands upon her, resting his weight on them, trying to get the feel of her into himself again.

Tools, bedrolls, kit, stores, rifles and ammunition had gone. She was picked clean.

" Would you believe it? " Bill said. " They've even siphoned all the petrol out."

The window of the cabin was open, and looking in he saw that nothing had changed, except in the rack above the wiper.

" Snowy, lad," he said, looking across the water, " they've took all your little bits."

" Chum," Snowy said, " I didn't expect anything else."

32

It was after midnight when Max awakened them and they crawled out of the canopy and ran into the dark of the dune watching a crowd of people splashing and trampling through the alders with torches throwing smoke and gold among the branches.

Rusty shouted to them, and they saw him standing in a cart, and behind him flame lit the rolling withers of a drove of white bullocks.

" Take long time," he said. " Everybody come a long way. The cattle's from the mountain."

" Rusty," Snowy said, " I don't know what to say."

" I promise everybody I get a truck for myself, for everybody," said Rusty, looking at the dozens of gathering figures, and more still coming through the brake. " So everybody come. If we get a truck, everybody get some food. Ecco."

" What now? " Max said.

" Now we dig under," Rusty said. " Then we get the animal and pull. In the morning, it's finish."

" Get cracking, lads," said Snowy.

Long-handled spades dug into the bank under Rosie's buried wheels, hollowing the slope, bringing her almost upright. Women carried the sand away in their aprons, others banked and stamped flat a path to the water, and another team filled the channel with stones.

Rusty went from group to group with a quiet word, but none of them seemed to need it. Men and women worked almost silently in darkness lit by blown flame, and when the tyres were solidly on the flat, teamsters brought the bullocks up in pairs and hitched their tackle, driving out along the path to take the strain.

On Rusty's signal the leading teamster cracked his pair over the neck, and they leaned forward, with the pair behind following, and steadily, as though thinking about it, each pair of bullocks thrust, team after team, until all of them, muzzles nearly in the sand, had lifted a black hoof to swing forward in a jingle of power.

But Rosie was in deep, and stubborn about it.

Rusty whistled, and instantly the quiet groups of men and women came running out of the shadow, forming a mass of hands and shoulders in a lift and pull.

A voice called out in high tenor, and a fine voice answered from up front, another replied in lower key, a chorus shouted, and the first voice chanted and the chant went down along the line and swelled, and suddenly stopped. The voice cried out again, in time with the lift and pull, and the teamsters shouted, and singers in the darkness were using their voices with the ease of pipe players, trilling on high notes, slurring to a minor key, all breaking on a sudden note, with only the creak of leather tackle in the pause, bursting in chorus the moment after.

And Rosie was moving.

Little by little, as though enticed by music, she crunched her way across the sand and presently was on the path, making gentle headway of her own. Snowy ran to climb up, taking the wheel with the feeling of having found himself again.

" O.K., Snowy," Rusty laughed. " O.K., O.K."

Max and Bill walked behind the singing crowd, picking their way in the mud, careless of the river that came up to their waists and tugged at their breath, leaving them sopped on the far bank, tender victims of the morning wind.

" I'll be God damned," Max said, listening to the song. " I never saw people like that."

" Ah," Bill said. " They can work when they've a mind to. Of course, they think they're getting something for it. I don't know where he's going to get 'em this other truck, though."

" Brother," Max said, " they're going to have that truck if I have to turn crook and do the rustling."

Rosie bogged a couple of times in deepest shadow of the marsh, and despite Snowy's doting on the wheel she snagged on tree roots hidden along the way, but each time the long-handled shovels piled the black mud and women scooped it up in double handfuls, and whips cracked again and then the song, with brutish muscle weighing and human spirit urging the great machine from inertia, and she moved as though flattered into it, seeming to go faster, easier each time until they reached the embankment under the road.

Snowy got down among a crowd of men and women covered with drying mud, all chopping down alders or else binding the longest withes in bundles, stacking them into a ramp. A pungence of spurting sap and a stench of black water mixed with the sweat of cattle and the smell of human bodies long in the same clothes and wet again in new labour.

" Rusty," he said, " how are all of 'em going to get something to eat? "

" They bring it," Rusty said. " Don't worry."

" O.K.," said Snowy. " We'll get some grub going. I'm starving."

While the ramp went up, he opened the box left behind by the ambulance driver, and built a fire in the shade of a tree up in the quiet of the road.

Bill stayed below with Rusty, watching the play of billhooks in green wood, admiring the dexterity of the binders' hands, that seemed merely to thrust a withe, and it was a knot with ends tucked, solid as a joint in metal.

Max sat apart, watching the scene without seeing it. A sense of hurry was in him. Everything was going on in a life outside this antheap, but he was not of it, and this little section of people made him feel his strangeness by ignoring him; or if he tried to talk to them, smiling, with dark eyes that looked beyond him, answering with a nod or shake of the head, or using a few words in language too thick to be understood. He was taken with a craving to get back to the world of towns and electric light and offices and desks, for this existence made him feel as though his elbow had gone through a window in history, giving him sight and sound of an age that disturbed his sense of order.

Rusty and Bill went up the bank towards the smell of frying sausages. Max caught it and went through the crowd, and came awake to see hunks of bread being handed out to stretching arms from a basket in a cart. He paused, pretending to allow passage for a couple of women, but he was watching the people with the bread. They all went away by themselves, standing against a brake, or sitting on bundles, picking small pieces from the heavy brown dough, putting it in their mouths and holding it between tongue and palate to soak it in saliva, chewing hard, and then swallowing as though the mouthful had gone to nothing. Not one that he could see had anything more to eat, and yet the smell of frying sausages seemed not to affect them more than the twitch of an eye now and again in the direction of Snowy's voice, and a harder pull at the hunk held always on a level with their chins, tucking the free hand under the opposite armpit, looking through the trees with eyes that stared too hard to see anything.

But every now and again there came that turn of eyes towards the fry of meat, no more than a twitch, and always the return, with the slightest move of the body away from it, perhaps in answer to rebuke from a troubled sense of courtesy ancient and delicate as blood.

Snowy held out a toasted slice with the sausage grilled in a tender crackle and a lid full of fried potatoes.

"There y'are, Maxie boy," he said. "In your honour, we ain't having tea today. We're having a go at the coffee, so you'll have to perform. I reckon we've got about enough grub for a couple of days. Ought to do us."

Max made the coffee and ate, watching the others eating, enjoying the fat crisp of fried bread, but he was seeing the brown hunk, and the eyes.

"Say, Rusty," he said, "what kind of chow these people down there getting?"

"They bring it," Rusty said, picking his teeth.

"I saw 'em," Max said. "But what do they get?"

Rusty shrugged.

"What they got," he said.

"Just that lump of gook they're chewing on?" Max asked. "Is that all they have?"

"They like," Rusty said.

"Apart from that," Max said, "what else?"

"What they get," Rusty said. "Better when the harvest come."

Bill wiped his lid with extra care, and looked at the dripping crust.

"Rusty," he said, "I've been meaning to ask you. Are all these from your place? Your neighbours, like?"

" Yes," Rusty said, and folded his arms about his knees as though ready for the lash.

" The same lot we had a bit of trouble with? " Bill asked.

" You don't have no trouble," Rusty said.

Bill put the crust in his mouth and crunched.

" Just shows you," he said.

Max found himself pouring coffee and wishing hard for Rosa, for times came when it seemed that the one sensible thing left to do was go to her, and hide his face in her lap with his arms about her, sicking the world from his mind.

33

Rosie broke through the bulrushes behind the power of thirty oxen, taking the ramp as steadily as though mistress of herself again, and Snowy could have sung. He turned her into the roadway in a chorus of voices and a patter of hands beaten in rhythm, delighting in the touch of her wheel and the sense of being one with her, mightily aware of gratefulness to Rusty.

But when his eye caught the rack above the wiper, a feeling came up inside him like a shaft, seeming to break through the top of his skull, bringing water to his eyes and an ache in the jaw from a clench of teeth bit tight.

A crowd waited for him on the main road where the alders joined a copse of beech, and he turned on to the smooth blue of tarmac with a feeling of complete relief, laughing at the people gathering round the cabin and throwing kisses to the women.

People formed themselves in a long line as far as the pool down in the marsh, and a food tin, the only vessel they had, was passed from hand to hand, given and taken like a chalice up to Rosie, and so she was washed a little at a time, the first splash to liquefy the mud, with men and women on their knees all round and under her, scraping and rubbing bare-handed, and another splash to rinse. Snowy took the can of petrol over to Max, out of the way.

" This is what burns me," Max said. " I'm like a clown at a circus. Standing around while the other guys do all the chores."

Bill worked with the tools Rusty had brought, and between them it seemed that only one mind was at work between pinpoint pupils of grey and brown, watching fingers glowing pink through grease, bending, hooking, twisting in a small wonder of machine surgery.

" All right," Bill said, and stood. " Let's try her. You'll have to take it steady. It's nobbut a botch job."

Snowy poured the tin of petrol into the tank, hearing the thirst hollowing out of her, and at a nod Rusty got the people up in rear. Snowy walked round her, not merely to assure himself that all was well, but to have the pleasure of touching her solidity, to know and convince himself that she was his again and ready for the road.

On the curve as they entered the village Rusty hammered on the cabin roof, but Snowy had already slowed for a barricade of logs across the tarmac, flanked by a quiet crowd of men and women grouping on each side with piles of stones at their feet.

Rusty spoke to a man in the crowd, and the logs were pulled aside by women, lifting from heels planted flat, straight in the leg, easily and without effort. The men looked on, making no move to help.

" What's this in aid of? " Snowy asked.

" The same men," Rusty said. " They make lot of trouble. The people wait if they came back."

" Let's get after 'em," Snowy said.

He knew, as soon as Rosie felt the speed, that extra repairs were needed before he could do any chasing, but knowing it made him angrier. The streets were quiet, but a different quality of quietness to the last town, for here, although upper windows were shuttered, the wood was splintered, most of the doors were gone and shop blinds had been blasted out of shape, lying over the windows in a series of rusted half blinks all the way down a long street bared of rubbish by the wind, but stale, unswept through the seasons.

He turned into the piazza, letting her glide down to the garage, and a small crowd of men looked round, and then ran, some inside, and a few round the back, leaving three bodies on the ground covered with sheets still in sharp crease from folding.

Snowy got down, hearing the people jumping soft-soled from the rear, and went over to the bodies, two, from the boots, grown men, and the other of a barefoot child. He stood, listening to the sounds of a crowd gathering, the whispers, the fleshy thump of feet on stone, a brushing of packed bodies and the sighing of women rattling beads in prayer.

"They shoot the men," Rusty said. "The little boy they run over."

"And they've gone." Snowy listened to the flatness of his voice in flight about the piazza.

Rusty nodded.

More women were hurrying across from the houses to drop on their knees and weep, and men bent over them making soothing sounds and patting their shoulders.

"We'll have to take her right down," Snowy said. "Take us all tomorrow. Suppose you make some coffee, Max?"

"Swell idea, Snow," Max said. "And suppose you take a look in the garage?"

Snowy looked over the heads of the crowd into the darkness beyond the tool benches.

Sunlight touched the colour in her face, tinting the brown suit, and something was sad in the way that she stood, in the set of her head and the bend of her knee, looking out of the window.

She turned and looked at him.

"Snowy," she said, without surprise, and smiling pleasant welcome. "I knew you'd be along."

"Hullo, Miss," he said, looking at her shoulder. "Where's the sparrow?"

"I let it go," she said. "Wasn't needed any more."

34

Snowy looked up at the night sky wondering what to do. He was beaten and he knew it; but though he knew he ought and tried to pretend he did, he felt neither shame nor any misgiving, but rather he was filled with savage want that sent him out into the piazza for a breath of cold air. But blue silence and the dark houses seemed to frame and isolate his feeling and the longing for her.

Somewhere to the north-west, thousands of miles away, he knew that Liz and the children were sleeping. He could see himself walking along the landing, looking in at them, listening to the sounds they made as they slept. At all other times that picture wrenched at something soft inside himself. He imagined the little hands moving in a dream as they always did when Liz and he tiptoed in on the way to bed for a last look at them. He saw Liz lying on her side, one arm bent up with the hand on the pillow and the other flat on the sheets, hearing the nervous pulse of her breath and the gulp when she turned, stretching, sleepily scratching her wrist, grumbling a little, drawing up a knee and letting it fall, settling down in a sigh with her mouth apart, knowing her lips would be cool as when she kissed him in love.

But now the vision came without feeling, as though it had grown too old, had lost vitality through too many hours of wishing.

During the afternoon in the garage the thought of her got in the way of work, making him look at a spanner for a long time until he had to force himself to think what he was doing. Through the smell of oil and petrol her perfume came in thrusts strong as physical pain, and the scent of her body that reached him, standing aside for her to pass into the house, reminding him of intimacies guessed at by other experience, stormed in his mind, in almost frantic bitterness of want, until he went to look at himself in the glass, and ask himself, soberly, if he were sane, or if perhaps without knowing he had not quietly gone mad.

But he appeared the same, and his work was thoroughly if slowly done, and the others treated him in a normal manner, yet he was surprised to find himself answering them as sensibly as ever, even with the torment swelling inside him.

Again and again he called at shame and felt its burn at the back of his mind, but he knew it was there only because he willed it, feeling that he should, more as a comfort in misery than from any desire to retrieve himself. He wanted to keep the feeling, but he also wanted to feel guilty about it, as though feeling shame for the way he was treating Liz were healthier, more respectable, than forgetting her altogether.

He heard a door open behind him, and turned, hoping she had come to find him, praying she had not, but in disappointment he saw Max looking about.

" Hey, Snow," he called, " come on in. Chow's ready."

" Not yet, ta, Maxie," he said. " I'll stay here with Rosie. She's not going out of my sight any more."

" O.K.," Max said, satisfied. " I'll bring it out."

He went back into the house Rusty had got for lodging, and felt his way through the passage to the room at the end. Bill was cooking in the light of a piece of burning waste floating in a pot of oil. Rusty lay on the floor with his head on Snowy's blouse, and Bill's blouse over him, for though the fire gave warmth there were no windows and the backdoor was gone.

" He's going to eat out there," he said. " Keeping track of Rosie."

" Ah," Bill said. " Well, give our lass a shout, will you? "

Max put his head into the passage.

" Oh, lady! " he yodelled. " Come and get it."

He heard the door rattle open.

" Here I come," she said. " If I don't break a leg trying."

She fumbled along the wall and entered the room, frowning to accustom her eyes.

" My," she said. " You got this fixed quick enough. I just got the dust out of mine. Where're you boys going to sleep tonight? "

Bill pointed to Rusty.

" Down there, Miss," he said. " We'll bank the fire. Best we can do."

" There's no fireplace in my room," she said. " Mind if I come in, too ? "

" Pleasure, Miss," Bill said. " Floor's got the same give all over."

Max sat on the window-ledge, leaving her the box. He felt sorry for her, in the loss of her bag and the unguessed happening at the camp, but unwilling to show it in case she should take it as acknowledgment that he had been wrong to take a drink. He was aware of the feeling between herself and Snowy, though it was not something to be seen. She was still as kindly, as cool, as obviously a woman used to her own way and her own manner of living, a different kind of woman, so much so that near her, despite her friendliness, he felt he had a chimney growing out of one ear and his shoes on back to front.

The thought of making love to her as a proposition had never occurred, but now there appeared something in her attitude, not by any means an invitation, but certainly a softening that roused curiosity. Thinking of it, Snowy was different, too. The old straight-grain quality was there still, the smile and the comical light in the eye, but he seemed to have changed, perhaps a quality in the voice, or a laze in the harshness of his normal manner.

She felt his silence, and, though she gave no sign, she was wondering how to patch the trouble, but beyond apology already made there was little to be done and she shrugged it away, sorry that in the misery of a wrecked village in back of beyond, among three people speaking the same language in one small room, two of them must be silent in a matter of pique.

" Like a bunch of kids," she said, out loud.

Max started to laugh.

" O.K., lady," he said. " For my money too."

" One supper, a gent," Bill said. " Take it out while it's hot, will you, chum? "

" For Snowy? " She took the lid from Bill. " I haven't done a thing all afternoon. Why's he out there ? You wouldn't eat with us the other night. Is it his turn tonight? "

" He's taking care of Rosie, Miss," Bill said. " Careful lad, is our Snowy."

She went out in the square, going towards the garage, and then, in a lull in the evening wind, heard him walking over in the shadow. She watched for a moment, feeling the lid burning her fingers. His hands were in his shorts, and his head was bent, as though he were looking at his knees in their slow pacing, and the colour of legs, forearms and head were darker than the twill, even darker than the night.

"Snowy," she called, "here's your supper."

He seemed to fling himself towards her, and then check.

"Oh," he said. "Thanks, Miss. You shouldn't have bothered."

"Nonsense," she said. "Where'll you have it? On the fountain?"

"In the garage, Miss," he said.

"That where you'll sleep?" she asked.

"Shan't sleep much tonight, Miss," he said. "I've got about fifty of 'em sleeping all round the place. I hope that lot comes back. I'll pay 'em for everybody."

"If only they hadn't taken my bag," she said. "You don't know how lonesome you can be until you haven't even got a handkerchief."

"Couldn't Rusty get you one?" Snowy turned, as though to go and find out.

"Look," she said, and took his arm. "I won't listen to anything about anybody as good as that. You're supposed to eat this while it's hot. Then I'll bring you out some coffee."

"Ta, Miss," he said, with the lid in his hands.

They looked at each other and he felt her fingers warm on his forearm, and the soft pressure tickling upwards to the elbow and above, watching the darkness of her eyes fixed always on his, tempted to throw the plate aside and break her with a kiss. But the hand dropped away and his arm was itching and she was hurrying back across the piazza.

He sat on the cabin step, listening to her footsteps, sniffling, trying to retain a breath of her. Having to chew seemed out of keeping with thought of her, and yet, because she had brought it, there seemed something, perhaps a fondness, added to taste.

Groups of men began padding across in the dark. When the crowd was still, he took them in dozens, placing them all round the garage, with a stronger section on the barricade across the highway. All of them had axes or pitchforks, but only two had shotguns, both old men with tall black hats pulled down over their ears, sucking empty pipes. He tried to borrow a gun, but they stood shaking white moustaches in the darkness, unyielding.

He found her waiting with the coffee when he got back.

"I've been trying to get a gun off these blokes," he said. "But they don't seem to know what I'm talking about."

"You're lucky," she said. "They're probably using home-made shot. Any place you hide it'll catch up on you. Here's your coffee."

"Thanks," he said. "Where you going to sleep?"

"In the kitchen along with the boys," she said. "I'm a toughie."

"I'd say sleep in the cabin, except I don't want you in a scrap if there's going to be one." He snapped his fingers. "All right, Miss. Have the cushions out of her. Easy."

"What about you?" she asked.

"I'm all right, Miss," he said. "Here we are."

He pulled out the heavy cushioning and hoisted it on his shoulder, following her over to the house. The passage was dark, and he waited while she struck a match, watching her silhouette going down to the kitchen door.

The match went out.

In darkness he heard the door open, and a minor trumpeting of tired men before she shut it, quietly, and waited a while, and then walked slowly back, opening another door near him.

"That's out," she said. "I can't wake them. In here'll do."

He put the cushions down and looked at the bare room, moon-lit in pale squares across the stone floor from a window with most of the panes gone.

"It's going to be cold," he said. "I'll go and get a fire going. What're you going to put over you?"

She pointed to a bundle.

"Rusty borrowed something, bless him," she said. "I don't mind things crawling about. You can always take a slap at them. I wish I had my pyjamas, that's all. I can't sleep in my clothes."

"I'll get the fire," he said, and quietly let himself out of the house.

He put layers of bark soaked in petrol over layers of coke ash in a charcoal burner and set it on fire. When the blaze went, he piled coke and bark, lifted it in tongs and took it over to the house.

She was on the cushions, wrapped, a dark shape when he went in, and he heard the move of her lifted head as he put the burner under the window. He stood back, watching the red glow spreading, feeling the heat, surprised to find that now he was near her the longing had passed, and in its place a wish to protect and comfort her.

Alertness came with a sound of voices outside.

He went for the door.

" Snowy," she called, in a whisper, " tell me what it is. Come back."

He ran out, and across to the garage, full into a small crowd.

" Now then," he called, " what's the lark? "

The men stood aside, showing him three coffins, pale in the darkness, and he smelt new wood. He led them round the building to the white outlines, standing in the breathy silence while they were wrapped one by one and taken away.

The cortège spread out through the cold light, in long shadows that crept across the housefronts, and the coffins glowed silver among them until they turned and were gone.

He looked about at a sound, and fear came, for quiet groups had gathered in the dark to watch bareheaded and he knew their eyes were on him.

But one old man still knelt. Snowy went over to him, feeling the life of the body warm under his hands, and gently pulled him upright.

" What's up, Dad? " he said. " One of 'em yours, was he? "

But the old man stayed quietly inside himself, keeping his head bowed, with hands pressed under his chin as in prayer, and though Snowy tried to see his face the head was too tightly bent, and the body too frail for struggle. Someone came out of the dark and took him away, and the groups passed farther and farther off until sound of their going was part of the night.

Presently he stood alone in the piazza, with the moon blue on the housefronts and rows of black windows, watching light creep across the muscles of the broken god in the fountain.

Except to sleep there was no good reason why he should go back to the house. He looked at it, imagining her inside that room, lying on the cushions with her clothes off, hearing her tell him to come back, but the feeling for her seemed to have gone, with his feeling for Liz, into a lost place, leaving him without desire except to sleep and be out of knowing.

He wondered why he should tremble for her one moment and dismiss her the next. But it seemed too mixed, and he was too sore, too tired to care.

He went back to Rosie. Her tailboard was down, but the floor inside was ribbed in steel, riveted, jagged with hard usage. The cabin seat was a sharp metal slatting, useless without the cushion. There was no straw, or shavings, or indeed anything except bare boards, or the stone of the street, and so he sat down on the stones, feeling naked, looking at the piazza from a new level and finding something silly in it.

He lay down, frowning at chill piercing through shirt and shorts, but happy to suffer, hoping perhaps that even Liz might forgive him if he suffered enough.

Yet, tired though he was, sleep was no match for the cold stone, and presently he got up, wide awake and dry in the eye, and went back to sit on Rosie's step.

35

If he slept at all, or if he only closed his eyes, he never knew, but he was back in the night with a warm hand squeezing his neck, and the rest of him frozen, in knotted knees and feet perhaps down there beyond a drowsy teasing.

" You booby," she was saying. " You big donkey. I don't know what I could do to you. I ought to leave you here and let you die of cold. Put your arm around me now. Don't let's have any more nonsense about this."

" I'm all right, Miss," he said, and tried to stand, but his feet were a long way down, and his leg had gone to laughing gristle.

" This way home," she said, holding his hand around her neck, pacing in time with his limp, surprised at his weight and the distance her arm had to go to span his waist. " I don't know what comes over you men. There am I waiting for you to come back and tell me what happened, and you're over here snoring like a hog."

He felt ashamed to be resting his weight on her, but when the blood was back in his leg he still kept an arm about her neck, feeling the shoulder muscle swell as she took fresh grip on his wrist. They went into the dark passage, and she pushed aside the door. Heat, and a faint perfume came at him, and as she stood close to shut the door the smell of her hair was rich about her and he realized it was unbound to her waist.

" Now," she whispered. " Get those shoes off, and lie down here. There's plenty of room."

" I'm being a lot of trouble," he said, making no move.

She took him by the arm and backed him against the cushion, pushing him so that he sat.

" Are you being coy, or just un-cooperative? " she asked. " The first time I invite a man to share the pillow, and all I get is resistance. Is it me, or the night? "

" No, Miss," he said, hearing the sigh of peeled garments, trying to unpick a knot in laces crusted with mud, " it ain't the night."

" Fine," she said, with a gesture of white arms in the darkness. " And look, would you like to make that Clarissa, or something, or just plain Mary Ann? That Miss thing's gone far enough."

" All right, darling," he said, but it fell from his mouth like a rock.

" Not that, either." She turned over, putting her arms under the blanket and he felt the movement of her legs burrowing behind him. He lay back, ashamed, feeling his heart thumping.

" I'm sorry," he said.

" Don't worry about it," she said, indifferently. " Good night."

He picked nervously at the edge of the cover and lifted it to slide under, feeling against his shoulders the roughness of the blanket she was lying in. With more confidence since they were not to touch, he lay down, feeling her warmth; and warming to her, he lay back, relaxing in a deep breath as tiredness crowded in, pulling at his eyes.

But suddenly his mind was clear.

The way to tell was by that funny shake now and again, and then waiting for breath, and again that shake, and a long breath with a little break in it, while the tears wet the pillow, the quiet tears that are saltiest.

She was crying, and he knew, because Liz cried quietly, too.

He became awake, as though he had never been tired, and his body was alive with no trace of fatigue. Staring into the grille of the window he wondered how to console her, fighting desire to turn upon her and put his arms about her, but it seemed too much of an advantage to take in her weakness, and he forced the notion away.

But she felt his wakefulness, almost hearing the snap of his eyes in the darkness.

" Oh, Snowy," she said, soft as a drawn breath, " in this wretched little place, with all this going on, and God knows what amount of it outside. Just pushed together in a dirty little room and we act like fools. And I'm sorry. After you've been so kind."

" Never mind, Miss," he said. " It's nice and warm. And it's somewhere to sleep, ain't it? "

" Yes," she said. " Somewhere. But wouldn't it be happier if we felt better about it? "

" Depends what suits you," Snowy said. " Don't it? "

" Does it suit you? " she asked.

" Certainly," he said. " But what about your husband? "

" I'm thinking about us," she said. " There isn't any roomful of people here."

" Just the same if there was," he said, and turned to her. " I wouldn't feel no different. I reckon you're wonderful. You're beautiful. You're a lot of words I can't get out properly. I can't say 'em, but I can feel 'em, though."

The voice playing touch with a whisper was not one she recognized, for its normal confidence was gone, with challenge in its place, as though he were daring himself to say things he had rather hide.

She lay still, waiting, and tears were drying, and thin fingers were alive at the edges of her spine making her want to stretch.

" What d'you suppose your wife would say if she heard you say that? " she asked, pleased at the restraint in her tone.

" She'd murder me," he said. " Can't say I blame her. If I

caught her with somebody, I'd do the pair of 'em. And burn the place on top of 'em, an' all."

" So it's one law for you? " she said.

"Tain't that, Miss." Snowy wished hugely for a cigarette. " I know when I'm doing wrong."

" Just what exactly would you say was wrong about this? " she asked.

" Well," he said, " if you look at it like that, nothing much, I suppose."

" You've been closer to other women in any crowd," she said.

" I wasn't feeling about them like this," Snowy said.

" So it's not entirely situation," she said. " Is your conscience bothering you? Because don't let it. It isn't even going to get the wrapper crumpled. Good night."

They felt the coldness come between them, felt it from their minds outwards, felt the heat in their bodies cooling, and the lines in their faces straightening, and their limbs growing inert, as though another body lay cold between them, shapeless, without weight or substance, yet real as ice.

Silence grew in the room, a blossom that might wither at a sound, and neither moved, barely breathing, restricting passage of air through nostrils that might whistle.

Then he felt despair at loss of a dream almost realized, of the wish nearly fulfilled, and struggled to assert himself against her, angry that she should be superior and yet respecting that strength.

" Never mind," he said, loudly, perhaps to convince himself. " I shouldn't have opened me trap at all. And if I did, I ought to have said I didn't care. That's what gets me. I don't even know me own feelings. I don't know what to think."

" Suppose you go to sleep? " The words came coldly again. She felt disgust at herself, at him, at the fact of having to live at all, but stubbornness would not allow a move away from him. It had to be, she thought, in or out of squalor, brutal or not, there could be no release, except the mundane compulsion of getting up in the morning. But still, despite his foreignness, there was gratitude. " You must be terribly tired. And you've got a long day tomorrow."

" It's all right, Miss. I'm happy," he said, and sat up, and then felt easy again, for with one movement made, all movement was possible, and muscle relaxed, allowing warmth to do its work.

"It's time," she said. "You're not happy very often, are you? I watched you while you were driving. And by the way, I wanted to tell you how sorry I was they stole your photographs."

"Thank you, Miss," he said. "I was sorry about your husband."

"Don't be." She dragged it out in weariness, as though to herself or the ceiling. "I've been playing Miss Muffet a little too long."

"Ah," he said. "Coming a bit rough on you?"

He felt her laughing.

"I just woke up," she said. "In just one little second I was thinking something else that I'd never have thought possible the moment before. The longer I live the more I'm amazed."

"It's all in the game," he said, wondering what she was talking about. "Feeling rotten about it?"

She wanted time to reply. The strength was back in his voice and his shoulders looked big against the light, solid, and that solid quality in some way weakened her will.

"Oh, darn it," she said, near hotter tears. "I don't know. I think it's better if you get hurt a lot all at once. Then it's too much, and too soon. You don't get time to feel it all. So you just say the hell with it, and go on your way."

"Never mind, matey," he said. "Don't let it get you down."

"Lie back there," she said. "Get some rest. You're going to be so tired."

He lay back and felt the warmth of her arm under his neck, and shock might have brought him upright again but her hand was on his shoulder.

"Sleep," she soothed. "Don't you like my arm there?"

"Afraid of hurting you," he said.

He heard the slight crackle of her smile.

"Snowy," she said. "Please. You're not that shy, are you?"

"I don't know, Miss," he said. "I've sort of got out of the way of it somehow."

"Out of the way of what?" she asked.

"Well," he said, "I don't know how to put it. Treating people, I suppose. Talking to 'em. Specially to you."

She was warned by his tone, but beyond an excitement she was trying to mute she was curious about the man, about his manner of thinking, finding something that inspired new tenderness in the rough quality that could be gentle, in the ungroomed strength of his black bulk outlined against the pale flooring.

" What's so different about me? " she asked, wondering whether she dare curl her fingers in his hair rather as she might with a pet dog. " I'm just like anybody else."

He was thankful for the darkness. That lazy tone he knew from Liz, when she was pretending to be practical, and had her mind on something else.

" I don't know it's so different," he said. " I don't know what to make of it. Sounds as if I was talking a load of toffee, don't it? "

" Tell me," she said.

" It's the smell of you," he said. " And you're so little. You're like Liz."

" Nice to hear," she said in the same tone. " But if that's so, what's so difficult about talking to me? "

In a sudden movement that was frightening he got up on an elbow, facing her.

" Tell you the truth," he said, " you're a bit too posh. I can't seem to get round it somehow."

" Posh," she said. " High-class. But that's idiotic. What's posh got to do with it? "

" Christ knows." He lay back as though all the words had been said. " I've got all sort of mixed up inside meself. I don't know where I am. There seems like something wrong somewhere, but I don't know what. Not Liz. Although, of course, she comes into it."

" Poor Liz," she said. " She's lonesome, too. How long have you been away from her? "

" Just over four years, Miss," he said.

She was surprised at the matter-of-factness in his voice, as though it were accepted in the same way as the door of a house.

" How does Liz feel about it? " she asked.

" Oh, I don't know," he said. " She don't say much. 'Sides, she's got the two girls. They keep her company, I suppose."

She had an instant picture of two little girls keeping their mother company, and then she sensed the hours going by after they were in bed, the knitting, and sewing, and the staring.

" How about you? " She moved her arm away and folded her hands. " Don't you ever get so you could yell? "

" Me, Miss? " The tone was cool with wonder. " What about? "

" About Liz," she said, and realized she was at the spring of a trap she had made for herself, led, almost without will, by nearness, and voice, and the silence of a dark room.

" I feel like getting drunk sometimes, Miss," he said. " But it don't do no good. I reckon I've got used to thinking about her. Thinking and wishing and never getting nowhere. I've either forgotten, else I've gone barmy."

She heard the lack of candour, the struggle to say something that might sound more palatable than fact, but the flotsam of hours of torment was in his voice, and perhaps it was sorrow for Liz sitting alone, or pity for him in need of her, but a quick flame of tears shook her, and she pressed her palms to her face praying for strength to control a ragged breath, and then it burst from her, and she turned from him and wept, reviling herself and yet helpless.

A shot cracked and another, a loud burst, and a clatter of metal, more shots and somebody was shouting and an engine spat and woke in a shudder.

Snowy threw the blanket off and grabbed his boots, a grey and black scarecrow of loose shirt-tails and tousled hair hopping on one foot to the door, tying a lace anyhow, thrusting on the other boot, slop-footing down the corridor and into the piazza.

He was just in time to see Rosie in tow behind another truck, and then she turned the corner and was gone, and shouting men were following.

Weak, sick, he stood looking.

Bill ran up behind him.

" That you, Snowy? " he said, in breathless unbelief. " Surely to God ye've never let 'em get her again? "

" Ought to shoot me bloody self," said Snowy. " Be out of it, and better off."

36

Adela Castelfalcone del Colavolpe tried to persuade herself that she really was walking of her own accord up a mountain behind a long file of peasants led by two soldiers, and followed by another, a silent man with grey hair and a glower she could feel between her shoulder blades.

Morning was up, in a massing blue mackerelled with puffs and tails of white all edged bright orange, and cold, for the sun was on the other side of the mountain. Wind blew the pine needles about her ankles, bringing the odour of tar, reminding her of steaming baths and hot towels, and coffee with a dash of orange petals.

They seemed to have been climbing for hours. When they started she was up front, just behind Snowy, but when they got out of the crowd in the piazza and went through the gardens a gradient loured in darkness and began pulling at tired muscles until pace by pace she fell behind and men were passing her by ones and twos and then in groups, and after them, women, bent-backed and loose-kneed, silent, without a glance for her, and slowly she eased her pace until she was last, and weary, and that was when the man with the spectacles tailed on behind her.

She was too tired to talk, too heavy of eye and head to worry much about anyone, but she felt the glower as she came on him, leaning against a tree with his feet crossed, and resented his lack of greeting until it occurred to her that the look in the grey eye was not recognition but dislike.

It had been obvious down in the piazza that they thought of her as a siren, if not worse, before the expedition started, for when she talked to Rusty he pretended not to hear, and Max had grinned at her, shaking his head, chirruping, making her wish she had the energy to hate him. This lumpy little man with spectacles had stood apart, arms folded, staring across the piazza resting on one hip, a leaden Napoleon, busy with a parade of cheap ill-will.

But thought of Snowy made her feel old and useless. Watching him run, trying to find her clothes in the dark, listening to the motors going away and the shouts, and the kitchen door bursting open and more running and shouting, and then having to dress, tortured by what might have happened to him, blaming herself for bringing him in the room at all, pitying him and sorry for her part in it, she felt snared, with no hope of struggling free, and each new incident another tightening, making escape more difficult.

It was out of the question to stay in the village, for she feared the peasants. The attitude of those she met on arrival had frightened her, and only the raid and the loss of her belongings and sanctuary in Rusty's garage had saved her, she thought, from attack.

Wherever she went, it seemed, on any level, there were enemies, and she felt too tired of living to want to fight back, for there seemed so little left to fight for, and the loss of personal belongings, even of chastity, seemed small matters compared with the hunger of thousands.

But out of it all there sprang this feeling of responsibility for Snowy, and a desire to retrieve pride by helping him.

So, here she was, footing it in shoes that wrecked her, up a mountainside in the early hours of morning, followed by a dreary little gnome in spectacles with a stare that seemed to be burning a hole in the back of her suit.

"Look," she said, "is there any reason for you to be following me?"

"I'd not like to see you tore limb from limb," Bill said. "Snowy got worried about you."

"Why should he?" Delight was in her, but she hid it. "I'm safe enough."

"Then why bother coming all the way up here?" he asked. "You know damn well they were only waiting on you down there."

"Nothing of the sort," she said.

"They know all about you," he said, as much to himself as to her. "D'ye think ye weren't seen leading him up the garden when ye thought everybody were down to it? D'ye think them blokes with Rusty are all daft, or something?"

"He had to have some place to sleep," she said, loath to argue, and yet forced to protect herself. "He didn't even get that."

" How can you be so barefaced? " He stopped and looked at her. " What's the use in messing about with the poor bloke? Ye know he's a wife and kids? "

" That has nothing to do with it," she said, and walked on.

" Of course it hasn't, for such as you," Bill called. " Ye think y'own the earth so you do as you like. Jezebel, that's what you are. A Jezebel, and y'ought to feel downright ashamed of yourself for leading a lad astray."

" Oh, go to hell," she said, angry at herself for challenging embarrassment, and yet amazed at gnomic fervour.

" And you call yourself a lady." The voice in rear dropped to levels baffling chords and breath, ending in a bubbling gulp.

Walking through tussocks spotted with flowering plants under winding ways already brightening in the sun, she found herself ready to give up, and sit down quietly, rest a little and make peaceful way back to the main road and trust to luck. She felt hot, in need of a bath, miserable to the point of tears, drenched in self-hate, and angry for something beyond reach of expression.

She stood still, facing the crest of the mountain not far above, where the figures of men and women were still outlined against the blue.

By turning her back she could leave them all to their several little ways, caring nothing for their opinions, forgetting them and their squalors, and return to the normalcy of her own way.

But his face lay between her and forgetfulness, the shame in his eyes, the pouched mouth, and the voice, a semitone, and that merely for yes or no. Never had she seen disgrace accepted as though it were a right, to be worn publicly as part of penance. At first she thought him joking, and, finding he was not, felt scorn rising against unbelief.

" But, Snowy," she heard herself saying, " what could you have done against a whole bunch of them, armed like that? It's not your fault? I'm thankful you weren't anywhere around. You might be dead this very minute."

" Wish I was," he said in that shell of a whisper. " I ought to be, I let 'em down."

She could only look at him in the darkness, wondering what to say to him, knowing herself helpless against the dictates of an upbringing beyond her knowledge and not to be criticized within the realm of speech. But that helplessness was only part of her responsibility, and she was unwilling that he should bear the whole blame, and thus she had taken her place when the expedition set off, determined that whatever happened she would have a part.

" Aren't tha' feeling too ripe? " The gnome was at her side. " Come over queer, have ye? Perhaps it's the height. We're up a good way here."

" I was just wondering if I wanted to," she said, watching the grey eyes steady on hers.

" Here," Bill said, for there was something of Pet in her, when she looked up a stairway. " Put your arm round me neck."

She felt an arm about her waist, and remembered a fist knuckling bone, and lumpy muscles fired in blue, and then she was lifted and carried as though she were a child. She laughed, despite all, with open mouth up at the green flails of the pines, blind with sunlight on teary eyes.

" No, no," she said. " I can walk. Please."

He put her down, and she kept a hand on his shoulder.

" Sorry," he said. " It'd be no trouble."

" I'm going to be all right," she said. " But, would you tell me? What happens the other side? "

" We find Rosie," he said. " The wagon. She won't go too far as she is. I'm betting she'll leave the road. Same trouble as last time, only worse."

" So we're short-cutting? " she asked, starting to climb. " Then what? "

" It's to be hoped we catch the blokes 't took her," Bill said. " She's worth a lot of money to 'em. They hid her before, but I doubt they'll have t'chance to do it again. She'll likely kill a couple of 'em this time, I do hope."

Bill was surprised at the change in her.

Snowy had looked round as if he had just remembered she was alive, but she had fallen back a long time by then.

" Where's she gone? " he asked.

Nobody had answered.

" Bill, mate," he said. " Go back and look after her, will you? I don't want her knocked about. I wouldn't trust none of this lot."

"Could you blame 'em?" Max had asked. "Outside of brothels, they don't go for whores, either."

"Listen," Snowy said. "I didn't even have me clothes off. Any surprise to you? Any of you? Now pipe down. Look after her, Bill."

Watching her coming up the slope had been an experience.

The mountain went down sheer into morning mist lit red by the sun, and the ground stared with white eyes of opening flowers among a black interlace of pines.

She came up slowly, each step an effort, carrying her hat in one hand, resting the other on the slung handbag looking as though she might have come straight from a town at home in the brown suit and silk stockings and shoes polished bright by the whisking needles. The hair was parted in a clear white line, smooth on her head in a bun at the back, but sight of her face almost stopped his breath, for it seemed impossible that a woman as clear in the eye and slim, chilled in higher colour by the wind, could be bent on ruining a man like Snowy.

But the way she gave him back look for look with one hand on her hip, and then turned with her nose in the air to go on, was all he needed for proof.

Now he was not so sure.

The lightness of her, the softness he felt through his forearms, that laugh near his face that rang true as sound metal to him, and the smell of her as much as all, swung his mind away into doubt.

"Have you any idea who these people are?" she asked.

"The blokes as pinched Rosie?" He shook his head. "Nay, we've not. But they'll have some idea who we are if ever we get our hooks on 'em."

"Probably some kind of smuggling gang," she said.

"It'd not surprise me," said Bill. "They're very welcome. They'll get bloody smugglers when we catch 'em."

"You're fairly confident," she said.

"No use being much else, is there?" Bill wiped the sweat away with his shirt-sleeve. "We can't go back without her."

"That why Snowy's so upset?" she asked, as offhand as she could make it.

" Not altogether, Miss," he said. " Twice in a couple of days is bad enough, but he was supposed to be waiting on 'em the second time. Had half the town doing sentry. Then they saw what happened, so they didn't bother any more, and most of 'em went home."

" You mean," she was frowning, " when I went to get him? "

" That's it," Bill said. " They all thought it were a match, and they all dropped tools. And, see, Snowy thinks he's shown us up in front of the whole town. So he has."

" But they were armed, and there were lots of them ! " she said. " I can't see it's such a terrible crime."

" Perhaps not," Bill said. " Weren't you the one as give poor old Max a mouthful about disgracing Uncle Sam, or some such? "

" Oh, now, please," she said.

" Then ye've to remember Snowy's Eighth Army," said Bill. " And Rosie came from Alamein. And that's different."

They were up on the crest among rocks, and pines that bent away from the wind, following a path between boulders. A line of peaks stuck blue out of mist miles away, and mist was rolling just below, covering everything.

" Just have to watch out for tracks, that's all," Bill said. " But them bare feet of theirs won't leave many. Funny thing, last time I were up in t' clouds wi' a lass, she were a Yankee, too."

" That I have to hear," she said, " from the beginning."

" She were a nurse on a plane," Bill said. " The Wichita some-fine-thing-or-other. I'll never forget her. We was boiling hot, what with plaster and blankets, but her hands was cold as dabs. Very quiet, she was. Spoke like you, an' all."

" I'm glad," she said. " Did you get her name? "

" Nay," Bill said. " I never. I've always been sorry. I bet she thought I were a bloke as never said a Thank You in me life. I never said it because I damn well couldn't. It's worried me, that has."

" She was used to it, I expect," she said. " Everyday affair."

" I don't give a damn what's everyday." Bill was watching tracks across the plough under vapour. " I'm just saying it's worried me. I wanted to say Thank You Very Much to her, and I couldn't. She even smoked me cigarette for me. Put it in me mouth and took it out again. And she wiped the sweat off me face. She was lovely, was that nurse. Ye'll never put me against Americans after that."

"You'll be making your wife jealous," she said.

"She knows," Bill said. "Tell you the truth, that were her only grouse, that I'd noticed how nice she smelt. So I went and chucked away nigh on three months' pay on a bottle of scent for her. She's saving it till I get home."

"Been married long?" She was wondering what sort of a woman could live with a muscular gnome.

"Five years," he said. "If I'd had any sense, it'd been ten."

"You like it?" she asked. "You're one of the few."

"I've one of the few wives, too," he said. "I don't reckon any man's a man till he's a wife and home of his own. There's nowt in this wide world like putting your own key in your own front door, and shutting the damn thing behind you, and saying to yourself, Our lad's home, in his own home, and damn the lot of you."

"I wonder how many had time to think of that," she said, and pointed. "Isn't that Snowy waving down there?"

"We've done this job in," Snowy called, when they were nearing the road. "They've got her craned up."

"They went to a bit of trouble, then," Bill said. "They meant to have her."

"Where does that put us?" she asked.

"Middle of Italy," Snowy said. "In the road. No transport. No grub. No money."

"I can fix the last one," she said. "How far to the nearest town?"

"Sixty or seventy miles," Snowy said. "We'd done better if we'd stayed at Rusty's place and waited for the boys."

"You wouldn't have felt so good," she said. "Where do we go from here? Back?"

Snowy shook his head.

Despite the sense of loss and sequent disgrace, pride was alive in him that not many hours ago her arm had been under his head, and looking at her fresh shapeliness he felt want grown again, stronger than all other feeling, turning away, fearing to show it.

"Straight on," he said. "Bound to meet something. It's these people I'm worried about."

A crowd sat along the parapet of the road, silent, looking for the most part down at the tarmac with their hands in their laps, and something of the very tree of pathos grew in the bend of their heads.

"They'll just have to go home," she said.

"They won't go." Snowy pointed to Rusty, farther down the road. "He's spoke to 'em till he's giddy. They won't take no notice. They're coming with us till we find Rosie. Then we all set about this mob. That's their idea."

"Have we any idea who the mob is?" she asked. "Might be a help."

"Deserters," Snowy said. "That's all we know. Ours, yours, everybody's. They've been a nuisance down here for a long time. Now they're going to shift 'em."

She heard the depth of sympathy in his voice, not so much perhaps for the problems that worried him, but for her, she was sure, and her part in them, that perhaps was becoming confused in his mind with the difficulty in their relationship, and she felt warmed blood and her hands shook, and she was forced to a deep breath, and a quick turn of the head.

"I'll help all I can," she said.

"But you still don't talk the lingo?" he asked.

"From now on," she said, "I'll speak better lingo than anybody. And faster. And I'll get results."

"Why didn't you want to before?" The ease, the smile, the quiet almost intimate approach made her feel as though she might be married again. "Feeling lazy?"

"Not lazy," she said. "Just playing a mite safe. I wanted to get down to that camp in one piece. Now I don't care any more. I have protection, even from anti-royalists."

"Like to see anybody touch you, that's all," he said. "You a royalist?"

She shrugged.

"I don't know," she said. "You get to a pitch when you just don't know what you are, or even who you are. It doesn't seem worth it any more. Any of it. Are you a royalist?"

"'Course." He pointed to the plastic badge in his beret.

" Got it right atop of me head, ducky. Take some shifting, too. But why would they go for you? "

" Because I'm posh, I suppose," she said. " Your word."

" The only one." He turned away, and walked uncertainly for a moment, and then with purpose, down towards Rusty. " Let's get going, Rusty boy."

As though his move were a signal, everyone got up and walked in groups, silent, in a slap of bare feet that emphasized the squeak of hobnails.

Somebody shouted up front and the crowd cleared in a crabby quickness for the sides, some jumping the parapet, others pulling themselves up the banks, leaving a stretch of tarmac glossed in sunlight, shadowed partly by a green overhang of trees. Snowy ran out in the middle of the road, waving his arms, tall, lean, brown-limbed in pale twill, but she stood looking at him, too surprised to move.

He dropped his arms and walked down to her.

" There's a lorry coming," he said. " Get in the side. It might be them."

He took her by the arm, and she wondered at her lack of will, walking to the shadow of a tree rough with white blossom, standing in the cool beside him, feeling the heat of him, knowing his strength, inclined to rueful laughter and yet careless, and still wondering why one man out of tens of thousands could upset her to a point where she could laugh at herself, and yet exult.

" Hold tight," Snowy said. " This is it."

A truck came round the corner ahead, a six-wheeled affair of blue enamel and chromium, making heavy weather of the slope with a coughing of steam from the radiator. It picked up a little speed as the road levelled, and then the sunlight was split by spinning grey rocks flung by the dozen, followed by a crowd of screaming men and women.

The brakes rasped and the truck stopped.

" Well, God feed the flaming ducks," Snowy said, looking at her. " It's old Pa Nincio."

The old man got down from the cabin and held his hands above his head, yelling for peace and quiet. Rusty added a shout or two, and then they talked for a little while.

" There," she said. " You see? Your friend Signora Nincio was worried about you. Rosie went through their place this morning, so she sent him after you. At peril of his life, he says. He really means it."

Snowy went down through the listening crowd, each head raised in interest towards the voices, grateful to them for their readiness to make way.

" What's on? " he asked. " I'll take care of Ma Nincio later. Hullo, Dad."

The old man danced on one leg, grinning, taking him in a strong hug.

" He says he thought you'd been shot," Max said. " He wants to take us in, but he'll have to drop us way outside the village. He's afraid what the gang'll do to him when they hear what happened."

" Let's get aboard," Snowy said. " Couple of hours, there won't be no gang. Tell him we're after 'em."

But the old man let Max say about half a dozen words and then stopped him in a violent display of hands and arms and a flow of words that left him staring.

" Just a moment," she said, pushing from behind Snowy. " Perhaps I can take care of this."

She spoke to old Nincio.

Snowy watched the colour going from the old man's face and his eyes darkening in surprise. The Princess spoke quietly, without flourish or use of hands. Even in the crowd an effect was plain, in the stoppage of all movement and the extra silence, as though people had drawn breath and were holding it.

Old Nincio breathed out in a long ahhh and then began to talk with matching quiet, and the crowd closed on them in a new excitement, for obviously he was pleading, and there seemed agreement in the crowd.

" Snowy," she called. " He says he'll only be helping you to die. He says they're a terrible bunch of people. They've murdered and pillaged round here till everybody's scared out of their wits."

" Just about time somebody turfed 'em out of it, then," Snowy said. " Tell him I've got to get Rosie back, gang or not. And we'll deal with them the same time. All we want is a loan of the bus."

She spoke and the old man listened, ear towards her, hand behind it, nodding every other word, and then looking up at Snowy and back to her.

He lifted his arms and let them fall in a gesture summarizing the fall of reason, but before he could speak the crowd came alive and turned as one, running for the back of the wagon, climbing up the sides, shouting and laughing as on a picnic.

" That's the answer," she said, watching them.

" I don't know where they're getting the strength," he said. " They've had hardly any sleep, and nothing to eat. Live on air round here, do they? "

" No," she said. " They've got children back there across the mountain, and they're hungry. And there's food down the road. And they trust you."

She was watching the bones of a bare foot splay on the hub, taking the weight of a climbing woman pulled up to join the laughter inside.

" Oh, Snowy," she said. " They haven't a soul in the world to turn to. You have to help them. There's nobody else. Please. Please help them."

He bent over her, and lifted her, and held her for a moment.

" You're dog tired yourself," he said. " 'Course I will. Upsi-daisy."

He put her into the cabin with Old Nincio and his son.

" Ask him to slow up when we get outside the village," he said, " just in case there's any of 'em still there."

She nodded.

He climbed on the step where their faces were on a level, and put his head close.

" I could eat you," he said. " Eat you all up."

" I'd want you to," she said, and smiled.

" 'd blimey," he said, and shut the door.

37

Max was worried about the time it was taking to get back, without wanting to be back there all that much, but because of Rosa and the baby and the news of both that might be waiting, and, beneath that, a thought of punishment, perhaps years inside that stockade wire while the child was growing up without him. Rosa was beautiful beyond a dream in a city full of wolves ready to take her away from him, not that he thought she could be tempted, but time was time, and she might feel different about him once she knew he was in prison.

The thought gave him that hurrying feeling, making him want to climb up in the clock of the world and make it go faster. Being with these people hardly felt the same any more, because they were set pieces in a kind of life that he had no right to be in, where Rosa was an alien, and the baby had no place. Even looking at them made him feel out of kilter, as though he were already behind the wire looking at free men through a spider-web of little barbs.

Wherever he looked, those little knots of wire poked in his eyes.

" Snow," he said, " what'll we do about transport to get back? "

" Borrow this," Snowy said. " Don't worry. We'll get you there."

" I wouldn't want to go without finishing this job," Max said. " Don't get me wrong there. But I'm having bad dreams about what's happening."

" About your old lady? " Snowy nodded sympathy. " I know. It's hard luck. And if I was you I wouldn't bother with us. We'll be all right. We'll get you where you want to be, then we'll go and find Rosie."

" You mean you've really made up your mind? " Max thought the voice was a little too light for serious business. " Wouldn't you do a whole lot better if you just went back and told 'em ? You don't know what you're getting into."

" Listen, Maxie," Snowy said. " Old Rosie's had a go at the best Jerry could give her all the way through Africa and here. And then I have to go and lose her to a lot of deserters? What am I? "

" Yeah," Max said. " And what am I ?"

" Ah," Snowy said. " Sorry, chum. But you ain't one of them. You've stretched your leave a bit, that's all. Got a bit of rubber in your pass."

The truck was slowing. Old Nincio shouted out of the side window, and the truck stopped.

" Come on," Snowy said. " Tell 'em all to get off and file up the village to Pa's place. We'll pick 'em up there."

Brown hands dug into dozing men and women, shaking them awake, and Max waited until they were all off, wondering again at the raggedness of them all, the thinness of women's legs and the boniness of their heads.

Snowy was walking ahead with Rusty, and Bill stayed behind to rummage in the toolbox, coming up with the biggest wrench Max ever saw.

" That's a bit better," Bill said. " Now there's a bit of sense in things. There's nowt like a good spanner if there's going to be a scrap."

" I still have the old elaterium." Max patted his pocket. " This is a hell of a note. Right in back of two armies, these guys can raise so much cain. Why don't somebody cut 'em down to size? "

" Don't take on, Maxie lad," Bill said. " We'll have 'em on the benches 'fore they're much older."

The truck started off at his signal, and Max got caught in a cloud of blue smoke from the exhaust, reminding him of the homing traffic jam down there at Third and Forty-second, with the lights just going up on the ad signs and stacks of pulp on the news-stand at the corner. He was on Queensborough Bridge again, the time Rosa and he wanted air and walked back from the staff party the night they got engaged, close together, enjoying their bodies touching, looking over the city, sniffing the river's morning breath, watching the little ships pulling barges full of the straight steel spines of other cities, turning to look across at all Manhattan cocking a stony snook at a sky green as apples, and a million windows throwing gold at the sun.

" Baby," he said, with his arms tight around her, " any time I stop loving you come on right back here and you'll see every one of them God damn things keeled over."

" Sh," she said. " I don't like that kind of talk."

" Maybe not," he said. " But I feel that kind of talk, so why don't I say it? "

" Because I don't want to hear it," she said. " So get to know it."

" Anything you say," he said. " But remember."

" I'll remember," she said. " It was the morning you broke my back on Queensborough."

" I didn't even start," he said. " You really want me to try? "

" No," she said. " Not Until."

" And after Until," he said, " you're going to need splints."

" That's something I always wanted," she said. " Come on. It's early. Or late. I'm due back at the office in a couple of hours. Let's run."

She was off, with her coat caught close to her, and then she was leaning against the rail, holding her side and pulling a face that was so beautiful he wanted to go right down and kiss the toes pink in the caps of her shoes.

" Oh, Max," she was crying. " Oh, honey, I have stitch."

" Yeah," he said. " And I have plenty of other things. So let's take it slow and easy. Else this family's going to fall apart before it even gets together."

He walked into the patio behind Bill and came out of dreams to find a crowd thick in the place, and somewhere the sound of women weeping, and a bumble of men's voices.

Snowy met them in the doorway.

" They've been back here," he said. " They done the youngest boy."

" What's that mean? " Max was shocked at the change in Snowy's face. " Done? "

" Done," Snowy emphasized. " Did for him. Done him in. Made him a job. Killed him. Shot him, having some grub in the kitchen."

" How about the provost department? " Max listened to the weeping. " This is still an army area."

"They won't complain," Snowy said. "She's trying to talk 'em into it now. Old Nincio reckons they'll come back and knock everybody off, coppers, too, and blow everything up. They believe it, and all."

"If they have that much respect for the cops," Max said, "what do we do?"

Snowy stared.

"What d'you mean, do?" he said. "Go after 'em, of course."

They went through the restaurant, pushing through the smells of a crowd of peasants, and into the broadcloth of villagers strung along the corridor, to the big kitchen, and as the door swung open they caught the hard monody of women's voices among lit candles and a waft of incense, and the voice of a priest, kneeling beside a draped valance, reading from a book.

Mother Nincio looked at Snowy through the flame of a candle with no sign of feeling except a softening about the lines of the face, at the temples, that might even have been humus of a smile, as though she were telling him that a lot of people were making a noise because they thought they must from habit, but she was not, because now she had discovered that silence is the pith of grief.

The men were arguing with the Princess in the chimney corner. The eldest Nincio girl was tying a black cravat about her father's collar, trying to see the knot through her tears. He was listening to the arguments with his eyes closed, hands over the arms of the chair, shaking his head from time to time as though he understood nothing, and each time his daughter dropped the ribbon ends and took his face in her bosom, and then released him, and went back to the knot.

"Shan't do a lot here," Snowy said. "Let's get out of it. Don't half make a meal of it, don't they?"

"That's what it is," Max said. "Three times are important, that's birth, marriage and death. Each one's a meal."

The Princess came across, making way through the women threading flowers into long garlands, meeting Snowy at the door.

"Wait till the priest's finished here," she said. "I believe I've got them to want to chase them. But they're so afraid. They're cowed."

"What time did Rosie come in?" Snowy asked.

" Two or three hours ago," she said. " They could only go very slowly, and they took the other truck to help out. That was when this poor kid went out and told them to leave it alone. Then they came in here and shot him."

" They don't know who they are? " Snowy looked across at Ma Nincio quietly sitting there. " If she knows, she'll tell you."

" They know plenty if I can get them to talk," she said. " And I regret to tell you they're mostly, or so they say, in British uniform."

" Jail birds," Snowy said. " What I thought. Tell 'em not to bother about making up their minds. We're taking this wagon, with all the volunteers as want to come, and we're off after 'em. Right, Maxie? "

" Right," Max said.

There was no change in her face, whitish in that light, with deeper lines about her mouth, but her eyes looked bigger, darker, full of light.

" I'll tell them," she said. " Give me ten minutes."

The crowd was still waiting outside; and as they pushed through, men raised their eyebrows and shoulders in query. Snowy pointed outside, and heard the quiet stir as they followed.

" All right, Maxie," he said, out in the patio. " Tell 'em the tale. See what you can get from 'em."

He went round to the wagon, and recognized Bill by the back of his shorts, deep in the hood, with Rusty on the other side, handing in the tools.

" Beats me," Bill was saying in his world of wonder voice. " I've not seen an engine out here yet as y' couldn't take a fortune in spuds out of. I don't know what makes 'em go. Must be something in the natter."

" They use' too much," Rusty said. " No rest. No maintenance."

" They could do wi' a driver or two, an' all," Bill said. " The way that young bloke drove this 'un were a fair disgrace to science."

" He'll be driving it again in a minute," Snowy said. " We're going to chase 'em."

" We know where we're going? " Bill asked.

" Finding out now," Snowy said. " How about some grub? "

" Suits me," Bill said. " I'm right clemmed."

They went into the restaurant among a quiet crowd of peasants lining up for brown loaves and slices of meat, smelling the fresh green of salad in wooden bowls full of chicory frills and sliced tomatoes, and went to a table pointed at by one of the younger Nincio girls, tears abrim, yet with a smile for them. Through the window they watched Max talking to a crowd of villagers, and then he came in, smilingly making way towards them.

" O.K.," he said. " I have it. Here's how it is. This bunch have a hide-out along the main route. There's a lot of 'em and they're all mixed up. They even have Krauts and Frogs in there. They have their own transport, and they just take anything they have a fancy for, hold up columns, raid dumps, grab off a piece of the farmer's harvest, take a share of his wine. Boy, they really have a business. And if the farmers don't want to ante, O.K., they get the thick end."

" Anybody know where they are? " Snowy asked. " The exact place, where we can go for? "

" Don't seem to be just the one," Max said. " They're spread around. But some of these boys know where we can get to know."

" What they doing there? " Bill was looking through the side window. " Burying him already? "

Two of the Nincio boys in their singlets were out in the front of the building, and a group of other men with their coats off were rolling their sleeves. A pile of picks and crowbars lay against the wall. The two boys were looking at the concrete facing of a shell hole behind a stack of rubble, and the discussion was causing excitement and drawing a crowd. A couple of the men picked up crowbars, and others formed teams with heavy mallets, and the wedge ends chipped into cracks in the concrete, and then the mallets began to play, but the crowd was thicker, and soon all they could see was the lift and swing of mallets.

" Maybe they're going to put him in the wall," Max said, while the plates went round. " They often do."

" Nothing they do that's daft'd ever surprise me," Bill said. " I'd have thought they'd let him get cold first. But perhaps they don't keep. They're a queer lot, altogether."

" How much petrol we got? " Snowy asked, in a mouthful of crude ham.

" Couple of hundred mile," Bill said. " If you drive. Anybody else, bar Rusty, eighty."

Rusty bowed his thanks, and then put his knife and fork down to stand up and bow with his heels together, bringing them all to their feet in a scrape of chair legs.

The Princess smiled at them, waving them down.

" Snowy," she said, " we're in luck."

" Glad to hear it," he said, helping her to sit. " It ain't above time. What is it? "

" We know exactly where they are," she said. " And just about who they are. So I suggest I go off and collect some real opposition and come back and meet you."

" What would you call real opposition? " Max asked, feeling appetite leave him.

" Combat troops," she said. " And lots of them. We're going to need them."

" Where'll you get 'em from? " Snowy saw the look in Max's eyes. " Ours or yours? "

" Ours," she said. " I'll go straight to the Commanding General. He ought to know what's going on right in the back pocket of his pants."

" Probably don't even know what's going on inside his bonse," Snowy said, still thinking of Max. " The way some of 'em carry on there. Why not just leave it to us? "

" Because they've got hundreds of men inside that mountain, and miles of galleries," she said. " And it's Tom Tiddler's ground for everybody. You won't ever get near the place."

" Inside a mountain? " Snowy looked from the Nincio girl serving him with eggs back to her. " What sort of a new lark's this? "

" No lark," she said. " And pretty dull skies, at that. They have a little army of their own in there. Guns, too. Snowy, please! You have to promise me one thing."

He looked across at her, feeling the others looking at him, afraid that he was going to give himself away because he wanted to look at her, and look, and look, and go on looking, and then throw the table through the window and reach across to her and take the time-glass loveliness in his arms and kiss, but looking at his plate instead, and wishing its white coldness were part of him.

" Anything you like, Miss," he said, cursing the sweat tickling his face.

" Don't move in till I give you the word," she said. " That won't be till I get back. Maybe tonight. Maybe tomorrow."

She knew, and irritably threw aside, the reason for the bent head, and the quick glance at Max, and then at the peonies' deep red among a snowfall of stocks, and another look at Bill, and then at her, a brilliant grey blaze in the redskin face and fair hair in a gilding from the sun's cloudy silver through the pane.

" How do we know ye'll get there? " Bill asked. " We might wait here like Soap till t' Crack."

" Somebody'll tell you," she said. " Or better, don't wait after tomorrow."

" All right," Snowy said, cold again at her tone. " We'll give you till twelve tomorrow. Then we'll set about 'em on our own."

" No." She pushed her plate away. " I mean, go on back to your outfits after that time. Don't mess with it."

" And leave Rosie with 'em? " Snowy sat back. " Look, Miss. Get one idea right. We don't go back without her, with you or without you, or your generals. And if you can't get the help, don't fret about it. One way or another, and we don't care how, we get Rosie back. See? "

" You're making an awful lot of fuss about a truck," she said.

In the sunlit motes he saw Rosie bumping over brown rocks, among the screech of near-misses and blokes folding like jack-knives and falling without another move and red-blue flashes among groups, and pieces flying away and nothing there in clear air, and Shiner hanging out of the other window shouting at the back of his throat like a woman with tears in his eyes, and the boys waving their rifles at him and opening their mouths wide with staring eyes filled with blood and frowning with their eyes going dark and falling, and Rosie rising in a blue wave under his hands, leaving him deaf, listening to himself trying to scratch the darkness.

" No, Miss," he said. " She ain't just a truck."

" Ye wouldn't talk to a sailor like that about his ship," Bill said. " I can see ye getting a nice mouthful if you did. Perhaps there's too many of us and that's why ye feel so belittlin'."

" I seem to have started something," she said. " All right. So she's a great friend of both of yours. But she's not worth your lives, is she? "

" Ain't worried," Snowy said. " If it gets as far as that, I'll think again. So far, I want her back, and I'm going to try. If somebody wants to stop me, that's his bad luck."

" Hear, hear," said Bill. " And I've been wondering. How are you going to get up to see them generals? Ye've no transport? "

" Have I not? " She turned to the crowd outside the window. " If old Nincio's on the level, I have the best transportation in this whole theatre."

The crowd had closed in and now were opening out to make room. A hole in the façade was almost in its original gape, and men were piling blocks on one side, allowing others to get inside the wall, with other men putting their arms round the waists of those in front, and pulling in a live tug o' war, backing pace by pace and bringing into the light a wrapped car, low on the ground, with sacking round its wheels. The crowd closed in, shouting, and the wrappings were passed overhead from hand to hand and dropped on the outskirts, and again the crowd thinned, this time to let them turn the car towards the gate, and from blocking the windows they edged round, leaving clear glass and a view of the crowded patio, and in forefront a black car with half a dozen exhausts and a blunt tail, and the eldest Nincio sitting against red leather at the wheel.

" Well, God stop me titles," Snowy said. " A racing job."

" Mercedes," said Bill, on his feet. " Hundred and twenty an hour on a mug o' tea."

" It belongs to one of the bosses of this gang," she said. " This place has been a dump for their goods. They have a cellar full right now. And you know why the Nincios treated you strangely the other night? They were afraid you'd get tied in with them, and you almost did."

" Who's going to drive you? " Bill asked, and in his voice she heard a small boy on his knees.

" You," she said on impulse, and in the corner of her eye saw a light go out in Snowy's face. " If you want to."

" If I want to," Bill said. " If I want to. Here, let's get at it."

He was half-way out of the room before she could say any more, and Rusty followed him.

" That leaves you and Rosie," she said, smiling.

" And me," Max said, offering a cigarette. " And if you're passing a PX, you might bring in a few of these."

" A bargain's a bargain," Snowy said, looking her directly in the eye, feeling a wash of envy that hurt behind his breast-bone. " Twelve o'clock tomorrow. After that, I'm on me own."

He watched her fingers crumbling bread and wanted to reach over and cram them all in his mouth.

" Oh, Snowy," she said. " Please don't do anything till I get there !"

" Twelve o'clock," he said, looking through the window.

She shrugged, and pushed her chair away.

" O.K.," she sighed. " Twelve it is. I'll write the place down for you when I get it."

" We'll be there," Snowy said.

He saw her eyes as she turned, and looked quickly at the peonies, thinking the same colour, wishing, envious, angry, and then as she walked away his eye was taken by a spot of vital milk just above her heel.

" Oy," he called. " Got a hole in your socks."

He was amazed at the swift turn, and she was hurrying to him, head up and arms out to clutch a handful of hair and drag his head back, and he felt the cool of her cheek laid against his and the drug of her perfume smelt close to her throat, and then she was gone, running behind a group of peasants.

Max was looking at him, cigarette between the fingers of one hand, propping his jaw on the other, with the little finger pushing up the tip of his nose.

" So O.K.," he said. " What're you sitting there for, stupid? "

" I like it," said Snowy. " Just the job."

38

Snowy reached the town with something of relief. His pass was overdue, and he was driving a civilian truck full of men and women armed with farm tools of every kind, with not a word to say in excuse if he were stopped by a patrol.

Rusty showed him the alley and he took the truck into a little courtyard with a well in the middle and a café in the far wall. The people got down, stacking scythes and spades against the well steps, and went off in a whispering drove with the eldest Nincio boy. Rusty gave them a nod and went down to the café.

" This is the safe place," he said. " Tonight we talk with other men, they don't like this things, then we get all together and we finish."

" That's it, chum," Snowy said. " What do we do for hard cash? "

" Hey," Max said. " Say another word and watch me get insulted. This part is strictly un affare Montemuro. E basta."

They drank chianti from a flask, brought from the back of the little shop that smelt of an age of garlic and strong tobacco, and a vinegary mist from wine in the open vat. Rusty talked to the landlord, quietly, as though their mission were routine.

" Taking it very calm, ain't they? " Snowy said.

" He's telling him what goes on farther south," Max said. " And the barkeep's telling him how much hell raising's going on here. He says the military police come in sometimes, but these thugs just laugh at 'em because there ain't enough of them. The carabinieri, that's the ordinary cops, are all sitting tight because if they open their traps they get knocked off."

" Very handy state of affairs," Snowy said. " They want a few of our coppers from home down here. Stop their larks a bit sharp, I can tell you."

" A few of the boys from the Tenth Precinct'd kick 'em around, too," Max said. " Which reminds me. What do we do to keep out of trouble? "

"That's what Rusty and Old Nincio picked this place out for," Snowy said. "I'm absent meself, from yesterday, chum. So we're in the same boat. We're in hiding, on the run."

Rusty turned to them, spreading a paper on the table.

"This is what we do," he said. "We got carabinieri, they got guns, and they know the way. We got all the men from the villages, and we got ours. Everybody want to fight these people. They all got their order. Six o'clock it is dark. Some go to some places and some go to the other. We go to this place where is keep all the transport."

He showed them a spot crossed with his thumb-nail, and traced the route.

"About fifteen kilometres," he said. "Perhaps we got to fight. So first we send in the women, and after half-hour then we go in."

"Send in the women first?" Max put his glass down. "What kind of a nutty idea is that?"

Rusty looked at him with soft eyes, head on one side, and with finger and thumb pinched his trousers in front to a peak, curling his fingers to wag it from side to side.

"This one," he said. "Very good, very nice."

"You mean they're going to lay 'em?" Max sat back shaking his head. "Why do these other guys always get the good ideas? So you're a crook, and the cops supply the lays? So you do it to 'em twice. Boy, that ain't a racket. That's a federal career."

"Where's the women coming from?" Snowy asked. "I can't see nobody fiddling about with this lot we brought. A stringier set o' mares I never see."

"Round the corner," Rusty said. "I show you. La Signora Inglese. Un bellezza."

A couple of carabinieri were looking in at the doorway, unslinging their carbines, grinning as though they were expected. The landlord opened his arms and slapped the table in welcome, kicking out a form for them to sit on.

Rusty spoke to them, and Max joined in.

Snowy listened to the give and take of voices, feeling loneliness cold at his elbow. The pass in his pocket seemed to be getting heavier every moment, and a sense of being haunted began to trouble him. It was discomforting to think that outside that door he could be put in prison just because the figures on a piece of paper were wrong; yet there it was, and, despite an effort to throw off misgiving, he found himself jumpy at the slightest sound, even when the old woman came from behind to change the glasses.

"What's wrong, Snow?" Max broke off in mid-stream. "Signora putting a curve on you?"

"No, mate," Snowy said. "I feel like a burglar somehow. First time I've never had a proper pass. I don't like the feeling."

Max put his head in his arms, laughing.

"Oh, baby," he said, "seems I've had that feeling for the last ten years. Like Adam before Eve showed up with that leaf gag. I'm even going to like that barb wire. Least I'm going to know where I am."

"Why don't you push off now, while you've got a chance?" Snowy shifted nearer. "Listen, you're taking a bigger risk than me. I've got an excuse. But if your blokes pick you up you'll be doing hurdles and high jump in one. We can take you on the wagon and drop you up the road tonight."

"Snow"—Max raised his glass—"you're a swell guy. And I'm going to drink to you. And how in heck d'you think I'd feel, leaving you and Rusty to bat this out between you? Besides, you ain't the only guy in love with Rosie."

The carabinieri were arguing among themselves in a whirring of fingers to stress points, as though the air between them were an integer in the argument to be prodded into shape. The landlord took off his apron in a whirling breeze of white and threw it on the floor, bunching both sets of fingers and joining them at the tips in a see-saw between the nose-tip and top-lip of the corporal.

"I'm going to give you three guesses what all this is about," Max said.

"Looks like a case of politics," said Snowy.

"Wrong again," Max said. "That battle is about who has the best whore house in town, and who's going to supply how many for which party."

"My missus'd like to hear about this," said Snowy. "She'd break my neck."

"Your missus?" Max watched the old woman lighting a

tub of candle in a saucer of water. " How about the Princess? Vhat's the score there? "

" Bowled for a duck," Snowy said. " Never even see the ball. 3ut that's outside my line."

" Not how I see it," said Max. " The way she went for the ›ack hair, boy, why, she wouldn't even leave you peanuts for he morning. I know somebody else like that. For Chris' sakes. What do I keep on doing to myself? "

Snowy watched him drink the glassful at a gulp, shutting his ›yes in a shudder.

" Maxie," he said, " do you ever think of having another voman? "

" Do I? " Max opened his eyes in surprise. " Why, sure. ead me to her."

" But what about your wife? " Snowy asked, and reached or the flask.

" Rosa? " Max considered, and shook his head. " She's grown up. She knows how it is. What I have, I have for her. What goes to other women is a lot of dirty water that just annoys ne. Period."

" Is that all? " Snowy asked.

" That's all, brother," Max said. " Ain't no more."

Snowy tried to see Liz, but she kept her back turned, though e could imagine the tone of her voice. Sitting back, thinking bout it, watching the old woman with nutshells on the knuckles of her fingers pouring wine through a funnel, he knew he could ever tell her, and it was a saddener, for that sort of thing eeded talking about, but she always made out it was rude and etter off kept quiet.

A crowd of civilians pushed into the place, with a man in a lue uniform and broad red stripes down his breeches and a ig silver grenade in scattered flame stuck in his cap.

Rusty shook hands with him and came back to the table.

" This the Maresciallo," he said. " Chief police. He take us o the house. He tell me he don't want trouble. The allies put im in the prison. He lose the job."

" If we don't get Rosie back," said Snowy, " that'll come utomatic. Tell him we ain't interested in nothing big. We just vant Rosie."

He watched the Maresciallo pulling faces and shrugging one shoulder.

" He say to get Rosie, you got to fight," Rusty explained. " Like I say, plenty of men, here, there, everywhere. They watch all the road. They got spies. They pay lot of people. We got to be careful."

" O.K.," Max said. " What're we waiting for? "

" Just to get dark," Rusty said. " And for the house to open. The police don't allow before seven o'clock."

" Back home I always said a cop is the best kind of a guy to know," said Max. " Over here, it's a must."

There was a move towards the door, and the Maresciallo turned to get there first, holding up his arms, talking to everyone as though he had authority, and getting silence, and when he finished a click of heels and a short bow from most.

" These boys plain-clothes cops? " Max asked Rusty.

" Corpo di Bon Costumi," Rusty said. " That's somebody what look after everything is good in the street. The women don't wear dress too little. The men don't do something bad. They make control the cocotte, also."

" Imagine that," Max said, going into the dark courtyard. " Corps of cocotte control. Some guys can't keep out of luck."

The crowd thinned, some holding back, others going through doorways and down alleyways. Rusty and the Maresciallo went on, into the main street, with Snowy and Max behind them, and as they turned into the shoplights other men filed out of doorways, all of them in raincoats, with felt hats that looked too big for them.

Snowy was surprised at the change in the town. He remembered it, in the months of passing through whilst the battle had gone on for the river, weary with wrecks of houses, piled with decaying refuse, lived in by a few people forever grubbing among the ruins.

But these shops were new, packed with goods, bright with light and lively with husbands and wives, and children in push-carts.

" I don't understand it," he said. " Can't make it out. A few months ago this was a terrible hole. We was billeted here for three weeks, and glad to get out of it. Now look at it. The boys wouldn't believe it if I told 'em."

They walked along the broad street between white lights, and turned opposite the church, down a side street smelly with garbage, and under an archway into an alley. The men in front stopped in a cluster about a doorway, and somebody rapped. Snowy looked up at a riband of sky, listening to Max breathing, feeling helpless, lost, out of it. The difference between searching for Rosie and this daundering in the dark was too wide to be explained, and though he felt something was wrong or out of place about it there seemed nothing else to do except follow on.

The door opened in a rattle of chains, with some whispering, and then a voice, that sounded too clear for a man's, in a loud welcome, and everyone went in to a yard that once had been a room, but a bomb had taken three floors out, leaving the walls and night for ceiling.

They went across to a long salon that looked like a small theatre, with red plush sofas spread over a black glass floor. A staircase went round three sides of the room to the second story, starting at the top in a curved sea-shell pouring out glass flowers among green waves lit inside by electricity that went on when couples walked upstairs, and out when they came down, so that colours never stopped lighting and pouring, up and down, in soundless waterfall.

Over the bar at the end of the room mercury strips lit a mosaic of a naked male, wearing the head of a white bull, lying at the feet of a woman bandaged in purple from neck to ankles, holding a lamp in one hand and a mirror in the other, with cherubim flying overhead pelting her with flowers.

"Boy," said Max, "what a concession. I'd like to operate the fruit machines in here."

"Blimey," Snowy said. "This can't be a knocking shop, can it?"

"Has all the earmarks," said Max. "Look at the strumps."

Women in black satin dresses tight to their bodies were talking to the policemen, and a dozen or more were coming downstairs, all in coloured petticoats that reached barely to their knees and long black net stockings with red satin shoes and heels full of glass chips that spoke in light.

The fattest woman Snowy had ever seen got up from a sofa, parting the group of men hiding her, and called out to those on the staircase in the voice that welcomed them on arrival. The girls hurried across in a brilliance of heels and stood together, hands about each other's waists or shoulders, a group of gold, black, brown and red heads in all heights and styles washed in the colours pouring down the balustrade and greening the floor.

Rusty came back on tiptoe. He looked tired, uncombed, black in the beard, and his shirt and trousers were soiled with grease, but his very unseemliness endeared him, and Snowy realized that his own appearance was little better.

" We look a nice mess here," he said. " Don't we? "

" So O.K.," Max said. " We look like bums. So who do we have to please in this kind of a joint? "

" We don't wait till tomorrow," Rusty whispered. " We go tonight. Plenty of trouble with the people. They don't wait for soldiers."

" What're we in here for? " Max asked.

Rusty opened his hands in a shrug.

" To get the girls," he said. " Everybody, they come. The Maresciallo, he try to make wait for tomorrow for more police, but all the people say tonight."

Snowy thought of the shopping crowds of husbands and wives, and prams full of children among the white lights and the plate glass.

" What do you mean, all the people? " he asked. " Them outside there don't look too interested? "

" Wait for one hour." Rusty wagged a forefinger across his chest. " You will see. Six month they got these criminal. They put tax on everything. They make bad things with girls, even the good family. They shoot people. Kill the children in the villages, and they don't stop. You will see how many people."

" Till then," Max said, " we just sit around the hard way."

" We got a drink," Rusty said. " And I bring the Signora Inglese."

" Is she English? " Max grinned at Snowy. " Something you have to live down."

" English," Rusty said. " Pure. I get a drink."

Musicians in white coats came through a door on to a platform near the bar in a pluck of guitars and violins, and a little man in a black coat and white satin bowtie looked at the patrons all round the room with a cash register totalling in his pale blue eyes, but his hands never stopped running along the keyboard.

Rusty came back with a waiter carrying a folding table, a tray and a bottle in a bucket, and Max felt in his jacket for some money.

"No," Rusty warned, "you don't pay. La Signora Inglese, she don't want."

"Who the heck is she?" Max said. "No woman ever paid for my drinks."

"Coming," the waiter said. "The lady she's coming. She like very much you drink, with her best wish."

"Speak English, too, do you?" Snowy said, liking the sound of it. "How?"

"I work five years London, Savoy and Berkeley," the waiter said. "Couple years the Plaza in New York. I wait to go back. I am sick for the big city."

"There's a complaint worth fostering," Max said, and raised his glass. "Fellow exiles, here's to the tall skylines and all the tender babes waiting under 'em."

The fat woman pushed into the ring, holding a glass above her head, but her size made the arm look as though it belonged to a doll.

"Whoa," she said. "Half a mo'. Nothing about tall skylines in this house, thank you. It was one o' your bleen bombs took ours away. We drink to houses all one story or nothink."

"Now listen, Mama," Max said. "The toast is tall skylines, and I'm a customer, and where I come from I'm always right."

"Well, you mush on back again, then," she said. "You're not a customer here, and I don't want your bleen wages neither. I don't allow no ordinary soldiers in my place. They can't afford it, one, and they can't treat a girl decent, that's two, and the last shall be first all the time. Where you from, New York?"

Max nodded, looking surprised at a voice deep as a man's, rising from a bosom that could seat the glass without spilling.

"Ah," she said, looking up at the coloured lights. "Well I remember it. Old Delmonico's, eh? I must've cocked my bleen leg over your grandpa's nut many a time. I was in vaude, them days."

" Long, long ago," Max said.

" 'Eighty-eight," she said. " I was in Chicago in 'ninety. 'laska 'ninety-one. Nome and Dawson. Frisco. Hong Kong. Johannesburg. Bloemfontein. Some o' you young blokes, you think you know a lot. How old am I, and not a grey hair in me head? "

" Couple of hundred," Max said. " Maybe crowding fifty? "

" Not even inside thirty year an' more," she said. " And I'll take on any bleen dozen in the place and send 'em home happy. How's that? I say a dozen? Make it two. See if I care."

She was tall as Max, with black hair cut straight below her ears, and a fringe touching her eyebrows curling away to the right. Her eyes were blacked all round with blobs of eyeblack on the ends of the lashes that left a fainter black line above the eyelid, and the nose was straight, the mouth was wide, full, painted bright red to match finger-nails bent over the tops of each finger, but there was not a line in the face, or any note of age, except the dark regard in eyes that seemed to go back deep into the head in long corridors with no ending.

But the bosom swelled up, almost on level with her chins, covered over with flounces of lace on a dress falling straight to the floor in a black velvet circle, with wide sleeves fastened at the wrists with diamond bracelets glittering thick with colour.

" Ah," she said. " Propped you, eh? You're not the first, either. Where you from, swaddy? "

" Bethnal Green," said Snowy. " What about it? "

" Bless you old jam tart," she said, trying to clap her hands. " Fancy, eh? Dear old Bef'nal. I was Kings Crost. Know it? "

" 'Course I do," Snowy said. " I done me time on the buses. The 14s. Remember them? "

" Oh." She closed her eyes, holding her sides, and in the catch of her breath was a holding back in all the seas. " The buses. 'Course I remember 'em. Every time I think of 'em I smell 'em. And every time I smell 'em I'm that there bleen homesick I could sit meself down and howl. Can't think of dear old London without 'em. Let's have a nice drink to the buses. Come on, Bruno."

The waiter peeled the foil from another bottle and started to pour. There was something in his manner that caught Snowy's eye, a certain sideways look now and again at all of them, but never higher than the sofa seat, as though he expected something out of the floor.

" What's up? " he said, bending forward. " Ain't we good enough for you? Work too long down the Ritz, did you? "

" Now then," she said. " Stop your bleen shouting. See? That's what a drink does for 'em. Leave Bruno alone. Been wi' me years, ain't you, Brun'? You want to kick up a row, go on out in the bleen road."

" Listen, Kings Cross," Snowy said. " I ain't being told what to do. I want to know what's up with him. Way he's looking."

" Worried," she said, and wriggled her seat farther into the plush. " Like me. Worried what's going to happen about this lot tonight. I suppose you know what you're taking on? "

" We been told," Snowy said. " We ain't worried."

" Ah, there you are," she said. " Bef'nal Green all over, that is. Ain't got nothing, so why worry. But I own this place. It's my bit o' bread and grease. 'Sides, I got to look after my girls. Where they going? They'll come down here and smash me up."

" Not after we get through with 'em," Max said.

" Please, Mister." The waiter put his feet and hands together, bending toward Snowy. " Don't think what I say is bad. But these people are so strong. We must be careful, eh? They are the worst type, the criminal, young, and they don't care. You can do nothing with them."

Max was listening to the music, wondering how that pattern of sound got mixed up among women holding out a rough moment of relief for sale, with the burdens of their trade seemingly stamped in their limbs, in legs wirily bowed meeting feet at ankles almost by accident, or in a worry of flesh, creasing at the knee in a raddle, falling to the ankle in gross stockings. Watching a woman with one foot on the sofa talking to the Maresciallo, scratching her leg under the short petticoat, he saw the dumple of flesh, and blue veins in a knot, and almost in a vision Rosa was coming out of the cabin down on Jones Beach in her white swim suit that got everybody turning their heads and bringing on the whistles, and she looking at him, one look, and then down at the board walk, smiling sort of under her breath, as though she knew what it was all about, but just would not let on.

"Now's your chance, Maxie boy," Snowy said, watching him. "It's all there, winking at you."

"Not for me, brother," Max said. "I was thinking. Imagine her finding me here with this bunch. Boy. I get sick to my stomach."

"What for?" The fat woman put her glass down, in a roll of her eyes nodding dismissal to the waiter, watching him go as though she had something yet to say. "Sick, what for? Because they ain't all a lot of bleen virgins? Eh? Make you feel any better if they was?"

"They might be in better shape," Max said, cold as her look.

"What's that got to do with it?" She spat in sudden stretch of chins and a poking tongue. "You don't pay for shape in here, cully. You're paying for the privilege of the use of 'em. 's why the likes o' you come in here, ain't it?"

She was bending forward, slopping her glass, and Snowy felt the sofa shaking under her.

"Now listen, baby," Max said. "Don't let's have any mess over this. I was talking to my friend."

"In company," she said. "My company. My drinks, what these shapes paid for. Shapes, eh? Have you had a look at yourself lately? D'you know what it feels like to come down them stairs, and see a room full of bleen people like you? Shapes? Perishin' Christ, look who's talking about shapes."

"Listen, dear," Snowy said. "The bloke didn't mean no harm."

"You listen, Bef'nal." She tapped his knee with the pads of her palm. "I've seen these blokes before, and I've heard 'em all before. Ever since I was old enough to cart me fat about. They're all the same. What did these girls ought to do? All go out and scrub floors for a living? For somebody else to go and walk over? What for? What're they getting out of it? Enough to keep 'em in their old age? Eh?"

"I'm just saying," Snowy said, "he didn't mean it nasty. If my old duck found me in here, you know what'd happen to me, don't you? She'd bloody crown me."

" And welcome, I'm sure," the fat woman said. " I'll tell you what's the matter with you. You ain't out of your baby rags. You're still a couple o' bleen school kids."

" I got a couple of me own," Snowy said.

" No fault of yours," she said. " You couldn't help it. But it don't say nothing for your brains, do it? "

" Hark at the towsing we're getting here," Snowy said. " Worse'n my Aunty Laura, you are. And she's got more tongue'n a cow's got swingers."

The Maresciallo leaned over the sofa to talk to her, but size stopped her turning to him, and she silenced him with a shaken fist, staring up at the corner of the ceiling, shouting as though at unseen crowds, and the little man with the pale blue eyes playing the piano nodded round the keyboard at the others, and the band thudded it out to drown her voice except in pauses, when the clear woman's part of it was a screech, and the low tone that came from deep in the lace hummed in the glasses.

" She don't want to travel," Max translated. " She don't want the girls mixed up in it. They'll come down and burn the place. What's she getting out of it except an empty cashbox, and a lot of excitement she don't want. And what's the girls going to get, except free bangs from a lot of murderers. She won't let 'em go."

All the women were crowded together behind the fat woman, all looking at her when she screamed, and then at the Maresciallo while he was explaining quietly, with all his fingers bunched together on his chest and his cap on the back of his head, looking down at her sometimes with his eyes shut, towards the roof at others, or frowning up at the seashell, rocking the top of his body from side to side, with the sweat glistening on his face and a smear of rouge on his cheek.

" He says anything that happens to 'em is all in the day's work," Max whispered, one eye and ear on the scene. " And the cops'll be in there too quick for any shooting to happen if the gals do their jobs properly. If the gals don't go, the cops are going to be fighting on their own and somebody's going to get hurt, and all the cops are married and why make widows out of respectable wives? "

" There's a lot in that," said Snowy. " He ain't so soft."

All the women threw up their hands and opened their mouths

in a long wail of disgust, half turning away as though unable to bear any more, and the fat woman tried to get up, driving her heels in the glass to attain balance, falling back in rage that mottled her face and shifted the sofa a good yard.

" The old guy says he'll see the government pays the gals," Max said. " They're saying they heard him the first time. Old Fatso's like to bust her cookies. Just look at that gal. Boy, she's fit to be tied."

With the band playing not for tune so much as noise to drown noise, nobody heard the outer door opening and it was not until the room started to fill beyond the outskirts of the crowd that the arrivals were noticed, and only then because one by one the girls were hoisted on shoulders, and carried in procession round the room and towards the door, kicking, screaming, scratching and hitting, but even so they were borne away high on shoulders, among men's heads jogging in rhythm to the drums and guitars that in a moment changed tempo to a one-two-three, one-two-three, one-one-one, one-two-three, drowning screams and laughter within the chanting of a hundred baritone voices, and black, blonde, red and brown hair flew in the greening light, passing into the darkness of the doorway among the shining heads of the carriers, and then were gone, leaving the Maresciallo and Rusty, both trying to talk to the fat woman.

She struck at them with her little arms, screamed at them in a lost voice of heavy savagery, shook herself in a grind of teeth, and tears dropped wet in little circles of light and they heard the obscenities of a past age of London's gutters rasp in her mouth.

The Maresciallo shrugged and took his cap, scratching long black hair over his bald spot, passing his hand over his face so that the flesh bunched like rubber. He put the cap on straight, smoothed his belly, did up the bottom button of his tunic, stamped to get farther into his topboots, pouted to say something like Behh', and marched to the door with his heels far apart and his toes turned out.

A helpless quality in the rave of little arms and fists bright with jewels, in the open mouth and bleared face blacked in running mascara, in the trembling of lace, in the helplessness of a childish whisper broken in sobbing made Snowy go to her.

"Just because they ain't got nobody to look after 'em," she wept. "'Taint fair. I wish I was young. I wish I was a bloke. So help me, so help me Christ, I'd blind an' murder 'em."

"Listen, matey," Snowy tried to touch her arm but she threw him off. "I'll do what I can, honest. Straight up, I'll try and look after 'em."

"Shut up," she said. "You, you, an Englishman, call yourself a Londoner, you sit down there and let it happen! Ought to be ashamed of your blood. Shamed of your mother."

"Hey, for Pete's sakes," Max called from the doorway. "They're miles off. You want to leave that doll in escrow."

Snowy slid across the glass to him and turned again when the howl began, frowning to see her lit in steady pale green with the big glass flowers glowing reds and blues, standing, hitting her thighs, looking up with twisted mouth and chins flabbing among the lace, howling a single note in the empty room of red sofas, with music stands fallen from the platform, and a shatter of glass bright on the floor by the bar, and a bull's skull grinning up at the woman with dark eyes that seemed to know everything.

They ran after the crowd down the narrow street, and into the broad main road, and stopped in surprise, for all the lights were out, but the church was lit with little electrics in different colours, and lights were in the trees and in banneroles stretched across the road, and the crowd was thick, all walking one way.

"Festa of some sort," Max said. "Kind of pretty, ain't it?"

"I'm sorry for that old girl," Snowy said. "Wasn't a bad sort. But what a paddy, eh?"

"Funny thing," Max said. "Sometimes you get the old yen, and you feel you could bang pretty damn' near anything that even looked like a woman. Then you get into enough of 'em to start a ball game, and all you want to do is to get out in the fresh air, or take a bath, or something. Human beings surely are the darndest people."

"'s quite right," said Snowy. "We're a bright lot here and there."

39

Rusty met them in the little café and led on, through a back door, to the truck filled with the villagers, and light shone on the badges of about a dozen carabinieri. The Maresciallo climbed into the cabin with them, and Rusty drove out of the lane and into the walking crowds, sounding the horn to clear a way, but beyond a turn of the head nobody appeared to trouble, and he went along almost at walking pace until he reached a column of more trucks, all filled with people, some of them with torches, and other torches were being brought to flame in bonfires along the kerbs.

" Snowy," Rusty said, " why don't you stay here with Max? Plenty trouble up there. If you are found, you get prison."

" I want Rosie," Snowy said. " That's all I'm here for."

" I get her," Rusty said. " I know her, and I get her. I don't get no trouble because I'm civile. You stay here, no? "

" No," Snowy said. " I'll get her first."

Rusty raised his shoulders and pulled a face.

" Bene," he said. " But don't say I don't tell to you what is."

" Don't tell me all of these people're going up there? " Max said. " This is the feste, ain't it? "

"Feste," Rusty laughed. " Plenty feste. Big feste. Vesperi Siciliani. E'. Tomorrow, we don't have more trouble with this criminal. Tonight, we finish, or they finish."

Max and he spoke, and Snowy listened, wondering again how anybody could make head or tail of that rattle of sounds, thinking of Bill driving for the Princess, and where they might be. There was something solid about Bill, he found, as solid as Rosie in many ways, and he missed him and the feeling of being able to depend on somebody, just like that week Liz went home to nurse her father and left him to look after the two girls, and the mess they were in the minute she turned her back. A longing for sight of her, for the touch and smell of her, and for the wholesome comfort of the easy chair, with the two girls on his lap, and Liz doing a bit of sewing opposite, listening to him reading them a story and all of them laughing away there at the funny parts, made him frown in sudden misery that hurt as much as treading on a pebble in stockinged feet.

They drove without head-lamps, and except for rays of flame from torches in the trucks ahead there were no lights, and little to see but the whitish flash of kilometre stones as they whined up the mountain. The village they passed through was dark, though the orange walls of the church were lit in electrics of all colours, with bright festoons in the trees, and whites stretched over the street. Then the road was steeper, rougher, and they slowed, and now shadows along the margins were more frequent, with sometimes an arc of fire on the blade of a scythe, or a glim of matchlight on a face.

"There's a heck of a lot of people up here, Snow," Max said, looking out of the window. "We've passed 'em all way up."

"Certainly," Rusty said. "I tell you. Tonight, you see something."

"I'm happy to see those churches looking so darn' pretty," Max said. "That's what we do back home. And just beautiful inside. All flowers and stuff. Certainly takes me back."

Snowy sat straight and turned at the note in his voice, instant reminder of the time Liz got the telegram about her mother. Oh, Bertie, look, look, and nobody told me and having to put his arm around her, and put her in a chair, hoping she would cry and get that white look out of her face and the cold from her cheeks.

"What's up, Maxie boy?" He leaned over the Maresciallo, feeling him pulling in his paunch. "Feeling a bit down on it?"

"Blue," Max said. "Bluer'n a son of a bitch. I feel I want to get going. Do something. Get some place. I ought to be back up there. I want to know what happened to Rosa and that baby. Hell, there's a world of things I ought to know and ought to be doing. And here I am, sitting in a God damn truck just because I have to do it. Don't ask me why. I just have to."

"Same here," Snowy said. "Tearin' about in the middle of the night half-way up a mountain ain't my idea of a lark, don't think it. But what else can we do?"

" So," Rusty said, " we start here. This the place. Now you see."

At a bend in the road, under the broken arch of a viaduct, the trucks were parking on the bulldozed rubble of a village destroyed months before. Torches whipped gold shadows among ruined walls and the canopies of dozens of vehicles, touching a pebbling of heads in a corner where a crowd was listening to a man standing on the back of a wagon, hemmed by silk banners and pennons rolling silver in the wind. The Maresciallo signalled his men and led them over, and the crowd of people rattling their scythes and rakes followed, among a confusion of others coming in on foot.

Rusty went through the edge of the audience to four ragged walls of a mansion. Fires were alight on the floors of the rooms, packed with men holding out their hands to the heat, tipping an ear toward the speaker, nodding at times, grunting agreement, looking round as they came in, a turn of the eyes and no more, as though uniforms were no longer important.

In the farthest room a dozen men were looking down at a sand-pit on the floor. Half bricks were stuck here and there, and an old man, in a black cape with long white hair falling about his face, drew his finger between them making a road.

Rusty stopped them in the doorway, and edged to one side, signing for silence as though he feared the man in the cape.

He was speaking as he might to a class of children, but so quietly that only when they stood still could they hear him, and all the time the half bricks went in, and then pieces of chalk, and finally lumps of red stone.

" The rocks are where these boys're hiding 'emselves," Max whispered. " The chalk is civilians, and the little rocks are cops. The old guy's telling 'em how to operate the whole thing."

" He is the chief judge from long time, years ago," Rusty said, behind his hand. " He was prisoner on the Lipari many years. We start in few minutes with the procession."

The Maresciallo came over with the old man, and the rest of the men broke away. Snowy found himself shaking hands, smiling into an old face that might have belonged to a woman for fineness of skin, remarkable even in that light; but though the eyes were laughing, they stared black under a straight spray of white eyebrows, and all the time the long hair was swept away with a motion that reminded him of Liz.

" How you do," the old voice said. " Tonight we have battle for ourself, no? "

" That's right, guv'nor," Snowy said. " They're a bad lot, so they tell me."

" So bad, the people don't wait for the allies," the old man said. " They are tired. They wait no more. Too long they suffer. Tonight, basta."

Max spoke to him in Italian and the old man threw up his hands in pleasure, talking in a rush, telling off points on his fingers. Shouting started outside, an ugly sound squelched by a pulse of hisses, and then a group of men came through the inner room holding two men in British battledress, both of them bleeding in the face, sullenly bending their rumps away from bayonets in rear.

The Maresciallo began talking to their guards, and the old man joined in, but neither of the prisoners looked up or said a word. Studying them, tall, well fed, shaven, with a lot of oil on their hair, in polished boots and ironed battle serge with watch-chains swinging between the breast pockets, Snowy saw a little glass dome, and sunshine on wax flowers.

He turned to catch Max looking at him, head on one side, with his eyebrows up and half a smile in his eyes. Anger made his face a mass of pinpricks. He could see these two greasing their hair while Shiner was still on the hilltop with the sun telling the time in the shadow of the little tower.

" A Kraut and one of yours," Max said. " Beats hell, don't it? "

Snowy went over to the old man.

" Half a mo'," he said, and turned to the two prisoners. " Which one of you's our lot? "

" Me," the shorter man said. " And you'll get to hear about it, an' all."

The quiet speech, as though he was accepting all things without struggle because of doom on its way, brought Snowy from anger to curiosity.

" Go on? " he said. " Where's this going to happen? "

" Not far away." The shorter man jerked his head at the mountain. " Just up there. They'll get to hear about it. They'll be burning houses all day tomorrow, you'll see. Done it before, do it again."

" What was your lot? " Snowy went close to him, and as he took the slack of the blouse in his fist, the carabinieri released their hold. " What army was you? "

" Don't matter to you." The shorter man grabbed his wrist. " Take your hands off."

" They want to know how many guys there are in the transport gallery," Max said.

" Find out," the shorter man said. " Go on up and find out. They got lots of Brens and Schmeissers up there. They'll tell you."

" Look." Snowy swung him round to face the fire. " Answer the questions, else I'll sit your arse on that. In the middle of it. How many blokes? "

" Wait." The old man in the cloak was holding up both index fingers. " Please. This is for justice. These prisoners must to be tried by civil court for crime." He turned to Max and spoke in the same quiet voice, and then smiled at Snowy. " Leave for the police. You have nothing to do."

Snowy took his hands away and stood back.

Age and wisdom were in the voice, and knowledge in the eyes, but something more was there to restrain him, a quality that he realized instantly was part of the Princess, an inner certainty, that had nothing to do with self-assurance though that was apparent, as though what he said was right, and had to be right only because he was saying it. In that moment he saw her, and heard her talking in the darkness, and the drag of her breath as she turned away, for once uncertain of herself and so weakened, making him feel he must go to her there and then, and comfort her, yet knowing the impatience, perhaps the irritability, of her reply, and he laughed to think of it.

" What, are you some of Ortesi's lot? " The shorter man was looking at Max. " You'll grin the other side of your faces when we've finished with you. Just getting ready to give you all you been asking for."

" Got your schedules knotted there, Joe," Max said. " We

don't belong any place except the army. And for the first and only time I feel proud about it."

"You better tell 'em they'll have to look out what they do to us," the short man said, and wiped some of the blood off his face with a handkerchief that fell in neat white squares. He seemed a little dazed, or drunk, not enough to make him unsteady, but there was indirectness in his eyes, and plodding in his speech. "They'll cop it when the boss hears, I'm telling you."

The old man in the cape finished talking to the corporal of carabinieri, and the guards settled on the prisoners with both hands, dragging them away backwards, disregarding their shouts and kicking feet, and under his anger Snowy was tempted to pull the Briton out of their grip simply because he felt himself demeaned by allowing foreigners to manhandle one better than themselves.

"They're for the firing squad," Max said.

"They wouldn't dare shoot one of our blokes," Snowy said. "Never mind how bad he is. They'd pinch the lot for murder."

"So who's around to stop 'em?" Max asked. "Listen."

The shouting had started again, and then the hisses for silence, but the shouts swelled, and a trample of feet, and single shouts, high-pitched, and the sound of dulled smacks, but then a brass band struck up, covering all except the gulps of the Maresciallo drinking from a flask.

"They start," Rusty said. "Come, we go to see."

He was troubled about the presence of the two men in allied uniform, fearing not only for their safety at the hands of the criminals but even more from the hotheads among his own people.

Impulse had brought him on the trip, generated as much by pleasure at sight of Snowy as by memory of happy days among craftsmen accepting him as one of themselves. He felt, and had comported himself as, a poor relation pitched into wealthy company, busying himself in details, taking all the menial tasks as his portion, deferring to any whim, acquiescing in any mood, thinking little since thought brought nothing, saying nothing except when spoken to, trying to realign his idea of created life and restore hope by contact with men more confident of the future, listening to them, watching them, moment by moment, hoping to find the secret of their faith. Loss of Rosie had been a personal matter, happening in sight of his home surrounded by his own people, and finding her had been accepted as a duty. But having achieved that triumph and losing her again by lack of diligence, always to be excused by the divine befuddlement of healthy passion, it was a shock to run headlong into a community angrily in arms, led by civic authority of a more ordered age, and supported by a resurgent carabinieri, for now it was no longer a flare-up between a couple of ordinary soldiers and a few peasants against evildoers in a remote area without the law, but a set battle between right and wrong, giving hope of that rebirth of public spirit that inside a maze of apathy he had prayed for.

Proud though he was, and excited by portent, he was worried by threat of danger to Snowy and Max, for there was little except their rough appearance to tell them apart from the criminals, and the sureties of the Maresciallo and himself might count for little if younger men, the infesting hobbledehoys in any crowd, took it into their heads to mob them, and for that reason he had got them as close to authority as he dare. But now he looked at them in new light, privately astonished at their meekness in the presence of the old judge and their readiness to obey his orders. It seemed suddenly, for no reason that he could explain, as though for the first time he was on a par with them, no more, no less, adding an excitement that was almost drunken in its impact.

He took them through the back of the mansion, climbing out of wrecked windows into the weeds of a garden fragrant with blossom persistent among neglect, wading through waist-high growth to a copse that edged the road.

Blaring brass was muted by a curve and by the slope, allowing the wind to be heard among the trees and in the grass, bringing the solace of a steamship calling down in the bay, reminding them that, come what might, some day, somehow, she and her sisters would be waiting there to take them home.

Torchlight scoured the trees a golden brown and marked the leaves in brightest green, and then a sparkle of brass turned the corner among a rumble and clash of drums and cymbals lighted all along by torches that bobbed in time to the beat.

Rusty withdrew to deeper shadow as the drumming approached and all three found cover behind a stump of a tree, watching through a screen of roots as torchbearers went by, dark under the flares, and then the files of the band, old men in farm clothes playing a collection of instruments of odd shape and size, throwing up a tune made of a series of spaced blasts strung along a boom-boom-arompity-boom of an assortment of drums, belted around the necks of about a dozen old gaffers all watching two bass drummers playing on drums each held horizontally by four boys, walking sideways to the line of march, and getting tidily in each other's way.

A flourish from the bass drummers' sticks started the smaller drummers in a ruffle, and the files turned inward, forming a circle, and then the boys swung the bass drums, and the bass drummers danced first on one foot, and paused, and then on the other, beating their own tempo, and the bandsmen lifted a foot and paused, and setting them down, lifted the other in time to piercing brays of brass that had no tune.

Boom, up with the foot, puhrah, boom, down with the foot, and up with the other, puhree, boom, and a pace forward, pahroo, up with the foot, and one of the boys falling over someone's hooves and getting a tap on the crust to remind him what he was about, pahrah.

Another signal from the sticks and the files reformed in a boom-boom-rompty-boom, and the band set off in short, jaunty steps that made a dance in itself, plummy cheeks among the brass, and a munch of little chins among the drums.

Under the drumming they were aware of handclapping, and now the narrow road was thick with people singing in a different rhythm, yet their end notes were always in the same tone and on the same beat, so that when the band was dancing the crowd walked, and when the band marched on the crowd started to dance.

Men and women weaved in and out of figures of eight, all dressed in curious finery streaming with coloured ribands gleaming in the lights, here and there a flashing of jewels when hands beat tambourines, and then a glitter of teeth when voices poured, always an overtone of laughter, and never ceasing the stamp and turn and arching of arms in the dance.

Snowy tried to speak in Rusty's ear, but a warning hand prevented his shouting. Max looked his amazement, making no move, remembering his father dancing at family parties after the wine had gotten into him, his shyness when they asked him where he had learned the steps, and his impatient refusal to tell. But here was the same dance, and Max was moved, and warm in his father's memory.

Foot by foot, as the dancers linked arms to go on, ranks of men came into view all bent under thick poles borne on their shoulders, and at intervals men out of the crowd on both sides ducked under, slipping between the ranks to tap someone and take his place, so that the platform they were carrying was always moving, but slowly, allowing stance and balance to a group of figures in tableau lit on all sides by petrol lamps swaying on rods, that cast yellow light and black shadow among sheaves of corn and heapings of flowers, polishing the bare legs and arms of masked women postured about a throne covered with silver paper. A dummy painted in gold leaf trembled with the movement, making the wheat ears dance in the triple tiers of its headdress, and from underneath the platform somebody worked the strings that opened and shut the mouth of its mask and turned the head to nod from side to side. In rear of the platform, more drummers were crowded, and a ring of men playing mandolins and accordions went around and around barrels of wine mounted on silver-papered wheels, and behind, in double files holding hands, still in their short petticoats, the women swung their hips in time to the tune, all of them singing, drinking from bottles passed by the crowd of men dancing all about them.

Rusty pulled Max by the arm, and went back through the copse, cutting across the grass and into a ploughed field sloping from the road, and the bay was blue far down, but all the land was dark.

" Half a mo'." Snowy looked at the other two black against the sky. " What's all this got to do with getting Rosie? "

" The hell of a lot," Max said. " They're all going up past this hideout. Then you'll see."

" I couldn't see no coppers," Snowy said, obeying Rusty's sign to follow.

" So what do we do? " Max addressed the trees. " Send them the news Western Union ? Or a bunch of delegates? "

" Can't see no sense in it," Snowy said.

" Happens plenty of times in the year," Max said. " One village church dresses up and visits with another. One time this procession started, these crooks shot a lot of the men, and raped all the gals. Some of 'em never did get to go home and ain't been seen since. That was a church procession by light of day, with priests. Can y'imagine? "

" Quick," Rusty said. " We going to be late."

They went over the plough and through a vineyard, coming out on a crest above the road, sloping before winding up again to the next ridge, with the volcano's crater colouring the clouds a gentle red over their heads only a few miles farther up. The procession was on the curve, just before going uphill again, rank on rank of torchlights and swinging puffballs of petrol lamps, and voices in echo on a thump of drums, and suddenly fireworks burst among the ranks, and round about, and torches went out.

" That gives the boys time to duck," Max said.

Two searchlights snapped on from the darkest part of the slope, with pale purple beams reaching the farthest point in the road, lighting the shadows of moving men, spotting and narrowing on the fallen platform and the figures dancing about the barrels.

They ran down the incline on to the tarmac edge, keeping outside the beams, and went full tilt into the Maresciallo and long lines of people coming down the slope. Rusty spoke to him, nervously it seemed to Snowy, and, listening, Max pulled him into the parapet, letting the dozens of people go on in a bare-foot scuff.

" Looks like we're going to get in their hair, see? " Max said. " Let's just sit back here. What d'y' say? "

" Everybody seems to know what I want to do except me," Snowy said. " What's the matter with going up and smacking a few of 'em in the nose? "

" Plenty, including they're wearing the same kind of uniform as us," Max said. " You wouldn't want to get fouled-up with a bunch of them corn-cutters, would you? "

The slope and the scrub they had to jump through took their breath, and the noise they made covered all other sound except now and again the crack of fireworks in light that helped them, and presently they were out on a brow about a hundred yards above the road with a clear prospect of the bay, up and across the beams to the farther slope, and on up, in darkness, to the crater capped with flame reflection on low cloud, and a ragged lip of gold about the rim.

One beam slewed over the road, across the slope, and they ducked behind a rock as the brilliance passed over them and down into the vineyard. The other beam narrowed itself, waited, and went out, leaving a night of surpassing darkness patterned with optic images, and then they saw headlights on the farther slope travelling down toward the petrol lamps and torches; and when their eyes were easy they could see the women dancing around the wine barrels, and figures jumping off the approaching trucks running down to join them.

They made careful way down through the scrub and into the vineyard, coming on a group of carabinieri watching through the leaf screen. A corporal motioned for silence with both palms flat to the ground, pointing to a hole in the lattice where they could see some of the old drummers going nearer to the platform, using their sticks in ones and twos, and little knots of people that presently were dancing up and down around the silver wheels of the wine barrels.

More figures were running from the arch of a tunnel lit by a curve of white spots in the roof, and then the beam came round again, playing full on the platform, showing the women's coloured petticoats, and the khaki uniforms of the men dancing with them.

As at a signal, the drummers broke into the boom-boom-arompity-boom, and started marching around the barrels, but a couple of the groups began to move along the path, into the heart of the beam, making huge shadows as they waved their arms at the drummers, staying there until the corps was level with them, and then, linking with all the others, hopping and skipping, followed by teams of men shouldering the wine barrels.

Again the beam winked and went out in coloured darkness, and when the arch was plain again, only one small light showed in the entrance.

A whisper from the corporal brought the carabinieri out of their hiding places and moving down hill and Max followed Snowy in a file behind the leaders, hurrying on until they were almost at the wreckage of the platform lit by a smoulder of torches. Other files were coming in from the darkness, and shadows could be seen up in the mouth of the tunnel a couple of hundred yards away.

"We stay right here," Max said. "Just in the event there's going to be a mess with the hicks. They're going to have trouble holding them babies."

An old drummer, with a drum on his back almost as big as himself, tiptoed across the platform, and pulled at the dummy on the throne, turning away with the head and a trailing of wires and handles. He stopped in the light of a torch and swung the drum to his front, took off the skin frame, put the head inside, fitted the frame on again, swung the drum on his back, spat in the middle of the platform, crossed himself, pulled both ends of his moustache, and marched off with his hands in his pockets and his sticks stuck in the front of his hat.

"G'night, Dad," said Snowy. "Mind how you go, boy."

40

Honeysuckle was silhouetted against the light in the tunnel mouth sprouting from gaps on both sides of the keystone, mixing its scent with smells of paint and motor oil, giving him a feeling that Rosie must be ticking over just around the corner waiting for him to climb in.

Files of carabinieri were shadowy down both sides of the tunnel with their feet bandaged in sacking, thrashing through loose earth beyond the ruts in a bustling whisper that almost covered a sound as though someone were whistling under his breath, drawn notes that swayed and went, striking high in a swinging wail, pushing through the rhythmic click of marching men.

Down at the curve, light shone in the blazing silver grenade in the Maresciallo's cap. Hand signs brought the files to a halt, but Rusty led on to the group. A smooth corner took the tunnel uphill, lit by a couple of electrics about a hundred feet apart, and in the darkness beyond a row of red bulbs formed a bar. Niches had been cut in the rock on both sides. Some of those nearest were full of splintered wine casks and iron hoops standing awry, but farther on light silvered on windscreens and fenders where cars were parked on either side, and the tyre tracks of their turnings were like chevrons in a length of tweed.

Now the whistling sound was clearer, seeming to come from up beyond the red bulbs, a chorus of voices and in pauses, the groan of a concertina.

"Having a rare old do, ain't they?" Snowy said. "Giving it big licks."

"They're going to be hollerin' for a priest next thing they know," Max said.

Some of the cars were manhandled down and pushed round the corner, passing by in heavy displacements of air that sharpened the odours of vinous wood and petrol. Carabinieri were hidden in the niches all the way up beyond the farthest light fall, and ranks of reserves stood in the bend. Snowy saw the Maresciallo's eyeballs moving from the rooflight up towards the red bulbs, almost hearing them slide, wondering again at the authority in the dumpy figure in down-at-heel top-boots and blue breeches with a scarlet stripe, watching an impress of fingers in fat cheeks, picking and smoothing perhaps in sympathy with an anxious mind.

Whiter light suddenly rimmed his chins, glittering in his cap badge, and he flattened inside the niche, staring into the fairway as though expecting an onrush. A metal door grated in distance, bumped clangily and doddered to silence that seemed to be stretching in weighted elastic, looping about the heads of restive men, making them feel they might never more use hand or foot.

Carabinieri were talking in a mix of undertones merging into each other and flattening in the roof like the breathy dribble of a loose tap.

The Maresciallo took off his cap and put part of his head and one eye around the corner, straightening instantly, signing to the men in rear; and as they moved, Rusty pushed to the front.

"Come," he said. "We keep close."

Long lines of men moved uphill in ranks of bobbing caps towards an open door glowing red where the bulbs had been. From below it looked small, but when the leading carabinieri folded back the metal leaves it became a gateway large enough to pass any vehicle, lit by warning lamps over the lintel shining on a white backing for a ramp turning down right and left.

A leading scout flung up both arms and jumped for the darkness. The files halted and became part of the walls, but the Maresciallo went on, up the middle of the ruts and between the silent ranks, putting out a hand to touch his men, murmuring to them under his breath, and the corporals followed on with Rusty behind, and Snowy and Max in rear.

A shadow fell across the backing and the Maresciallo halted, putting out his hands as though about to conduct an orchestra, raising an index finger in warning at the general swing of rifle muzzles, with his little finger half-way up in modified assent.

A woman walked directly under the flooding red of the lamps, bent double trying to force her arms into a military overcoat. Blonde curls hung over her face, but not thickly enough to hide the darkness beneath her eyes, or the cheeks flabbing from both sides of the nose and disfiguring her mouth. The bulge of moons about her neck went down into a silk slip tightly wrinkled with the bulk of her breasts, falling loose to her knees, and gaiters of flesh draped down her legs, puddling over the tops of her shoes.

The Maresciallo's hands fell helplessly among the folds of his breeches. Either the sound or the movement froze her, for she stood still, bent over, one arm behind the one poked out in front in a muddle of serge, staring through coils of hair that blew out and almost into her open mouth as she breathed.

A corporal went towards her, but she shook her face free, throwing her head back in a scream little more than a cough, dropped the coat and ran back the way she came, calling out in the same tone, gathering the silk about her knees with one hand, holding her bosom with the other, caring nothing for the Maresciallo's impatient clucks and snapping fingers, or the undertone yelps of the carabinieri massing in the gateway.

"That's one of them bramahs from the knocking shop," Snowy said. "I thought they was on our side?"

"Maybe she wants to call the front office," Max said. "But she ought to have somebody fix that throat. Sounds real sore."

She was screaming, beyond the curve of the ramp, as though smoke were pouring from her mouth, and dozens of the marching carabinieri were mimicking her, until the Maresciallo turned about and shouted once in a scarlet show of teeth and staring eyes. He motioned Rusty into the left-hand file, waiting until Snowy and Max were in step behind, and then turned, hurrying on around the bend.

" Well, God stiffen Wapping Stairs," Snowy said. " Me, taking orders from an Eyetie copper. Good job the lads can't see me. I'd never hear the last of it."

Dark, cool from a movement of air bringing a whiff of coffee, a cave opened at the ramp's end, lit by one strong light hooding its beam on an orderly work-bench along the far wall.

Cars and lorries in stages of dismantling ranked in shadow alive with files of marching carabinieri, all going towards light coming through glass over on the right. With a tap for Max, Snowy jumped off the ramp and doubled across to the lines of trucks and lorries, hearing Rusty call out.

Only three of the biggest could have been Rosie, and the feeling that heated him made his legs tremble, making him want to laugh as he ran blind for the first, and found it to be an American six-tonner, on to the second, a military caravan, and then slower, with something telling him to save his breath, to the third, a panzer workshop. Looking up, hating the spotty camouflage and the shuttered ugliness of it, everything he detested seemed brought together and locked inside those steel slats.

He knew the layout of the machinery in there, reminding him of shops at home alive with songs shouted above the working lathes, and he knew the smell in there, the same anywhere in the world, of grease wipers and turpentine and petrol.

A feel of tools coming handily to the grip, and the joy of a close job under a spotlight when time ran in a bland oil of absorption, and half-hours in the tube with the evening paper going home to a hot supper, a call at the pub for a nice pint before he opened the gate and heard the girls running to meet him, everything he wished for and all he dreamt about seemed crushed under the sharp-cornered weight of it, and the warmth was out of him.

" Snowy," Rusty was calling. " Please. Snowy come, come. Plenty more next place."

" Ain't even going to think about it, mate," Snowy said. " Got a good mind to walk out. I'm browned."

" But this only for wash down." Rusty fluttered his hands at wet patches in the flooring. " Plenty more. If we stay down here, we get trouble."

A rapping of shots sounded musically among the metal, spaced automatically as if the firers were taking aim.

" Trouble's what we have," Max said. " Let's go."

Running in and out of the parked ranks, they reached a glass partition at the end of the tool-bench, pushing through a crowd of carabinieri waiting outside the sliding door, and went in to a corridor lined both sides with glass, to the right looking out on a roadway, flanked by offices on the left, some of them lit by tube lights, others dark, and two at the end untidy with fallen chairs, and tables heaped with newspapers.

A man in green uniform lay in the last doorway with light glossing red along the rim of a little pool, and winking in new steel studs on the soles of his boots.

" Somebody's had it," Snowy said. " Mind where you're treading."

" Kraut," said Max. " Jesus."

Rusty swung open the heavy door, letting out a blare of sound, of women screaming and laughing, of men shouting, of smashing glass and splintering timber, and, under all, the hum of a heavy turbine.

A plank roof painted white reflected green circles from rows of lights, and at the end wall a switchboard eyed with dials was shut away behind a brass rail. Tables and forms were wrecked down the middle of the room, and about a dozen men were fighting near a barrel stove, with threes and fours grovelling among cots along both walls, rolling in and out of the lights, watched by naked women huddling together in clusters here and there, and waiting carabinieri darted in to crack a skull with a rifle butt or kick at someone on the floor.

A group of carabinieri stood guard on a couple of dozen men in stages of undress sprawling near the wine barrels, and in front of them the Maresciallo directed the struggle, pointing where help was needed, turning to the screaming women to shout for silence, staring at the roof with hands outstretched until they stopped, and fisting his forehead in rage when another group started.

" In his glory, he is," Snowy said. " Talk about it for years, he will. Drive everybody barmy."

Rusty edged quietly around the furniture, standing against the wall near the carabinieri guard, talking to him. The prisoners were mostly asleep, but those able to move about bore marks of severe handling, and a pile farther along covered in bedding showed feet, bent arms, and the tops of heads, all still.

Heedless of the fighting, many of the women were looking about for clothing, pulling out boxes from under beds, opening cupboards, feeling textures coolly as in a bazaar, tidily closing lids and fastening doors, putting on what they fancied and helping each other into overcoats, screaming in laughter at overlong trousers and bursting shirts.

But others, mostly the younger girls, held close together with their arms about one another, shivering, silent for moments when the Maresciallo shouted, and then, following one wavering shriek, all of them pressed together, eyes shut, mouths wide in a scream that rang in the ears.

Snowy noticed how short they were and the caked mud on their feet and legs, the long hair at knee length thick enough to hide their bodies, except for a thigh and a leg, firm as though hammered, or smoothly polished arms and shoulders, or a perfect breast offering a teat the size of a rosebud.

It surprised him that he could look at them without feeling, except perhaps pity, wondering again at other times when it had seemed, beyond the dream of Liz, that any woman of whatever age or shape was all he wanted in the world.

" Healthy-looking babes," Max said, watching him. " This bunch certainly had the ends tucked in. Look at the way they been living. Wasn't a sonovabitch didn't have a broad to do the chores and press his pants. If he ever got time to get into 'em."

Rusty came over, nodding at the fight moment by moment, quietening as carabinieri dragged bodies away.

" This the fathers, brothers of the girls," he said. " Nipoti."

" Relations," Max said.

" Relations." Rusty nodded at the groups of girls. " Lot more. The Maresciallo promise they fight. So now he keep the promise. Then we go next place."

Carabinieri ran in at the Maresciallo's whistle, pulling at those till fighting near the stove. On a sudden thought, Snowy went ver to the prisoners.

" Any you blokes our lot? " he called. " Eighth? "

" One here," a voice shouted, and a hand was up. " What re you? M.P.s? "

" No," Snowy said. " Reemee. Had a breakdown wagon in ere the last couple of days? Seen one? "

" Find out," the voice said. " And get burst."

Rage that took his breath sent him at a run along the line, alling over sitting men, or treading on shins that rolled beneath is weight, or yieldingly in torsos, hearing shouts as he passed nd caring nothing except to find the man. But then lights tore lashes, passing to darkness and a buzzing pulse, and he came wake to feel booted feet kicking him.

" O.K., Snow," Max was saying, and he felt himself pulled lear by the collar. " Surely was a finisher. Lose any teeth? "

Snowy felt the bump on his forehead, trying to stretch an aching eck.

" No," he said, and stood. " What was it? "

" You took a rabbit punch somewhere along in there." Max odded at a group of carabinieri using their rifle butts in the hadow. " But I wouldn't give you any odds of finding him ight now. He's a gone goose."

A door near the switchboard slid back in a rattle of steel plates, etting in bright light over the shoulders of a group of civilians. The Maresciallo hurried down to them, shouting orders as he vent, and the carabinieri began rousing the prisoners, getting hem on their feet, and herding the women into a corner at one nd, raising brows with closed eyes and tightened mouths when hey were screamed at, and fists with lacquered nails tried to beat side the rifles.

" Come." Rusty had been watching the arrivals. " Finish ere."

They ran down, jumping a wreckage of tables and beds, seeing he bodies beneath them, and halted on the edge of the crowd. ooking at the floor, the Maresciallo was listening, picking his ower lip, while an old man talked in a loud scatter of words, lividing his glances between the sleeve of his jacket, slapping it now and again into little puffs of dust, and the purplish tip c the Maresciallo's nose.

" They come from the other place," Rusty whispered. " Plent trouble there."

" What's he saying about the volcano? " Max asked. " I don get it."

" He don't like," Rusty said. " She don't be quiet."

" Well, now, just listen to that." Max looked at Snowy. " Eve wonder how Jonah felt, fooling around in that fish? Here's u loused up inside of a volcano. And who'll give a damn? "

At a series of orders from the Maresciallo, part of the cara binieri marched off with the prisoners, leaving half a dozen o guard over the injured with a couple to look after the womer and the rest followed the civilians out of the switchboard doo Rusty held back until the rear files had gone.

" We wait," he said. " Then we have plenty time."

" I can do with it." Snowy sat on the brass rail. " Never bee knocked clean out before. Very funny feeling."

" Right," Max said. " I got knocked out once. I was nu about a kid in high school. We used to meet in drug stores an movie houses. But when we were through, she always aske which way I was going, and had a date the other way. Took n time to catch on. Get it? She'd let me pay the checks, but sh just didn't want to be seen around. That's the kind of knocko that really knocks you out. And it lasts."

" Wonder what the Princess is doing? " Snowy said. " I' bet Bill's having a rare time in that racing job."

" He's maybe having himself a time with her," Max sai " She'd worry."

It was not anger, or helplessness, or weariness that Snow felt, but a mood that seemed to blend all three, together with a impatience to be away and yet a disinclination to move. A wis to defend her was pegged by a certain shame for the manner his feeling, and knowing that she was impatient of champions, fre even of any responsibility for his feeling for her, smothered t jealousy he felt for Bill.

Thinking of him, the sharp grey points behind the ste spectacles, the voice and the bush of hair outside the fore-and-a cap, made him grin.

" Lucky people," he said. " Wish she'd took me. You could do ninety easy in that bus."

" She couldn't have said it plainer if she'd put it over the P.A. system," Max said. " And I'm talking about a piece of tail, not autos. Why didn't you? "

" Ain't my cup of tea," Snowy said, and jumped down. " How about it, Rusty? "

Rusty turned from the doorway, but the smile whipped from his face, looking not at Snowy but just behind, and he pointed, throwing up his arm in a shout of angry dismissal.

Snowy looked, and stepped back in surprise, for a few of the women had crept close, only a foot away, leaning on the rail, watching them, and the colours of the switchboard lit their eyes, tinting whole curls among untidy heads of dyed hair.

A tall girl in a khaki overcoat looked at Max through black ringlets combed down both sides of her face, showing the bridge of her nose and a pale mouth, and spoke to him in a little girl voice.

" They think the coppers'll pinch 'em," he said. " They're afraid to be up here, and they want to go down with us."

" Poor little cows," Snowy said. " I don't blame 'em. Anyhow, I promised the old mother judge down there I'd look after 'em. Tell 'em yes."

Rusty shouted at them, and they went backwards hang-dog, looking without expression at all three in turn, but in his mind Snowy could only see the two girls going pace by pace towards the kitchen door, one eye on Liz sending them off to bed without any supper, and the other on him, hoping he would say the word that never came.

" Don't make too much trouble," Rusty said. " We got plenty help from the police. We want more. This bad woman. Leave alone."

" Who started 'em off? " Max asked, and waved at rifles and machine-guns gleaming sleek blue in the racks. " And if they hadn't come up here, how many of us'd got into this place, anyway? "

Rusty shrugged away a whole philosophy.

" Va bene," he said. " Now we go."

He led through a corridor, passing a workshop office, and out into a cool chamber that might have been any city garage for size and orderliness. Vehicles of all types were parked in bays, each with its own bench of tools, and a travelling crane left festoons of shadowy links across concrete driveways that ran on, round a bend.

" Hey, Rusty," Max said, as though it were injury, " what's the story? God damn it, there's more stuff in here than we got outside."

" Two years war," Rusty said. " Two years deserters. They take the truck, the car, the lorry. Bring here. Sell to civile. Anybody. Now it's finish."

Overlaying his words, sound of rifle fire rapped in echo along the driveways, followed by a rumble of explosions and cries that might have come from a playground. In silent periods the turbine hum seemed louder.

" What do you say we go down there? " Max turned to Snowy, and paused, open-mouthed. " What the heck's happened, Snow? What's wrong? "

Snowy was staring across the concrete at a bay beyond the line of pumps.

" I can see her," he said. " There she is. I've gone all of a slop. It's Rosie. My Rosie."

41

Max was amazed at the change in Snowy. He had thought first of all that the big fellow was a quiet, slow sort, painstaking and a mite dull, opinionated in a small-town way, but kind enough and, all things added, a pretty good type of trucker. His relationship with the Princess was a joke to be excused, nothing serious, but pointing up a lack of experience with women, and his awkwardness in denial was simply foot-shuffle shyness tangling with a lusty want.

But the business over Rosie, useful and important though she might be, was something he did not altogether understand, for here was a beat-up old repaint job, as near a jalopy as Brooklyn to Flatbush, talked to, petted, cooed over and generally treated like a prize cow, in a manner he considered unhealthy since there were limits to what could be said to a truck. But Snowy looked and sounded as though he meant what he was saying, and that was plenty, and none of it sounded like the Snowy he thought he knew. Even his appearance had changed. The eyes were clearer, there was colour under the tan of his face for the first time, and the withheld feeling about him had gone, and in its place an energy that could be sensed leaping out of him, making the very tools seem to jump as he touched them.

Yet, all the while they worked, rifle fire had been getting louder, until it was obvious that not very far away a battle was on, no longer a sniping affair, but set and vicious.

Rosie had been taken down almost to her bare bones. Her parts were lined up on tarpaulins spread round her chassis, and the engine was mounted on a bench, with the canopy showing the tell-tale camouflaging that Snowy had seen, neatly folded and hanging from a roof-bar. Leaning against the wall, with both headlamps hanging from one side, like earrings, her radiator seemed to be looking up at her body swung from the crane overhead with all the anxiety of an acrobat's wife.

"Made a lovely job of her," Snowy was saying, busy with the magneto. "Didn't they, gel? Eh? Look at her laughing. These blokes knew their stuff, I'll give 'em that. I'll also give 'em something else ever I catch up with 'em."

"Must have had a pretty good engineer outfit down here," Max said. "I can't get over it."

"Germans," Rusty said, working on the engine. "Some Italian. But plenty German. They work clean. They build this place for panzer divisions. First Italian army, then German. Very good."

"You like 'em, Rusty?" Max asked. "Krauts? You can't."

"Like or not like, what's a difference?" Rusty twirled a hammer, looking at the head tracing a broken silver circle. "These are German, and they are good. So? What difference I like or not like? Is for little baby this like or no like. For a man it must be good or bad work. Per forza. If it is good, I like. No good, I don't like. E basta."

" Here," Snowy said. " What's basta? Bastard? "

" Enough," Max said. " That's all. Enough. Basta. Maybe he's got something, at that."

Watching the two men working, the quick movements, so precise with an almost regal aspect of skill rich with odours from a thousand litanies of sweat, a sudden craving rived him to be working again in the store over on Sixth Avenue, among the smells of bath soap and pine tar, and a linctus brewing in back, and the heavy buses going by and shaking the place till all the little bottles woke up and elbowed one another. He yearned for the fineness of glass jars and measures, the gentle pull of a balance, an enjoyment of laboratory routine in a white coat, and the cheery salute of a cop's nightstick as he passed beyond the amphora in the window.

He looked around the walls, hacked out of rock and painted over, with shelves of strange tools, and bay after bay of engines and trucks, hating it all, detesting his unwashed body stinking with the ash of bygone energy, a needly jaw and greasy hair, the tiredness that made his eyes simmer, ashamed of his uselessness before the two mechanics, envious of them, contemptuous of himself, unable to find light of hope except in prayer for Rosa.

Motor horns sounded in harsh squirts, bringing movement from the big room, and shouts, and a couple of carabinieri ran down the steps looking along the driveway leading to the ramp. A convoy of trucks wheeled into the parking space, and stopped with running motors. An officer jumped down, waving at the two carabinieri, and they pointed up towards the battle, shouting, moving towards him, but he was aboard before they were anywhere near, leaving them to look up at faces blank as their own, packed tight in truck after truck. The clamour of their passing was giving way to the turbine hum, and the carabinieri had been joined by more, with a chorus of women venturing out on the stairhead, and they were startled by the oncome of an engine that from its pulse might have belonged to an aeroplane.

Snowy looked across at Rusty, and both men straightened, looking at each other.

" Give you one guess," Snowy said. " On a million pound cash. No I.O.U.s."

Headlamps flicked on and off in bursts of golden light, bringing nearer and nearer a massive beat of power that in a rapturous roar fell silent, making thin song of the turbine, leaving a sense, unfelt before, of space.

Snowy looked at the dusty shape, enjoying its quality, surprised at the pile of stuff in the back seats, waving at Bill's grin behind the windscreen.

But the seat beside him was empty.

The world dried out and left him dry, sucking up and wrinkling, twisting inside, making even his skin feel sore, letting him stand weak, distrustful of his legs, trembling in the arms, feeling the stares of those standing near and defenceless, willing for them to watch and share his misery.

Max saw the change and, despite a smile bitten off short, felt sorrow tumble through him for some element of fineness suddenly smashed and irreplaceable. He wanted to go over there and clap the big fellow on the back, but deeper sense warned of a wild animal's sudden turning rage and the strangle of big hands.

" What're you two looking so daft about? " Bill leaned over the side of the car. " What're you playing at, anyway? Shops? "

Snowy turned away, flapping his arms in a brisk warm-up.

" Come on out of that," he said. " Get your bloody shirt off, and get stuck into it. Been playing the gent too long, you have."

" Dearie me," Bill said, hauling himself out of the red leather seat. " We are in a temper. Ah, Rusty, lad. How's it going? "

" Magnifico," Rusty said. " We find her, Rosie."

" Rosie? " Bill looked at the parts spread about, and up at the crane. " Whatever did you do this for? There wasn't all that wrong with her. Good gracious me."

Snowy listened, eyes tight shut, resting his weight on a wrench.

" Look," he said. " This is how we found her. If you'll look very careful, you'll see they'd started spraying her. Whoever took her down knew his kit. All we got to do is put her back. Can you understand that? Or are you up the wall?"

" I'm with you," Bill said. " But y'ought to have said something before, not stand there looking soft."

" Lancashire." Snowy went back, as though in penance, to the bench. " Lancashire. That's where they come from. They pop out of some hole up there, and you can't catch 'em. God 'blige my Uncle Charlie."

" As you've had to be, many a time, I've no doubt," said Bill, rattling the tool-box. " Else I don't know how ye'd have got on. Terrible to be born a cockney. Never get over it. Half a brain makes it worse, of course."

Snowy felt a weary hope rise in him to think that now Bill was back Rosie would be on the road many an hour sooner, bringing him so much nearer the unit, and mail from home, and fresh dreams, and new longing to have the kids around him and his feet back in the fireplace.

Setting about the carburettor was another way of taking his mind off the ache somewhere inside, a hurting, raw place that she had gone, not without saying goodbye, but simply that she had gone.

A new meaning seemed to have got into that word She, a shade, nothing he could fix, some new thought that came as he said it. She, She, and yet there seemed to be no words for it, but only a feeling.

Alarm came slow, growing in pressure somewhere between his shoulders, an impulse sprung, he knew, from another pair of eyes, at first frightening and then warming, rising in delight that seemed to flame in colour against the wall he stared at, making him blink hard to assure himself that he stood there in a world not of images but real, and himself no dreamer, but awake.

He turned exactly to where she leant against the bonnet watching him, wrapped in a long coat with her hands in the pockets, resting one sheepskin boot on the other.

" Snowy," she said, in a voice high with make-believe hurt, " I never was so disappointed in all my life. I come all the way back here, and you don't even ask where I am, or anything. Oh, Snowy. How could anyone be so forgetful? "

" Sorry, Miss," he said. " I was just going to ask, only you know what a beauty he is. Talk English to him, he's done."

" English," said Bill. " Hark at that. The conceit of it. The airs on it. I'll tell ye what. If it weren't for our *Manchester*

Guardian keeping you decently informed, ye'd all end your days in a thicket eating one another's tattoos."

"Are you hungry?" she asked.

"Hungry?" Snowy looked at Max, and then at Rusty. "If I look anything like them two, Miss, I'm dying. I reckon I've gone past it. Till I see it."

"There's a meal going on in there." She nodded at the big room. "I'll call you when it's ready."

She pushed herself off the car, looking at him, and all the way through, no wrinkle, no frown, no smile, as she might at someone she had seen a little distance off.

"Do you have a can-opener?" She turned to Max.

"Surely," said Max, pulling out a knife.

"Follow me," she said, hooking a finger. "While I'm away, Bill, you can tell him what happened."

Snowy waited until they had gone up the stairway.

"Why didn't you tell me she was standing there?" he burst out. "Made me look a right mug."

"Natural state," said Bill, unmoved. "Have I to do your looking for you now, then? You'll have plenty to worry about soon, besides her."

"What're you nattering about?" Snowy was surprised at his seriousness. "What's gone wrong?"

"There's a couple of battalions of our lot coming up here," Bill said. "I heard one lot's Highlanders. They was brought back out of the Line to rest, so ye can tell what sort of state they'll be in. The Yanks're sending some, so are the Poles."

"Blimey." Snowy pulled the crane chains to the bench. "Let's get out of it, chum. I don't want to argue the toss with that lot. How d'you know?"

"She started it," said Bill. "She's a right 'un. Passed all the coppers, all the sentries, stalked inside the place as if she was the G.O.C. She wasn't in there, I'll swear, not ten minutes, and things started happening. I got marched in some big bloke's office. He was a Yankee. Asked me questions. Got straight through to our lot. Talked to our C.O."

"That's tore it," Snowy groaned. "Right down the middle. What he say?"

"Well, I said we'd only broke down, see?" Bill nodded at

Rusty, and all three lifted. " Then the Provost Marshal's lot started pouring in. We passed 'em on the way back here. Biggest troop move I've seen outside the Line. They're going to clean the place up, and put everything on two legs behind wire. Good luck to 'em."

" 's right," Snowy said. " What's all that kit in the bus? "

" Stuff for us, and blankets, grub, overcoats and such," said Bill. " I went home with her." He put the tool edge-down on the block, tapping it gently in double beats, thinking. " It were coming on dark when we got there. Through a big garden. We went in a side door to a room with half a dozen candles. I've never seen owt as pretty. Lovely house, proper lovely. And a staircase that ought to go up straight to Paradise, the way it were made. The tooling'd fair twist itself in your heart. Ever hear the saying, Show me how they live, and I'll tell thee what they are? "

Snowy shook his head. A pain that he thought was hunger, and knew was not, like a sickness without wanting to be sick, had been busy whilst Bill had been speaking. He wanted to talk about her, hear about her, think about her, and yet more than anything he wanted to run beyond sound of Bill's voice, so fat with knowledge of her, that should have belonged only to himself.

" She's lovely," Bill said. " It's a lovely house. Not because what's in it. It's the way y' feel in it. That's all."

The difference with the woman with the suitcase and the woman in the house was still troubling Bill, for, although she fitted right enough into everything she did, it was only in the house that he saw her properly, and the one way he could think of her now was in blooms of light, that just touched the edges of everything, firing a diamond in the corner of her eye while she talked to an old man with white gloves, holding a silver tray against his chest.

" She's a different lass at home," he said, trying to explain himself. " It's well-nigh unbelievable. A few hours' driving and you're in marvels. Come up here again, and where are ye? What's that noise going on? "

" It's only a bit of a do up there," Snowy said. " Eyetie coppers, and the lot that had this place."

Bill looked round the garage, taking in the detail.

" D'you mean to say this weren't ours? " he demanded.

" Never," said Snowy. " And nothing in it. Everything you can see was pinched."

" Well, upon my sam," said Bill. " Some right carry-ons, I must say. When y'come right down to it, we're slow, y'know. Dead slow, that's us."

Max came out of the doorway in a hurry, and, looking about, grinned at an oil tank, picking up a piece of scrap-iron, thumping the sides until the metal trembled.

" First service," he shouted. " Volcano special. Hurry, hurry."

" I've had a bite," Bill said. " You two go. I'll get this done while you're away. You'll find soap and towels on top of that stuff."

While Snowy was washing he tried to make up his mind how to act when he saw her, what he was to say, and how to say it, but all the time a face kept looking over his shoulder and whispering that it was useless, that he might just as well go in there and look and talk and say what he wanted, because, one way or another, he would end up making a fool of himself. Conscience was running its way at the back there, telling him that his feeling was wrong, and that Liz was entitled to every thought, and any he could spare ought to go to the girls. A quick notion of another man feeling for her as he felt for the Princess brought him to stare down at the bubbling water, and then shog the whole problem away for impatience at the bother of it.

Rusty noticed his preoccupation.

" Don't worry, Snowy," he said, clapping his shoulder. " Couple hours, we finish. Go home."

" That's right, chum." Snowy waved at the lines of vehicles. " And you take your pick out of this lot. Anything you want, it's yours. But where's all your pals? "

Rusty looked about, thumbs under his armpits, grinning, snapping his eyes, drawing in a breath that seemed to go on for minutes.

" Ah, Snowy," he said. " I take three lorry. No more to starve, eh? My pals, they all here. They don't leave. When I want, they come."

" That's the sort of pals to have," Snowy said. " Now let's see what's on in here."

What he expected to see had made no impression on his mind at all, but what he saw on reaching the doorway pulled him up short, brought a whistle from Rusty, and a grunt from both as they cannoned.

Some of the tables had been righted, laid with bedsheets, and dressed with dishes of red apples, with crockery and cutlery stacked at both ends. A wine barrel stood at the foot of the switchboard, and glasses and mugs had been lined on the platform.

A doorway on the other side was open, and the Princess was under the light, ladling out soup in swirls of steam that hid her now and again, stressing the copper of her hair, tidy as ever, with the big bun coiled on her neck. Coming out of the door and winding all the way round the wall, a queue of women, mostly in trousers and military overcoats, could be told from the men by their hair. In a bathroom opposite, shower stalls were busy with women, and others were dressing, binding their heads in coloured towels, and more still were waiting, leaning against the wall, looking tired and ready to sleep as they stood. Snowy saw a girl's face looking up almost in fright just before the water fell in a jewelled cone about her, making a pinkish ghost inside a lacy crystal that grew a forearm and a drooping hand.

" I could do with one of them," he said. " You could scrape it off me."

" Come," Rusty said, and went inside, pushing among the women, pointing to a couple of stalls, and talking apparently to nobody, because nobody answered or took any notice. Snowy followed him, careful to keep his eyes on where he was going, smelling the odour of water on flesh, reminding him of warm afternoons and a green depth on tiles in the swimming bath. Rusty took a pair of sheets from a pile in the corner, and borrowed a lump of soap from the woman next door.

Snowy got under the shower, savouring the blasting agony of a mountain freshet for the few seconds before all breath had left him, and stepped out, blind, frozen almost to paralysis, and felt himself taken by hands that first pulled him on to a board overlaid with a sheet, and then began rubbing soap into him.

At first he thought that Rusty might have gone crazy, but,

opening his eyes, he found two of the women at work on him and leaving nothing to chance.

"Well, God peach me," he chattered. "What a do, eh?"

"Leave alone," Rusty warned. "'At's a business. Very good."

"Telling me, chum." Snowy was sinking under a merciless lathering. "Ain't took a bashing like this since my old ma had the handlings of me. But she did leave me a bit of meself here and there. Oy, nark it."

He got back in the shower, hearing Rusty yelling and the women screaming, just long enough to lose the soap, and leap for the length of sheeting, first binding himself in the slack, towelling as fast as his arms would move, but still careful not to look about, conscious of a dozen women all round.

Again, he wondered if it were tiredness, or hunger, or if there were too much of a good thing, or what it was that prevented his being roused by their nearness. A glance, side to side and under cover of wiping his face, to see if there were not a couple of them ready to make him change his mind, assured him of their utter disinterest. Even the two women had left Rusty and were wringing underclothes with their backs turned.

He went out, careful to look nowhere except at the doorway, buttoning his shirt, feeling better than he had for months, and yet a little flat, for he was loath to think that he could openly undress and bath in a room with a lot of women, and attract less attention than what they were finding in their hair.

Talking and a rattle of cutlery on enamel plates gave warmth to the room, and light falling on red apples brightened everything, making it more homely, until even the hum of the turbine seemed to fall restfully in place. He saw the Princess looking at him from the other side of the stove, smiling and nodding at Max, as though they shared a joke, and then invitingly holding up a plate.

"Who's been taking a shower with the girls?" she called when he was near. "I rate pretty near top as a scrubber. Why didn't you let me know?"

"Couldn't," Snowy said. "Too cold to open me mouth. 'Sides, I was took care of by experts. I'll be black and blue for a week. What's this? Steaks?"

" That's right," Max pointed to the kitchen. " You want to see something? Go and look in that ice-box out there. They had the area champ for quartermaster."

One of the women helped him to a fillet steak, fried potatoes with chopped onions, tomatoes and runner beans, another brought him a crusty baton of brown bread, and the Princess filled his glass from the wine barrel.

" Question is," she said, sitting opposite, " where do we go from here? "

" Soon as Rosie's ready, we're off," Snowy said. " And if there's anything left in that ice-box that'll come too."

" I promised everything to the girls," she said, a little uncertain. " They're hungry people. They have children down there."

" Children? " Snowy looked at the rows of shaded faces. " Them? "

" Them," she said. " Most of them are in this business for the money. Didn't you know that? They make more in a month than a couple of lifetimes out on the farm. Then they go back home, and buy some cattle, and they're settled for life."

" What about the husbands? " Snowy asked. " Ain't they got anything to say? "

" Marriage is a contract in this country," she said. " You both work for the good of the family you're going to have. There's no love in idleness or dreams in a cottage. And if you're both born poor, then you've got to do the best you know. Not every woman has the courage. Or the health. Those who have just capitalize on them, that's all. If they're down that far."

" God bless 'em," Max said.

Snowy tried to think of Liz going off with the two girls. He tried to think of it, but thought seemed to stop. He could see Liz with her hat and coat on, standing in front of the hall mirror putting what she called the finishing touches to her hair, and generally pulling herself about, and he could see her going down the road hand in hand with the girls. But to think any further than that was like looking at a barrier. A vision of her down in that room with the red plush sofas made the food in his mouth seem dry.

" I'm glad it don't happen to us," he said.

" Make up your mind, Snowy," she said, looking at him in a

way that reminded him of a steady fall of cool water. " Any country that's destitute'll have the same thing happen. Don't let's kid ourselves. No kind of claptrap's any use. If the men can't bring it home, the gals will. They have to."

" But if everybody's so poor," Snowy said, " who's going to pay 'em? "

" There'll always be plenty of loose cash for that kind of utility," Max said. " Like cigarettes and the movies. It don't cost all that. Asiatics have the same idea, but they use opium."

She shivered, drawing the coat tighter, looking down at her hands.

" I don't know why I have to feel so high and mighty about it," she said. " I never thought of myself as a utility. That's the big, strong, male mind at work again. Does it make you feel good to think that way? "

Max waved at the tables.

" There it all is, lady," he said. " Whether I feel good or not, or even if I think. There it is."

" Yes," she said. " I guess that's about the answer."

Snowy wanted to go over and lift her on his knee to try and nurse that note out of her voice. Something had hurt her, but he was unable to make up his mind what, and asking questions could have made it worse. He looked down at his plate, and carefully packed his fork, wishing he could think of something to say that might carry his feeling to her or even fill the silence.

None of the women had moved from their places. Some of them had put their heads in their arms and looked asleep, and a couple were pecking at long rolls of crochet. In the corner, a group of carabinieri were watching a card game with no more noise than the slap of play. Steam went bumping through a pipe out in the kitchen.

Something peculiar about the quietness made him drop his knife and fork, listening, and then he knew.

" Oy," he said. " Notice anything? "

Max shook his head.

" The turbine," Snowy said. " It's stopped."

Perhaps he spoke too loudly, or a note of alarm was emphasized, but the tables awoke in movement and a mumble of talk sprang to an hysteria of questioning, and then forms scraped and toppled. Women were screaming, more were trying to hush them to silence, and carabinieri called soothingly along the gangways.

Glass panes flew, the stove toppled, spilling embers, and the chimney-stack broke loose in sections among clouding soot and a crash of sound that shook the floor, throwing people headlong among falling furniture.

42

Bill felt the ground underfoot swell up and saved himself by rolling under the engine bench, crouching there until a cloud of small stones had blown by, waiting for the roof to fall. Moments passed in darkness thick with dust, and through it all he was thankful that Rosie had been covered ready for the test run. Clearing air and colder currents brought him out, feeling in the darkness until he touched the next truck, running his hands over the dashboard to find the switch and turning on the headlights in a smile of relief.

Dust was still rolling, but he could see the racing car, and he ran across, turning all her lights on, and then hurried down the bay towards the stairhead, turning on headlights as he went. At the end of the inspection pit he found a spotlamp and battery and took it with him, reaching the stairs when the first women were coming out.

They screamed at him, screamed at the light, screamed as he passed them, and their screams joined all the others along the corridor and in the room. He steadied the bright spot on the floor, letting the women push past him, wondering at the terror in their faces, cold at sound of their voices.

Max had a girl over his shoulder and another holding his arm.

"Hi, Bill," he said, "what happened?"

"A damn big bang," said Bill. "That's all I know. What's the damage here?"

"Lots of noise," Max heaved his burden farther over. "Snow got a whole lot of soot in his chow. That's all."

Carabinieri advanced with their rifles held across their chests in a cordon, driving the last of the women towards the door. Snowy was behind, carrying the Princess in his arms with her hands swinging loose as though she had fainted.

" Now what's up? " Bill went towards him. " She's never hurt, is she, by God? "

" I hope to Christ not, Bill mate," Snowy said, looking down at her. " Went out like a light. Let's get her in the air."

" There won't be a doctor for miles," Bill said. " Bloody fine country. There's nowt in it, except a damn lot of flaming trouble."

Carabinieri had grouped the women in the sweep of the racing car's headlights. A draught from somewhere blew the dust in patterns round about, but the air was almost clear and certainly breathable.

" We're not buried in, then," Bill said. " That's a mercy. How is she? "

" All right, I think." Snowy stood up, looking at Rosie. " Take us a bit to bolt this down. Why don't you and Max take the racer and run her down to the town? Find a doctor."

Bill patted the racing car's sides.

" Why don't you? " he asked. " I'll get Rosie going quicker'n you can. You and Max go. Leave Rusty here with us."

" Just where is Rusty? " Max was looking about in the crowd. " Oh, Rusty? "

Women turned among themselves, and carabinieri moved in and out of the light, calling into the darkness. But all the faces turned back, enquiringly, blank.

" Who saw him last? " Snowy asked at large.

" When he went to supper with you," Bill said. " Was he hurt? "

Snowy picked up the light.

" I'll go and see," he said. " You finish Rosie."

" Wait a minute." Max held Snowy's arm and took the lamp. " You boys go ahead and fix the wagon. I've been useless long enough. I'll find Rusty."

Snowy let the lamp go.

" O.K., chum," he said. " Any nonsense, give us a yell."

" Lose my voice if there is," Max said, starting off. " That solid beat'll be my knees and teeth."

The Princess looked as though she were sleeping. A group of the women stood round her, and some of them had taken off their coats to roll them up for a mattress and pillow, and others chafed her hands, or waved towels, believing they were clearing the air.

Snowy looked down at her for a moment, and then went back to Bill, surprised to catch himself feeling as he had on the night that Primula came, when Liz was having a bad time and he sat in the waiting-room by a gas fire flicking pale blue, without wanting to smoke or drink, praying for her inside his head and pretending not to, and hoping he was not suspected of it.

"It's a dead faint, that's all," Bill said, trying to be cheerful. "I'm well up in them, never fear. She'll come right as a trivet, you'll see. Poor lass, she's dog tired, what wi' tearing about uphill and down dale, and nobody looking after her. A lass'll have need of a man, tha' knows. Somebody to swear at her now and again and keep her in trim."

Both men were conscious of the crowd of women silent about them watching every movement, tensing in sympathy as Rosie's body was lowered into place, grunting little squeaks when tools clashed on the floor, murmuring often in apprehension, and breaking into a high-pitched Bravo! among a patter of clapping hands when at last Bill nodded, and Snowy stood up, throwing sweat off his face, triumphantly patting her sides, ready for the road.

From time to time Bill had been aware of Snowy's glances across at the Princess, and then into the darkness at the stairhead, obviously thinking about Max and Rusty, and he was not surprised when Snowy, wiping his face, came around deliberately to his side of the bench.

"They've been away too long, mate," he said. "I don't like it."

"Send the coppers after 'em," Bill said. "Standing here doing nowt."

"They've got their orders, same as everybody else." Snowy counted four carabinieri, with rifles in the crooks of their arms, on the edge of the crowd. "Leave this and look for 'em. Eh?"

"I'm on," Bill said.

As they left, a dolorous cry went up, smothered by sharp orders from the corporal, but when they reached the stairhead and looked back they found half of the women close behind, and scattered pairs hurrying through the criss-cross beams of the headlights.

" Never mind," Bill said. " They'll be useful, if it's only to kick up a row and scare t'bogeys off."

Striking matches, they found their way along the corridor into the big room, and paused at the doorway. A white light was on in the kitchen, and they heard the sound of chopping, and a clatter of steel.

Glims from a half-dozen hurricane lamps spotted a path to the far door, lively with the shadows of many people bowed under heavy loads going out towards the tunnel mouth. When the last had gone, and the big room was still, Snowy jerked his head, signing to the women for silence, and went on tiptoe towards the kitchen.

Hung up on a bar, the spotlight threw heavy black and white relief in its lit area and such darkness beyond, that women padding through barefoot appeared in the circle as if by magic, and, passing, obscured the bulk of men working on the butchery table, carving joints from hung carcasses, throwing bones in copper vats that were being emptied into a tarpaulin.

Stripped to the waist, Max was knifing a side of beef with easy motions that sang, and beyond him Rusty was checking men and women rolling joints in sacking.

" Oy," Snowy called. " You're a fine couple. You had us in a fair tizzy out there. Why didn't you tell us? "

" The heck for? " Max said, still craving. " I took a look at you a while ago, and, boy, you looked like Castor and Pollux, Inc. So I came right back in here. Can't you see? I'm the happiest guy in this whole continent. Maxie's busy. For once in a long, long whiles."

" Where you taking the stuff? " Snowy asked, as empty-handed men and women pushed by to come in. " These're Rusty's lot, ain't they? "

" Sure," Max said. " He's got a couple of beautiful new trucks all picked out for himself, and they have 'em loaded way below the axles."

Rusty opened his arms, laughing up at the roof.

" Ah, Snowy," he trumpeted. " I'm so happy. Is everything

so good. Meat we got. Vegetable we got. Tin of stuff we got. Truck and lorry we got. Everything we got. No more we hungry."

"That's right," Max said. "He's in a huddle with the angels. And if you could've seen these babies just now, when we called 'em in to get all this stuff away, you'd probably be, too. They just went right down on their knees."

Snowy took Bill by the shoulder and turned him round.

"We'll be ready in a couple of ticks," he said.

They went out, surprised to find that the crowd of women had gone, and stumbled their way into the garage.

"Well worth while," Bill said, flat.

"What?" Snowy looked at him, a little surprised.

"This job," Bill waved his hand toward Rosie. "I'm glad I came. It's not been much of a leave. But now I'm satisfied."

"Ah," Snowy said. "That's something, anyway."

"Remember that poor little love in that place where Rusty lives?" Bill said. "Worried me, she has. Now she'll have a nice big plate of grub inside her, and I've helped."

"That's right, chum," Snowy said. "Good old Lancashire. Couldn't fight the war without you, could we? I can't think why you don't all go and live on your own somewhere. Nice and comfortable, with your throats cut."

"Hark at the cockneys." Bill nodded at the Princess. "Flattering themselves by poking fun at others. It's an old dodge, is that. How're you feeling, all by yourself, here?"

"I've had the most wonderful sleep," she said, combing her hair. "I'm a little ashamed."

Snowy watched the plaits being separated over her head, marvelling at the interplay of fingers, thinking of Liz with the comb in her mouth, standing at the window doing the children's hair before they went to school.

"Long as you're all right," he said, "that's the main thing. Where's all the girls?"

"They went off somewhere," she said. "Along towards the way we came in. They said you'd taken all the stuff I'd promised them."

"Ah," said Bill. "More trouble, like as not. We'll see they get their share. Feeling all right, love?"

" Fine, fine," she said, off-handedly it seemed to Snowy. " I just didn't like passing out like that. Nobody else did."

" Nobody else had the caning you had," said Bill. " All said and done, there's nobbut one end t'candle, and that'll burn quick enough."

" Stop nattering," Snowy said. " Give us a hand here."

Bill was a little surprised at both Snowy and the Princess, for while he had no sympathy with any deeper feeling than what he called friendliness between either, at all events he knew that such feeling existed, and he expected to have the satisfaction of showing open disapproval on noting the signs. But neither of them looked as though it mattered if the other were alive, much less in tender thought, and it annoyed him to think he might have missed a quarrel he could have enjoyed.

The Princess was back in the old mood, heartily sick of herself and her surroundings, moment by moment finding herself caught in gusts of surprise that she could have been so stupid about coming back, whether from a sense of responsibility towards these people, or for whatever reason. She wanted more than anything to be away from them, out of this cavern that stank of mould and gunpowder, and get back into the air, and the road and home. She was almost physically sick of their rough talk and habits that seemed, since she awoke and found herself alone, to have become marked beyond all palliation. Hating the weakness that had made her sleep, she tried to put distance between herself and Snowy in particular, trying to loathe the ugliness of his dirty hands, and the drips of sweat falling off his nose, fighting hard to shudder in distaste at long muscles in sudden knot, closing her eyes in nausea when he scraped his throat. But she could only pretend to be sick, knew she felt no real hatred or distaste, and found herself wishing she could press a finger-tip on that muscle and test its quality, wanting to laugh at the vigorous impatience behind the spit.

Snowy was uncertain how he felt, but he was angry at somebody for something, without knowing who, or why; so, to make sure primarily of himself as a workman, he took thorough charge of the tools, picking them up and putting them down as if he meant them, at least, to know who was the master, until the cavern rang and rang again, and in the healthy pealing he thought he heard assurance that some part of life, at least, was changeless and solid, speaking words of hope for a happier day.

"Well," Bill said at last, "we're to be right thankful, tha knows. Whoever took her down had some respect for his job. Not a happorth of nonsense in the lot. And I had me doubts."

"That's right," Snowy said. "Knew his stuff, and no larks."

"When do we go?" she asked.

"Couple of minutes, Miss." Snowy turned to her, sitting with hands about her knees, bright in the eye, and looking, he thought, fresh as a daisy. "I don't know how you do it."

"What?" She frowned, unclasping her hands. "What's wrong?"

"Nothing, Miss," he said. "Only how you look. Anybody'd think you just come out the front door. I feel like a moggie just crawled through a knothole."

"What's a moggie?" She looked at Bill.

"A tomcat," said Bill, reprovingly. "A fine thing to say, I'm sure."

"Snowy," she said quickly, preventing an outburst, "what do you suppose that noise was?"

"Don't know, Miss," he said, pointing with a spanner. "That's where it was, and that's where all the coppers went. Hope nobody got hurt."

"Do you suppose it's serious?" she asked. "Nothing's happening?"

"Don't know nothing about it, Miss," Snowy said. "And I ain't poking my nose any more in it, neither. All we want now is a nice drop of petrol and we're off. Nobody more pleased'n me, tomcat or no tomcat. Of all the blinkin' sauce."

Bill went away with a couple of empty cans towards the pump.

"Don't be hard on him, Snowy," she said, watching him go. "He told me about his wife. I wish somebody felt like that about me."

She saw him pause in turning a bolt, and then put weight on the ratchet.

"Lots of people feel like it," he said, in separate efforts of the turn. "Trouble is, they can't say it."

"I know it," she said, and jumped down. "But I'd love to hear it. I don't know how it is, but we all seem to go around giving ourselves hell for really nothing at all. Flaying ourselves just for the fun of living. And it never was much fun, either."

"That don't sound like you, Miss," he said, looking at her.

"How do you know?" She was smiling. "How do you think I ought to sound?"

"A lot perkier than that," he said. "I don't reckon you've got a lot to be sorry about, take it all round. Tomorrow night you'll be home. You'll have your little girl to bath and put to bed. You'll have your health and a roof. Thousands of others won't. Wait till I'm one night away from home. I'll give it perky."

"Ah, Snowy." She smoothed herself down with the flat of her hands, all the way down slowly, lightly, and then lifted them wide away in a gesture of flight. "It's too easy to talk. You've got somebody to go home to. I haven't. Health and a roof is fine if there's someone to share. My daughter's beautiful and adorable, but there's still an awful lot that's missing. There's something in knowing you're wanted, that nobody else'll do but you. I'm so sick of standing around wondering when it's going to be my turn."

"But, Miss," Snowy said, "I thought you had a husband?"

"I had," she said. "But not the way I mean. Never. I thought it'd be wonderful to share everything, and tell everything. Not to be able to wait till you could get back home and spill every last syllable, and go to sleep, nights, just empty. That's what I dreamt of, always. It didn't work out."

Looking at her, pale in the headlamps, standing against the hard criss-cross of beams along the driveway, Snowy thought he could hear in her voice a note he knew well enough from Liz, a special tone that was more to be felt than heard, of pleading for a little more sympathy than usual, or perhaps an invitation to be curious and ask questions about some matter she was keeping to herself, that she considered he might share, but only if he pressed her, coaxingly as though parting a baby's fingers.

"I didn't like asking you about him," he said, and went across to her. "What happened to him?"

"He's gone," she said. "Escaped. Like so many hundreds more. He'll turn up at home sometime. More weeks and weeks of worry. He's no criminal. He'd have got out pretty soon, anyway. It's this phoney romantic sense they all have. A bunch of

Monte Cristos. In fact, they were just a lot of little jackasses in topboots doing what they were told. My fault, too, I guess. I saw it coming. I should have done something."

"You had the baby to think about," he said, watching a clear iris, almost gold in the light. "House and a job to do."

She laughed out loud, up at him, and walked away, still laughing.

"Oh, Snowy," she said. "If only you knew. We don't look after homes. Only common women do that. Farmers' wives and housewives and housekeepers and maids. Why, didn't you know? We only get interested when the work's all done. As for my baby, bless her, I adopted her last year. She was pulled out of a ruin. She isn't mine. Not really. Oh, Snowy. I can't even love her properly, because she's not."

Tapping the heavy steel against his palm, watching the chain turn, he felt the blood rise in him, wanting to go to her, and feel inside the swathing coat to find the shape of her and take her, tightly, but he jibbed because of the grease on his hands, and it seemed the wrong place to say what he wanted to, too cold and wide, and light.

She looked as though she might be praying, but she turned in a quick swing of skirts and he was amazed at her eyes, glittering white.

"I want something that's mine," she said, loudly, that crackled in the roof. "I'm sick of houses, and sticks of furniture and all that junk. I want something that's mine, that's a part of me, that couldn't come from somebody else. Don't you understand, Snowy? Don't you? Something that belongs, that's mine. Mine."

Bill was coming back with the petrol, whistling, and she heard him, and turned away. Snowy went over to collect the tools and clear up, finding that tidy racks brought a sense of satisfaction, almost of contentment, as if an array of orderliness outside helped promote a feeling of order within.

"They've nigh finished in there," Bill said. "So I told 'em we'd drive round and meet 'em."

"Right," Snowy said. "How are they?"

"Jumping for joy," said Bill. "Old Rusty, he's kissed everybody a dozen times, and now he's started a second dozen. They've a convoy of wagons loaded. He's took tools enough for a base dump, and he's loading oil and petrol on another. Right hand of all that's good, is old Rusty, and he'll not care who knows it."

" He deserves it." Snowy looked across at her. " All right, Miss. I'm just going to start her up."

" I'll stroll on ahead," she pointed, walking away, and, remembering the tears, he nodded to himself, almost hearing Bill ask questions.

Rosie started, clearing every other thought from his mind, for now, cool against familiar leather, with his hands comfortable on the slim width of the wheel, he felt himself once again master of power he could call by pressing his foot, given, it appeared to him, from affection that he returned by encouragement in a voice keyed by sound of her engine, in words shaped by her response.

Bill watched him run out into the fairway, hearing him whisper between the hums and has of Rosie's turn, and grinned, happy to think of a job well done and promise of a good drive home behind an engine running in silk.

" What's today? " Snowy asked. " Saturday or what? "

" Don't know," Bill said. " Might be. What's the odds? "

" I like keeping up with it," said Snowy. " I don't like going on day after day, all the same. Monday, I used to like going down the market in the lunch hour and see what I could pick up. I had some lovely bargains. I got a smashing bit of carving for our parlour one day there. A dollar the lot. The bloke said it come from a Burma temple. It was all little carvings of girls, they looked like, with only a pair of trousers on, holding their hands funny. Liz never went a lot on it. Bit too much tit for her liking."

" Pet's the same," Bill said. " I brought home a calendar once. I just turned me back. She had it in t'boiler fire, no arguments."

" Ah," said Snowy. " They won't have it. Tuesday I always let go by. Never much to a Tuesday. Wednesdays, Liz and me went to the pictures."

" So did me and Pet," said Bill. " That's damn funny."

" Thursdays, I either went down the dogs for a couple of hours, else round the club if there was boxing." Snowy put her into the straight and waited for the wheel to swing. " Summer, I used to go swimming. Fridays, I helped Liz with the shopping. When the kids got older, we used to go second house of the Empire. Saw some lovely turns there, too. Shilling's worth in the gallery, that was us. Fish and chips after. God love me."

" So far," Bill said, " you're nigh a dead spit of me, except me or mother did t'shopping. And I used to go to the club for billiards. What did you do of a Saturday? "

" Finish work at one," said Snowy. " Go round and see the Spurs if they was playing at home, else I used to go down the allotment and give the spuds a kind look." He was watching the driving mirror, backing Rosie for a wide turn. " Saturday night, we used to pick out a show, and go and queue for it. Sunday morning, take the kids down the road for an airing before dinner. Nice read of the paper after, and a snooze till tea. Then we either had somebody come round and see us, else we went round and see them. Else we just went out and had a nice little drink on our own. Best part was taking the kids out."

" Ah," Bill said. " Lovely times, them."

" Time they was back," Snowy said. " Sometimes I reckon I dreamed 'em."

" Strange they can't leave well alone," said Bill. " You're going along very nice, and then all of a sudden some bloke gets an idea, and before you know where you are you're out here. And no hope of getting back."

" Never mind, chum," Snowy said. " Get the job done first, argue after. I'll argue, all right."

Minutes had gone by in trying all her gears, and operating the crane, but then Snowy put up a thumb and winked, taking her slowly past the pumps and the stairhead, and into the parking space to turn on the ramp. They saw that all vehicle lights were on, with hand lamps lit on the edges of the driveway, flushing the path.

Rusty's convoy of trucks, nose to tail, stretched along the middle lane, pointed for the ramp, with some of the cabin doors hanging open as if the drivers had just got out.

But there were no people.

" Probably still in the kitchen, stuffing themselves," Bill said. " I'll go and see."

Snowy got down and went over to the convoy, hearing Bill clatter across a scrap heap, swearing as he went. The trucks were all new, and packed full above the tailboards, covered over with tarpaulin and roped by an artist. The last vehicle was the panzer workshop, and mentally Snowy shook Rusty's hand for having the sense to take it. Mulling over its equipment, he tried to think of a repair job beyond its scope, and, with pictures of stripped gears in mind, he turned into the space behind the driveway.

All the women were huddled together, and all the people with Rusty were farther down, separated by a group of unarmed carabinieri.

Rusty stood in the clear space, thumbs in his belt, looking down at his boots.

Scarlet tops of military policemen's caps were lively in the darkness at each end of the company. Two of them, with white crossbelts, stood at ease with automatic rifles slung.

The Princess was staring over the head of someone sitting on an upturned chest. She moved slightly, as though wanting to turn, and yet afraid.

" Snowy," she called, in a thin voice. " Snowy? Is that you? "

" Yes, Miss," he said, going towards her. " What's the lark, here? "

" You'll find out, Snowy boy," a voice said, that he recognized because it never stayed in the same tone two words at a time. " Remember me? Dincott. Nipper Dincott. 't your service, Snowy boy. I'm the boss here now. Where's the other bloke? "

43

Sometimes a moment comes in a man's life when the thinking part of himself, as it were, goes from the flesh to a place high overhead, and rests there, looking down upon his body in its surroundings, seeing all things in detail, not only immediately but even far back to first memories, tracing the pattern of his life straightly from then to now, remembering the shape of an aunt's hat, the scarlet glow of paper round an Easter egg, the smell of mimosa, and disappointment almost to tears in a palm cross that was only a dried reed with a knot in it, too limp to stand upright, never mind hold a man.

Without wanting to, it seems, he sits there watching himself and the people he knew, feeling knuckles cracking against his face in his first street fight, and the surprise that such hurt existed, and on to the freeze of fingers on a milk churn in dark mornings, and the schoolie trying to teach him the meaning of π. Snowy found himself remembering a French coin somebody gave him instead of a shilling when he was selling newspapers, and the disgust of old Mrs. Brickney when she found it in his takings and dropped it in the pocket under her apron, telling him always to run his fingernail along the milling round the edge if it was too dark to see, and how God could let such cowsons live was more than she could fathom, because if ever she got her five claws in his scrag, she took her oath she would bash the spit out of him with the other five, and case him and his dirty-bellied cow of a mother, too, if ever she had the face to toe her marks.

He saw his first pale day at the works, ashamed of his tea can on a board with all the others, and sneaking it off when nobody was looking to hold it over the smithy fire and burn the newness out, and then swing it against the wall to make dents, but so hard that the lid got stuck, and old Charlie McIlwaine let him have a share of his, with rum in it, that got him drunk, and went home with him to try and explain to Ma, but all he got was both edges of her tongue and he went off showing the patches in his blue dungarees, laughing down the alley.

Her face came near to him, now, the day he got back from work and she came in the wash house and looked through the window to tell him to go about quietly because Dad was upstairs ill. Looking at her through suds drying on his face, watching her head drop little by little as courage left her, and then the big tears falling.

And the memory of night-time, and a girl in a short coat walking her long, beautiful legs across the brilliance of a roadway in rain splashed with rags of greeny blue and scarlet from the traffic lights, and watching those legs getting longer and straighter, going away from him into the darkness, wishing he knew her warmth, wishing, wishing, until she had gone. Thinking of Liz now, in a veil that blew about her and touched his face lightly as her kiss at the altar, and the first handful of confetti dripping from her mother's grey glove flying in coloured clouds, and hands slapping his back and voices under carriage wheels, getting quieter, until he could only hear the horses' hooves dull on wood blocks, and the rustling of her dress when she took his hand and pressed it under her breasts, and said Darling in a voice she had never used before.

So many memories, half of them not even thought, but only running together at the back there, one thing bringing up another and overlaid by the next, all rushing in a river bright and strong, pouring through the mind in a few moments of silence, resting up there, looking down at a body grown older through it all, until this moment.

And each happening, every thought and wish, and all the dreams a part of it, a flourish of leaves, full of vital sap that hardens, now, in this moment, giving further strength and impetus of spirit to do and say and know what, by those memories, is right.

Snowy felt the strength come in him again, and with it a clean anger, that all his work, and all the work of men he knew, and the great machines pounding in splendid willingness of effort, and Liz and all the quiet women slogging away at home, and old Shiner and the other lads lying there, and the convoys going through the night towards the Line, and the blokes in the slit trenches trying to keep their eyes open, all of it, all the singleness of it, put at nothing by this rotment leaning against the fender, one polished shoe on the step, and the other on the floor, playing with an elastic band round his fingers, watching it through the smoke of a cigarette hanging from the middle of his mouth.

Rage came inside, with an edge that seemed to slice through fine as a wheel on a bacon cutter, piercing and widening, and never going back, making him set his teeth, and smile.

Wonderingly, he could feel himself smiling, and in wonder, he stretched out his arms and laughed, seeing the Princess turn towards him, and stare for a moment, and then turn her back.

"Glad to see us again, Snow?" Dincott looked up, laughing, too. "That's the hammer. Nothing like good fellowship and old pals, eh? I was only telling the blokes just now. You're the sort we want in charge of workshops. One of us. Eh?"

Snowy nodded, from helplessness to think of anything else. It was in his mind that all the cards had to be played by himself, and, remembering the punch in the jaw, he knew he had to protect Bill. Thought of the Princess he put worriedly away.

"That's right," Dincott nodded, quietly satisfied. "Using a bit of sense, eh? Nothing like it. Drop of vinegar on your bacon, ain't it? Just gives it that little extra shove, don't it? Where's the bloke with you?"

"We lost him," Snowy said. "Never came back."

"Pity." Dincott shook his head. "Tck. What a shame, eh? Never mind. All come out in the wash, I suppose. I see she's still working for the firm."

"Been a good pal to me," Snowy said, weakly, it sounded to him, and he cursed himself. "She's all right."

"'Course." Dincott said it as though he was certain. "I give you this. You're a picker. Wish I'd seen her first. Still, you never know. Everything changes, don't it? She might wake up one morning and say to herself, I'll give the Nipper a go today. See how we get on. Eh? You never know, do you?"

To his surprise he was still smiling, but the lines of the smile were aching, and he wished he could stop.

"Well"—Dincott smacked his knees, and stood—"won't get far this rate, will we? Here's Rusty off home with his tribe, and I'm only sorry I can't go with 'em. Won't half be a turn-out when they get there."

"You're going to let them take this stuff, then?" Snowy asked.

"Certainly," said Dincott, as if any other answer were silly. "They've done all the work and saved us a lot of trouble. Now they'll go home, and all they do is pay us our little bit every month. Fair's fair, ain't it? Don't work for nothing, do we? Eh?"

Rusty looked at Snowy in a fraction of a moment, the sort of look they might exchange across a faulty motor, each knowing what was wrong, with too much respect for the other's knowledge to say it in words.

"How they going to pay?" Snowy asked. "They're very poor."

"They are now," Dincott said. "But they won't be when

this lot gets there. 'Sides, if this was a bank, they'd have to stump up, wouldn't they? So they stump up to us. Same thing. All right, Rusty boy. Get ready to follow us out. Snow, there's a couple of jobs you can do for me. All right?"

"Right," Snowy said. "What?"

"Job of towing." Dincott appeared to have no doubt of acceptance, or fear of anybody wanting to do something different. "The police trucks go first in case of trouble. Then Rusty's lot. Then you. That's the order of march. Look."

The quiet word made him turn to meet a pair of eyes that still, even in that light, seemed to spin round and round in opposite directions within themselves, and then stop, looking deep inside his head.

"Don't let's have any bright capers, will you?" The shaky voice was quieter than usual, still lazy, still with a sound of laughing in it, but there was another sound, too, that he could not quite define, except as a threat. "Capers waste time. If you're in with us, you're in. But no capers. I can't abide 'em. Neither can the lads. And they're very touchy. Especially after this caper tonight. Did you hear the row?"

"What went off?" Snowy asked, knowing she was listening.

"One of our safety measures," said Dincott. "Went off professional, didn't it? Brought everything down. Road, cliff, everything. That's why we're here. They can't touch us. Take 'em a day to get their troops round here. All we've got this side is a lot of their coppers. Soon deal with them. Then we'll be gone. Easy, ain't it?"

Snowy felt a withering of hope. The slight movement of her head touched in him a sorrow beyond telling.

"Always providing we get out of it," he said, hoping his voice was normal. "Where do we go?"

"Follow the police trucks." Dincott nodded at the redcaps. "They'll show you. They're our police, so you don't have to worry. All good blokes, well paid, and happy in their work. That's all 't matters, ain't it?"

He went over to Rusty, joined by a couple of the redcaps. With surprise Snowy saw them salute as they halted.

The Princess swung round and her coat billowed, lightly running to him.

" Look," she said, staring emptily at him. " If that creature comes anywhere near me I'll go insane."

" Hold hard, Miss," he said. " Leave it to me. Don't say a word. Just follow the band."

" For God's sake don't say anything about Bill," she whispered. " He's after him."

Snowy smiled, in a happy relief of stretched muscles.

" I know where my money'll be," he said. " And I'll have a few bob on myself, same race."

" Snowy," she touched his arm. " Please. Don't do anything. You have a family."

For some reason he was angry with her for reminding him. There was a fine notion in his head that any effort he made would be for her sake, that he must be gallant and appear so, for her and none other.

" Don't you worry about me, Miss," he said. " Just watch points. And Rosie. Did you see Max? "

She shook her head.

" Not a sign," she said. " When I got here, these trucks of police were just coming in and I thought they were ours. But when they started pushing everybody around and then this brute showed up I almost died."

The group broke, and Rusty came over with Dincott. Redcaps were running down towards their trucks, shouting and waving, and the men and women began to move.

" My heavens," she said. " They're Germans."

Rusty stopped with his feet astride, as if he were trying to convince himself of his ability to stand upright.

" Snowy," he said. " For everything, caro mio, everything, I thank to you. Goodbye."

Without waiting, he turned away and hurried to the end of the column.

" Now then," Dincott said, " you follow the convoy. Take it steady. My blokes are on the road all the way. Anything that don't answer the questions'll get it. Just do as you're told, Snow, and your old lady'll still be married. Off you go."

Snowy turned away, taking her arm.

" Come on, gel," he said, feeling her half resisting. " This way for the *Skylark*."

" That's it." Dincott put his hands in the pockets of his beautifully-creased trousers and rattled some coins. Snowy saw the outline of his skull under the beret, and decided which tool would make an end of him, and suddenly he was cold and warm at the same time, raging and yet in peace, for he knew what he had to do, but it seemed to him that the decision had been made elsewhere and handed down to him almost as an order. " Bit strange, ain't it, Snow? Don't know how it's done, do you? Eh? Little bloke like me in charge of things? Look at her dial. She loves me, look. Don't try and kid me, dear. Nipper knows."

" Oh, for God's sake," she said, " let's go."

Snowy wanted to talk, but impelled by the tears in her voice he led her off along the convoy and back to Rosie. People were still milling in little groups around the backs of the trucks, climbing in and being helped up. Redcaps watched them, sometimes lending a hand with bundles, or making a knee for the women. Rusty sat in the cabin of the leading truck, with the light on, staring directly ahead, and Snowy watched him in compassion, and with a warmth of friendliness that made his rage hotter, and yet colder.

Dincott strolled, a neat silhouette trailing cigarette smoke, waiting until the people were aboard and the convoy line was clear, and took a whistle from his breast pocket, blowing two blasts and waving to the police trucks.

Rusty switched off the cabin light, and signalled through the window, starting up and moving off almost in one movement, making Snowy smile despite his feeling. One by one the convoy moved away, checked by number and by driver, and when the last had gone Dincott turned and came across.

" Snowy," he said, almost sorrowfully. " What did you do to my Mercedes out there? The black 'un? She won't go."

A blither of questions flew through Snowy's mind.

" Well," he said. " There you are. Your blokes don't know enough about the job. Laying up a car like that takes experts. You had her in that wall too long. No grease, no oil. So what happens? One trip, and she's burnt out."

" Ah, ha." Dincott lit a cigarette from the butt of the other. " Well. What happened to that Yankee bloke? "

"He hopped it somewhere." Snowy felt her elbow in his side. "Couple of days ago."

Dincott was looking up at him with a straight face, and eyes that were dead, and yet bright, as though he had stopped living just to look.

"Snow," he said. "I don't think you've took it in, after all. And that's a big pity, because I reckon you'd be useful. Don't you want to go on leave? Couldn't you do with a month at home?"

Snowy nodded.

"Well, then," Dincott spoke in gentle chide, "use your common. I can get you a month at home. No risks. Lots of our boys've been back. I'm just back myself. There's boats doing the trip nearly every week. Nipper fixes everything. Passes, papers and cash. Specially cash."

Snowy could only look at him, listening, helpless, feeling Rosie at work under his foot, seeming to feel her looking sideways at Dincott, and growling, a wary animal waiting its moment.

"Talk about it later, when we get back," Dincott said. "When you've seen how we live, you might change your mind. But no capers. Don't forget. I've put her up there with you just in case you was feeling like a caper. I won't tell you what'll happen to her."

From behind, a truck pulled out packed with women, showing blank faces and blonde hair momentarily in Rosie's headlights, followed by a car full of redcaps.

Dincott grinned and nodded.

"Follow on, Snowy boy," he said. "Do it right."

Snowy went up the ramp and turned into the tunnel, seeing that most of the niches were empty. He felt her finger-nails in his arm at the curve leading up to the entrance, for there were bodies sprawling among the ruts at the side, but they passed too quickly to see shape or colour, and the lights of a car behind were warningly-white on the roof.

Redcaps were waiting in the arch, and as he slowed, going over the stone kerb, he felt the touch of fresh air, and breathed deep, realizing the muddy taste of the chambers, grateful for a sense of new vitality bringing a spurt of hope.

Instead of going downhill to the right, the way they had come, the guide truck went to the left, following the rise of the rock, with white flicks from a redcap's torch to lead the way until Snowy flashed his headlamps in reply.

" There's an awful lot of those men," she said. " Could they all be Germans? "

" Not all of 'em, Miss," Snowy said. " But far's I'm concerned they're worse'n ordinary Jerries. Did you notice anything in there? Before we started? "

" No." She was looking up at him. " I was too frightened. If they hadn't let me travel with you, I don't know what would have happened. What did you notice? "

" First of all, Bill and Maxie was spare," he said. " Got down to it, somewhere. But this I'll take a gospel on, that all Rusty's people weren't on them trucks. Else I can't count. Where'd the rest get to? "

44

Bill watched Max pull the automatic out of his blouse and gently squeezed his shoulder until he turned.

"Ye'll never hit him at this range," he whispered. "Save it for later."

They were looking through the slats of the battery room at Dincott talking to a redcap near the pumps. Other redcaps joined them, and the group went from truck to truck, inspecting them, and switching off the headlights, going back on the near side, and up the stairway.

" Let's go," Max said.

" Give 'em a chance to clear out," said Bill. " Ain't it surprising, eh? A bloke like that. A jailbird."

" What the heck does it matter what he is, as long as he can do the job? " Max said, trying for patience.

" It matters a damn lot," Bill said. " Ye can't have jailbirds doing as they please. Not where I come from, any road."

" Jail doesn't enter this thing," Max said. " Enough bad luck and all of us can get in jail without any trouble. I ought to have been in there a couple of times. I stole bread from my own pa's place when he got laid off. I stole meat, too. And I've stolen money. See? But I didn't get caught. And I suppose you'd call me a guttersnipe if you saw where I was raised. I had the arse out of my pants. What's a guttersnipe? Ain't he a man?"

"Certainly," Bill said. "And don't give yourself a lot of airs about this, that and the other. I've had cardboard in m' boots. And I've felt t' wind on my behind more'n once. Y' telling me nowt. But it's what ye make of yourself. And he's a guttersnipe."

"But it don't matter what the guy is," Max insisted. "He's doing the job, ain't he? The guy has brains. Anything else is second."

"What's happened to Snowy, I wonder." Bill was anxious, pulling ends from the cigarette. "That lass's a handicap. She's too much of a lady to be shoved in wi' that lot."

"Ah, my eye." Max turned away from him, and wheeled about again. "You know what the real difference is, don't you? Dollars. Just dollars. If her pa, or somebody, didn't have the dollars, she might have been down in the whore house along with the others, or on a farm, or just sewing dresses. That's all, brother. The other stuff is strictly mularkey."

"You have it your own way," Bill said. "A guttersnipe's a guttersnipe, and a lady's a lady, and that's that, and ye'll not alter it. Anybody'd think he was your best pal."

"Ah, for Christ sakes." Max took off his cap, scratching his head. "Bill, please, listen to something. I hate his guts. But I'm just saying it don't matter what he is, or where he comes from. Can he do the job? That's the one that carries the dough."

A tall girl, barefooted, had run down the stairway, looking about, nibbling the knuckles of her hands and then putting them to her cheeks, bending forward a little, up on her toes in hesitant paces, as though she were afraid of the silence but more afraid of making a noise.

"Looking for us," Max said, and swung the steel blinds far enough aside to get his hand through and rap.

She turned, opening her mouth, covering it with both her hands, staring in terror until he put his head out, and she might have fainted, for her eyes went up in whites, but then she took hold, standing erect, running gracefully towards them, falling on her knees to take Max's hands and kiss them, talking in whispers. He picked her up, and jerked his head at Bill.

"O.K.," he said. " They've gone. Rusty told a few of these babies to hide up and wait for us. So it's our play. Let's go."

The big room was empty, littered, and dark, and they hurried through, almost feeling the appeal of bodies lying under wrecked furniture. Out in the parking space they were almost mobbed by men and women running to meet them.

Max put up his arms, calling for silence, and they formed a ring.

" What'll we tell 'em? " He spoke as though the words cost money. " They're like kids. We can't give 'em a lot of nonsense."

" Tell 'em the facts," Bill said. " That's all they'll need. We're all in a muck, and we've to do best we can wi' what we've got. That's that, and that's all there is to it."

Max spoke quietly, and as he paused someone here and there supplied the word he searched for, and he nodded, smilingly repeating it, and making them smile, and becoming serious again the moment after. But when he finished, they all looked at one another, and turned to him, shrugging, and a woman spoke.

" She says we don't have to worry," he translated. " They know what they're in for. But they want to get us out of here, and join up with Rusty. Apart from that, they don't care what happens, because they was raised on trouble, and they'd feel bad without it."

" Right," said Bill. " I'll pick out the best truck there's here. What happened to all them coppers? There was millions of 'em. And who's outside waiting for us? "

Max spoke to them, and a group of men set off at a run.

" They'll find out," he said. " What's first? "

" See if there's any grub left," Bill said. " I'm right clemmed."

He picked an American truck that wanted only a few repairs, and settled to work on her, finding he had an attentive audience of men and women, all squatting a fair way off to be out of his way, but near enough to see what he was doing. When he had finished, he switched on the lights, and they clapped their hands. But when he started the motor, and moved her out of the bay, they began to dance among themselves, and the childishness of it, the rampage about so ordinary a matter as getting an engine to go, made him angry, and impatient, and yet he was touched by a quality of helplessness, mixed perhaps with envy of spirit that could openly express itself unchecked by fear of comment.

Women came out of the big room, carrying a table-top piled with bread and dishes of meat, and behind Max and the tall girl brought trays of glasses full of wine.

"We been having more fun," Max said, red and watery in the eyes with laughter. "They've been telling me what they'll do to 'em when they catch up with this Dincott mob on their own. Did you get her started?"

"Ready when you are," Bill said, inclined to feel proud of himself, and then angry with the thought as a fancied weakness. "Ye'd best tell 'em they've to catch 'em first."

Max handed the wine glasses round, refusing to give up the tray to the many hands offering to relieve him, puzzling over the problem of Bill, at one moment reasonable, at another intransigent, and decided to say nothing lest he upset the partnership altogether.

Bill, munching a thick sandwich, was sorry for his sharpness, but he thought it foolish to say so and be misunderstood, especially since Max appeared not to have noticed, but he resolved to be unusually gracious next time and square the debt.

A man ran down the ramp, shouting as he came, and instantly the group was on its feet to face him, food and wine forgotten. Bill watched the tall girl, and wanted to wipe the crumbs from her mouth.

"More trouble," Max said. "Some guy's headed in here. Not Dincott, and not the police."

"That's all right, then," Bill said. "We've nowt to worry about. Or should we hide again?"

"The heck with it," Max said. "If there's going to be trouble, let's have it in the open."

"I'm with ye, lad," said Bill.

A crowd of armed men were coming down the ramp, led by a man in a jacket with a fur collar, bareheaded, and as far as they could see without weapons. He came directly across, stopping inside the flare of light, and his party blocked behind in a shuffle of feet, thudding their rifle butts on the stones.

"I am Ortesi," the man said, in good English, as though he expected them to know. "Where is this Dincott?"

"Too late," Max said. "He's gone. And we wish we knew where."

"What are you?" Ortesi had looked at Bill, and addressed Max. "American?"

"I'm an American soldier," Max said. "What's it to you?"

"I am Ortesi, as I said, and I arrest you, and your confederate, and these people. They have no right in this locale." He spoke seriously, quietly, without moving his body. "A court will try you. If you are judged guilty, you will be shot."

"Where do this lot get their ideas?" Bill was eating the sandwich. "I've never heard anything like it. Tell him about them Highlanders on their way up. They're the lads we'll answer to."

"You will answer to me," Ortesi said. "To my justice."

"Look," Max said. "We came here with the carabinieri. If you want trouble, take a trip down the road. They're waiting for you."

"We finished two outposts of this Dincott," Ortesi said, turning to look at the wings of his party. "We shall find him later. But first you shall be tried."

Max looked down at Bill, and laughed, and the more he looked at that expression of serene disbelief the louder he laughed.

But he stopped when a couple of the men took him by the arms. Two more lifted Bill from his seat. The others rounded up the men and women, kicking away the debris of the meal to clear the floor.

"You have had much to enjoy," Ortesi said, and sat down. "Now it is time to pay. All luxuries have a price. Your names?"

Bill went on eating. Max was looking at the tall girl.

"It is immaterial," said Ortesi, and shrugged in a motion of hands. "Two criminals, A and B. You are charged with desecration of Italian soil, with rapine, and with prosecution of policies inimical to the welfare of the people."

"Don't look now," said Max confidentially to Bill, "but here we have a nut."

"I understand you," Ortesi said. "But I confine myself to this accusation. Do you plead?"

Bill suddenly had a cold feeling that the man meant what he said.

Any aspect of the meeting that might have been comical now became one of concern, since he remembered being present at a court-martial when nothing appeared to happen, and officers spoke so quietly, and yet almost unbelievably a man had marched out to serve years in prison.

" What's your authority for this? " he asked. " I'm a British soldier, don't forget. I'm not a deserter. As for the rest of that damn nonsense, you're cracked."

" Attaboy, Bill." Max clapped him on the back, and then was thrust aside by the rifle of one of his guards. " What's going on? "

Ortesi spoke over his shoulder to the men and women in a tone which implied that their understanding of language, in the first place, was a distasteful fact, and that to be noticed at all was in the nature of a dispensation.

" You wouldn't believe what this guy's saying to 'em," Max said, high with wonder. " You want to know? "

" No," said Bill.

" He's telling 'em they're all going to die," Max said in the same voice.

" You understand Italian? " Ortesi looked at Max.

" My father took out papers," Max said. " Sure I speak Italian."

" Naturalization papers? " Ortesi raised his hands and let them fall. " So, in addition to criminal charges, there is also another. You are a traitor. That is more serious."

" Look," Max said. " Just who in heck d'you think you are? "

Ortesi stood up.

He was about an inch taller than Bill, with black hair curling over his head to a clump at the nape, ears inclining outwards as though pressed, a flattish nose, bony cheeks, and a mouth turning down in deep lines that looked self-imposed, perhaps from a desire to add a note of strength to his appearance.

" I will tell you," he said. " Your bombs destroy my house and your shells and your bullets and your boots ravish my land. I have property without value, and no hope of compensation. In my own house I am outcast, without a roof or walls, my goods are destroyed, my animals are eaten and my servants go away. Everything has gone. Except only hate. Hate of foreigners. Hate of polluters. Hate of the Goth, and the Hun, and the Saxon. Hate of the American. Hate. Hate."

The voice started conversationally, but midway had come a crack, and the body almost crouched, the hands came out of the jacket to beat the air, and the eyes stared until the spitty whispers stopped in phlegm, and a sudden fit of coughing.

" Hey, Bill," Max spoke behind his hand, " give me cover when I draw."

Ortesi waved his hand, as though excusing himself for coughing.

" Emotion makes me to be upset," he said, reaching for breath. " Now you see why I am here. These gentlemen with me, they are the same. But I lead them because I possess the hate. Again we shall see the sun through our own air, free of contamination, free of you, living or dead. Because even the dead we will dig up and burn, and throw the calcine in the sea."

" That's a programme," Max acknowledged, in slow, respectful nods. " How are you working the schedules? Because the way it looks to me you got started the wrong end. We're a couple of G.I.s. We got pushed into this thing. We'd just as soon be home, minding our own business. In fact, now I come to mention it, we'd prefer that. What do you say, Brother Bill? "

" You're dead right." Bill had his eye on a tyre lever about a yard out of reach. " Tell him, while you're at it, what I think of this damn country."

" Your opinions are worthless," Ortesi said. " How do you plead? "

Max looked at the young, fairly-well-dressed armed men in the company. All their faces looked the same, without expression except in the stare of the eyes, direct, impersonal, seeming to add another quality to the silence.

" We're not doing any," Max said.

" I second that," said Bill, and took off his spectacles.

" Very well." Ortesi folded his hands, looking at the knuckles as though in surprise. " Criminal A, you are charged as traitor. Your father evaded his sacred duty as an Italian, and robbed the body politic of his services and the produce of his labour. You, his natural issue, and therefore an Italian citizen, condoned his defection, and took arms against your own flag. Witness, your uniform."

He spoke in Italian, over his shoulder, and the men nodded, murmuring.

"The verdict is guilty," he said, as if it were something to do with the temperature. "I concur. Criminal B is in a different category. He is British, and therefore shares guilt for the crime of trespass upon Italian soil, and the destruction of our property. It is enough. I do not introduce or pursue the charge of rapine."

"Rapine?" Bill frowned at him. "What's that?"

"You are not acquainted with the formalities of your language," Ortesi said.

"When you get in the hay with your hat on," said Max. "Rape."

"Me?" Bill felt for his spectacles, and put them back, struggling to find words. "Me? Rape? What, with this blowsy lot of frisgigs? I'd not waste me spunk. Be damned to ye."

"O.K.," Max said, putting his hands together. "Any time now."

The men and women were being forced into a packed space by three of the guards, using rifle butts on the slow movers as ploughmen prod cattle. A team of about a dozen guards waited near the wall in the shadow, talking and laughing quietly among themselves, passing a cigarette from one to another.

"The court's verdict is death by shooting," Ortesi said, turning about. "Have you anything to say?"

"Plenty," said Max. "Even if this is a joke, you've left yourself open to charges under Martial Law, and there's a raft of witnesses."

"There will be none," Ortesi said. "You are all guilty. You all share a crime in consort. You will die."

"But listen." Max pointed to the men and women. "They're a bunch of peasants. They don't even know the scores. What kind of justice is that?"

"My justice," Ortesi said, and kicked a crust spinning into the cleared space. "The justice of a Roman. There is no such thing as a peasant. There is one who lives an Italian life by Italian ideas, or there are foreigners and enemies. Those who eat and drink with enemies are of the same blood. They die. By my justice."

" You mean," Max nodded at the group, " women, too? "

" We have shot more than two hundred women," Ortesi said. " What should we do with criminals? Crime has no sex. It has only punishment."

" Well, Max lad," Bill said, " we'll have to look slippy."

Out of the corner of his eye Max saw the flash of an uppercut that caught the guard square on the chin. As he dropped, Bill reached out and took his rifle.

Max stamped on the instep of the youth on his left, and Bill poked the foresight of the rifle full in the right-hand guard's belly. The tall girl leapt at Ortesi, gouging her fingers into his face, and Bill saw the men and women breaking through the ring, fighting with a savagery that appalled him into watching them.

" For Christ's sake," Max shouted, " don't stand there. Get going."

Two shots were fired from the team by the wall, but they were afraid of hitting their own people, and edged in, trying to use their rifles as clubs. Bill and Max fired over their heads, and went, back to back, towards the truck. Ortesi was defending himself from the tall girl, but she had him by the muffler, and with her head down, his groping hands could find nothing but her hair, and he was pulling; but hard as he pulled, she pulled the muffler harder and his mouth was opening, and then they were covered.

More shots cracked. Max fired two from his rifle, not in aim, for the fight was thick, almost in darkness, and then stood, irresolute, but he saw with satisfaction that peasant strength was telling, because gradually the fights were being isolated, and many were struggling on the floor.

Bill started the truck, pressing the horn.

Max and a couple of men with rifles were shouting to the others, and the knots were breaking into running figures that stooped to pick up rifles, or paused to kick at someone kneeling, or gathered about a figure, lifting it, and coming on.

Max ran to the cab.

" What d'you say we take this guy along? " he shouted. " This Ortesi? "

" If she left anything of him." Bill had the truck on the move, held on the brake. " I'd not like to find her waiting up for me."

A number of the faction were on their feet in the shadow, with their hands behind their necks, cowed by the rifles swinging round at them, but there were still a few on the ground, and under the engine pulse Max could hear groans.

" Mama," he said. " Always trouble. Always somebody has to be hurt. Somebody has to act big, so somebody has to get hurt."

The last man climbed up, and Max saw blood on many of the faces that smiled down at him, and he wanted to reach up and pat them.

Bill started as he got in, wheeling for the ramp.

" Ye didn't bother to find that bloke, then? " Bill slowed, looking back. " That's him, standing up, ain't it? "

He saw the flashes of rifle fire, and heard the bullets, putting his foot on the accelerator, taking the ramp at speed only excused by superb driving, and turned in to the entrance.

" See? " Max was nodding. " That's what you get for being big-hearted. Nobody shows gratitude any more. What's wrong with everybody? "

" Nowt much wrong wi' them in t' back," Bill said. " I've seen a bit of scrapping here an' there, like. But them women. They can't half use 'em."

" Yes sir," said Max. " They certainly go for the things that matter."

A tremor shook the truck, as though she had gone over a rough patch, and while Bill was changing down, another, that rocked them badly, tipping the wheels, bringing them down hard. The driveway was filling with dust, and again they tipped, but this time they heard a sound as though a train had stopped suddenly in a scream of crashing metal, and while the roadway split in front of them, rock was bouncing on the cabin roof.

Bill put his foot down, and went into the dust, watching the wall a yard away in the headlights, feeling the downhill tilt, and sensed the levelling, slowing to take the turn. The upper reach was clearer but rock was falling in chunks, and he felt his way between the ruts, and then the air was almost clear, and thankfully he went for the archway.

A convulsion shook rock, road and truck.

The wheel was wrenched from him. A fender scraped the wall. He got the wheel again, and felt the tyres bounce across the kerb at the entrance, and then an explosion without flame lifted him, and the engine was racing without moving the truck.

Max pulled at the door, but it was jammed. He cracked the rifle butt through the windscreen, and when it was free of glass he climbed out, and Bill followed.

Rock was closing down, clamping the body tight, with no hope of freeing her.

Bill climbed back in the cabin, and, using the rifle butt, broke open the wooden rear panels, seeing the fingers come through from the other side to rip away the boarding. He waited, helping the first woman through, and then jumped down to catch them as they fell.

Two of them were dragged through and lifted out, to be carried a little distance away.

The rest stood near, watching the rock settling, and the metal cracking under the strain, first the tubulars, and then the chassis. The headlamps were still alight. The ground shook. Some of the women were sitting at the feet of the men, arms about their knees.

Bill was suddenly aware of being cold.

"Well," he said, "here's a fine how-de-do. They must have mined the road."

"Night," said Max. "On a bare mountain. And baby, I'm thankful. I think we could do a whole lot worse'n get right down on our knees."

Bill reached up to take off his cap, and found himself bare-headed.

"Funny," he said. "I were just thinking of my old mate. He'd have said the same."

45

Rosie had given him the notion, but it took a little time to soak in. He had seen her so plainly glancing sideways and growling, but it was much later that it ripened, and in richest impatience he realized she had been trying to tell him that she would make scrap of the police truck any time he let her know, and then in comfort they could go back and find Bill and Max and Rusty.

The threats, still clear, in Dincott's voice did not deter him, for he was used to the school bully, the street bully, and the bully at work. He knew that man to man he would enjoy battering the life out of him.

But the thought of failing, and thus leaving the Princess to be handled by others, apart from Dincott, weakened his will. To think of her being ill-treated, or that anyone might speak rough, or behave badly in her presence, made him feel not merely angry, but blood-mad, until he had to clear his eyes to see the road.

She was sleeping in the corner, against a cushion bent up for her back, with the soles of her feet pressing against his side. Her eyelids were dark, and the lashes were wide on the cheek, and her mouth budded as she breathed; and when Rosie changed down and was quieter, he heard the pop of her lips, a delicate, womanly sound that reminded him in raw hurt of times when he had wakened to hear Liz in a dream, feeling for her hand, warm, pliable, helplessly his, and in a smile had settled to sleep.

Everything she did seemed to have some shadow of Liz, until there was torment in being near her, but wretchedness when she was away, and he knew, staring at the mauve stream of the road, that he dare not think of a time when she would have to leave him. A thought came that he might go with her, and hide away somewhere, but achingly he knew it to be foolish, for some part of him was determined on Liz and the children, and going back and fore to the job, on realizing his dreams of being and doing, the part of him that knew this wish for life with a Princess to be fit for laughter and a ribald snub. Yet, in that knowledge, even hearing the laughter, a part of him was envious that other men might have such women, to treat, as far as he could judge, only as cattle, breaking their tenderness without cherish or any thought of love. Rage came on to think of it, but always the stable self leaned back and smiled until in despair he threw aside all thought, concentrating on the road, that seemed as friendly, as embracing in trouble as Rosie herself, as though perhaps the road and she were man and wife so much they were part of each other.

Torchlight flicked ahead, and as he approached the tail lights of the truck, he was surprised to see a crowd of civilians standing about the redcaps, all pointing and shaking their heads.

Here might be his chance, he thought, but there were too many women in the crowd, and Dincott was farther up the road with a bodyguard, standing, looking at a wall and gateway.

Snowy leaned out of the window and instantly felt heat that he knew was unnatural; and then, with a sense of shock, he saw that the wall along the right-hand side of the road was a wrinkled mass of smoking earth that moved, shedding rocks and pebbles, threatening at any moment to encroach upon the roadway.

Dincott waved him on, climbing upon the step.

" It's a rotten job, Snow boy," he said, and breathlessness seemed to unite his voice. " We'll get out quick as we can. But it's important, see? Here you are."

He got down by the gateway and went inside the garden.

A square white house stood about fifty feet away, surrounded up to the height of the bedroom windows by a smoking wall of earth. The back of the house was down, and the façade was cracking, and while they stood there tiles slithered off the roof and bounced from the paving in splashes of terracotta.

Dincott pointed to a building at the side, almost engulfed, showing only the double doors.

" It's in there," he said. " Try and get it out, will you, Snow? It's a carriage. We've got the horses safe."

" Not enough towing cable," Snowy said. " Want this wall down first, before she'll go in here."

" Fair enough," Dincott said, and went outside, shouting.

The Princess woke up, disturbed by the voice, and stretched, putting her feet down, startled, looking about in sleepy fear.

" It's all right, Miss," he said. " Take it steady."

Men were running with tools, and they started picking at the wall on either side of the gateway, knocking out ragged blocks of mortar that women lifted and carried away.

" What on earth's going on? " She jumped down, and took his arm. " It's so hot. Why, Snowy, it's lava."

" That's right, dearie." Dincott called from the dark garden. " Lava. And it's messed up my little abode, and I'm very put out. First bit of hard luck I've had, this is."

" One little touch of nature," she said. " That's something you can't hoodlum your way through."

Even the man swinging a pick among the wreckage of the gateway was frightened by Dincott's face, white in the headlights, with eyes that were plain and pale, fixed, and a mouth that opened only at one side, seeming to jerk among a set of nerves all its own.

" Shut your face, you stuck-up bitch," he said. " Else I'll give you something to open it about. Get up there, and don't give me no more lip."

Snowy felt himself on the football field again, with the ball at his feet, taking that one quick look to see where his men were. He saw how the redcaps stood, and knew himself helpless. From the corner of his eye he saw the look she gave him, upwards, a second or so long, a shake of her shoulders, as though she cast him off with Dincott, and he heard her climb up in the cabin and swing the door shut.

" There it is, Snow," Dincott said, perhaps with regret. " I can't abear no woman mouthing back. Don't take it hard. She's all yours. I only let her off because of you. Don't forget it. Ready? "

Snowy was thankful, in the expulsion of a breath, that the window was up and she was inside, beyond hearing, and he shifted an icier peg on a board that he knew must be added and one of these days paid off.

" I'm ready," he said, surprised at the normalcy of his voice. " I'll back in. Tell 'em to shift anything in front of me. I'll need all the pull I can get."

" All right, Snow." Dincott seemed confident that all was well. " We'll have it as bald as Ol' Mother Riley's."

Men had picked down the lava in front of the coachhouse, dodging the weight on the roof that moment by moment pushed forward, bursting rafters and cracking tiles in a stench of hot pumice. Snowy walked among shrivelled growth, hearing it whisper against his stockings, seeing the dark dispersion of leaves and grass as he made way with the grapnel. Men had propped the doorway with logs, and redcaps switched on their torches, allowing him light to enter. Smoke filled the place, but he could see enough to fix the hooks in the axle of a wooden coach, and when he was sure of purchase he took up the slack and ran out, through the sigh and flutter of the garden, and up to the cabin.

She turned a little farther away from him, looking through the window on the other side, and quite suddenly, laughably, he could see Primula sulking after being smacked.

" Never mind, Miss," he said, starting to turn out. " It's all going on the bill. He'll pay for it. Too many of his own blokes standing there to do anything."

" Don't let there be any trouble," she said firmly. " There's just one thing more you could do for me."

" Say the word, Miss." Snowy was watching the slack taking up in the hawser. " Here she comes. Shan't be long now. What did you want? "

" Any time you get an opportunity," she said, " just slow down and drop me off. Anywhere'll do. I can make out."

" Pick your own time, Miss," he said, treating it as routine. " It's marvellous walking country, anywhere round here. We're only about twenty miles from a light, and it's proper crawling with all sorts of lovely people. I'll drop you, Miss."

" On my head." She turned towards him. " I never really understood the meaning of killer. That's the only living creature I've ever been frightened of. Doesn't he frighten you? "

" Oh yes, Miss." Snowy put Rosie in gear. " I frighten very easy, I do. Anybody even looks at me, I go straight up the wall yellin' for my ma."

He felt her hand on his arm.

" Snowy," she said, so that he could just hear. " I'm so glad you're with me."

His impulse was to turn to her, but the shouting outside disturbed him, and he merely touched her hand, and got down, surprised to find his shirt sticking in the heat, and stopping to pull it away from his spine. He felt a tap on his shoulder. He looked up.

A couple of faces were laughing at him from under the shadow of Rosie's canopy. They were Rusty's people, and there were more behind them.

The backs of the crowd of civilians in front he saw, thankfully, were turned. He got out in the light, buoyed by thought of friends close at hand, picking up the hawser as he went.

The crowd of civilians were ill-kempt, and, from their eyes, sleepless. But the quality of their clothing was more of the city than he would have expected, and so was their manner. They readily made way for him, until he got to the front of the circle, full in the strong light, stopping for a moment to suit his eyes, and then straightened in amazement.

Dincott sat on the driving seat of a cream carriage heavily scrolled in gilt, all curling upwards to a profusion of gold leaves on the roof, and surmounted by a coronet. Men in leather aprons were busy with scarlet harness in the shafts, and at a whistle the shouting rose again, and among it the stamp of hooves and jingle of bits, and the crowd broke apart, letting in three pairs of greys all caparisoned in scarlet saddle cloths, with white cockades in their headstalls.

" Bit of all right, ain't it, Snowy? " Dincott leaned over the side, patting the scrollwork. " I found it a few months back. Had it ever since. Lovely job, ain't it? They knew what they was doing, didn't they? "

" Is this the job? " Snowy ducked to unhitch the grapnel. " This is what we come all the way up here for? "

" Certainly," Dincott said. " Very important. I'm getting married in it. And I promised the kids down there they'd have a Cinderella job, and they're going to have one. They don't have nothing decent, no parties, or nothing, only a lot of this guts-aching church business. So I promised we'd have a do of Cinderella, and ride 'em round. D'you mind?"

" No," said Snowy, at loss.

" All the same if you did, chum." Dincott took the ribbons

and cupped the whip, sorting the handful as though born to it, standing up for one of the old men to wrap a huge fur rug twice round his waist, buckling it in place with a belt. The old man leaned over to lift a coachman's cocked hat for Dincott to catch neatly on the butt of the whip.

In a khaki shirt, and with a bulky train of grey fur, Dincott put the black hat on, back to front first, but the crowd laughed and stamped, and the old man clambered up again, pulling the peak round, shoving the cockade in front.

"Where are you, Snow?" he shouted. "Don't I look a boy, eh? Wish my old ma could see me now. She'd be the doin' of me."

Snowy was surprised at the attitude of the people. Nobody appeared to be afraid of Dincott, and certainly not of the red-caps, for groups of them were standing laughing among the crowd, and he saw one of them take a cigarette from a man, and then give him a light, talking in the friendliest manner.

"This was my village, Snow, see?" Dincott said. "Came up here to be out of the way. But now we've got a job to find another place because this stuff's coming down on top of us, and a bit too fast for the reckoning. We thought we'd have another month or so."

"So now where you going?" Snowy asked.

"I'll show you all in good time." Dincott looked about, and pointed. "Up there you'll find a lot of carts full of their furniture and stuff. I want you to tow it down for 'em. All right?"

"Anything for a quiet life," Snowy said. "What would you do without me?"

"Ah," said Dincott, twirling the lash. "That's what I've been telling you. Always pick a bloke from the Smoke. Can't beat 'em, can you? I've got all the wagons I want, and I've got a few good blokes, but not enough of 'em. The rest of 'em's light labour. Put a red cap on 'em, they think they're out for the day."

"Why shouldn't they?" Snowy asked. "If they see you looking like that? You're supposed to be the boss, ain't you?"

"However I look, they know who's the boss." Dincott took off the three-cornered hat and fanned it across his face. "Don't you get any funny ideas, either. I've just had to deal with a couple of blokes with funny ideas. I'm still laughing. They ain't."

Vividly, and in a moment, Snowy saw him, sitting on a soap box with pram wheels, goading small boys to pull him uphill, and then letting them jump on to take the run down. He saw him in school, always with a handful of coloured chewing wax, and a side pocket stuffed with new comics, always able to buy hot drinks, and never without a roll of pennies to play toss.

The old man came up, waving his hands at the coach, and then at the horses. The stableman had made no attempt to harness them to the shafts.

" That's it," Dincott said, and undid the buckle, letting the rug fall. " Just how the luck goes, that is. The wheels at the back don't belong to it. They got smashed. These front ones ain't safe. You'll have to tow us, too."

" Let 'em all come," Snowy said. " If we had to bust the gates to get her out, how d'you get her in, the first place? "

" Now, Snow, Snow." Dincott shook his head, looking sadly at the sky. " Can't you see all that stuff rolling down there? It's covered up the front of the house. You come out of the back gate. Don't you know the front from the back, yet? Where's your broughtin's up? "

" Well, they do everything a bit awkward round here," Snowy said. " You never know."

" Not much of a burglar, eh, Snowy? " Dincott signed to the redcaps and they came on the run. " You'll get used to it. As long as I get this lot down to them kids, I'm happy. Few years' time they'll be the grown-ups. Can't let 'em down, can I? "

" Thinking of hanging on here, then, when it's all over? " Snowy asked.

Grey or brown, or something between, and shifting all the time inside, seeming to spin first this way and then the other, and stopping on a sudden, the pupils of Dincott's eyes sucked themselves into clear points, and the steady look was startling by its fixity, and confusing, for the slightest cast in one eye tended to convey an effect not simply of seeing the object, but of looking all round it, as though able to judge of its importance in time and space.

" Far's I'm concerned, Snow," he said, as he might in a confidential matter, " it's been all over a long time. A very long time. And what's going to stop me hanging on ? "

" They're after you now," Snowy said. " There's a couple of battalions scratching about down there."

Dincott patted his shoulder in dismissal.

" That'll last a couple of hours, or a couple of days," he said. " How far'll they get? Who're they looking for? Me? I'm up here, chum."

Some of the men standing near looped the hawser, and he went back to take it on the drum, climbing up on Rosie, pretending not to see the men and women crowding against the rear wall, hoping that none of Dincott's people would jump up to help him. But they stayed below, looking at him big-eyed, as he could remember watching tram drivers changing the trolley arms.

Dincott passed by with the redcaps, pointing up the road.

" We've got to get a move on, Snow," he shouted. " This stuff's closing in on us. How d'you want these carts? "

Snowy jumped down, glancing in the cab as he passed. She sat against the cushion with her face turned in shadow, still, and he wished her asleep, feeling about her, he thought, smilingly, as he had for the baby in her basket when he tiptoed through the kitchen, home from work, laughing at Liz pulling faces and shaking her fist to stop him making a noise.

A long line of two-wheeled carts piled with furniture, each with its group of women and children, went on into darkness. Here, away from the chatter of the crowd, Snowy heard the sound of the lava, a tumult of rock in molten pressure under moving earth, and the tiny spill of pebbles in helpless fall.

Children sat close to their mothers; and seeing the whiteness of their faces turned to him, Snowy felt a certain pride in himself and Rosie and their contempt for any obstacle, even to the threat of burning land.

" Right," he said. " Get these hitched up to the police truck. I'll take the strain at the back and hold 'em steady. Jack the carriage up on the crane. And Bob's your uncle."

Dincott nodded, turning to the redcaps.

Snowy doubled down to the carriage and had a close look underneath. In rear it was mounted on cartwheels, but spokes were missing in the front pair and the axle turn-table was newly broken. He thought regretfully of the piteous tumble across the garden's stonework willy-nilly in Rosie's expert clutch.

A redcap was watching him, leaning on the fender, as though wondering whether to talk or not. Snowy signed to him that the carriage was to be taken nearer to Rosie.

"It's all right," the redcap grinned. "I'm no' one of these heathens here. Wha' are you wantin' done?"

"Get 'em to take her up to the crane, will you?" Snowy was aware of pleasure in listening to someone else speaking English. "How did you get mixed up in this lark?"

"Oh, I don't know." The man was laughing, twisting the knot on his revolver lanyard. "I got married and came back to see her, and sort of stayed. And there y'are."

"Like it?" Snowy strolled back, keeping pace with the men shifting the carriage. "Going to stay out here, too?"

"Oh, aye, I think so," the redcap said, almost scoffingly. "Nothing to go home for, is there? I've a nice place here. Having a kid soon. Everything's fine."

Snowy dropped the grapnel and watched the men fixing it, taking the chance to look more closely at the redcap. He was sunbrowned, shiny in the face, and heavy in body with that unmistakable solidity of good living. His tailored uniform and civilian boots, both of regulation pattern, would have passed him anywhere, on surface, as an ordinary, perhaps smarter than most, military policeman.

But there was still something about him which eluded distinction, that he realized was inherent in them all, but only to some extent in Dincott.

The carriage was hung by its front axle, with its rear wheels off the ground, and when Snowy jumped down to make sure that all was snug he started to laugh, for Rosie looked as though she were crouching away from the cream and gold thing swung on her tail much as a cat before leaping off in a squall.

Dincott went by with a crowd of redcaps in the truck, pulling the carts behind with women and children perched all over them. Redcaps standing along the road flicked their torches to stop the procession when they were about to pass Rosie, and Snowy turned her, fastening the end cart to her forward winch, feeling himself the while under the eye of the redcap and knowing, from movement inside the cabin, that the Princess was watching.

A woman's laughter, free, and strangely beautiful in the smoky darkness, brought him to stare, but then he heard Dincott's voice, and he came into the headlights, arm in arm with a young woman in a plain white dress wearing a flowered shawl about her head.

" Snow," he said. " Got a fare for you. Let her ride up front. She's going to be Mrs. Nip. For the time being. What's up? "

Snowy was staring at the girl. The white dress was tight, her waist was narrow, her breasts were setting gentle weight on the cloth, and the hips swelled, dimpling with the fall of the skirt. Brilliant teeth were in a smile, and her eyes glinted, watching him, full of knowledge, perhaps of sympathy.

" I was looking at her," Snowy said, uncertain what to say, unable to look anywhere else, and knowing he was only a few feet from the Princess.

" Ah," Dincott nodded, almost in approval. " Right piece, ain't she? Smashing cook, an' all. Wasted on these blokes. She don't wear nothing underneath, you know. Fact."

" Well," Snowy said, " some of 'em's lucky. But wait till she's forty."

" Plenty of time." Dincott closed an eye. " She's sixteen next month. They come to the boil very quick out here. Going to take her? Think she'll start a battle with your plate o' kippers up there?"

" Nark it." Snowy felt himself blushing to think the Princess might hear. "There won't be any trouble. Tell her to climb up."

Dincott took her by the arm and hurried to the other side, talking to her in what sounded to be fluent Italian, and she, answering him in laughter, made Snowy long for just a few words of the language, enough to make her show those teeth.

" He's a boy," the redcap said. " He's got 'em spotted everywhere. This one's a picina though, ain't she? She's legs right up to her elbows."

" I wasn't looking at 'em, mate," Snowy said. " Sixteen-year-olds don't interest me."

" Pity," the redcap said. " You don't know what's tasty."

Myriadly lit, a stabbing rage came to gouge him deep inside on raw nerves, stretching the skin of his face as though between gripping fingers. Shame that he had felt drawn to the girl, disgust that he shared any feeling with the redcap, anger that Dincott should possess her, and bleakest sense of his own want, and the wishing, and praying without thought, and the heart-thumping craving for the blessed ease of a woman, the feel and gloss of her softness, and the lunacy of dreams, knotted together, running in battering confusion, bringing him into a sweat, and then empty and weak.

He held on to Rosie's bonnet, drawing in a breath, and perhaps the redcap knew, for he turned, quickly, and walked away.

Dincott came back.

" Got plenty of these, Snow? " He pushed the cigarette package into Snowy's pocket. " Made a fortune out of 'em, I have. So don't go short. Ready? "

Snowy nodded.

Dincott looked at him across lighter flame, the long pale look that saw all round and far in distance.

" Right you are, chum," he said. " I don't have to tell you no more, do I ? About capers? "

Snowy shook his head. Contempt for himself, heavy as a stone, was in his throat.

" You're a funny bloke, you are, Snow," Dincott said. " One minute you're all smiles, and next you're black as the ace. Something upset you? My bit of olly-olly? I only wanted her to ride with you because she'd be out of the way in case of trouble."

" Expecting something? " he asked.

" Always," Dincott said. " So I'm always ready. Now, look. My blokes are posted all along the road. We don't go past that place in the tunnel. We turn off. You'll be told where. Plain enough? "

" Let's get cracking," Snowy said, and left him. With softening inside, he saw that the Princess was sitting in the middle. The girl rapped on the window, waving as Dincott went by, and then turned, sighing, and settled in the corner. The Princess folded her hands.

He waited, sensing her desire to talk, but for some reason he was unwilling to start, and without knowing why except that, suddenly, he was embarrassed.

Torches flicked, and the carts were lumbering on the move. He felt the strain of the tow, and geared Rosie for the incline, noting the impress of wheels in lava already piling across the road, hearing it scrape on the offside as they turned a corner, watching a mother, high on the cart in front, clutch a child's hand pointing up at the crater.

" Snowy," she said quietly, as though she had taken a long time to choose her words, " how do you suppose we're ever going to get out of this jam? "

" Don't know, Miss," Snowy said, in relief, and heartily. " But I ain't worrying too much about it. Hadn't been for these women and kids, I'd have rolled him and his coppers in the road a long time ago. I believe he put this bride in here in case."

" In case what? " She looked at him in alarm.

" Just in case I tried," he said. " He knows I couldn't with her sitting there."

" My God," she said, shaken with it. " Give me that wheel, that's all. Have you forgotten everything? And that boy they shot? "

" We'll have all that out, Miss, don't worry," he said. " But this kid's only sixteen."

" Doesn't signify," the Princess said. " Absolutely not. Sixteen or sixty, when you look like that, there's nothing more to learn. Dincott has plenty to answer for. I'm going to try and contact those soldiers."

" Miss," he said, keeping his eyes on the road, " you're in my charge, and I'll have you know it. You're going to sit where you're sitting now, and you're not going to move till I say so."

" And just supposing I don't? " she said, with her shoulders off the cushioning. " Who do you think you are? Another Dincott? "

He looked down at her, laughing, and at wide, angry eyes, dark, and yet full of light, laughed the harder.

The steering column shook under his hands, and he felt the flooring rise against his feet. The carts in front had tipped and were rocking back and fore. Above a sound that might have been thunder, he could hear the women screaming. He slowed, making the line taut, steadying the cart, and then looked out of the window, but there was too much smoke to see very far.

The girl in the corner was running beads through her fingers, talking to the Princess in a frightened little voice. Again the rise in the flooring, as though Rosie had jumped a fence, but now the screams were louder, and he realized they came from Rusty's people in the rear.

Without warning, the smoke was thickened by a greyish-brown powder that slashed across the windscreen and then cleared, leaving them on a golden road in a night of clear red, watching the woman on the cart in front sitting with her fingers wide in terror, staring high up in the sky.

"It's the volcano," she said, quietly pointing to the girl. "It's in eruption. And this little thing's quite sure it's all on account of her, because she's been a baddie, and run off."

46

Max looked at the women, marvelling at the wealth of their quietness. Perhaps they might have been sitting there forever with their backs against the rock, one leg crossed over the other, knuckly hands passive in their laps, looking at no particular thing, but keeping their faces towards the bay, not frightened, or even watchful, but as if they were aware that what they were waiting for was nothing new, and nothing old, but simply another curiosity in time, as with a hard rainstorm, or an outsize potato, to be shrugged at, and forgotten.

Yet in the womanly patterns of them all were active and lovely threats of toil, and obedience, and a knowledge of ancient recipes livening on floury fingers, shy, and then volupt submission to one randy male, and natal hymns, and brown children swaddled in sumptuous fat. He tried to guess what might be in their minds, but even the youngest faces had the same unlit promise of a new candle, as though their spirits were at distance, leaving a vital force of flesh on guard, not even vigilant, but simply to exist, and it struck him that here was a quality which might explain their competence with hard living, perhaps the very touchstone of healthy survival.

Sadly, as with music, he realized that this islanding of the spirit was part of his father, the silent man patiently looking out at the sunshine, protecting himself from the unjust with solitude that grew with him inside his dreaming mother.

They were all waiting up on a knoll overlooking the road. The ground was still shaking, no more than might have been caused by the passing of heavy traffic, and almost unfelt, but it tickled in the mind, bringing thought of a globe spinning in a firmament, a lot of air that in the hand was nothing, turning on a pole that nobody had ever put a spade in, on an axis that by a little push might tip, like a pegtop, and scutter into nothing.

" I'm telling you," Bill said, sitting up. " Sooner I'm out of this damn country, better I'll be pleased. I can't understand how they put up with it. Volcanoes, mind, right in your backyard. Daft lot."

Max looked up at the crimson shaft glistening out of a sparkle of gold around the edge of the crater, watching the colour changing into clouds of ash blowing away in the strong wind.

" When she changes," he said, " we want to duck. There's going to be lots of ash around here. Maybe it'll be another Pompeii all over."

" Nothing'll surprise me," Bill said. " If we'd had our wits beside us, we'd not be here, messing about."

" What could we have done?" Max felt sudden exasperation. " These girls are tired. Anyway, we have to wait. We don't know the country."

" We know which way we come," Bill said. " We could have been half-way there by now. Supposing that damn thing blows up? We'll look bright, squatting up here, won't we? "

The women were moving, rolling farther back in shadow, and one of them, making signs with an open hand, was crawling towards them. She pointed down at the tunnel mouth, about two hundred yards away.

In the dusty bloom of the headlights dozens of figures were moving about, and in phases of the wind they heard them coughing, and laughing, and then a voice was speaking, and the figures stood still.

" Ortesi finally got out," Max said. " They must have had a pretty sweet time in there."

The figures were walking along the far side of the track leading down to the road.

Max and Bill flattened themselves, looking over the edge as the long file passed directly underneath, well spread out.

Bill felt his ankle shaken, turning to see a woman jerking her head at two men creeping down behind the rock, letting him know by a fixed smile and nodding head that they were friends.

Max and he crawled over to them, and in whispers they told Max all he could understand, and then spread their arms about the women, talking in a fury, and laughing up at the sky, all without a sound.

" They're from Rusty," Max said. " They've got stuck down there, a mile or so, on a side road. They met our two boys, and they've gone on to tell Rusty what happened to us."

" Rusty? " Bill said. " Where's Snowy? "

" Ain't with them," Max said. " Nor that Dincott guy. I hope nothing's happened to Snowy. I certainly hope nothing happened to that boy."

" If he tried any nonsense with her"—Bill looked up at the flame—" old Snowy'd have a smack at him, ye know."

" That's what I'm afraid of," Max said. " Dincott got fresh, and Snowy just threw one at him. That'd be all. What'll we do? "

" Go down and try and find some of our lot," Bill said. " That there Ortesi bloke's down there, an' all. I don't know who to pick for t' worst."

" Look, Bill"—Max was taking a lot of trouble with the ends of a shoelace—" I'm not trying to slide out of this. I want to see Dincott cut to size, and this Ortesi, too. But I want to get back to my outfit more'n anything in this world right now. If I get screwed up with the Army and some of that justice they have, I'm going to get what Dincott's bunch'll get. To the Army, what's the difference? I hate to think that. Suppose I had to argue about the difference between me and a guy like Dincott? "

" That's all right, lad," Bill said. " Matter of fact, we're all loose now. Snowy and me's two days over the edge. What, will ye get on th' highway and thumb a lift? "

"That was the general idea," said Max. "I can't stand to think of it, Bill. Honest. Imagine. Same sort of trial as Dincott!"

"We'd best start off," Bill said. "I want to find Snowy."

Max went over to talk to the men and women.

Bill looked about, wonderingly, trying not to think that Snowy might be dead somewhere down towards the dark silence of the bay in this smell of burning hair and pepper.

"They won't go by the road," Max said, returning. "They say they're happy to go over the campagna, but the road's just hopping with murderers. Follow 'em?"

"Anything to get out of here," Bill said. "I'm right worried about old Snowy."

They went over the rock, striking across land that from the feel of it had never been ploughed. With the shift of smoke, they saw the terrain lit in red, and a grey fall, as though solid, straight down from the sky some miles beyond.

Barely to be noticed, at first a touching on the cheek like a dry snowflake, and then a harsh whirl that scratched their faces, ash began to fall, and they saw the billion sprinkle falling black against the glow just before it struck.

The men and women went down the hill together, and a man turned, speaking to Max, pointing.

"He says it don't matter in this if we keep together," Max said. "Get on the road and stay close. He's a stranger in this part of the country, he says, and he has to see where the heck he's going."

"I could have told the damn fool that, first off," Bill said. "I don't know why we don't go off on our own. We'd get a damn sight more done."

Max took the long strings of a woman's gown, and turned to Bill.

"These people'll find their way by what they were born with," he said, keeping the patience in his voice. "Stay close. We don't want to start looking for you."

"Fat chance," said Bill.

But within a few minutes the extent of his ineptitude was making him angry. Max had gone up a place, leaving an old woman between them. She looked tightly corseted, but he was surprised when her thumb dug into her spine, perhaps to move the ash that powdered about their bodies, for he saw not rigidity beneath, but the yield of malleable flesh. He looked down, watching the comfortable fall of her bare feet, trying to keep pace, but his boots slipped, and he often stumbled, falling back, having to stare down to catch the juggling of her heels, round and veined as a couple of old ivory billiard balls, leaping in and out of her skirt. They were following a track a little paler than the earth on either side, but so narrow that a yard away in that light a townsman's eye would have lost it.

He tried to check himself from bumping her when they stopped, but still bumped her, apologising to her quick smile, and then lost her when they started off, until in rudest anger with himself he found space to be grateful when she took his hand and swung him in front of her, taking him by the waistbelt and pushing him along with little cries of O! and E! as she might with a stupid bullcalf.

They halted on an incline. In the pause they heard the ash, falling hard, a brittle sound, not unlike breeze in elms, but steadier.

A man felt his way back to Max, pointing. His face was grey, stuck with dust and sweat, and the movements of his mouth sent out little grey puffs.

"O.K.," Max said. "The road's just below. Hold on going down. It's steep."

Slowly, a pace at a time, they went down, but now everyone held on to the waist in front, leaning back to take the strain of anyone missing a step, careful to try each rock before giving it full weight, finding comfort in the steadying grip front and rear. But then the incline was too steep, and holds broke, and everyone had to sit down. For a long time, it seemed, they went inch by inch, over rocks, through beds of small pebbles and little white seashells, passing weeds bobbing mournful comment heavy under brownish powder.

Max was grateful when one of the men pulled him upright, laughing, skipping on the flat to show him the roadway. But his feet went in flake to the ankles, sending up clouds of powder that burnt the nostrils, making them sneeze.

"This stuff's inches deep," he said. "If it keeps on for a couple of days? Or if it gets any heavier? Holy smoke, what a mess. There won't be any traffic up the Line. How can they do any hauling if it's like this?"

"Depends on the wind, don't it?" Bill looked anxiously about, and then, with his fingers drooping, down at himself. "We're in a nice mess, an' all. Ask him how far we've to go to t' nearest town."

"He don't know," Max said. "He don't come from around here. Best thing is to keep to the road and just keep going till we hit bottom."

"And how about Snowy?" Bill asked.

Max raised his arms, screwing up his eyes in the fall.

"Where in heck'll we look for the guy in this?" he demanded, and impatiently spat. "Let's get going."

They set off, all the men in front, and the women behind, arm in arm, with Max and Bill sandwiched between them, heads bent in the quick dust.

"This past couple of days I had more to do with women than any time since I was in high school." Max's voice was dulled in the clouds. "So what happens, I go for nice, long walks. Mama mia."

Waves of ash leapt beside them with a sound like tearing canvas, and bullets wheezed overhead. Bill went flat, taking the two women with him, both struggling for a moment until Max's shouts brought them still. Together they all crawled to the rock face, crouching there, stifling their coughs, hearing now plainly, now faintly, the sound of heavy rifle fire.

"Either the troops caught up with one of 'em," Bill said, "else Ortesi's having a go at Dincott. That suits me."

"Long as Snowy's not in it," Max said, "I don't give a damn. Who'd shoot at us?"

"Spares," Bill said. "They're hitting the rocks up there. I'll bet we're a good few hundred yards away."

"Don't make me feel any better," said Max. "Eruptions in back of us, bunch of geckos in front, and this stuff all around. Nobody knows the trouble I's seen."

Two men came back, hands outstretched, feeling their way, turning when a woman hissed at them, grinning through thick masks, excitedly pointing the way they had come.

" Some more of their own folks down thereaways," Max said. " Shall we go see? "

" Wasting time here," said Bill, and got up. " 'Sides, more of our lot we can collect better for us."

Happily as schoolchildren, the men and women set off, hugging the rocky side of the road, talking among themselves, perhaps unaware of the threat in bullets that still ploughed waves in the roadway. Bill had a feeling of being naked, of wanting to curl up in a tight ball and roll along in the ditch.

A cool draught sprang up and surface dust swept towards them in greyish-brown clouds. Wrapping their faces, they crouched against one another, coughing, closing their eyes tight, but not tight enough, for the grains got through, itching the eyeballs, bringing water that they blinked to clear, and in blinking made a thin paste that stuck to the rims and eyelashes. Blinded and stifled, they tried to burrow farther into the rock, feeling the fine stuff growling in their ears. Women were retching, trying to scream, and retching again.

Then the wind was cold, fresh, and free of dust.

Under a bronze sun, the land went down mistily all in the shade of purply-brown, trees, fields, and villages, except for hint of a red roof here and there, and the dark green of a sheltered cypress. An enormous curtain of ash was sweeping out towards the sea, smoothly as on rollers, trailing a spindrift of dust that sprouted more houses and vineyards, and farther down, whole villages, all of them sending up clouds of grey smoke as though on fire.

The rock behind them was embankment for a road forking off the one they were on. About a couple of hundred yards ahead another road went down to the left, crowded with a string of lorries in a confusion of angles, as though they had stopped in a hurry.

Nothing moved, and there was no sound except the long breath of receding ash, soft as distant waves, and the lowing of frightened cattle somewhere in the dip. But there were no outlines anywhere. Everything was covered in a purply-brown fur, and the canopies of the lorries were uneven and made ragged by falls momentarily sending down riffles of powder that trailed gracefully as lengths of net.

Bill could feel the woman shaking under him. Looking down, he saw the tears dropping into dark holes in the dust. He tried to turn her face, but she resisted him, though not enough, for he saw the shadowed eyes and the clean tear tracks down the side of her face and into her hair.

Anger came hot inside him to think of this woman, deprived of comfort, and bereaved of dignity, having refuge only in the warmth of her own tears, lying in a ditch for fear of two gangs of ruffians pitting strength in defiance of law that had shaped her gentle ways. He watched the movement of her shoulders, and a sob wrenched out of her that she crammed back in her mouth with helpless gestures of her hands, nervelessly moving in effort to control herself and then lapsing, as though tired of the struggle, into sobs that blew the dust in clouds about her.

He crawled farther up, taking her by the shoulders, cupping her face, using a loose sleeve to wipe her cheeks.

"Never mind, love," he whispered. "Everything comes to a finish. Ye'll be all right. I'll not let 'em touch ye."

"Damn it, Bill," Max said. "They're real gone. Hungry and tired."

A stone rolled down from the embankment just above his head, a simple sound, a small stone, and yet everyone crouched, looking upwards. A hand came into view, open, showing the palm. The fingers spread and closed in the sign of greeting, and opened in the two-fingered V. An arm followed through the embrasure, and a shoulder, and then the side of a grinning face.

Rusty was looking down, laughing wide.

He made a mouth to silence them, and frowned, nodding, to tell them he was coming down, pointing to the convoy, shaking his head.

They waited, watching the tip where the fork reached road level nearly hidden by a clump of weeds, knowing that Rusty had to move down in full view of any sniper on the other side.

Then the weeds shook, and the leaves dropped beards of powder that hung down and trailed off, and Rusty broke through behind the shaking stems, crawling on all fours towards them, followed by a couple of other men, all of them laughing quietly to themselves as if the joke were on someone else.

He gave a hand to each in greeting, sitting back, tiredly rubbing his eyes.

" Cristo mio," he whispered. " Just a job. The redcap fight with somebody. I don't see who it is."

" Was it Ortesi? " Max asked.

" Ortesi? " Rusty shrugged. " First, we get lot of shooting. Nobody knows who is. Then we get this polvere. We go away. Nobody hurt. Then I see you. I'm so happy. Where is Snowy? "

" Went off with Dincott," Max said. " Safe to get up, d'you think? "

" Not safe." Rusty shook his head. " Everybody, they hide. Wait for the night. Sleep, no? The carabinieri, they come to find us, then we safe. Look the poor girl. Want to sleep."

" Hell of a place to bunk down," Max said. " But what'll the carabinieri say about all them wagons and stuff?"

Rusty's face seemed to gather together, looking him in the eye.

" Nobody say nothing," he said. " Everybody very happy. I am happy when I find the Snowy. Then I go home."

Rifles were firing again some distance away, bursts and single shots, and more bursts, tiny sounds, less important than any nearby snap of twigs, but still the women drew together again, with eyes that frowned their fear.

" Look." Bill stood up. " If they're having a go down there, why don't we get in the lorries and shove off? Likely we'll meet some of our coppers coming up. I'll feel better doing thirty mile an hour than squatting here like a pouter."

" I'm with you," Max said. " Come on, Rusty. Let's go."

Rusty turned to the men and women, getting them on their feet. As though being able to stand upright and stretch, and beat the dust in clouds out of their clothing were start of a new life, the men and women began talking and laughing among themselves as children without care.

Rusty made deep tracks down the middle of the road, lifting his feet in rolling powder. Out in the open space where the fork joined the main road he held out his arms, whistling. For some moments there was no movement, but then, from the most unexpected places, up in the rocks, in trees at the roadside, out of patches of grass, and from the side road among the convoy, men and women came out beating themselves into streaming grey fumes holding laughing shadows. They halted when Rusty talked to them, and turned about, hurrying down to their tasks.

"Rusty has the stuff, all right," Max said, as they walked, carefully, to avoid the dust. "And I didn't see anybody argue with him yet."

"A guv'nor is a guv'nor wherever ye find him," Bill said. "Besides, he's an engineer."

Canopies were shaken to rid them of dust so that drivers in rear should not be blinded, and one by one the lorries were backed up on the main road, and turned to point downhill, in a fog that blew up high in the wind. When they were in position, Rusty went along the line checking drivers and complements.

"Snowy got with him three men, three women," he reported. "Everybody else, I got. I go in first truck. Where you like to?"

"Anywhere suits me," Bill said. "I'll go in the last, if you like."

"Better," Max said. "I'll go in the middle. Then if there's a mess we have three chances of keeping 'em together. Right?"

"Good, good." Rusty nodded happily. "So I drive very slow. Don't stop for nothing except only carabinieri. Bene?"

"Bene," Bill said, and looked at Max. "There y'are. I'm talking the lingo. Can't say no fairer, can I?"

He saw Max get up in a cab with a driver and a sleeping woman beside him, and went down to the end truck, coughing in his own dust. He swung the door open to climb in, and paused, catching a movement in the fog.

"That you, Rusty?" he called.

He saw the sweep of a skirt, and then the face of the woman in the ditch. She put her hands together, nodding with her head on one side.

"Well, well," he said. "Want to come in with me, love? Come on, then. Up you get."

He helped her in, with a man at the wheel, and a woman.

"We'll have to squeeze up, like," he said. "But that'll not hurt us. Good job we've not all had breakfast, else we might have a bit of trouble fitting in. Eh? What a damn fool. Ye don't understand, do ye?"

He listened, not altogether happily, to the engine, and when they started off, watched the driver's practised handling, sitting back completely satisfied, and suddenly weary. Both women were fast asleep, aloll with every movement of the springs. He put his arm about the woman next to him, putting her head on his shoulder and resting his cheek on the dusty headcloth, feeling himself going to sleep but unwilling while the driver remained awake.

He jolted wide awake at a sudden shout, looking about for cause, and then cringed away from a fury that struck the window, blotting out the light. For moments on end they watched the brown swirl, seeing the tail light of the lorry in front when the wind relented, edging closer until they were only a yard from the tailboard and the comfort of its nearness.

The driver nodded across the wheel with his eyebrows up, lifting one shoulder in disgust. He started when the red ball moved away and stopped when it came near, and started again when it moved, and then stopped, and started and stopped, and started and stopped, in a moan of engine and a screech of brakes, stopping and starting, a few yards at a time conforming with the distance of that little red eye in a purply-brown sleet. And all the time, both women slept with the quality of children, never stirring, soft of breath, with their skirts high above their knees from slipping in the seat; and looking down at hams the colour of wheat husks, the driver caught Bill's eye, closing his own in a clown's grin, wagging his fingers up and down as though they hurt.

Bill was seized in bitterest rail at thought of Pet, lying white at home, knowing how she prayed for health, and what she would sacrifice to be either of these women if only for a few hours. He was saddened to think of these rich, and her denied, with always a thought behind, but never allowed full play, of coming home to a singing girl, and a house crisp with a woman's touch, and this sturdy comfort at night.

Something in the thought took rage away, and staring out at the falling ash there appeared to him a similarity, as if his life were being sketched and coloured, and the bright red points going away and coming near, but never near enough, were prayers always at point of fruition, yet always to be prayed for and dreamed again.

Light was paler, and purply brown had changed to grey, and for a period they went through mist reminding him of mornings when streets were silver and all the lamp-posts were hung with diamonds.

Splintering glass jerked him back to see the windscreen cracking and crinkling through its length. Both women awoke with in-drawn screams, silenced by the driver's curse as he pulled the truck to a halt.

The tail light in front had gone out.

Rapping on the window brought the driver round. Bill saw the brass butt of an automatic rifle crack peremptorily on the glass. The driver opened the door and jumped down, turning to help the women, sleepily falling over the controls.

The door on Bill's side swung wide, letting in the fog. Red-caps and the long shadows of uniformed men made a dark grouping. The man at the door dug the foresight of the automatic into his leg.

" Aus! " he shouted. " Vite! Quick! "

Bill helped the woman down the steps, and with her arm heavily in his, turned in answer to pressure just below his ribs, and walked towards the group.

Rusty was already there, he saw, and then Max arrived among a crowd. Men were being made to jump off the rear of other trucks, and they heard shouts, and sound of women weeping.

One of the redcaps spoke in Italian.

Nobody answered or moved.

He spoke again, and then Rusty held up his hand.

" What do you know? " Max lifted his hands, rocking on the balls of his feet. " We headed into it."

" Who are they? " Bill felt the woman come closer to him, and patted the back of her hand.

" Dincott's bunch," Max said.

47

Snowy looked into the fog, remembering early turns at work, walking among the office cleaners, listening to them talking with their heads in pale nets of breath, hurrying along on bad feet, on heels over at the side, turning off to tap on big glass doors, calling goodbye to those walking on.

He remembered looking up at dark buildings down long streets, and seeing lights go on, a few here, and there, on different stories, thinking of the women with buckets and brooms getting business ready for another day, scrubbing acres of stone flooring, polishing miles of wood, sweeping tons of rubbish, singing to hear their voices roll down empty marble corridors and hang, echoing in lift shafts, giving themselves a little moment of grandeur, and revelling without fear.

Early days, when he worked as electrician's mate, listening to those voices, and sang falsetto up the shaft in reply, and the language that weltered back with a clanging of brooms on iron gates for good measure. He thought of all those women, wishing himself among them, walking now, in the dark morning, as they always did, rain, snow or shine, getting up at three o'clock and leaving the children's breakfasts, going off to get business ready for another day. In his mind he seemed to see Liz in her lodgings, that room shared with two other girls, and old Aunt Laura in her little room over the grocer's where everything smelt of biscuits and piccalilli, and all the tens of thousands of other people in their little rooms, all getting up and washing and doing their hair, all coming out of doors from little rooms to join that numerous shuffle in the dark mornings.

Happiness came to feel the Princess warm against his side, fast asleep and heavy on him with all the trust of a dreamer. The girl slept in her corner, a crumple of white, stained with dust and troubled with snores that seemed to worry the back of her nose.

He was sorry for the women and children on the carts. In moments when the dust was blown away he saw them clustered, barely to be told from the bundles they sat on except for the movement of a child, or the stretching of a sheltering arm. Mile on slow mile the procession went, always downhill in fog too thick to see the other side of the tarmac. At times a redcap stopped him with a flashing torch, and twice he passed a truckload of them drawn in to allow passage. All their faces were brown in the fog, and all of them looked up at him with the same expression, not of surprise or of expectancy, and certainly not of welcome, but something between the three, mixed with a quality he could not define, noticed in the man up at the village, and now plain in all of them.

A torch blossomed white in the pinky-grey cloud, and, as he slowed, a redcap jumped on the step, grinning and tapping on the window.

"We're stopping here, chum," he said, when Snowy lowered the pane. "This is home. Hot baths, and the best of everything. Feel better already, don't you?"

"Shan't be sorry," Snowy said, warmed despite himself by the man's cheerful manner. "What about the girls?"

"Special department," the man said, as if it were really a serious question to be spoken about in lower tones. "It'll be a bit of a mess-up tonight because of this muck floating about, but tomorrow morning we'll all be off to the other side where it ain't falling. It's the wind bringing it over, see? And we're copping it a bit unlucky."

"Where you from?" Snowy asked.

"Tell you when I know you a bit better," the man said. "I hear you're muckin' in with us? Very sensible. You won't be sorry. I've put more'n two thousand quid in the bank since I've been here."

"We'll have to see about all that," Snowy said. "Who told you?"

"The boss." The redcap waved him into a courtyard, towards lit double doors in the far wall. "'Fore long you won't be talking to me. You'll be up with the nobs. Straight through, and turn at the far end."

As they passed, Snowy saw trucks parked diagonally along both sides of the courtyard wall, but they were too shadowy to collect detail. The Princess was awake, he thought, from the different pulse of her body, motionless, but no longer torpid in sleep. On the other side, the girl was looking about, smiling at her reflection in the windscreen, drumming her heels impatiently, glad to reach a place she obviously knew, and preening herself for a position she thought she held, for as they neared the gateway and people began to wave, her head went farther and farther back, until, when they were in the light, she was inclining her neck the merest half inch this side and that, acknowledging their greeting.

Redcaps went on ahead, signalling the way, but long before he was ready to stop the girl had turned several times, glancing first at the Princess, and then at him, never a full turn or a direct stare, but a glimpse, as if she imagined that any weathercocking of hers were enough to command attention. Then she turned, full on Snowy, fluttering her hand, speaking, he could have sworn, in the back of her nose, but remembering her snores he grinned at her, and she sat back staring at him with her hand against her mouth.

" She wants you to stop and let her off," the Princess said, and moved, sitting up, trying to bind her hair. " She's in a bad temper with you."

" I see she was slicing it off a bit chunky, there," Snowy said. " Don't take 'em long to get the bells on their toes, do it? Little mare, I'd slap her backside."

" She'd probably enjoy it," the Princess said. " How about Dincott? "

" Don't worry, Miss," Snowy said. " I'm saving it up for him."

A sergeant redcap gave him the stop sign and came round to the door.

" Lovely job," he said, patting Rosie's fender. " Just what we've been wanting. But you're cheeky, ain't you? "

" What d'you mean, cheeky? " Snowy climbed down. " What're you talking about? "

" You heard," the redcap said, but his smile had gone. " Ain't this the wagon we knocked off a couple of nights ago? "

Snowy nodded.

" And you chased her? " The redcap was smiling again. " And pinched the boss's Mercedes out of the osteria down there?

We've heard all about you. Then you went and pinched this? What, was you thinking of starting up on your own, was you? "

" What's it got to do with you? " Snowy leaned against the fender, wondering at the anger he felt, determining whether to hit him on the chin or keep on talking, but above his eyeline he saw her frown and move her head. " Were you the bloke who pinched my photographs? "

" No chumbo." The redcap looked confused and turned away. " That's all been dealt with. Ask the boss. He'll tell you."

Petrol lights were yellowish in the smoky air, hung between archways all round the sides of the courtyard. A crowd of people had gone into a room lower down with the girl in white. Dincott was standing under a lamp, signing papers one after another, reading them with the pen in his mouth, and signing in a couple of loops. A few redcaps stood in the closed doorway at the far end. There was no sound except a sudden shout of laughter from the crowd inside.

" Where do you suppose we are? " she whispered.

He shook his head at her. Dincott had finished signing, and with another man in plain clothes was walking slowly towards Rosie, talking seriously, with a pointing finger, as if the civilian wanted reassurance.

" Snowy," he said, holding the civilian by a wrinkled lapel, with a loop of broad black braid through the button-hole. " This is Gippi. Second in command. Anything to do with the running, grub, vino, everything, see him. He's going to show you your quarters for the time being. All right? "

" Shan't be sorry," Snowy said, and looked at the Princess.

" Don't worry, boy." Dincott waved a hand that dismissed all doubt. " She's been took care of. We attend to everything. I hear you wanted to know what happened to your photos? "

Snowy nodded.

" Very hard luck," Dincott said. " I went down there to do a job, see? Always travel on me own down the main routes. Saves a lot of trouble. When I saw the wagon, I says to myself, just what I want. So I sent the message, and while I was doing my stuff some of the lads done the job. But they was no good."

"I'd like to get my hands on 'em," Snowy said. "Any chance?"

"First, they didn't take enough petrol, so they had to put her away." Dincott went on talking in the same tone, ignoring the question. "Then they let you get her again. And to crown it, they started shooting people what was useful to us. Then I found out they'd done a few jobs of their own, on the quiet. Nipper don't allow it. Eh, Gippi?"

"Bad," Gippi said, in a voice deep as a cough. "Very bad. Everywhere we like to make the help. Everywhere we want plenty friend."

"See?" Dincott looked as if he felt there were ample reason to clear him of any charge. "So I shot two of 'em, and the mechanics are on half pay."

"You shot two of 'em?" Snowy frowned at him.

"That's right, Snow." Dincott looked from Gippi to the first lamp, and then at him, smiling. "Dead. Happened before. And they knew it. How about a nice bath?"

"Come," Gippi said, "I show to you." He looked up at the Princess. "Come, please."

"See you in a couple of hours, Snow?" Dincott patted his shoulder almost proprietorially. "I'd like to get the line of march straight, and there's a lot of work for you. We've got about seventy miles to cover on bad roads, round to our other place. And if the wind comes back this way again, it'll be a shocker. Couple of hours?"

"Right," Snowy said, and wondered again at the calmness of his feeling.

Dincott opened his mouth to talk to the Princess, but she passed him without a sign. His grin changed to a half snatch at a snarl, and back to a grin, for Snowy was watching him, reminded of a dog tantalized with a bone.

"You'll have to train her, Snowy," he called out, "else I will. Then she won't be no good to nobody else."

Snowy hurried after her, hearing the voice doubling under the archway and wishing he could stop it. Both figures turned into a doorway, and he followed, into a stairwell lit by a dip, but brighter up the stairway.

A crowd seemed to be talking, laughing, and there was clatter of plates, and violins playing a dance tune. They went on, up to the top of the stairs, and were met in the corridor by an old woman in a long, white apron, and a neat cloth round her head that made her face darker and her eyes larger, waiting with a petrol lamp.

They went behind her, blinded by the light, seeing nothing except the mosaic floor under shielding palms, listening to the comfortable pad of her bare feet.

"Ecco," she said, and opened double doors on the left.

The man called Gippi bowed at the waist.

"Please," he said. "The bath is ready. The clothes. Everything what you want. She is your servant. Some food when you want. Very good kitchen. What you like. So I come in two hours? No?"

"Thanks," Snowy said, and looked at a square, grey room, with plaster filigrees in the panels and a high, painted ceiling.

A bed, under a curtain of gold brocade, took almost one side, and opposite candles ran grease on a dressing-table covered with cut-glass bottles. The floor was soft with a grey carpet. Light came from a white room next door. One long window was shuttered.

"Where's my room?" Snowy asked. "This is hers."

"Please," the man shrugged. "This for you. Nobody else come. Is the order. Everything the best for Signor Snow."

As though to settle the matter, he bowed, kicked the wedge out and quietly closed the door. Snowy heard him go along the corridor to the next room, and talk to the old woman.

Buckets rattled on tiles among splashings of water. The Princess was standing with her back to him, hands clasped in front, looking down at a bottle on the table. He felt helpless, and angrily as though he were taking advantage of her smallness and lack of bad temper or any complaint.

A shadow moved in the doorway. The old woman bent a knee, holding on to the jamb, speaking in hesitant half-whispers, half-gulped words.

"They even have these poor little things frightened out of their lives," the Princess said. "She wants to know who's going to take a bath first. You or me?"

" I'm dirtiest," Snowy said. " You go first."

She went into the next room as if she might not have heard, but as the old woman closed the doors, he heard her laugh, and one leaf opened.

" Somebody put my suitcase in here," she said, putting her head out. " Clean clothes. I had to tell you. Think it's safe to talk? "

" How d'you mean, Miss? " He went over to her, attracted by the whisper. " Safe? I'd like to see anybody play about round here."

" You don't think someone's listening? " she whispered. " I expect the whole place to burgeon out in ears. Long, furry donkey's ears."

" That's all right, Miss," he said. " Let's give 'em something to use 'em for. Know any funny words? "

" Lots," she said. " I'll match you."

She shut the door and he went back to the high chair by the dressing-table, looking at the light making pretty colours in the crystal, and the tassels on the perfume sprays, and the little cupids flying around the mirror.

He listened to the susurrus of drawn silks, watching the come and go of light under the door, feeling a numbness coming on him, and a desire never to move but simply to sit there, watching, listening, intent. But the meaty stench of his body came warm from his open shirt front, bringing him to realize his condition, the greasy twill permeated with ash, grimed hands, a two-day beard, and spiky hair. Bending forward to look at his face, he was stricken to see its colour and the patches beneath the eyes, and sat back, wondering how she could talk to him, or even notice him, in such a state.

Almost with fear he realized that he was in the bedroom of a woman from another region of life, someone he had spoken to, and sat next to, and thought about, though always with reserve as a creature set apart, not quite as a foreigner, perhaps, but certainly never as someone he could treat coevally and remain at ease.

Ripples of water coming now and again, and a line of song in a voice that surprisingly reached into him and hurt for desire to protect its womanliness, and the glissant rumours of her laving hands, became part of a strange fever that moment by moment grew in heat and discomfort, bringing him to feel that even the furniture had come to life, looking at him with side glances and sneers to make him aware that he was intruding in a place that had always been reserved for intimacies of another order of people, where generations of elegance had been conceived, perhaps born in this very bed, and there dying with nothing changed but the linen.

Voices that might have come from the furniture told him to go and find himself another room where he would be comfortable on his own, without having to worry what to do with his hands, or what to say and how to say it.

He tried to imagine what Liz might do if she came in now and found him sitting there, listening to a woman enjoying a bath next door, with not so much as a key turned between them, but either he was too tired to think hard, or else she was too far away, for his mind stayed full of the sounds of towelling among little sniffs and indrawn breaths from effort, and the belling of stoppers put back in glass bottles. The sough of the hairbrush brought a vision of the two girls taking the papers out of their curls and then waiting, ribbons in hand, until Liz was ready for them.

Again and grievously some prong of shame reached through, making him feel he should move, and with it an almost sickening desire to go to Liz and hold the compact yield of her, and flatten his nose against her cheek with a long, hard kiss of prayer to absolve him for a state of mind that he knew was wrong, but could not, or would not, fight.

And again the stopper rang in the bottle next door, a tiny bell, exorcising visions, bringing a flood of notions, and memories of perfume, a look across the heads of many people, the white line of her scalp through gold and copper, the twirl of her fingers, a broken sigh as she slept against him and the electric satin of her hand on his arm when she turned to him in fright, throwing upon him the trust of protection and melting him with honour.

There were footsteps in the corridor and taps at the door.

A redcap stood in the light of the old woman's petrol lamp, holding out an armful of clothes still fragrant from the hot iron, and a bottle.

" Here you are, chum," he said. " Boss's compliments. Cigarettes, matches, and a little drop of o-let-us-be-joyful."

Snowy took the whisky and pointed inside the room.

" Put 'em down somewhere, will you? " he asked.

" Cer'nly," the redcap said, and walked in, laying underwear and clean drill neatly on the counterpane. " You're one of the blokes brought in that big breakdown job, ain't you? "

" What about it? " Snowy stood in the doorway. " What d'you mean, one of 'em? How many more was there? "

" I don't know too much about it," the redcap said, turning quickly, ill at ease. " I heard there was three or four of you. Had some trouble with Ortesi, didn't you? "

" Never heard of him," Snowy said. " Only trouble I've had was with Mr. Dincott. You looking for some? "

" Now listen, chum." The redcap squeezed past in the doorway. " For Christ's sake don't get awkward. Don't start rubbing the Nipper up the wrong way. Take it all as it comes. You won't do yourself no good, I'm telling you. He's got you, and he'll hang on to you. And if he don't, you're a goner."

Snowy looked at him, trying to exact the quality so noticeable in all of them, and yet there seemed nothing out of the way about him except the cut and finish of his uniform and a robust air of well-being. The man was grinning at him, and turned away.

" Think you'll be able to identify me, do you? " he said, good-humouredly. " I wouldn't bother. Couple o' months' time you'll be all settled down. One way or another. See you in the mess."

The old woman came out of the bathroom with empty buckets, and picked up two more that steamed, taking them inside, looking at him as she went in, nodding to tell him the bath was ready. In the mourn of her eyes he sensed the tale of years of willing work beyond the clock, with no reward except the stretch of her days and blotting sleep.

" Ta, Ma," he said. " I'll be there."

The Princess came in from the bathroom with her arms about a pink bundle that she dropped on the bed. Her hair was in a plait swinging as she walked, and her toes glinted in gold sandals mousing under a long blue gown that caught shadow in folds and crumples.

With all the gentleness of flowers her perfume reached him, touching a yearn, a need, some far-away desire that might always have been there, but if felt unthought, or, if thought, put aside, a singular desire for beauty that might be worshipped from distance and yet held in the hands, for a dream undreamt with lovelier form than reality, sometimes to be sensed and always replete with melancholy.

"Snowy," she said, listening to the redcap going away, "do you think we'll be disturbed for a while? I so want to lie down. Just flat, and feel myself collapsing in on myself."

He turned the key in the door to the corridor.

"When I've had me bath," he said, "I'll sit out there, and I'll lay nobody comes anywhere near you."

She grasped his forefinger, turning aside, shaking her head, watching the leaves of candle flame quivering as she moved.

"Please," she said, "don't do that or I'll come out there with you. Remember what happened before? You come right back in here."

He picked up the clean linen with his finger-tips, but the garments were smooth from the iron and slid off his arm. She hurried to him, and took them one by one, and preceded him to the bathroom.

"I hope that didn't sound like an invitation to the waltz," she said, with her back to him, putting the armful neatly on the table. "I never know what you're thinking. And I don't quite know how to handle this situation, either. But I expect I'll learn."

"I ought to have got a place of my own," he said. "Shouted for it. Stamped me foot."

"If you had," she said, going into the bedroom, "Mr. Dincott might have been stamping on both of mine. I'm grateful you're here."

She had almost closed the door. He watched the handle turning.

"Snowy?" Except that the tone sang along the tiles, he would not clearly have heard. "Promise you won't leave me till we're out of this. I'm scared of him. Nothing else. Just him."

He felt a rage that seemed to grow bristles under his eyes, and he saw the outline of the skull tight beneath the beret.

"That's all right, Miss," he said. "You go and have a nice lay down. I shan't kick up a row."

The door closed.

The crocodile suitcase lay open on the floor, and he nodded as he might to an old friend.

He dropped his clothes off where he stood and got into the hot water, stretching out with his head hard on the porcelain, feeling the heat pulping fatigue, swelling his fingers, hurting his feet. The wound scar in his belly awoke in a bite of teeth and he put his hand down there to steady the pulse, feeling it easing, drawing a deep, thankful breath, knowing his need for sleep.

A report, loud as a rifle shot, sounded close to his head.

Minutest ripples clouded the bath water, and he felt the shuddering underneath him, hearing shouting beyond a rumble and crackle that passed away.

He sat up, listening.

The water settled.

In the wall by the window, a ragged gape was black from ceiling to the tiling dado.

"You all right, Miss?" he shouted.

"Why surely," the calm voice was surprisingly near. "I'm hoping somebody we know's broken both his necks."

The nearness of her voice made him wonder if she might have been listening to the sounds he was making, but he shook his head at the thought. Nevertheless he tried to move quietly, and swore under his breath when he slipped and sat down, appalled at the noise he was obliged to make in effort to keep quiet, and finally gave it up as a bad job, lathering with her soap, calling himself a fool for wanting to kiss the tablet because it had touched her, and then groping for courage to pour cold bucketfuls over his head.

The door to the corridor opened without warning, and the old woman came in, bringing clean towels, and a tray of glasses, putting them down with her back turned and picking up empty buckets to go out.

"You don't mind what you see, do you, duckie?" he said, grabbing a towel. "What a turn-out, eh? Things ain't your own round here."

" Case of when in Rome, ain't it? " said a familiar voice. " That's what the boss says."

The redcap was leaning against the doorway grinning.

" Feeling better? " he enquired. " Boss asked me to come up and see if you was worried about the shocks. We've been having 'em the last couple of days. 'S why we moved down here. Stone-built house, see? Get out of it all together in the morning. Where there won't be no shocks. Any complaints? "

" Only about you," Snowy said, wrapping the towel. " Gawking round here in your rubber dabs. Don't want to be bothered for a couple of hours, like I told you. I'll let you know when I'm worried."

" Cake," the redcap said, nodding next door. " Don't blame you, either. Where d'you find her? "

" Come a bit nearer, and I'll show you," Snowy said, feeling a blush starting that might have come from a fire deep down inside. To know that she could hear gave him the same feeling as seeing someone spit on her.

" Snowy," she called, " would you be kind and ask if there's some coffee, or something to drink? "

The redcap lifted his finger to the old woman and said something in Italian.

" She'll bring it," he said, as she hurried out. " You don't half blow up quick, don't you? No offence meant. None intended."

" All right," said Snowy, carefully choosing his words. " Sling your flamin' hook. Quick."

He slammed the door. Clean clothes, though slightly too small, and the effect of the bath brought a new state of wakefulness. He wondered whether to stay in the bathroom until the coffee came and then saunter in, or whether to bank on her falling asleep if he kept quiet and not have to go in at all, or if he should call out an excuse and then go downstairs to have a look at the house and all the people in it.

Anything, to keep away from her.

" If you want a comb," she called, " I have one here."

He looked at the toilet bottles, and little brightly-coloured woman's things on the table, feeling as he had on the morning after the honeymoon, waiting for Liz to finish dressing, too shy to watch her, and too ashamed of shyness to leave the room.

Taking a pull at his waistbelt, he breathed long, and in the breath strode to the door, and entered.

She was lying on the bed, still in the blue gown. The brocade cover and a neat pile of white sheets were on the chair. The pillows and the bedsheets were pink, catching a silvery gloss where they wrinkled.

"I brought my own linen," she said, watching him. "I always do. You never know what you'll meet on the wayside, do you? And they don't have any soap, so they can't launder."

"Good idea," he said, for some reason unable to look at her. "Why don't you try and get some sleep? I've got to go down and look at Rosie."

She sat up.

"Now, listen," she said. "If you're going down to Rosie, so am I. I'd rather wait in any morgue than here by myself. Please, Snowy!"

"Can't do much harm for a couple of hours," he said, and shifted the pile off the chair. "How about a drop of whisky?"

"Have some in your coffee," she said. "Then perhaps you'll sleep. Who was the man you talked to out there?"

"One of the mob." She shook her head at the cigarette and went on biting the end of her little finger, watching him. "I don't know what it is, Miss, but there's something about 'em. All of 'em. There's something I can't quite put me finger on."

"What do you mean?" She roused, frowning. "Something you've heard?"

"No, Miss," he said. "Something I'll swear I can see, but I can't, if you see what I mean? It's something about 'em. The way they set about things. Way they talk. I can't make out what it is."

She was smiling at him.

"Oh, Snowy," she said. "Surely. Doesn't it hit you? They're doing something monstrous. Despicable. Don't you think they know it? When they talk to people like you, don't you think they feel it? A sporting nation breeds that kind of a conscience. They'll do anything to bribe you or frighten you into joining them, just to make them feel better about themselves.

They're sly. They're all sly with guilt and the filthiest kind of shame. They can hardly bear to look at each other for thinking of the guys in the fox-holes up there. It's what makes them crueller. They're trying to crush it out of their consciences. That's what you can see. They're sly. That you could never be."

He got up, hearing the pad of bare feet next door, and went out to take the tray from the old woman. She looked up at him with the eyes of a child, and whispered a question.

"Come inside, old dear," Snowy said, nodding in the bedroom. "We'll fix you up."

The Princess called her. He saw lines go smooth with amazement as she turned and hurried in, falling on her knees, talking in a whisper never far from tears, and he stood there, holding the tray until she had finished. For a while she nodded, listening to the Princess, and then she got up, and curtsied, and ran on spread toes past him into the corridor, closing the door.

"They have some people locked up." The Princess motioned to the bedside table, leaning across to pour the coffee. "I asked her to go and find out who they are."

"Sure she won't split on us?" Snowy took his cup. "Ta. Thank you, Miss."

"You don't know these people," she said. "They hate Dincott and the rest of them. But as she said, what can they do? Except sweat it out, and hope for the wrath to fall on him."

"Yes," he said. "I'm waiting for one little chance. That's all."

"Now, Snowy." She stopped pouring, looking at him square, with only a little space between them. "You promised me. Did you forget you have a family?"

"No, Miss." He was looking at her and trying not to blink. "I ain't likely to."

"That's fine," she said. "You're in a class of your own as a husband. And I mean that."

"Just what I ain't, Miss," he said, and turned away from her. "That's what I meant. Every time I think of you, I get carved up thinking of them."

He heard her put the cup down and lie back.

"I hope I can think of something so I don't have to cry like a fool," she said. "Come and sit here, and let's talk."

He sat at the foot of the bed, near the end of the pink turn-down, almost shocked to find that the sheets were silk with big monograms bumpy in the corners.

"Don't you like silk sheets, Snowy?" She was amused by his sudden stare. "I didn't know we were going to meet, you must remember."

"Never had the pleasure, Miss," Snowy said, feeling the qualm again, and wishing himself far away. "Something I'm not used to. I've even forgot what ordinary 'uns feel like."

"Ever feel sorry for yourself?" she asked, still smiling, but differently.

"Me?" He laughed, and she laughed with him. "Blimey, I should say so. Not exactly sorry for myself. But it's a long time, and I start thinking about all the time I'm throwing away. For nothing."

"Not for nothing," she corrected, sharply. "Somebody had to stop them."

"I tell you, it's such a shocking muck-up you don't know what to say for the best," he said. "Except, the big blokes'll come out bigger, and we'll all be the same as we was, only worse off by four or five years. Perhaps six, the way we're going on. That's a dead cert, that is."

"Well, let's try and get a little sense into this thing about thinking of me," she said. "Just because we've been bundled in together doesn't mean we have to go crazy."

"That's quite right, Miss," he said. "Like a drop of whisky in that coffee?"

"No thanks." She covered the cup with her palm. "I'd go off and wake up next week if I did. I'm probably talking nonsense because I'm tired. Darling. What's the use? It's no good."

"What ain't, Miss?" The furniture seemed to be laughing at him, and the rest of what he wanted to say was lost in a dry throat.

"Us," she said. "You only think I'm attractive because I'm a woman and you're overdue. Any woman would have been the same in these circumstances. But when you look at me like that, I don't know."

"I know I'm not good enough," he said. "That's why I didn't say anything before."

"Somehow I feel a lot older than you," she said. "Sometimes I could be your grandma. What do you mean exactly, not good enough?"

"All hands and feet," he said, with his hand in both of hers, feeling like an electric battery in heavy charge. "I don't know where I am. How I feel."

"Feeling's only a matter of a little while," she said. "Love's different. Love's deep, where you can't seem to feel anything any more. And it weighs on you from outside and bursts through from inside and it leaves you so you could die, and it's there all the time. There's no such thing as not good enough."

"You couldn't live my kind of life, Miss," he said. "I couldn't live yours."

"That's all a matter of what you've gotten used to," she said. "It doesn't take long to shake down. But we weren't talking about living. We were talking about love."

It was obvious now, and alight, as though someone had switched something on inside his brain, except that a small doubt remained, shaking its head in shadow. He could see that living together would make the sort of feeling he had for Liz, but that love was what he felt for the Princess, a rare and distant emotion found in the stories about knights and fair ladies in school books of big print and coloured pictures, so good to read, though never part of ordinary things like beetroot salad and napkins on a line and walls with broken glass on top. That much was clear. But the little doubt was still raising its finger at the back, there.

Because he remembered having this feeling for Liz, the same need to see her, and be with her, not even to talk to her but only to know she was there. Sharply, now, he recollected telling her that he was not good enough, unworthy he heard himself saying, and her telling him not to be such a fathead and kissing him.

"I don't suppose I know too much about it, Miss," he said. "I never was over bright about anything like that. Give me a set of tools, and I'm in. But put me in a place like this, and I'm up the wall."

"I'll admit it's pretty awful." She looked about, smiling. "But why should it affect you?"

" I don't feel right in it," he said. " I only like what I'm used to. This belongs to other people. Your sort."

" Oh, Snowy," She drew the name out long in laughter. " I never heard anything so ridiculous. My sort of people? Just what kind of people are they? "

" Like you are," he said, doggedly. " No use trying to dodge it. You fit in here. You feel all right here, in this kind of stuff. I wish I did."

She reached out and handed him the comb, and unthinkingly he took it, dragging it through his hair, but it was dry from the bath and it stuck up almost straight. He felt the bed shaking, and looked down to see her laughing quietly, and then out loud, helplessly.

" You're just like a teddy bear," she said. " And I want to hug you but I can't. There's your beautiful Liz standing right behind you. And I'm as certain as I live, if she knew about this, she'd want my eyes."

He felt cheated and, in a childish way, mutinous at thought of Liz interfering just when everything seemed right, though he was unsure what he inferred. He evaded argument by tearing his mind from it, but there occurred a notion that here was the chance to find out all he wanted to know about another sort of woman. Even as the wish took shape, he found that his anger against Liz was almost at a point where he could swear out loud.

" I reckon Liz'd understand, Miss," he said. " We're not doing any harm, are we? "

" We're not doing a lot of good." She rolled over, drinking coffee. " Bill, you remember, that warty old sentinel, he called me Jezebel. My goodness, that's just how I feel. I know you're dynamite. But it can't happen. I don't even know why it's important that it mustn't. It mustn't. That's all."

" Because of Liz? " he asked. " Or your husband? "

" Both," she said, and lay back. " But you and me, too. Especially me. I often wish I'd played around. This morality business always had me a little mixed-up. I don't know if it's good or bad. It works two ways, I guess. But I'm pretty sure I know what puts a gal on the town."

He watched her mouth shaping the words, wondering how it

would feel to kiss her, or what she might do if he tried. She was looking up at the gold drape over the bed, talking as much to herself as to him. The quietness of her voice and the appeal of the tone seemed for all time to be part of the room, in accord with the furniture and the pink silk sheets, but beyond him, far away, too far to be understood or listened to with any mite of sympathy.

But then he realized that she was just like Liz that night coming back from their first holiday together before they were married, rolling home on the last tram, all by themselves on the top deck watching the lamps passing by and miles of dark squares of closed windows, until she turned into his shoulder, gripping tight, startling him in the strength of her tears, whispering that she hated going home to be all by herself again, day after day, wanting to get off the tram then and there, and find a room and sleep together, never mind what her mother might say, if only to have that memory for comfort.

Without the tears or the strength of hands, it was still the same sort of voice.

And suddenly he thought she was Liz, changed in some way, but Liz, brought to a place beyond his knowing, flooded by springs that filled and weighted her, low, stretched by gentle agonies that took her breath and coloured her cheeks, turning to meet him with slack hands and half-closed eyes, whispering things he never heard.

Memory scraped and tore, destroying misgiving, inclining him without volition towards her, but she turned from him, shaking her head, and that reminded him again of Liz, writhen, one side of her mouth drawn down waiting for him, and the vision struck, hungrily, wanting to know again the softness and dearness, the rage of attainment, the fine heat and viscous bubbling in the ram and plough of flesh held tight and yet unfelt.

He thrust his face against the curve of her shoulder, feeling the lobe of her ear against his mouth and the warmth of her seemed to burn, and her perfume mixed with the scent of her hair, occluding reason, bringing a new feeling of utter peacefulness, as if lying beside her, barely touching, savouring, evaluating her beauty were all he had ever wanted from life, and all he would ask.

There were taps on the door in the corridor, and about the same time buckets began clattering in the bathroom.

He rolled off the bed, and stood, almost in one movement, with thudding heart and a mind riddled with panic, ready to see Liz, herself, come in. But the moments passed, full of reassuring noise from next door, and then the taps sounded again.

He went over, trying to look as if he might have been reading a paper, and quietly turned the key, squinting through an inch of cool darkness at the top of a man's head, and a tray with bottles and small glasses, lit by the petrol lamp.

He opened the door farther, standing so that he covered her, and put out his hand for the tray.

Rusty was grinning at him.

He opened the door wide, but Rusty's instant glare stopped him from closing it.

His delight was obvious, even in the shaking tray. " No time. Bill, Max, everybody, they downstairs. We wait till good time, then we go. I come for you. Goodbye." He kissed his hand to the Princess, and pattered off barefoot, shutting the door.

Her eyes were wide in astonishment.

Snowy turned away from her, feeling quick pain that he would never know the fineness or extent of her ordinary emotion, much less the sacral feeling he divined.

He heard her go next door, listening to the whispers of the old woman, and laughter that sounded like Rosie ticking over.

She came in hurrying, more beautiful than he remembered her, close to him, taking his hand.

" What do you think? " Her eyes were bright with laughter, staring, coloured by reflections of candle flame in the mirror. " Everybody's down there, and they're all set to go. Dincott's people can't tell the difference between our paisanos and theirs, anyway, and they're all thick as thieves. They're going to get all the gates open, and if those mobsters try stopping them they'll hit plenty of trouble."

" Why didn't they do it before, then? " he asked. " Why wait for us? "

" Not enough of them by themselves and no guns," she said. " There were only the servants of the house and a few people from the village. It was Max and Bill and Rusty and our boys and girls that started the whole thing. I have to dress."

She seemed immediately to sense the desolation that grew in his mind at any hint of her leaving, or any widening of the distance between them, even to putting on thicker clothing.

Boots were loud in the corridor. They heard a bucket fall next door, almost as a signal. She stood on tiptoe and kissed his cheek and would have run, but he caught her, and forced back her head with a kiss in the bud of her mouth, and let her go, turning as the footfalls stopped, and someone whistled.

When she had gone, he opened the door.

Dincott and three redcaps stood there.

"Time for a talk, Snow boy?" he said, and walked in, stopping to point at the rumpled bed. "Didn't waste no time, eh? That's the hammer. Nothing like a nice rub out. Now look, this is business. Pour a drink, Krolly. Krolly and Piet's both Jerries. That's Andy. He's a Greek. This is Snowy."

All three nodded, laughing. Except that Krolly and Piet were fairish and as tall as himself, and that Andy was broad in the shoulder, shorter, with black hair combed flat from forehead to neck and glistening all the way, there was little difference between them and those he had already seen.

And in all of them, the fat of good living seemed polished into their skins.

"We start at four," Dincott said, looking at a slip of paper. "Two police trucks first, then three lorries of our stuff, three lorries of yours, one police truck, four private cars, three lorries of our stuff, three of yours, 'cluding the workshop, then another police truck, and then you. Behind you there'll be nothing except the Cinderella job. The second convoy starts half-hour afterwards. I've put you in the first, just in case of trouble on the road. You can either go forward, or turn back, see? In between the two. Any questions?"

"What d'you mean, three of mine?" Snowy watched them grin.

"Come off it, Snow." Dincott looked at the candles through his drink. "'Member what I said about capers? You know's well as I do, your mates are all downstairs there. Very happy and comfortable, mind. Full of Nipper's hospitality. They've all said they want to work wi' me. Just like you did. I've told 'em about capers, and they looked as if they understood. Just like you did. So you'll all be working for Nipper, see? Only on different jobs, in different places. Then if any of you play any capers, you'll all get a steak tea. Only one of you won't be there to eat it, see?"

"Yes," Snowy said, cold in the spine.

"And look, Snow." Dincott put the glass down, leaning on his elbows across the chairback, pointing a half-bent index finger next door. "I've told you. I can't tell you no more. You work a caper off on me, and besides doing one of your pals, I'll do her."

"You don't want to talk like that," Snowy said. "You want to wait till it happens first."

"Just what I don't want." Dincott got up. "Mind, I'll have a real game with her."

"No need for it," Snowy said, colder still. "If you want a job out of me, you leave her alone."

"That's the bargain," Dincott said. "Leastways it would be, if I wasn't the boss. You're not doing me any favours. You're doing what you're told. If you wasn't going to be useful, you wouldn't be here. As for that highclass cow in there, she's only here because she's part of your job. I don't know what you're doing with her kind in the first place. She won't stick by you, y'know."

"I got a wife and kids," Snowy said, aware that the redcaps were closer to him.

"Not out here you ain't." Dincott drank the lees of his glass. "Last of all, I've give you this little talk because of your pals downstairs, see? Because I can't abide capers. There's too much going on. The biggest part of my lads are doing a job down at the docks tonight. That's where I ought to be, not playing about up here. And you could be helping me. But if you're bent on a caper, you've got to be learnt."

Some strange difference was in him. The voice had climbed between two tones in edged sound under his tongue. His face, perhaps, was paler, and a tic was pulling at his mouth. His eyes were in shadow, fixed, liquid in red refraction. But he was shaking, as though with a malarial bout on him, and when he wiped his mouth his fingers quivered, until he bunched them in a fist.

Snowy felt his arms grabbed and twisted behind by the taller men, and his feet were pulled away from the rear and bent at the knee, so that he swung, suspended at the same height as Dincott.

Instinct called on him to fight, but even as he tensed, he remembered her, and shut his eyes.

Fists beat into his face, cutting his cheeks, sending the stabbing soda-water pains down his nose. He was remembering old lessons, pouching his lips to save his teeth, and then a blinding pain below the breast bone ripped his breath away, and they dropped him.

Praying for breath, for some hold on his lungs, he lay on his side, clear in mind, but helpless to move.

" There you are, Snow." Dincott's voice came from distance, normal again in genial waver between two octaves. " Easy, ain't it? That's just to learn you. Both your pals had the same helping, so you can't grouse. I didn't do you in the eyes because you've got to drive. That's the caper treatment. Now have a nice wash, and a drop of Scotch, and you'll be a different man. All for the good of your soul, Snow. You'll be called in about an hour."

He heard the door groaning in the draught.

He was aware of being lifted, and then the chill of a cold towel on his forehead, and stings when bruises were cleansed of blood. Gradually breathing was easy and without pain. Inwardly he was laughing, for he remembered feeling like this, stiff in the face and mouth, and sore in body after many a fight round the streets, and hearing his mother scolding, though not hard, for she knew it was useless.

He looked up.

Her eyes were glazed in a peculiar shine, though not of tears. Her face seemed drawn down towards the jaws as though each muscle had gone hard. Even when he grinned at her, there was no relaxing.

" Hullo, Miss," he said. " Right lot of boys, ain't they? "

" You couldn't hit back," she said, looking above his head.

" I'd have got a bit more if I had." He got up, flexing his arms, feeling his chest, punching in a shadow-box, dancing. " Ain't done me any harm. Knocked a bit of paint off, that's all."

" Because of me," she said. " Just because of me."

He went to her, taking flaccid hands, lifting her to stand.

" I've had this all me life, Miss." He held her by the arms, gently shaking her. " You don't want to worry. Honest. I'm all right. All that's worrying me is how I pay it back."

" You're going to? " She was looking up at him, but, it seemed, beyond him. " You mean it? You do, don't you? "

Snowy frowned at her, for a tone of surprise in the words implied suspicion that he might be content to accept the disgrace, and, further, that she was willing he should. Apart from waves of crushing ice in his mind at thought of those unanswered fists, and aside from murderous blight corrupting sense at memory of restraining hands, despite a frigid lust to avenge both, a warmer, thawing anger sent blood through his head until he felt too hot to stay inside his skin, that she should think him capable.

" Miss," he said, lunging at words. " You don't think I'd have that, do you? Stand there and let them hit me? Who d'you reckon I am? I'll wait ten years. I don't care. Twenty. But I'll have 'em. I'll have 'em all, one by one. What d'you mean, going to? "

He saw the colour darken her face, and her shoulders sank a fraction, and she was smiling softly, perhaps in relief.

" I'm so very glad," she said. " And so happy. I know you did it for me. It was wonderful. But we have to get away. We have to think how. All the time. Threats mustn't stop us. Nothing must. I can help. I have this."

She showed him a revolver under the pillow, and nodded through the bathroom door.

" Rusty gave it to her for me." She patted the pillow flat. " All we want now is a chance to use it, and get away. Fast."

Suddenly he was bleak.

Depending on a revolver and not on himself was disappointment enough, and that she had doubted him, even momentarily, was worse, but heinous fault was in this presumption that he wanted encouragement of any sort, especially in that tone of voice, the inference that he was to be assaulted without reply, and then led by the hand and pushed into rebellion as though he were some lesser order of male. She took her place among the gold brocade, the silken sheets and flying cherubim, all of them shouting patronage, and sufferance, permitting him the grace to feel aware of himself, and unwanted, perhaps alien.

Bottles fell on the table and the candles went out. His feet slid and he fell, holding the floor, that moved loose as skin. Both shutters split apart with glass falling in dismal scatter. A booming tumble of sound piled up among ear-tingling whipcracks of breaking stone sending out a reek of hot metal; and frightened women were screaming down in the courtyard.

Her hand touched his shoulder.

Instantly he turned to her, forgetful, avid to protect, and, despite the tremor of the flooring, he found her, and they fell together, scrambling in the darkness until he took her tightly in his arms, hearing the noise subside, and whimpering chatter from people hurrying about beneath the window.

She moved, perhaps to free herself, but he kept her. He felt her breathe out.

She moved again, an impatient gesture telling him more than words.

Her hands, that had not yet touched him, moved lightly to his shoulders, and drew apart. Her right hand, luminous in light from the courtyard, rested near his eyes. Perhaps, because the fingers curled easily with light polishing long nails, whitening lines creasing the soft palm unused to work, speaking of a way of living that, he acknowledged, he was unfitted to know, or perhaps it was only because it looked helpless, summarizing her dependence that she seemed to forget, but some perverse quirk devoid of feeling other than resolve to have his way made him tighten his arms still more.

Strange silence came between them, as though neither was able to give word to unfriendly and accusing thought, relying still upon near memories of kindliness, hopeful that this mood might pass and be forgotten. But Snowy found himself compelled, if only because of tacit refusal in the averted face, either to dominate or make her plead.

He tore at the gown and pulled it back, shocked immediately in astonishment at the exquisite texture of her skin. Persistent, defiant, intent upon a profanation of that other world, he threw his weight upon her, and felt her yield wildly and convulsively, in bursting tears that first startled and then sobered him.

Dismayed and cold, he heard her whispering his name, and felt the softness of her hands touching his face, but her passion lacked the strength, and ease of ingress, and the warmer harbouring of another well-remembered, and he was thinking of her husband, a shape, no more, and gold cherubim and thick carpets in big houses full of radio voices that talked all the time and never said anything, living that life he could never know.

And behind it all, only this, that was nothing.

Suddenly he was glad, and free of any regret, and the happier feeling created a new, impersonal tenderness for her, and he took her deeper with all his strength in fierce desire to console her for emptiness he no longer wished to share, perhaps in purge of memory; but even as force narrowed in royal flame, another memory wrenched him from her seeking mouth, twisting his head away from her, turning him ever into the darkness, calling, calling for Liz.

48

Redcaps marched out of the courtyard gate and another company was standing at ease opposite the stairway, listening to a sergeant reading from a sheet of paper. Behind the ranks, in the light of a bright arc, men were at work beneath the cream and gold carriage that waddled under their handling in deprecating squeaks on four new motor tyres. Four scarlet wooden wheels leaned, glistening, against the wall, and both axles were sending up a stink of burning paint and grease from a bonfire near the chapel. The doors and windows were open so that the crowd under the cloister might hear, allowing incense to wave blue rags among petrol fumes from the supply pit and the aroma of coffee from a buffet table in an ordered mass of twinkling glass and silver near Rosie.

A chant began that made people look uneasily about as if in doubt of their surroundings, dropping on a knee, reproachfully turning their heads, but only for a moment, towards the sergeant, still reading in a clear voice that ended on the same note, with a pause, and then a word of command that straightened the files with their white-gloved hands lost in the skirts of their overcoats.

The crowd in the cloister broke under pressure of people coming out of the chapel. Redcaps linked hands, making way for half a dozen girls carrying bouquets of carnations. A double file of redcaps marched down and halted, facing each other, and at a command raised their automatic rifles in a ceremonial arch for the girls to duck under. Free of the chapel, the crowd began shouting, tossing flower petals and white sugared almonds into the procession.

Dincott, in a frogged tunic and red trousers with a wide gold stripe, stood on the chapel steps for a moment looking at a veiled woman on his arm, and then at the crowd, laughing at their cheers, nodding to the redcaps grinning at him. Waving his hands, trying to catch an almond, grabbing at a flower, he went on, through the arch, and, once in the open, took his bride's hand and led her to the buffet. Glasses were handed out on trays that went into the mass of people and were flung away empty, clanging on the stone. Corks spat and bottles foamed, and among the shouting and laughter toasts overlapped, unheard, and glasses by the dozen were thrown up to spin silver, and burst on the cobbles, bringing groans from the barefoot and a general clearing of the crowd. The files of redcaps finished their glasses, handing them to white-coated waiters running along the ranks, and at a command turned and marched off, giving the bridal couple an Eyes Right as they passed.

A white touring car backed in through the gateway, clearing a path with a blaring siren until it reached the carriage, stopping below the coachman's seat. Mechanics fastened a couple of bars from the front axle of the coach to the car's luggage grid, and screwed down the clamps. At a signal, the driver started testing in a wide turn, gradually putting on speed, and the faster he went the louder the applause of the crowd massed, and craning over each other's shoulders, under the archway.

Dincott waved him to a halt, and went, glass in hand, to open the door.

"Just the job, Snow boy," he said. "Couldn't have done better myself. Have a drink."

Snowy looked at the glass, and hesitated too long.

"Ain't you going to drink my health, Snow?" Dincott still smiled. "Can't you let bygones be?"

Snowy took the glass.

"Thinking, that's all," he said. "I've got to drive, don't forget."

"Safety first, eh, Snow?" Dincott watched him drink, and put his hand out for the glass. "Won't do you no harm. Best champagne in Italy, that is. Specially pinched from the General Staff. Good health and good luck."

Snowy could see the Princess, sitting next to Max in Rosie's cabin.

"Wish I could say the same," he said.

"You will, Snow boy." Dincott straightened, holding out his arms. "I don't know what's matter with some of you. Everything in the world for nothing, and you don't want it. Why don't you be sensible?"

"What did you want to do that to my mates for?" Snowy asked him, direct. "I don't mind getting a towsing myself, but there was no need of knocking the Yank about. And you've got the finest mechanic in the Army here, and you bust his glasses. So now he can't see what he's doing of. That's clever, ain't it?"

"Either keep his mouth shut and his eyes open," Dincott said, "else he can keep his mouth open if he wants to, and I'll shut his eyes for him. I'll get him fixed up with glasses, don't you worry. When I think he's ready for 'em. But take a tip, Snow. Good job it didn't happen to her, ain't it?"

The lines of lamps under the cloisters were going out one after another. Down at the buffet table, women wrapped crocks and glasses and a couple of men were kicking empty bottles spinning into a refuse pit. Snowy watched them, trying to think what to do, but it seemed madness to say, much less do anything, because of what might happen to her, and to the others. But Dincott's voice, and his attitude, all he had done and all he was doing, gored and savaged his mind, making him feel as though he were inside a cage with the bars all round and digging into him.

Dincott gave the empty glass to a redcap, and pulled off the black tunic, showing a khaki shirt with the sleeves rolled. Snowy watched his eyes as though they were in the boxing ring.

" I know what you're thinking, Snow," he said. " A left lead, and a short right. But it won't do you no good. Listen. You're the only bloke I want out of this lot. They're all Jerries or Poles or How-de-do. But you'd make a marvellous boss behind here while I'm doing the job up front. We're the only two talk the same lingo, for a starter. If I could get you with me, we'd be a marvellous pair. Can't you see it? "

Snowy realized he was listening to a pleading, meant in cold blood.

" Listen, Snow." Dincott stopped buttoning the cuffs of his shirt and came closer, looking up at him. " I've built all this on me own. It's easy enough, once you've got a few of the blokes with you. You go on collecting 'em. If they get barbary you dish out the caper treatment, else you knock 'em off. Most of 'em like being told what to do, specially if they're paid enough. But you got to have brains back here, and blokes like you, mechanics and things. And that's what I ain't got."

" What about them blokes in that tunnel place, up there, then? " Snowy asked. " Nothing much wrong with them."

" And they got themselves pinched," Dincott said, in contempt. " That's what I say, see? No sentries, nobody on the look-out. So a few carabinieri creep up there, and they're all in the nick. My blokes was all out doing jobs, and very big jobs, too. Took a bit of time to round 'em up. That's where a bloke like you comes in. I wouldn't bother back here if you was with me. We could be big pals, Snow. I'd like a good pal. We could do what we liked. Go where we like. All the brides you'd ever want. All the booze. Jewellery. Money in the bank. Fix up your wife and kids. You could be home in ten days' time for a nice month. Don't you believe me, Snow? "

Hard against the grain, and terrifyingly, he did.

Despite every cry of instinct, he felt himself drawn by the appeal in the man's eyes, and the persuasive warmth of his voice. Again, plainly, he saw him as a wide-mouthed boy with a rippling of pennies in his hands, lording it over a group of urchins wide-mouthed as himself, buying where he could not entice, learning penny by penny the rudiments of power by blandishment, or purchase, or by force.

"After what you did to me just now?" he said, wishing his voice were more certain. "I reckon you've got a neck."

"Ah, but Snow," Dincott's face was remorsefully puckered in a smile of regret, "look at it from my side. You've got that snotty cow working on you, and a couple of pals downstairs. Well? When in Rome, do the Romans, and when in doubt, do 'em all. See? I had to. I didn't hit you hard, on purpose. But I had to give both of them a right doin' because they wouldn't listen. But when your pal Bill found out that when he give me a mouthful the Yank got a love-tap, and when the Yank warbled and see Bill getting paid for it, they both give over. That's the way we work, Snow. And nobody's the worse off. That's the beauty of it."

Gippi was standing behind a redcap under the archway, fussing with clothes on hangars, looking at the surface on a pair of shoes, waiting until another redcap brought up a chair. Dincott went over and sat down. Gippi knelt, pulling the patent boots and red trousers off, and the first redcap held out ironed drill trousers to be put on. The second redcap helped him into polished brown shoes with a shoe-horn, and laced them. Dincott waved the red trousers on the hangar.

"Wedding clobber," he said. "Give 'em a bit of colour. Put a uniform on, and they think you're Christ."

"I thought you were married," Snowy said.

"So I am." Dincott was helped into a battledress blouse. "Seven or eight times out here. It's a bit of all right, boy. Makes a nice break. Get sick of doing the same old thing all the time."

"That's bigamy," Snowy said. "Ain't allowed. The heads won't have it."

"There's a lot of things they won't have," Dincott said, "till I say so. What harm's it do. Makes everything respectable.

Everybody's happy. Don't cost a lot. She gets her lines. I get what I'm after. That's business."

He pulled on the beret. Snowy saw the neat outline of his skull in a freezing of the blood.

"Now then," Dincott said, slapping his palms together, rubbing hard, "where are we? Snow, you drive your wagon in front of me. They're all formed up out there, so you'll just slip into place. Then me. Gippi'll drive the car. We're going very slow till we get down to the village. That's where the wife comes from. I promised her the ride. Show herself off to all her pals. Sweeten her up, see?"

Snowy nodded, and turned, suddenly cheerful, towards Rosie.

"Tell the Yank to get out of it," Dincott said. "He can sit in the back of the car."

Snowy paused, almost feeling hope draining out of his finger ends.

"Ain't you done enough to him?" he said. "He's all right up there."

Dincott was shaking his head, laughing.

"Be more comfortable in the car," he said. "For me, that is. Your other pal's coming, too. Looking bright, ain't he?"

An aftermath of the plexus punch caused Snowy pain and hard breath for months on end. Two redcaps had come out of a room behind Dincott with Bill between them. His eyes were almost closed in purple sacs, his nose looked broken, and his lips were cut.

Two more redcaps brought Max across from Rosie. One eye was swollen and the eyebrow was gashed. The nose still bled and his teeth had gone through his bottom lip.

"You can't say I treated you bad, Snow," Dincott said. "In a week's time they'll be chirping like a couple of birds. Not a mark on 'em."

"I'll have you," Bill said. "You mongrel's bastard."

The redcaps grabbed them both, twisting their arms, entwining their legs in a practised drill.

Dincott strolled to Max, and deftly, effortlessly, punched him square in the nose. The crack of fist on flesh seemed to bounce along the floor in Snowy's mind. Dincott had turned and was looking at him with his mouth half open, and his eyes rounded in unspoken question.

"And if you're feeling like saying anything, Snow," he said, at last, "they'll get one apiece. That's how we do things. All you got to remember is, I'm the boss."

Max had fallen on all fours, and the slow blood dripped red cogs on the stones.

"But good Christ Almighty," Snowy shouted. "How can you treat blokes like that? You'll get nothing out of 'em."

"You'd be surprised, Snow boy." Dincott signed to Gippi, and he trotted over to the boot of the carriage. "They'll be's gentle as lambs, and they'll work like cart horses. And in a couple of weeks' time, when they get in with the other lads, and they know me better, they'll be's happy as larks. I know what I'm doing, Snow. All for their benefits. Mine, too."

Gippi came back with the caped coat over one arm, holding the tricorne.

"Put 'em on, Bill boy," Dincott said.

Bill looked about as though half asleep, tiredly unsure in his own mind what was required of him. Gippi opened the coat, nodding invitingly.

"Come," he said, in his deep voice, mild, almost kindness itself. "Put the arms. So. This the hat. Ma guarda, che bello."

The caped coat was much too big, and the hat perched.

Snowy looked, and turned his back.

"Wipe his dial for him," Dincott said, pointing to Max. "Get him in the car. Up you get, Bill. You're the Lord Mayor's coachie today. Off you go, Snow."

He saw Bill turn towards the coach, and put one dusty boot on the step in a trailing of braided cloth, holding on for a moment and grunting as he pulled himself to climb.

"Up, the old red roses!" he shouted. "Up the First!"

Blindly he went across to Rosie and felt his way to the door.

She was crouching in the corner, with her face away from him.

Rosie's turnover came as a song in a beloved voice, reminding him of other times, and some notion entered his mind that she was trying to soothe him. But anger stuck, tormenting, breathless.

A redcap waved him on. As he reversed, he saw the girl in white come out with her arms full of flowers and get in the coach. Dincott followed her, and talked to Gippi through the window.

Bill was sitting on the box in a huddle of gold-braided blue cloth, with the three-cornered affair pushed on the back of his head, and not a move.

Max, bareheaded, was helped into the back of the car, and a redcap slammed the door.

Outside the gate he was signalled into position behind a truck full of redcaps in a convoy stretching all the way downhill and round a bend. In the driving mirror he saw the white car pulling the cream and gold coach turn out of the gate and creep up behind, and another truck-load of redcaps in a bristle of automatic rifles wheeled into place in rear.

A whistle sounded.

Arms appeared out of side windows all the way down, waving the rearward drivers on, and the convoy started at a crawl, supervised by redcaps on motor-cycles.

On the left of the road, mist was still purplish-grey out to sea, but the wind had shifted ash from roofs and out of the cypress trees and off the cabbages, making red patches and dark blue flares and long rows of pale-green spots on a yellowy-grey plain, and beyond all, the town went up the mountain in a clumsy stairway of white and pink and pale-blue blocks, with a glim of sunlight in the golden dome of a church at the top. All across the plain were little puffs of dust where women worked stiff-legged in the fields, and on the right the mountain curved in a long sweep of bare land up into a deep brown fog bloomed by morning light, walled flat by the wind, rolling in its play subtle as grass.

She moved, and, without looking, he knew she was wiping her eyes.

" Cheer up, gel," he said. " We'll get out of this."

" I'd have shot him," she said. " But I was so afraid they'd shoot you."

" That's where they've got you, Miss," he said. " Best to keep everything to yourself, and wait. Can't make out where Rusty's got to, though."

He found comfort in the pressure of her fingers, only sign of her feeling since that tiptoe touch of a kiss on his cheek just before they went out of the room.

He wondered at himself. The sense of guilt, so strong not long ago, was gone. In its place an irreproachable fondness for her, for the way she looked, and how she put her hands, and the smell of her, and the glitter of her tears, almost the same as the feeling he got when he carried the children sleeping with their heads heavy against his neck, and their arms hanging loose.

Memory of her whispers, of the plunge and bridle of her thighs, and the triumph in her voice when she cried out and her hands fell from his shoulders, all remembered, moment by moment, plainly as he saw the road, and yet not as though it had happened to himself, or between them, but as if it all belonged to someone else. He could not convince himself that he had been close to her, and neither did he want to, for then the thought of Liz was bearable. It was strange, this feeling of knowing deeply and in detail, and yet of being able to deny it life, treating it as though he had been standing aside not even watching, but just knowing, and heedless.

But the great relief was riddance of the desire to be with her, to share life he had thought was richer in experience and surrounding than his own. The wish to possess and use, and live among the things she was used to, or even to be with her at all, was gone, leaving space where shame seemed to pour small drops.

All along the desert road and across the sea, and all the way up here, had been one long dream of Liz, and now she seemed more desirable than ever, and the children more to be loved, the house more livable, and even the ash tree next door, that darkened the kitchen and caused trouble between Liz and the neighbour, seemed like an old friend.

He had an itch to go back to being himself, alone with Liz, and the kids, and dreams of both, and the life they would have when he got home.

" I hope the wind brings that stuff down again," he said. " You'll have a chance of slipping off. Once you're away, you'll be all right."

She was looking at him, and he felt the smile.

" Brush-off," she said.

" No, no, Miss." He tried to protest, but he knew what she meant. " We'll never get anywhere while you're here for him to mess about with. You know that. You can see where we are. All you got to do is get down to that place where we met the coppers and get them and the troops to follow us up. I couldn't leave Bill and Max. You and Rusty're the only chance we've got."

" I've put the revolver in the door-pouch," she said. " That's one good friend you have. The other one's me."

He felt her nails biting deep in his arm, so deep that he almost threw her off, but he let them stay, going deeper, more hurtfully, and then deadening.

" Rusty's people," she whispered, and took the nails away.

Lines of peasants were walking along both sides of the road in the same direction as the convoy.

" How do you know? " He tried to look at them, but they were too far below eyeline, and covered by their bundles.

" Look what they're wearing," she said. " Black and red. They're not from around here. Where's Rusty? "

A motor-cyclist redcap was pushing them roughly in to the side of the road, expecting no remonstrance and getting none.

" How in God's name can they take it? " She stamped in anger. " Where else in the world do people get treated so? Why don't they throw rocks? "

" And get a bullet for it? " Snowy put his arm around her. " They like living best, Miss. You keep your mitts out of this. I don't want you messed about."

He felt her hand travelling flat across his back.

" Oh, Snowy," she said. " I wish. I wish."

The truck in front stopped. A redcap came alongside, waving her farther into the road's edge, and presently the white car went by, with a glimpse of Max lying back in rear, and a view of Bill's tricorne above the golden scrolls of the coach.

A brass band started to play, and people were shouting.

The convoy moved again, and they found themselves heading slowly across the main street of a village, on a road going up the mountainside, but the coach had turned left into the square guarded by both truckloads of redcaps, crowded among cheering people waving little flags.

"How d'you start understanding them?" she said. "They know what he is. And look."

"It's the girl, I expect, Miss." Snowy halted at the redcap's sign, closing in to the rear of the lorry in front. "She lives here. 'Sides, if he's been kind to 'em, they'll cheer to save 'emselves trouble."

"Kind," she mewed. "And they know too well she's not his wife."

"They had a church service, Miss," he said. "That's as much as I had."

"You were married in church?" she asked. "Anglican?"

"Don't know, Miss," he said. "Liz did all that part. She's the church lot in our family. She's off there every Sunday. Now and again she used to rake me out of it at seven of a Sunday morning. Sunday, mark you." Snowy emphasized it with a tightened arm, happily surprised by the answering pressure. "I like a night out now and again. So she says, all right, provided I get one Sunday morning here and there. If you've got to be a savage, I'll see you're a good 'un. The kids are old enough to go with her now."

"And they all say prayers for you," she said.

"I hope so, Miss," he said. "I don't know it does much good, mind. But it makes nice thinking."

A redcap looked up, waving his arms and pulling faces to make him reverse.

"Something going on," he said.

"Run them down." She moved away from him. "Don't bother about me. I'll take a chance."

"What about Bill, and poor old Max?" He was turning into the backs of the crowd. "And look at these here. Thick as you like. I'll pick my time, Miss, don't you worry."

Dincott was talking to Gippi and a civilian among a group of redcaps near the coach. The crowd, mostly of women, still thronged, chattering and laughing among themselves with their faces towards the girl in white.

Snowy got down in answer to Dincott's wave, and the group strolled to meet him.

" They've had a bit of hard luck with these shocks, Snow," Dincott said. " These lids all got stuck. Could you do anything with the wagon? "

Gippi pointed to the level part of the square. A few workmen were hammering crowbars into the surround of an iron shield lying flush with the paving. A series of neatly spaced rows of them made that part look like a chessboard.

" They got wheat in the store," Gippi said. " The iron get fix. Want explosive for move it."

" Explosive, me foot. Try and pull it off, or something, Snow," Dincott said. " Try not to bust it, else we'll be unpopular. One less to put the harvest in for next year, see? "

Snowy went to look at the granaries, and found the men trying to cut through rock to come at the heavy iron lid. Earth tremors appeared to have jammed the stone against the lid-frame.

" Tell 'em to stop messing about with them hammers and chisels," he said. " Get some firewood and pile it on top, and make a fire. Not too big. Just enough to heat the metal. Then splash a lot of cold water on it. Then I'll pull it on tow, and we'll see."

" There you are," Dincott said, and clapped him on the back. " Brains, that's all they want. I told you, Snow. You're the bloke for this job."

Snowy pretended confusion to cover an enormous lifting of the heart.

At least three of the men in the crowd were Rusty's people, grinning at him openly.

" Get it off first," he said. " Then we'll start cheering."

Going back to Rosie, he saw the black skirts and scarlet petticoats in among the crowd of women about the coach, but he feared that elation at boiling point inside him would show in his face, and so looked down, watching the colours from the corners of his eyes, passing Bill and Max without a glance.

" Rusty's lot are all here, Miss," he said, when he got in the cabin. " Men and women."

" Be careful what you say," she said. " Hardly open your mouth. He's watching you."

He took Rosie nearer to the granaries, and dropped the crane tackle. Men and women were carrying headloads of firewood, dumping them under the eye and cough of Gippi. Still the women chattered and laughed around the coach.

Men came out of the wine shop with bottles and glasses, handing them up to the redcaps in the remaining truck. A girl reached a bottle up to Bill, but he refused. Max got out of the car to take a glass, and immediately was surrounded by women all making consolatory sounds that ohhd and eehhd across the piazza.

Snowy watched the men piling green sticks and bundles on the iron lid, laying other bundles cross-wise on top.

A discussion started with Gippi, and the men crowded round, using voices, hands and eyes, everyone trying to outshout everyone else. Gippi broke through them all with his fingers in his ears.

" What's up, there? " Dincott called, and came across. " Want smartening up, do they? "

" Essence," Gippi said. " Petrolio. They want some petrolio for the wood. It don't burn."

" Get 'em some." Dincott turned away as though disappointed. " 'Course it won't burn. And get a move on."

Redcaps brought up cans of petrol on the run and sprinkled the bundles, laying a trail of splashes to a small pile of twigs. Gippi put a match to it, jumping back from the orange burst, and the crowd shouted, watching the trail flame, and flung up their arms when the fire blazed, joining hands and starting to dance in a ring that got bigger as women and children ran from side streets in flurries of skirts and thin brown legs, shouting as they came.

Presently the square was cut in two by a slow circling of people dancing in unison, chanting a song that in its minor tones and odd rhythms spoke chillingly of other times among these orange walls and red roofs and grey stones.

Men and women came from cracks between houses carrying logs and bundles of twigs, throwing them down and going back for more. The crowd about the coach had dwindled, but a few older women stood at the door talking to the girl in white. The redcap truck came back loaded with tins of water.

At Snowy's nod, Gippi sent the men in to rake the embers away from the lid, and others carefully poured water, making a great cloud of steam that drew screams from the dancers and halted the circle.

Snowy made the tackle fast to the ring in the lid, sweating in the sudden heat, feeling the iron burning through his boots, and went back to Rosie in silence broken by the crash of brushwood dropped near the coach, self-conscious under the weight he imagined he felt of hundreds of eyes, seeing in him a workman of miracles.

Rosie started in a whisper, taking the strain in a purring disregard of all resistance, gradually raising her voice to fortify the argument of her tautening cable. In the murmur of the crowd, backing away, fearing the steel would snap, he heard excited prelude to a sudden raving of men and women, hugging and kissing one another, and Rosie's voice told everyone how easy it was to pull a lid out of the ground and make it roll like a hoop.

Redcaps were lifting boxes out of the opened bricklined chamber, piling them up on one side.

"I thought you said it was wheat?" Snowy said to Gippi.

"The others, yes." Gippi waved at the other lids. "This one, no. He got plenty stuff, there. Molto roba. Everything, it hides, everything safe. If he lose something, he burn plenty house. So is everything safe."

"I can well see that," Snowy said. "He's a proper case, ain't he?"

"The biggest, greatest," Gippi said. "I don't speak this English so much, but for the Dincott, il magnifico, plenty words I got."

"Same here," said Snowy.

"Good." Gippi linked arms. "Everybody they love the Dincott. He is so strong. I am glad you work for us. We make plenty things and lot of money."

Shots rapped out, making the village sound empty.

Everyone seemed touched by a moment of sleep, looking at each other in a small dream of fear, and then they awoke in a rush to be away from the open space and into the alleys, with no sound except the slap and thud of bare feet. A truckload of redcaps turned out at Dincott's signal and went up, full speed, towards the convoy. Drivers were jumping down and running away from the stationary trucks, shouting, holding up their arms. Single shots were ragged among an imperious rip of automatic fire, and bullets were ricochetting off the paving and digging chunks out of the walls.

Snowy ran, passing Dincott and the redcaps, towards Rosie. " Getting her under shelter," he shouted, and saw Dincott raise his finger.

He let her freewheel down the slope and turned into a yard, with the solid stone of a house to protect her.

" Just going to get Bill and Max," he said. " Don't move from here."

The second redcap truck swung round and went up the mountainside. Max and Bill were sitting on the step of the white tourer smoking a cigarette between them.

The girl in white called out of the coach window in a high, broken tremolo. Dincott waved at her and spoke to Gippi. Snowy chose his time and ran across the square.

" Careful what you're doing, Snow," Dincott shouted.

" I want to talk to my mates, that's all." Snowy pointed to the coach. " Why don't you shift this? "

" That can stay where it is," Dincott said. " It's finished with. Your mates'll go in the truck with the boys. Me and her'll come with you on the wagon."

" How you feeling, chummie? " Snowy gripped Max by the shoulder.

" O.K.," Max said. " Great life."

" We're waiting for t' second house to go in," Bill said, trying to look at him, but his eyes were almost shut. Tricorne and cape had been thrown off. " Any idea what time it starts? "

" I was just saying," Max said. " If I don't have the clocks figured wrong it's around theatre time back home. We were half-way along Broadway. Who do you think's battling up there? Carabinieri? "

" I was hoping it's our troops," Snowy said. " But I don't think so. We'd have seen something of 'em long before this."

" I certainly hope it's any kind of combat troops," Max said. " That'll be candy for us."

" Till we're stood in front of a court-martial," Bill said.

" You know," Max passed the butt to Snowy, " I just don't care what happens to me any more, so long as something can happen to this Dincott. I don't see what can, the way he has the cards stacked, but I'm just hoping."

Firing, that had stopped, broke out again in a different part of the mountain. They saw the redcaps change direction, going farther left, beyond sight. The second truckload had debouched from a grove of trees, shaking dust off themselves, appearing to wander, rather than advance, towards the top of the rise above the convoy.

Dincott stood up, pointing, giving orders. One redcap went running to mount the motor-cycle, and a second got on the pillion behind him. They went off in a straddle of legs and a thin blue fog.

Gippi was talking to the girl in white, with one foot on the step, patting her knee. Dincott went to them, climbing past Gippi, sitting beside the girl with his arm around her waist.

"O.K., Snow," he called. "I don't know what that was, but it wasn't much. I've called 'em all back. Fetch the wagon over, and we'll go up there. I'm wasting a lot of time."

Snowy and Max looked at each other straight, deep in the eye, in one eye, and then the other, and in between, seeing nothing, reading each other's hatred, sharing sympathy that suddenly and without words touched deep.

Each put out a hand, and each took heart from the grip.

"I'll take care of this boy." Max nodded at Bill. "He's cooked without his glasses."

"I'll see the pair of you right," Snowy said. "So long, mates."

The girl in white was leaning against Dincott, looking up at him, watching the motions of his mouth as he spoke to Gippi. He felt a sudden disgust at all thought of passion, and profoundest contempt for the swooning darkness of her eyes. He went across the square cursing houses, silence, light, sky, himself, everyone, but acknowledged himself at loss for a good reason, except that Dincott could command such worship from the girl in white, and he none, not even a glance. Even though the Princess was dear to him, and knowing they had been so close, seemed not to matter any more. There was something empty in it, he found, whereas the feeling between the girl and Dincott was full. He was reminded then that Liz had often looked just like that, but at those times he seemed to have taken it as a matter of course.

He got up in the cabin. She sat, looking at him, smiling, head on one side, trying to gauge his mood.

" Dincott's coming with us," he said. " So's the bride."

" Any room on the other side of you? " She appeared unmoved. " There's a gun there, in case you forgot."

He thought he heard accusation in her voice.

" I ain't forgot nothing, Miss," he said. " Except there's Max and Bill to think about. There's you. And there's Rosie. I've got to get the lot of you away."

She put her hand on his knee.

" Don't be angry with me, Snowy," she said. " Please."

Quick, and hurt, he looked at her, seeing at once her tiredness, her willingness always to carry the fight, and, more than all, her silence in trouble and lack of any complaint. He felt ashamed of himself to think he could bring that note into her voice, and the lash got to work, for underneath he felt a deeper shame for having taken advantage of his strength, and it was salt on the raw that she had said nothing, but with tender hand flat on his cheek, and smiling eyes, had kissed him that cool kiss after he helped her fold the silken sheets.

" I feel like a dog," he said.

She went close to him, with her arm about his shoulder.

" Think that's a good idea? " She jollied him with little shakes into a grin. " Does that face hurt you? It's real pretty."

He shook his head.

" No, Miss." He put his arm around her, and felt her draw warmly into his side. " It's about last night. I shouldn't have even tried."

" Don't let's go into it," she said. " Don't let's even think of it. Just let's think how good it is to sit here like this. I wish it could go on. That's the best part of a wish, just thinking about it."

He looked out, through the gateway, across the empty square, seeing the round, black mouth of the granary bawling at the greyish clouds, the piles of firewood round about, and the orange shutters on the house opposite, and women and children poking their heads out of the alleyway, and carefully, step by step, going into the square, bent at the waist, necks stretched, looking about and ready to run, gradually straightening and then walking off, calling to others and laughing, perhaps, at their fear.

" Fine way to live," she said. " When you're frightened at every shadow and every sound. Darling, I have something to say to you. Just keep on looking out there while I say it. Then don't think about it again. Ever."

So warm beneath his hand, so small in the crook of his arm, and womanly in the couchant beauty of her thigh, there came again the desire to protect her, and with it, in rising misgiving, a further want of her, taking strength from memory and the thrust of livening blood.

" I wish I could always be with you," she said. " I know how Liz must feel. That's the reason why I don't regret anything. She wouldn't want to be angry with me. I'm certain of that. She'd have no reason to. But it's crazy. The things I love in you I've wanted from a man as long as I remember. I never found him, so I never got them. Somebody to lean on, sometimes. Just like this. And know he's around the place. Last night happened because I wanted it to. I'd be willing to live any kind of a life to go on like that. But we can't. And it's stupid to think it, anyway. I'm going to pray to God I get a child. I don't dare hope for a son. I want you to know that was the only reason why I came back. I had to."

A shouting of many voices was faint through the open window, sustained, higher than cheering, without joy, and too harsh for gaiety.

" Stay here," he said. " Don't forget you've got this."

He took the revolver from the door-pouch, but she moved away.

" No." She shook her head, looking at the wall. " I wouldn't want to touch it. You take it."

He stuck it back in the pouch and closed the door, doubling to the gateway.

The square was crowded with quiet people facing towards the coach.

Children ran about on the outskirts, trying to push through and getting chased away.

A single voice was shouting, and then the arms went up, and again the strange outburst of sound, as though all mouths had opened to scream as long as breath would last.

Over the heads he could see the gold leaves on top of the coach, and someone standing on the bars that fastened it to the car. A man climbed up on the coachman's seat wearing the tricorne, greeting the yells with a kiss of his hands, and in relief Snowy saw that he was not Bill, wondering, idly, what he was doing.

There was no sign of movement up on the mountainside, and the convoy was still there, stark, matt khaki vehicles against the pinky-grey ash.

In unbelief he saw the man in the tricorne pull a petrol-can up on the seat, and tip it, splashing the glistening rags over the coach top, letting it dribble into the well of the coronet. Bundles of sticks were being piled all round the coach until they hid the windows.

Almost in silence the crowd drew back and those in rear broke free, running for the sides of the square and the high doorsteps. Windows were opening in a squeak and crash of shutters, and people were leaning out.

Grey smoke puffed on the other side of the coach.

Snowy ran headlong, with no breath in him, only a soreness in his chest, and people looked round at the hard clouting of his boots, scattering out of his way. A couple of men were splashing petrol on the twigs and logs walling the coach, and the far side already crackled behind a spuming curtain.

He went for the tourer, pulling open the door, letting the brake off, and, in the hugest grin of relief, felt her glide. She started up, and he got her in gear, watching the coach in the driving mirror bumping over the cobbles. He took the car in a wide turn, stopping among the iron discs of the granaries, and, with the engine running, got out.

The door and windows of the coach had been roughly boarded over.

Someone was beating on the glass.

He ran back to the tourer and felt for the crank handle under the seat, shouting when it came cold to his grip. Going back to the coach he knew that people were running and screaming, but he stuck the end between the cream panels and the boards, levering with his boot on a golden scroll, wrenching, hearing the wood split, and the nails screech, ducking as the boards fell.

The door burst open, and the girl in white was heavy in his arms, limp.

Dincott jumped out, grabbing him.

"Snow," he said, without voice, "I knew you was a pal. I knew it. I'll do anything for you. I'd give me blood for you. I'll show you."

He looked about at the running, gathering crowd.

"As for this lot," he said, "I'll burn the place to the ground, and them in it. They want a lesson. Where's my boys?"

But the villagers came to them, silent, with clawing hands, too many to fight off, too strong for denial. Snowy was dragged backwards, trying to keep his feet, and then he was free and Rusty came shouting among a group of armed men, with Bill and Max close behind.

Dincott fought legs and arms free, but he was lifted high overhead by a dozen hands, and in a red grimace he dropped from sight. Gippi was lifted, screaming unheard, and fell. The girl in white was naked except for torn stockings and a few white rags hanging about her neck.

Women bunched their skirts between their legs, craning forward, screaming high-pitched from swollen faces to see the dark scissure of her thighs pulled apart and mocked, and the incredibly white grace of her body and the tanned limbs jolted and dangled, made clumsy by the boorish clutching of any hand that could reach her, and then in a spread leg arc, she was thrown, and the sky was empty and so were the hands.

Rusty dragged them back among a group of quieter men.

"Nothing to do," he warned, with a finger over his mouth. "Nothing. Lascia. Leave alone. We wait for the police."

"But what's going to happen to 'em?" Snowy was watching the backs of the screaming crowd. "You can't have that girl smashed up! She's only sixteen."

"Leave." Rusty shut his eyes in all finality. "Leave alone. Nothing to do."

Snowy saw the Princess run out of the gateway and into the crowd. He ran towards her, breaking through a group of men edging away from the revolver.

"Stop them," she was saying. "I have to stop them."

The crowd was milling about the space where the three had fallen, and now he followed her terrible stare.

Men were pouring petrol into the grain pit. Shrieks, magnified by the length of the chamber, could be heard above the clamour; but even as he moved, the men crouched, and one struck a match on his nail, crawling on his belly to the verge, and with a deliberate gesture of the thumb flicked the stalk into the hole.

A flame blew in a sheet and went out, with thick smoke.

Light flitted on the chamber walls.

Screams lifted, and then were drowned in the screams of the crowd, and they drew near, trying to look in.

Snowy went to take her by the arms, but she shook herself free, staring, not at the pit, but down at the revolver. Again he tried to put his arm about her, and she turned from him, looking up and around at the mountainside desperately, tragically, making him want to pick her up and carry her away.

She raised and turned the heavy revolver, still looking at the mountainside, and with both hands pulled and pulled the trigger into the thick of the crowd. He leapt at her, burning his hand on the barrel, afraid of breaking her fingers, and she struggled, cursing.

But then he had her.

Rusty and a few more ran in front, threatening the crowd with their rifles. A couple of men were kicking near the smoking pit, and a woman was on her knees beside one, with praying hands stretched to the sky.

"Quick!" he shouted, lifting her. "Get over to Rosie. Let's get out of it. Where's the other two?"

Rusty stared, and the crowd became still.

Max lay with his head on Bill's knee, and blood came thick from the pocket of his shirt.

49

Shiner was with him all the while, all the way up the mountain, curving to the top until they met the troops, just like the other time, and all the way down into the grey plain, foggy in travel, like November at home. But this time it was Max's head in his lap, not Shiner's, and Max at full length on the seat, not Shiner, and Max's blood sticking between his fingers, and Max's groans driving him mad, not Shiner's.

Rosie seemed to know. Fine feeling lay between them, hand and foot of him, wheel and button of her, smooth interaction that chose the flattest part of the road, gently disengaging from bumps, on his part almost without thought, apparently without effort on hers, both intent to keep the wound from spilling.

Long before the road joined the main route he saw at right-angles the heavier breath of traffic between the Line and the Base Dumps rising, darker, mixed with the road's dust in a broad flume curling off into mist.

Max awoke, and turned, trying to get up.

Snowy dropped a hand on his shoulder.

" Steady, the Buffs," he said. " Don't rock the boat, mate. You'll be all right as long as you stay there quiet."

" Hey." Max seemed comically surprised, and, for all his pallor, unusually vigorous. " What happened? "

" I'm taking you to one of your hospitals," Snowy said. " Don't talk too much. You got shot."

" That's what I figured." Max closed his eyes. " Well, maybe I'm cockeyed, but I'm glad, Snow. Who was it? "

He saw her face again, and felt the hot barrel, but his mind lurched away from it.

" One of 'em down there," he said. " Still, we've got to get you put to rights first. How d'you feel? "

" Fine," Max said. " Kind of sleepy, but fine. Where's the rest of us? "

" In the back." Snowy patted his shoulder. " Get off to sleep, else I'll wallop you."

" You want to lose your marbles? " Max made an effort, relapsing. " I'd lift you one off the floor. Get to lift myself first."

He appeared to sleep, quietly, gradually in depth, and his face was free of lines, making him look younger by years.

In a cold draught of fear straightening his neck, he realised that Shiner had looked just the same, younger, quieter, and yet with as much humour on waking, as much vigour in voice. His eyes seemed to turn away by themselves from thought of that last clicking of teeth and jerk of the legs.

He tried to form a prayer for Max inside himself, but the words made nothing, and were going nowhere, without shape or direction, attacked all the time by disbelief somewhere at the back there, of no shape or size, but still, as though he could see it, shaking its head. He tried to think what Liz said when she was teaching the children after their bath, or what they said in church, but the voices were just the same as those on the radio, only in sing-song and whispers, saying a lot and nothing, talking in a way that made people screw their eyes up, and just sit there, thinking of something else and hoping it would stop, or dive for the knob and turn it off.

A section of infantry marched towards him, rifles slung, flat-footed, bent at the knee, old timers, looking into the pack of the man in front, busy inside themselves, no expression on any face, careless of where they were or what they were doing, carrying their strangeness into strange country with an air about them that said it was only for a while, until somebody unnameable said it was all over.

Snowy grinned, despite himself, and changed down to approach the corporal, bent under a cradle of mortar bombs, leaning out of the window to catch his eye, waving the convoy to a halt.

" Browned off, Corp? " he called, hoping sympathy might establish goodwill. " Having a nice holiday, are you? It's all free, y'know. Get paid for it."

" Holiday? " The corporal looked up through sweat dripping down from his eyebrows. " Some bastard'll pay me for it, I can tell you. You're all right in there, though. Got something to laugh about, you have. You can talk."

" Ah," Snowy said, instantly sensitive. " We've had a bit of a do up there, an' all."

The corporal's eyes fixed.

"What's going on?" he asked eagerly. "They found 'em, have they?"

"'Course," Snowy said. "The Yanks came in one side, our lot the other, and the coppers in between. Done 'em a treat. Any M.O.s anywhere about handy? Got a casualty here."

"Just down the road." The corporal pointed farther down. "First house. You'll see the sign. Much more to do up there, is there?"

"Depends where you're going." Snowy could feel the eyes of the section questioning him. "Our blokes're well in where we've just come from. Got a lot of prisoners. All over time you get up there, I expect. So long."

He saw an officer running towards him, and gave the starting signal, unanxious for questions, if only because of Rusty and his people on the trucks in rear. The officer raised his hand, shouting, but he pretended to be busy with the gears, and passed by the remainder of the company, watching the officer in the driving mirror looking up at the convoy, truck by truck, frowning.

The house was just below the embankment, with the red cross of a Regimental Aid Post sign stuck in the ground beyond the front door. A sergeant came out, eating a sandwich in a whole-hearted manner that made Snowy's mouth swim with hunger.

He carefully propped Max's head and slid out of the seat, putting the head down, thankful to see the quiet movement of the nostrils.

"Shot wound here, Sarge," he said. "Yankee. They asked me to bring him down. His own ambulance wasn't there, see?"

"I'll get the M.O.," the sergeant said, still munching, and without any surprise.

Bill and the Princess came hesitantly round the side.

"How is he?" Bill looked in for a moment, and turned to him. "Ye'd best talk to her. I've done all I can. She's chunnering about giving herself up."

Snowy stood in front of her, but she refused to look up at him.

"Now look, Miss," he said. "If you do anything like that, we're all in it, specially Max. Keep it quiet; let's get him to one of his own hospitals, and he might get away with everything. They can't prove he wasn't done in the Line. That is, once we tell 'em a tale."

"I was crazy," she said. "I ought to be punished. Those other men."

"You've had all your punishment." Snowy saw the medical officer coming out of the doorway with the sergeant. "Go back, and keep quiet."

The officer went round to the driving seat, nodding at Snowy's salute, and climbed in. Bill and the Princess went down to Rusty's truck. Snowy waited, listening to the officer talking. The sergeant ran into the house.

"How did this happen?" The doctor put his head out of the door. "When, and where? Why wasn't he treated by his own M.O.?"

"They're all mixed up up there, sir," Snowy said. "Proper Fred Karno's, it is. Us and the Yanks, and Eyetie coppers. Nobody knows who's who."

"Many casualties?" The doctor took it without argument.

"I don't know, sir," Snowy said. "We was in convoy, that's all I know. Is he bad, sir?"

"Not all that bad." The sergeant hurried out with an orderly, both carrying trays full of steamy silver dishes, and rolls of cotton wool. "I'll pack him up and make him comfortable. Where were you told to take him?"

"A Yankee hospital along here somewhere, sir," Snowy said, at magnificent random.

"That's right." The doctor filled a dish. "About thirty miles. He'll last that comfortably. Can't understand them sending him down like this, though. There're two other R.A.P.s up there."

"Ah," Snowy said. "But we wasn't all in the same part, sir. Half a dozen roads and villages up there. Some of our blokes're right on the other side, miles and miles."

"I think I'd better send him down in my ambulance," the doctor said, throwing out a wad of red wool. "I ought to put a stitch in that eye, too."

Snowy could see forms filled in and names and times and places, and Max bound hand and foot behind them.

"It'll save me a job, sir," he said. "I got this convoy to take through. But I was hoping I might be in line for a tin of pineapple juice and a few smokes down this hospital. The Yanks've got it all, you know, sir."

" Unfortunately," the doctor said, and climbed down. " Make out a docket, Sergeant." He sluiced his hands in a bowl. " All right. He'll do until you get there. It's along here on the left of the road. Where're you going? "

" Not allowed to say, sir," Snowy said, promptly and fat with moral right. " Sorry."

" Well, Christ," the doctor grinned. " All right, get your docket and push off."

" Thank you, sir," Snowy said, and put into his salute all the relief that was making him hot and ready to dance. The orderly ran out with a couple of grey blankets.

" Might's well make a job of it," he said. " Get him the other way round, he'll be that much better off. Take his feet, will you? You can keep the blankets. They ain't on charge."

The sergeant came back with a label, and waved Snowy away.

" Upupup." The admonition was fatherly. " Don't want a lot of split-arsed mechanics messing about with the patients. Get on with your own job."

Snowy ran down, hearing the sergeant and the orderly arguing, and climbed up on the step of Rusty's truck.

The Princess and Bill sat beside him.

" He's all right, Miss," he said, heating in the appeal of her eyes. " Honest. The M.O. said he's champion. He's letting me take him down. That'll show you."

" You have to let me come with you," she said. " That has to be."

" Get in the back, Miss," he said. " That's all you got to do. Rusty, you turn right at the end, here."

Rusty nodded, a profound movement of the head, an acceptance directed at all and at none, signifying that he knew, as they did, that down there by the big sycamore on the corner he would leave them.

He looked as though he was using the flesh of his face for a wall, twisting and cramping all its muscles in unexpected forms to give an impression of no matter, but his eyes looked over the top, without guard and beyond discipline, roving along the breadth of the windscreen, fearful of rest, blinking and blinking to hide themselves in looks at the roof and out at the grey fields, or anywhere except at Snowy.

But from the muscular bulk, from the black beard, from the ashy head, from the stained twill, there came a subtle and affecting knowledge of sorrow.

Snowy knew.

He winked at Bill, and jumped down.

" All aboard," he shouted, more to clear his throat than to warn.

He heard the chorus of voices answering him along the length of the convoy, and went back to Rosie, hearing the sergeant and the orderly still arguing, with something in their words and the tone of their voices to suggest that it was part of an older argument that had always been.

" If we'd had half of that stuff the war'd been over a couple o' years back," the orderly said, dull, rueful, pulling down the harsh woollen sack hanging below his waist belt. " Look at his jersey, and look at mine. Same with everything else. We can't touch 'em."

" Got nothink to do with it, I tell you," the sergeant said, letting the words go as though each was a separate uprooting. " Nothink at all. And what's a jersey got to do with it? I've never heard a bloke talk so much cock in all me life. Hopeless bloody mess, that's what you are."

" See?" The orderly nodded at Snowy as if part of eternal truth, at last, were manifest. " Comes of listening to his self. And three stripes up, to give him the rights o' making other people's lives the same stinkin' misery his is. Don't know too much about it, that's his trouble. Givin' everybody the twits."

" Go on in," the sergeant said, wearily riding the mumble. " Go on in. Get your sterilizin' done, do. Drop yourself in, while you're at it. A good stew-up'd be the makings of you. Bloody mess."

" Every word of what you're saying's bein' took notice of." The orderly's voice was strained in lifting the trays. " Not the way you think. The day'll come, though, just the same." He paused in turning, slipping his eyes at the sergeant, and back to Snowy. " He's the bloke thinks Gillingham's in Surrey. That ought to tell you something. Surrey, mind."

" So it is," said the sergeant, as if it had all been said before, a little subdued, but dogged. " Been there many a time."

" In the car." The orderly winked one side of his face completely shut, with the free eyeball up, searching the clouds.

" Yes, in the car," the sergeant said. " We wasn't all a lot o' paupers, like some o' you. Had many a picnic out there."

" Now, there's something I don't doubt," the orderly said, in blandest satisfaction. " Wherever you was, there'd bound to be some kind of a picnic, I'll lay my dyin' oath."

Snowy carefully closed the door and started up. Max was pale, and the gash in his eyebrow was raw clean, and he seemed to be in a heavy sleep, with no movement of any kind.

" I suppose he's all right, Sarge, is he? " he called out of the window.

" He's well away," the sergeant said, and passed his hand over his bald head, professionally fresh of voice, throwing out a foot as if he, personally, stood between Max and any threat. " Won't have no trouble at all, not with him. Get him down there, turn him in, and go home. So long."

Snowy started the convoy, watching the sergeant listening, and the orderly's mouth sharp at work as they paced slowly into the house.

Under the darkness of the sycamore he stopped, signalling the convoy on. In the mirror he saw Rusty wave to the trucks in his rear. One by one, and slowly they came, crowded with men and women, with the green and white camouflage of the workshop last of all.

Rusty turned out, and stopped his truck just in front of Rosie. He went around on the near side to say goodbye to Bill and the Princess.

Snowy got down in the warmth, looking up the way they had come.

A bronze light glowed high in the falling ash, making gold triangles on the ends of houses, touching haycocks and vineyards with gold leaf, spreading sharp cuts of black velvet just beyond, and the road polished silver all the way up.

Rusty came round and looked in at Max, putting a hand on the toecaps of his boots, but he was pale in sleep.

" Ciaou, amico," he said.

Snowy looked along at the convoy, crowded at the back of each truck with men and women in groups of brown faces and eyes bright black, one after another, like the portraits in the window of a seaside photographer. But many of the women wept, holding out their rosaries to assure him of their thoughts, and others put their hands together as in prayer, pointing the fingers towards him and returning them to place between their breasts.

Rusty stood in the brilliance of the tarmac with his shadow long before him, holding out his arms in a massive wide-fingered gesture that seemed part of the grey mountain and the golden leaf of the vineyards.

" Fratello mio," he said, in a strange voice. " Non ho parole."

" So long, Rusty boy," Snowy said. " Keep 'em turning down there."

He was grabbed and shaken, and then Rusty was walking away.

Rosie felt cool, as though she knew his sadness, and she started quietly, rolling almost without sound past the people bending to look in the window, smiling and blowing kisses with square brown hands among groupings of brown faces that glittered tears, shouting Snowi, Adio, Babbo, Ciaou, Grazie, Grazie, Snowi, all the way down to Rusty, standing on the corner, holding the main traffic for Rosie to take her place in the stream.

Snowy held out his right hand in the V sign, watching light on a cracked finger-nail, and through the dust he saw the bitter motion of hands shaken in answer, and Rusty's face breaking as Rosie swung away.

But the moment he was on the road he realized he was back in the life he knew, of time, and responsibility, feeling, in the speed and accuracy of down-Line traffic, that sense of worry he seemed to have lost that came back twice as strong to think that others had been filling the artery day and night while Rosie had been nosing down the side roads on holiday.

There might have been something aloof and superior in the shapes that passed him, anonymous in dust that never settled, brushing by, rough as city crowds in a station treat a couple going on holiday, him in his white trousers and strawyard and her in a white dress and panama, putting them in their place for going away and leaving more work for those left behind.

" Come on, Rosie," he said. " Wake your ideas up, gel. Don't start crawling about."

He took his place in the queue to cross the bridge, watching the engineers sweating with the girders of another, and rattled over the pontoons, wishing there were time for a swim, and he was going up the ramp on the far bank when the sun went out, and the ash was thick again. He switched on all the lights, speeding until the red eyes of the truck in front were just beyond Rosie's headlamps, and settled to a spell of close driving, welcoming release from having to think about himself.

The wide street of a town opened in rows of little oil lamps inside the shops, and in amazement he recognized the buildings and the church of a couple of nights ago, picking out the alley with the house of red sofas at the end of it, wondering if the girls got back and sorry not to be able to stop and find out.

On, up the mountain, and down, turning, always turning, watching the scarlet rearlights in front, seeing the down-Line passing on the other side in flashes of their headlights regular as the turn of a lighthouse, and somehow as comforting, as if they were saying in one voice that nothing could stop them, nothing had, and a volcano could take its turn and try, and here was the answer, one after another, without pause or break.

Ash got lighter, and the wind was visibly blowing green through the orange trees, and then he could see the fruit, and presently there was no ash, and no fogginess, but clear sky, and earth rich in neat furrows under evening light.

He saw the canvas walls of an American traffic post, and the white helmets of M.P.s on duty, and waved himself out of the traffic line.

" Where's your hospital, chum? " he called. " Got one of your blokes in here."

The policeman gestured him into the fork on the other side, leading away from a pillar thick with Fifth Army American Unit signs.

A corporal climbed up and looked in.

" Hi," he said, and looked down at Max. " How d'you pick him up? Man, he sure looks bad."

" One of your ambulances got it on Route One," Snowy said. " We had to cross over and come in down here. Took us a bit of time. The roads are jammed."

" Sure, sure," the corporal said, as though the map were in

front of him and the whole business had been marked out. " Don't we know it? I'll have a boy take y'up."

Snowy waited until the motor-cyclist gave him a round-arm signal, and followed on, admiring the broad leather belt and the polished holster, but the bright spot where sunlight caught the white helmet made him think of Shiner, still up there among the olive trees even now, with night coming on, and through all the nights, always.

He was grateful for the darkness, and happy to see the shaded red cross of the hospital, feeling like a poor relation among all the ambulances, quietly white and tidy on the arrival park.

The policeman went into the reception hall, and talked to a nurse sitting at a desk, leaning across at her, smiling, but she was glum, as though she knew what he was after. She got up, pinning a dear little cap further into her hair, and came across to the glass door in a click of white heels.

Snowy looked up at her.

" Sorry to trouble you, Sister," he said. " We've got one of your soldiers out here. He's wounded."

She called to a man in a white coat looking out of a door, and Snowy went back to Rosie, and leaned across to tear the label off Max's blouse.

A couple of civilians and the man in white came out with a stretcher, opening it down by the step. The policeman came out, looking on. They took the blankets from under Max's head, and Snowy held them warm against him.

Head first they drew him out, and carefully turned to put him flat on the stretcher, covering him, and lifting him, and walking heavily away.

" So long, Maxie chum," Snowy said, with the label tight in his fist.

" Did you know the guy? " the policeman asked, and sounded puzzled.

" No, no," Snowy said. " Just talked for a bit, that's all."

" Would that British soldier come in here, please? " The nurse called from the top of the steps in that American voice, so invitingly feminine that he wanted to reach out in the dark and catch each word as it flew, and taste it.

Max had gone, in a thudding of swing doors.

Snowy went in and faced the desk, and the top of her little cap.

" What happened? " she asked, with the pen ready.

" We came down from the north, Sister," he said. " Right behind your lines, we was, on the ammunition route. There was a bit of shelling. Not much. But one of your ambulances must have copped it. He was in it. Some of the others got took off. I was given him. So here he is."

She was smiling.

" We just had a convoy in," she said, looking at a pile of papers. " I'll get his detail from that. He hadn't anything else with him? "

" Nothing at all, Miss," he said. " You don't expect it coming out of the Line, do you? Specially in a smash."

" True enough," she said. " You look as if you could do with a little treatment, too. What was wrong? Catch some blast?"

Snowy felt the swellings on his cheeks.

" No, Sister," he said. " Talking too much."

" That's how you learn," she said, and opened the book in dismissal. " You want to pick your date next time. And thanks, anyway. You've been swell. Good night."

The policeman had started his motor-cycle.

" Hey, Joe, you want a cup of coffee?" he shouted, over the engine noise. " Follow me around."

" No, thanks," Snowy said. " Got to hop it, quick. I can find me way, don't worry."

" O.K.," the policeman waved and moved off in a dazzling cloud. " So long."

Bill lifted the Princess down from the rear, and went out of the way to the other side of the cabin.

Snowy saw her coming, almost unseen in the darkness, but suddenly all tenderness was gone and she was just like anyone else, to be spoken to and passed by.

She put a hand on his arm.

" Except for this," she said, " I regret nothing. I hope you don't."

" Never," he said, but he felt a thousand miles away from her.

" I'll stay here, or near as I can." She looked up at him. " I'll look after him all they'll let me. Everything I can do."

" Don't forget," he warned, " he's a casualty out of the Line. You don't know him."

She stood away from him, looking over towards Rosie's sidelights, and he saw the glint on her eyelashes. Her littleness moved him to touch her shoulder, but almost as though she were unaware of it she moved a little farther away.

" Dear Rosie," she said. " I'll often think of her. There's a little bird out here, called cingallegra. And it says ' Io non lo so. Io non lo so.' Every question you ask, every doubt you have, it answers for you. Io non lo so. I don't know. I don't know. I'll never hear it without thinking of us."

Nurses in raincoats came into the foyer, pulling up collars and tugging at belts, hurrying out to the darkness and feeling for the steps.

" God," one of them said, breathing deep. " Doesn't that smell wonderful? "

" I hope that laundry finally got here," someone else said. " I'm getting kind of sick of wiping off on old pillow slips. I'd just as soon use a towel."

" Nobody 'preciates y', babe," another voice said. " Face up to it, now. No use asking for a palazzo on Fifth, either."

They turned the corner and the darkness was quiet again.

" Poor kids," she said. " So far from everything. I'll write to you, Snowy."

" I'll give you the address," he said.

" I have it." She held his hand a moment. " I'm unhappy we have to say goodbye. I was hoping we could go home. But I have to stay here. I don't know what I'll do if anything ever happens to him."

He took her by the arms.

" Nothing will," he said. " Safe as houses. Don't cry, Miss."

" I'm beyond it," she said. " Edmund. I love the sound of it. I love you. Darling mine. Goodbye."

She slipped away, leaving him staring about to see where she had gone.

" Wait a minute, Miss," he called. " I'm going to see you again, aren't I? Where shall I find you? "

He saw her moving against the dark sky, over on the corner where the nurses had turned.

"Non lo so," he heard her whispering. "Goodbye."

He went to sit in the cabin, looking out at the deep unbroken blue, a little hot, feeling as though he might have said more, but, under all, conscious of relief.

Bill got in quietly on the other side, and folded his arms.

"Well," Snowy said, "now we can get off home."

"Lovely woman is that," said Bill. "She's off her head about Max. I had a rare time with her."

"He'll be all right," Snowy said. "But what about us, three days overdue?"

"Four," Bill said. "And nothing to show for it, 'cept two fat eyes. How far off are we?"

"You go to sleep," Snowy said. "I'll get you there. You're with the Eighth now, y'know. They can't lose us."

"Pity." Bill's voice was gently reflective. "Mr. Dincott was Eighth, too, I suppose ye'd guessed? Somebody to be right proud of, was that. I doubt if we ever had owt in t' First to touch it."

"'Course not," Snowy said. "We bred 'em in the Eighth. Bred 'em and chucked 'em out. They didn't ought to have done him like that, though. Or that girl."

"Wish I'd been the bloke as struck that match," Bill said, in an ordinary tone. "Not for that poor lass. But I'd have trussed him first and gathered his gravy."

Snowy let it all go in one comfortable push, leaning back against Rosie, holding on to the wheel as if it were a strong root going down into soil he knew, that he was part of and happy in, tasting his command of the road with a relish that was almost physical.

Down at the fork he watched the traffic patrolman boiling coffee over the stove in the tent, waiting for the pointsman to signal him into the pale khaki stream of wagons and trucks coming out of the darkness in pair after pair of dusty white eyes that slewed off for the main route. He joined in at the twirl of the pointsman's arm, wondering how many thousands of vehicles had given it practice, and settled behind a tank-conveyor even bigger than Rosie.

"There's something on," he said. "Armour's going up. Looks like a new Div."

Bill was fast asleep.

He looked at the nodding head as he might had Shiner slept there, and almost with as much affection, inclined to wonder at it, and yet glad, and willing that it should grow.

The old feeling, of wanting to remember Shiner and to keep his memory apart, resenting any talk of replacing him, was gone, and in a curious way he felt that Shiner himself had done something to make it so.

Somehow, but he was uncertain why, it was easier having someone to talk to almost as he talked to Liz, sharing the work almost as he shared with Liz, for then his need to be with her could be kept in bounds. That empty feeling after Shiner's death had been all the worse because there was nobody to share a parcel with, or read out bits of her letters to, and share the jokes. That was when he seemed perished inside for want of her, when he looked at her letters for hours on end before opening them, just feeling them, wanting to put his fingers where she might have held them, trying to think her thoughts.

But now there was somebody to write about, and so lengthen letters that never went over on the second page of the airmail form however hard he tried, for all the hours of chewing a pen and writing of love, love, love just sickened him, especially since he knew that every word was read by censoring officers.

A new mate to work with and talk to until it was time to go home, and here he was, doing thirty miles an hour in the middle of nowhere, sleeping like a good 'un, and dreaming, he hoped, of Pet.

He picked out a tune among the many Rosie was singing and sang with her under his breath, applying himself to the road regardless of hours or miles in a study that was almost sleep itself.

Torre Fiore came out of the night in white letters on a pale blue traffic sign, and he reached across to shake Bill, taking the turn with one hand, going for the lamp outside the monastery gate.

"Come on, chum," he rallied. "Get 'em open. We're home. This is it."

He answered the sentry's shout with a double touch on Rosie's horn and put her through the gateway in fastest purr, stopping her among a crowd of mechanics on the night watch coming out of the messroom with mugs and plates.

" Decent leave, Snow? " a voice called from the bright lights of the refectory. " We heard you was scuppered down there."

" Who, us? " Snowy was reaching in Rosie's bonnet. " No fear, boy. We had a spanking leave. Spanking. Where's Sar'n Whitmarsh? "

" Gone in for some grub," someone said. " You better get a move on if you want some. Ol' Philippo's just packing up."

" Come on, Bill mate," Snowy said. " Hungry? "

" I don't rightly know," said Bill. " But if tha' put a steak i' front of me now, I'd not know whether to cuddle it or frame it."

Sergeant Whitmarsh looked up as they came in.

The butts of his knife and fork stayed on the table. First he frowned and then his face went flat as if a hand had passed over it, setting white lines where the frowns had been, and his eyebrows went up, and up, and the staring pale-blue eyes got colder, first looking at Snowy's face and then at Bill's and back again, with one cheek bulging in an unchewed mouthful.

" Well, God stiffen my Aunt Nellie's fluebrush," he said. " If I'd ha' known it'd come to that, I'd never ha' put you together. Bright pair o' tea-leaves, ain't you? "

" Thought we'd surprise you," Snowy said. " We had a bit of scrimmage with some blokes down there. Tried to pinch Rosie."

" Better go sick, the pair of you," Sergeant Whitmarsh said, in a friendlier manner. " I'll sign a special."

" I'm all right if Snowy is," said Bill. " How about some chow? "

" Chow? Yankee, eh?" Sergeant Whitmarsh pointed his knife at two places, and nodded to the messman. " You've heard, then? They tell you out there? "

Snowy looked at Bill, shaking his head.

" We ain't Eighth Army no longer." Sergeant Whitmarsh applied himself to his plate, elaborating salt on half a potato. " Adjutant give it out tonight. So this ain't a unit no more. It's an outfit. You're a couple of Yanks. We're Fifth Army."

Bill's eyes closed right up in a grin and he sat back.

" What's happened to the Eighth? " he asked.

" Gone out of business," said Sergeant Whitmarsh. " Soon as Monty went home, they put the brokers in. They couldn't wait to do us. Jerry couldn't, but They did."

He went around the turn of the plate with a crust of bread.

" How was things down there? " he asked.

" All right," said Snowy. " I got some snaps. Looked all right, didn't it, Bill? "

" Champion." Bill was looking at Snowy's face. " They smashed up the First, just the same."

Snowy watched a fly going round the electric light bulb, remembering fighters coming out of the sun.

" I won't take the Eights off of Rosie," he said. " I'll go loose first."

" Didn't happen to bring a little drop o' something back with you, did you? " Sergeant Whitmarsh made it sound like an answer in profoundest agreement. " I could do with a drink tonight. Try and get some heart back in me."

" We've a couple of cases." Bill got up. " Rusty's pals give 'em us."

" We met him down there," Snowy explained. " Doing all right, he is. Fifth Army, eh? "

" Yankees," Sergeant Whitmarsh said. " For the time being. Ain't hardly creditable, is it? "

" We come back with one." Snowy made way for the messman to put a plate of stew in front of him, looking about for Bill, sucking his fingers. " Shove it down, chum. He's coming."

" Mutton stew and starlings, that is, Snow," Sergeant Whitmarsh said. " I got me cartridges yesterday. We didn't half have some sport in that there tower. I never see so many bats. Here, and no wonder they never took that littlest bell. It's only a lump of metal and a clapper. Ain't worth a sausage."

Bill came in with a couple of bottles and gave them to the messman.

" Chianti and cognac," he said. " There's some champagne there, too. Do for tomorrow."

Snowy heard the corks come out.

" We dropped in on Ma Nincio," he said. " Poor old girl. Her youngest boy got his pictures. Got shot by a deserter down there."

"About time they chased a few of 'em up," Sergeant Whitmarsh said. "There's a job I'd like."

Snowy trod on Bill's foot under the table.

"How's things been going on here, Sarge?" he asked.

"Same as usual." Sergeant Whitmarsh looked at the colour of the wine, and turned his mouth down in appreciative awe. "Trust old Rusty to know what's good. Here's to him."

Snowy held up his glass and waited until Bill's was filled.

"And here's to Max and the Fifth," he said. "May they always stick together."

"Hear, hear," said Bill. "And I hope that babe of his's a right little puddin'."

"What's this in aid of?" asked Sergeant Whitmarsh.

"This pal of ours I told you about," Snowy said. "Real boy, he is. I liked old Max."

"Ah," said Bill. "There's nowt wrong wi' right folks. Eighth or Fifth, it's all one to me."

Sergeant Whitmarsh stood up.

"I ain't going to sit here listening to no blasphemy," he said. "'Sides, I've got some work to do. You know you're on the road tomorrow, you two?"

Snowy looked across at Bill, and winked, seeing a dome in the light bulb.

"Hear that?" He picked up his glass. "Us two and Rosie, eh? Where, Sarge?"

"Up Route Two, about forty mile or so." The sergeant fastened his belt. "House all to yourselves. Only it ain't got a roof. But there's running water. Kick off at Reveille. See me 'fore you go. Right?"

"Right, Sarge," Snowy said. "No sense going to bed just for a couple of hours. I think I'll have a nice wash, and write a letter."

"There's some mail for you." Sergeant Whitmarsh took the other bottle, using it on the table as a walking-stick. "Want it now?"

"I'll have me wash first, Sarge," Snowy said. "Feel fresher."

"Doubt there'll be any for me." Bill got up with the chianti flask. "Won't have had time to catch up. If you don't want any more of this, give it to t' cooks. That stew was good."

They went over to the cookhouse, watching the orderlies swilling down. Tables were stacked with tin trays, and old Philippo and two juniors were filling others. He pushed his white cap farther back and grinned at them.

" 'Sera, signor," he shouted. " Sta bene? "

" Hi, Philippo. Have a glass of this with old Rusty." Snowy went in, holding out the bottle. " You remember him, don't you? "

" Certainly." Old Philippo nodded, unhooking a mug from the rack. " He is well, no? "

" Rusty's all right." Snowy looked at trays full of little birds lying on their backs with their legs tied over their breastbones, and dozens more in a pan. In the roll of their heads and open beaks he saw Max, and quite suddenly in the rounded drumsticks he caught a glimpse of the girl in white with her mouth bleeding, arching in a faint on a mattress of hands. " Whose idea's this, Philippo? "

" Sergente, he shoot for tomorrow, the dinner." Old Philippo took his cap off, raising the mug. " Gian Rustizzi, tanti respetti. My good health for everybody."

" Bill, draw the rations, will you, mate? " Snowy said. " I'll get petrol and stores. I'm glad we ain't here tomorrow. It'd corpse me to eat one o' them. Don't take none for the meat ration, mind."

" What d'you think I am? " Bill turned away for the ration store. " I'd rather see 'em flying about any day."

" And watch him on the scales," Snowy called, from the doorway. " He'll do you on tea and sugar if you ain't careful."

" You attend to your own damn business," Bill said. " Think we're all like you cockneys? "

Snowy went across the yard and into the refectory, sniffing the comfort of machine-tool odours, nodding to friends looking up from the lathes, making his way towards the stores.

" Rosie," he said to the storeman. " She wants the lot."

" It's all out there," the storeman said. " Sar'n Whitmarsh checked it."

" Primus an' all? " Snowy looked down the list. " I don't want to get all the way there and find I've left half me stuff behind. My mate wouldn't thank me, you know."

"Took it all out meself, Snow boy," the storeman said. "What d'you reckon to this Eighth business?"

"Very empty job, you ask me," said Snowy. "Still, I don't mind the Fifth. You might find yourself dishing out gum and baseball bats 'fore you know where you are."

"Be the most pop'lar bloke in the district," the storeman said. "Run me own car inside a month. You're lookin' well. Nice range o' tints?"

"We had a Dolly-dye sun down there," Snowy said. "D'you mind?"

"Sign here." The storeman slid the register at him. "How was Shiner?"

In the neat array of spares and tools from floor to ceiling along yards of shelves in the big room, heated, it seemed, by smells of new rope and oil-paper packings and turpentine, and dully quiet with the glass door shut against the murmur of the lathes, he could almost hear windrush in the olives and the doves flying up among the pink flowers on the cote, knowing, and feeling the pull of a thought that here was where Shiner would prefer to be.

"Just the job," he said. "Thanks to you and the lads."

He went out from the brightness of the refectory and into the yard, seeing Rosie's headlamps and windscreen throwing off little points and bars of light, and her green paint shadowy in the darkness and yet alive, and something in her stillness reminded him of the people in the square, standing, watching, ready.

Sergeant Whitmarsh stood by the tailboard watching Bill stow the rations.

"It's all there, Snowy," he greeted him. "And half a dozen duckboards to keep your tootsies dry, up there. Your mail's in the cabin."

"Ta, Sarge," Snowy said. "I got a good mind to shove off now. Be up there time it's light. What d'you say, Bill?"

"Suits me, chum." Bill finished tying ropes and dusted his hands. "Anything you say. We've a lovely lot of stuff in here. Ye'll be that pleased."

"Well," said Sergeant Whitmarsh, "if some Yankee general drops on your necks for inspection, I want him to see we can still lay out a kit, and no half larks about it. Else I'll have the skins off o' the pair of you, and a bit sharp."

" Don't you worry, Sarge," Snowy said. " He'll find out, all right. But what about Rosie? Think he'll say anything about her Eights? "

" I don't know, boy," said Sergeant Whitmarsh. " But you can tell him, with my compliments, that if she hadn't wore 'em in the first place you wouldn't be in no position to answer the question."

" Ought to tack him down," said Bill.

Snowy helped to fasten the tailboard, and took a lot of care to make sure all was snug, punching creases out of the canopy, fiddling with chains and generally wasting time until even he was getting impatient of it.

He knew that he was preparing himself for sight of her handwriting, that would make him feel almost the same as sight of her, uncertain of the state of his feeling towards her, to be ashamed and ask forgiveness, or to say nothing and take everything in his stride; but whether or not, it had to be gone through, and so he walked around to the cabin and opened the door.

Green in light from the dashboard, the letters were propped against the wheel immediately over the red notch.

Bill grinned at him.

" I got a couple, too," he said. " I'm savin' 'em till we get there."

Snowy got in and shut the door.

He picked up the letters in his right hand, knowing that Bill was watching, determined to show nothing either to him or to Sergeant Whitmarsh standing below.

But the big loops and the round e's brought her close, so close that he could see her resting over on her left forearm to dodge her shadow, with her tongue tip just showing, moving with the nib, and her lips forming the words as they were written, and the special curls for My Darling Husband Bertie.

Somebody was shouting at the gate and Sergeant Whitmarsh went away.

" Forty mile up Route Two," he said. " So we can pop in and ask about old Maxie."

"Ah," said Bill. "Now you're talking. Everything's turning out very nice, d'y' know. Me with two letters, an' all."

Rosie started quietly, and turned about, and all the time he kept the letters in his right hand, unwilling to put them down, as though the act of release for sake of doing something else were putting Liz second in importance.

Bill switched on the headlamps, and as they straightened for the archway, Sergeant Whitmarsh came out waving his arms, signalling them on.

"Come and show 'em how, Snowy," he shouted. "Got a tow-job stuck right outside, there. Just shove her off the road, that's all."

Snowy nodded, and put Rosie through the gate.

Another breakdown wagon had backed away from a truck it had been towing. The front wheels were down in a shallow rut at an angle from the body, in an attitude that reminded him of a woman sitting over to one side with her knees crossed. She seemed to be looking at him in surprise from empty headlamps white from Rosie's, and suddenly he thought of the Princess and felt that unutterable yearn of pity as for someone beyond reach of help.

Rosie went closer and closer, and pushed, until her front wheels were almost off the tarmac, and then Snowy reversed her, and turned, ready.

Sergeant Whitmarsh held up one thumb in the light, and changed it to a finger that pointed north.

Snowy let out the clutch and released the wheel, spreading his arms wide, with the letters, still in his right hand, fretting in the breeze outside the window.

"Here y'are, Sarge," he shouted, as they rode the dip. "Look. No hands. Anywhere, anytime, anyhow. That's Rosie. So long!"

A cool headwind blew the letters against his knuckles in gentlest reminder of their presence. He brought them into him, and the act seemed to fetch Liz and the children, and the house, and the job, and even the lamp at the end of the road, a little nearer, almost enough to put his arms around them all and call them his own. Forty miles farther north, forty miles nearer to Liz, another trip along the miles of road from Suez, and old

Rosie, with her nose in all of them, was laughing away singing a dozen little songs at the same time as though she knew all about it, telling him not to worry because come what might there was not a doubt in the wide, wide world that one day she was going to stop right outside the front door.

At home.

Caronte
Rotondi
Ponte Grande
Iodi
Venice
Trefdraeth
London.